MW00442685

JONATHAN JANZ

THE NIGHTMARE GIRL

This is a FLAME TREE PRESS book

FLAME TREE PRESS
6 Melbray Mews, London, SW6 3NS, UK
flametreepress.com

Distribution and warehouse:
Baker & Taylor Publisher Services (BTPS)
30 Amberwood Parkway, Ashland, OH 44805
btpubservices.com

Thanks to the Flame Tree Press team, including:
Taylor Bentley, Frances Bodiam, Federica Ciaravella, Don D'Auria,
Chris Herbert, Matteo Middlemiss, Josie Mitchell, Mike Spender,
Cat Taylor, Maria Tissot, Nick Wells, Gillian Whitaker.

The cover is created by Flame Tree Studio with
thanks to Nik Keevil and Shutterstock.com.
The font families used are Avenir and Bembo.

Flame Tree Press is an imprint of Flame Tree Publishing Ltd
flametreepublishing.com

A copy of the CIP data for this book is available from the British Library and the Library of Congress.

HB ISBN: 978-1-78758-131-9
PB ISBN: 978-1-78758-129-6
ebook ISBN: 978-1-78758-132-6
Also available in FLAME TREE AUDIO

Printed in the US at Bookmasters, Ashland, Ohio

JONATHAN JANZ

THE NIGHTMARE GIRL

FLAME TREE PRESS
London & New York

‘Fire being the seed of all existing things, to which they must in time again return, has suggested to generations of pyromaniacs the alarming idea that if humanity could only be consumed entire then it must, as a matter of course, arise from the flames renewed and purified.’

Richard Cavendish

Man, Myth & Magic

Thank you, Peach, for being my daughter. You are pure joy
and love, and my love for you grows every day.
Thank you for being you.

PART ONE THE TORCH AND THE TINDER

CHAPTER ONE

"If I didn't know you better," Joe said, "I'd think you were calling me out."

Michelle wouldn't look at him. "It's not calling you out, honey. It's constructive criticism."

"Doesn't feel much like it to me. Feels like you think you married a loser."

Michelle did glance at him then, a finger to her lips to warn him off rousing Lily.

"It'd take a sonic boom to wake her up," Joe said, but he threw a look in the rearview just to make sure. Their two-year-old daughter was conked, her mouth open and her face turned sideways, a spill of long black hair tumbling down her cheek.

"Let's just drop it," Michelle said.

"You're the one who brought it up."

She sighed. "Well, it was frustrating, Joe. Aren't I allowed to feel frustrated?"

He willed his voice to stay even, but it took an effort. "You don't think I'm mad about it, honey? Maybe I should shout some cuss words, smash a few beer bottles over my head so you know I'm agitated."

"Smartass."

"I wanted that contract more than anybody. I work for two months with a client and those Wilson jerkoffs come in at the last minute and undercut me?"

Some of Michelle's angst seemed to dissipate. "I know you're disappointed, dear." She shook her head, tapped her fingers on her legs. "Maybe it's the name."

Joe felt the skin at his temples tighten. "It's not the name."

"Joe Crawford Construction just sounds so…"

"Accurate?"

"Boring."

"Thanks a lot."

"You know what I mean," she said. "It's not catchy."

"And Azure Horizons is?"

She shrugged. "You have to admit Azure Horizons sounds more interesting than Joe Crawford Construction."

"Azure Horizons sounds like an airline company," Joe said. "Or a Latino porn star. Take your pick."

She made a pained face. "The Wilson Brothers are no better at building houses than you are."

"They're idiots."

"But this is the third time in as many months they've outbid you."

"Underbid, honey. There's a big difference."

"So lower your bids."

He clenched his jaw, forced himself to pay attention to the road. They were nearing town, the Marathon gas station up there on the left. His eyes flicked to the fuel gauge. Nearly empty. They'd have to stop.

"I've explained this, honey," he said, taking care to keep his tone low. They'd have to wake Lily when they got home, but it was usually best to let her sleep as long as possible. When she didn't nap, she was more frightening than a terrorist on crystal meth. He went on. "If I put forth a lowball bid and the client accepts it, what happens when the project gets going and the costs start to rise?"

"You do what every other contractor does and raise the price."

"I don't do business that way."

"You won't do business at all unless you adapt."

It hit him like a punch to the gut. Michelle was seldom this way to him, but he'd made the mistake of dreaming aloud of the new car he'd buy her once the contracts on this deal were signed. The ragged edge in her voice was her unvarnished disappointment talking. But that didn't make it sit any easier.

She sighed. "Sorry for being selfish."

"Are you?" he asked without looking at her. The gas station was a hundred yards up.

"You know I am."

"I can be like everybody else and overcharge for materials and drag my feet to inflate my labor fee, but I'm not going to do that." He signaled a left turn. The gas station looked busy. All the pumps but one were occupied. He said, "What you're talking about, that's dishonest. I tell people the price, and I try to steer clear of overages. If that makes me some kind of chump, then so be it."

She smiled wanly. "It's like I'm sitting here with my dad."

He pulled into the station and sidled their black Tundra next to the vacant pump. Cutting the engine, he turned to her and said, "I'll take that as a compliment."

Michelle's smile grew a little brighter.

Joe rolled down the windows and climbed out. He didn't like the gasoline fumes wafting in toward Lily, but he liked the prospect of her and her mother baking in the unseasonably hot early April afternoon even less. He left the door ajar, swiped his card, and chose the cheapest grade of gas. As he waited for the all-clear to start fueling, his gaze wandered over to a maroon van parked on the other side of the pump. There was a blond woman pumping gas and another blond sitting behind the wheel. He saw what looked like a kid's car seat behind the passenger's seat.

Joe's pump said "Please proceed" in a pleasant female voice, so he did, inhaling the gas fumes as he pulled the trigger and braced it to remain on until the tank was full. He felt a pang of guilt at enjoying the fumes so much – his mom had always warned that sniffing them would kill brain cells – but he couldn't help it. He'd always loved the smell.

A plaintive cry tore at his ears, a child's cry, and for a moment, Joe thought Lily had awakened. But when he glanced to his right, he saw his daughter still snoozing peacefully and realized it was the kid in the maroon van doing the bawling. He took a sideways step and saw that, yes, there was a little boy in the car seat, and he was indeed wailing. Little fella couldn't have been more than a year old and had hair the color of bleached straw. He noticed, too, the pretty young woman in the driver's seat was glaring up in the mirror at her boy with a grim look on her face. She didn't look so pretty anymore. Or very old, for that matter. She couldn't have been much over twenty.

Joe's eyes shifted to the lady at the gas pump and saw how it was more clearly. The little boy belonged to the younger woman. The woman at the pump was the grandma – the very young grandma. Probably forty-three or forty-four, just a couple years older than Joe. Of course, from the way the grandma was dressed, she didn't much like the thought of growing older. The denim shorty shorts and the tight white top showed so much leg and midriff that the lady could've posed for a nudie magazine with minimal fuss. The shorts were so tight Joe worried her female parts might suffer from oxygen deprivation. But she wore them well, there was no doubt about that. Grandma looked thirty or so, until you got to the face. And though it wasn't a bad face and might even have been called attractive, there was a hardness there, a fierceness that suggested she'd seen much of life and wouldn't put up with anybody else messing her over.

The little boy in the van continued to wail.

Joe saw the look on the young mother's face and felt a ripple of misgiving sweep through him. The young mom, her blond hair pulled back in a ponytail, was staring daggers at the kid in the overhead mirror now. Joe glanced at the young grandma at the pump and thought, *Hurry, lady. Your daughter's at the end of her fuse. I've got a feeling the toddler in the backseat isn't a stranger to fussing like this, which means his momma's nerves are as frayed as old wires.*

"You gonna stand out there all day?" Michelle's voice called.

Joe blinked, returning to himself, and glanced at the gas pump. Stepping over and leaning into the open doorway of the pickup, he said, "It's three-quarters full. Can we get Lily home and into her crib without waking her up?"

"It's probably better if she does get up," Michelle said, checking her watch. "It's five now. If she doesn't wake soon, she'll be up all night."

Joe nodded. "You're right. She'll be cranky th—"

A flat, solid sound popped in the spring air. Joe felt his guts squirm. Michelle's face paled. She was staring at something beyond him. He knew what it was even before he turned, knew it yet hoped against hope it wasn't true. But when he did crane his neck around and peered through the windshield and saw what was happening, it was as though Joe's internal organs turned to mush and settled in the pit of his stomach.

"Joe," Michelle said in a small, breathless voice.

Jesus Christ, he thought. *Jesus Christ.*

The young mother stood in the van's open side doorway. She raised her hand again, her face twisted in a snarl. She was spitting sibilant words at the little boy through bared teeth. Her eyes were enraged and full of white.

His whole body numb and shaking, Joe pushed himself away from the pickup, and his view was momentarily washed out by the late afternoon sun glare boiling off the van's windshield. But he still saw a flash of brown skin as the young woman's arm whipped down, still heard the sickening, meaty smack of bony fingers on tender pink flesh. His heart thumping, his gorge a bursting mass of heat, Joe stumbled over the concrete island on legs he couldn't feel. He was distantly aware of the young grandma's eyes on him as he drifted around the corner of the van. The scene that awaited him was worse than he ever would've imagined:

The young mother, athletic and curvy and all brown skin. Her right palm rearing back like a sledgehammer, her eyes ringed with hideous white coronas, her gleaming teeth those of a Rottweiler with all the gentleness conditioned out of it, who only knows how to lash out, who only knows how to rip and maim.

Beyond her were the faces of several bystanders. Though Joe wasn't looking at them, he could make out their faces in the background. Like horrified constellations they stared at the hideous scene, but not one of them moved. Women. Men. A couple children of maybe four and seven. The faces gaped, but they were frozen in that tableau. Some modernized version of a Bosch painting come to life.

But the worst of it, by an inestimably vast margin, was the sight of the little boy, too young to know exactly what was happening or to understand the injustice of his situation, but old enough to know he didn't want to be hit again. Old enough to cry and writhe in his seat while the snot and saliva formed bloody whorls on his lips and his chin. The collar of his baby blue T-shirt, Joe saw, was purpled with sweat and other fluids Joe didn't want to think about.

The woman was beginning her striking motion again when Joe reached her. Until this moment he'd known people like this existed, but perhaps he'd deluded himself into believing their crimes really couldn't be as detestable as the papers described. A mother really couldn't willingly harm her child.

What he did do was catch her by the wrist. So powerful was her downward swing that her arm descended another few inches anyway, but Joe was a good deal stronger, and he had enough adrenaline sluicing through his body to stay her slap before it landed on the toddler's already swelling face.

For a split second, it seemed she would relent. Her white, deranged horse's eyes flicked to his and registered what might have been astonishment.

Then her left hand curled up in a claw and tore ribbons from the side of his neck to the shelf of his jaw. The pain was incredible, but the instinct for self-preservation won out. Before she could get at him again – and she was already retracting her scythe-like talons for another vicious swipe – Joe jerked her sideways, away from the squalling toddler and his heartbreaking tears. She staggered, nearly fell, and Joe almost came down on top of her. There was someone batting at his shoulders, a voice shrilling at him to *Let Angie go! Let Angie go!* But Joe's only thoughts were of preventing more abuse to the child in the van and of saving what was left of his own looks by immobilizing those lethal fingernails.

They were halfway between the pumps and the gas station. A car had stopped about ten feet shy of running them over and sat there idling impatiently. The young woman was thrashing in his grip and spouting obscenities at him, words like *cocksucker* and *motherfucker* and other things so foul he didn't even know what they meant. Beyond the shrieking harpy he could make out the pink, full-moon faces of onlookers who'd stepped out of the gas station to spectate. On their right flank, the crowd from the small parking lot had closed in, perhaps to get a better look at Joe's bloody neck.

The young woman – Angie, the grandma had called her – reared back and let loose with a gob of spit that slapped him in the cheek. Meanwhile, the grandma was tearing at his arms, his shirt, now interposing herself between him and Angie to pry loose his fingers.

"Let my girl go, damn you!" Grandma whacked him across the chest, the shoulder. "Let…her…*go*!"

Joe threw her a look. "Tell her to stop carving me up with those nails of hers and I will."

The grandma seemed not to hear him. She hauled off and swatted him across the bridge of the nose, and god*dammit*, did that hurt. Angie was still flailing about, her arms like electrified nunchucks, and now she was kicking at his legs, rearing back like an NFL placekicker and booting him with all her strength in the left shin.

Joe stifled a cry of pain and gave her a shake. "Stop it, damn you, and I'll let you go!"

Angie aimed a knee at his crotch and only barely missed neutering him.

For the love of God, Joe thought. *I'm in the middle of a sordid daytime talk show, the kind where guys hump their sisters and the bodyguards have to work overtime.*

He spun Angie away from Grandma so he could avoid the older woman's bruising slaps, but she kept at it, revolving with him in an unceasing attempt to disengage him from her daughter. A gas station attendant, a young guy with longish brown hair, had finally exited the building and was now just a few feet away from the scrum. The young guy's face was etched in a disbelieving mask, but he looked like he could be an ally if he'd snap out of his stupor.

"Help me," Joe managed in a strangled growl. The young guy gave him a reluctant nod and ventured to put his hands on the grandma, but no sooner had he made contact than the woman whirled and slugged him in the mouth. The dull thud of her knuckles on the young guy's teeth would've made Joe wince under ordinary circumstances. But these were not ordinary circumstances. *The Twilight Zone has landed in Northern Indiana,* he thought. *Forget about ordinary.*

Angie was grinning crazily at him now and actually snapping at his forearms with spit-flecked teeth. He dodged her first lunge, but on the second, those gleaming white teeth sank into the meat of his forearm like it was a filet mignon. This time Joe did bellow in pain and, without thinking, he shoved the young woman away. The force of it surprised them both and her teeth came loose with a disgusting *schlurp*ing sound. She landed in an awkward tangle, her wrist pinned under her side. Joe heard a gruesome wet crack and made a futile wish it wasn't a broken bone. But her pinched features and her inhuman wail of pain suggested otherwise.

The grandma shouldered past him and fell at her daughter's side. Grandma cradled her daughter's thrashing head and shot Joe a look of such venom that his stomach performed another somersault.

"You'll burn for this," Grandma hissed. And so venomous was her expression and so resolute was her tone that Joe experienced a moment's guilt for shoving the young woman. But he'd tried, hadn't he? He'd tried not to hurt her. Surely everyone could see that.

He looked up at the young gas station attendant, but there was no help there. The poor guy was doubled over, his hands on his knees, his mouth frothing so much bloody slaver that he looked like a college freshman suffering the aftermath of his first drinking binge. Damn, but the grandma had done a number on the kid.

Joe scanned the faces surrounding the scene, but they were like shell-shocked soldiers fresh off an unexpected air raid. No help there either. Joe turned and saw Michelle, who stood ramrod straight about ten feet from the truck, her hands pressed together at her lips, concern and horror showing in equal parts in her big brown eyes.

Then Joe remembered the boy.

The toddler was still crying, but it was an exhausted sound now, the kid's face livid with anxiety and hurt. Joe exhaled shuddering breath and crossed to the boy. He reached out and endeavored to mop the blood off the kid's lips but only managed to smear it. Joe patted his pockets in the bleak hope there'd be a handkerchief there, but of course, there wasn't. Joe never carried one. His father had, but Dad was dead twenty years now. Joe glanced dismally at the van floor and saw nothing but crinkled fast food wrappers and what might've been an empty wine bottle. There was a green pacifier just visible beneath the passenger's seat, so Joe plucked it from its nest of dirt and hair and proceeded to wipe it off with the front of his shirt. He became aware of the little boy's gaze. Joe met it. The kid's blue eyes – no doubt his mother's – were swollen with tears, but they were watching him curiously. Joe's lips trembled into a smile. He checked the pacifier one more time to see if it was free of grime and decided it was good enough. He reached out, placed the pacifier in the kid's mouth. The kid accepted it eagerly and began to suck. Joe felt tears stinging his own eyes and had a wild urge to kiss the boy on the cheek.

But that was when both women fell on him.

They slammed him like an inrushing tide. Joe's forehead cracked against the van doorway, his midsection pushed into the side of the boy's car seat. There was a surge of shouting voices, the sense that a melee was forming behind him, and as Joe spun around, he saw this was the case. There was Angie, there was her mother. But their attention was now on Michelle, whose trance had finally broken and who was now nose-to-nose with Grandma. Both women had their index fingers jammed into each other's faces, their hoarse shouts merging in a hell's chorus of recrimination. Angie was cocksuckering and motherfuckering a half dozen bystanders who'd converged on the van. Present also was the gas station attendant, who despite his split lips and his bloodied front was gamely demanding the women get the hell off the premises. Joe admired the young guy's pluck. Also haranguing Angie were a tall, skinny man of perhaps seventy, a stocky mother with curly brown hair and a small child at each hip, as well as a grizzled man in a faded Grateful Dead T-shirt and black leather chaps. This guy, who looked to Joe like a thinner, healthier Jerry Garcia, was almost as animated as Angie herself, and gesticulating so wildly that Joe worried he'd knock the young woman unconscious.

Then again, maybe that would be for the best.

Just when Joe thought the whole situation would explode like some violent sports brawl, the sound of a child's screams reached his ears. He thought at first it was the toddler in the van, but no, he saw with a glance, the boy was merely watching the spectacle with a look of polite interest now.

Then Joe remembered Lily.

"Honey?" he said to his wife. She whipped her head around and looked for a moment like she'd unleash her vitriol on him too – dear God, he'd never seen her so fired up. Then something like coherent thought seemed to seep back into her pretty face and she made for the pickup truck.

The gas station attendant, God bless him, took it as a cue to restore order. He pointed at Angie and her mom in turn. "You and you, get your skanky asses in that van and get the hell out of my station."

Frantic loathing showed in Grandma's eyes. "This place isn't yours! Terry Overmeyer owns it!"

The attendant nodded, his bloodied lips twisting into a flinty smile. "That's right. And he'd tell you the same damned thing. You think he'd be okay with a woman assaulting a baby at his station?"

Grandma's face scrunched in mocking denial. "Angie never assaulted that child. It's called discipline, you stupid shit, and it's none of your business anyways."

"She beat the crap out of him, and you know it," the Jerry Garcia clone said.

"Bullshit," Grandma answered and took a step toward him.

"We all witnessed it," the older man said. Joe looked at the man's white hair and formal Sunday clothes and felt a desperate wave of affection for him. The older man nodded at Joe. "We'll all testify on this man's behalf."

"Fuck you too," Grandma said.

Angie was massaging her wrist. She shouted at Joe, spit flying from her lips, "You're the one attacked me, and you're gonna pay for it. I hope you got a good lawyer, you son of a bitch."

"You're not fit to be a mother," a woman's voice said.

Joe saw that this had come from the short, stocky woman, the one with a child on each flank. The woman's lips were trembling, but there was steel in her unflinching gaze. Joe gave silent thanks for her support.

"You go to hell," Angie said, but some of her spirit seemed to have been stolen by the woman's firm declaration.

There was a pregnant moment when no one spoke. Joe felt unspeakably weary and feared he might throw up. But when Grandma broke the silence, she said, "Come on, Angie. Let's get out of this hellhole."

Angie started to follow her mom toward the van, then she stopped and stared at the white-haired man, who Joe now saw was punching numbers on an older cell phone. "What're you doing?" Angie asked, with what might've been a glimmer of apprehension.

"I'm calling the police," the white-haired man said.

Angie's mouth worked for a moment. Then, looking like a spoiled child who's just been deprived of a toy she covets, she said, "Good. Tell 'em Angie Waltz needs to file a complaint about this asshole." A nod at Joe.

"Get out of here," the attendant said, pronouncing each word slowly. "Now."

Angie's lips pressed together, whitened, her nostrils flaring with pent rage. But she went then, stalking over to the sliding side door of the van. Without so much as a look at her son, she slammed the van door shut. Joe jumped a little, the racket of it something felt in his bones. Grandma was at the wheel now, and as she gunned the engine, Angie climbed into the passenger's seat. Joe could see his wife and daughter on the other side of the pumps, Michelle bouncing Lily gently and soothing her. Lily was two, but she still insisted on being held like a newborn when she got worked up like this.

The sight of his wife and his girl did his heart good, reminded him that life maybe could get back to normal, that he might not go to jail for accidentally breaking that little punk's wrist.

But when Joe glanced up at the van, which had started to roll forward, he knew how far from over this was. Angie Waltz was glaring at him with a look that made his flesh crawl. She didn't just hate him, she didn't just want him to suffer. The look on her face in the moments before the van veered onto Washington Street made him think of real-life courtroom clips he'd seen, the ones where accused murderers shrivel under the baleful stares of grieving loved ones. The measureless look of hatred often present in the loved ones' eyes…that was how Angie Waltz had looked at Joe before they'd pulled away.

Joe watched the van grow slowly smaller as it rolled toward whatever place of misery the girl and her son called home. Probably Grandma's house.

A horrorshow of images unspooled in his mind:

The squalid house awaiting the little boy.

Unchanged diapers.

Unwashed dishes.

A hovel full of raised voices and bitterness and nicotine.

Neglect and abuse.

Jesus Christ, Joe thought. He realized he was weeping quietly. *Jesus Christ, son. I'm sorry. I'm so sorry.*

CHAPTER TWO

The second policeman showed up around nine-thirty that night.

Joe expected it, of course. After all, he'd had Michelle call the police just a few minutes after they got home from the gas station, and they'd dispatched an officer – a young guy not much older than Angie Waltz herself – to take their statements. Joe had known that wouldn't be the end of it, known it even as he was rocking his daughter to sleep and depositing her gingerly in her crib. But it still struck Joe as surreal to see the big black police car roll to a stop along the curb in front of their house. The cop inside – a husky black man in his late-forties – engaged the emergency brake before climbing out, which Joe took as a good sign. The man was cautious. Joe's house was near the crest of a steep hill, and though the cruiser probably wouldn't go rolling to the bottom unless it was rear-ended, it always made Joe relax a little when folks used their emergency brakes.

The cop climbed out, adjusted his belt buckle, and ambled around the rear of the cruiser. The man's pants were navy blue, as was his shirt. He wore no hat, but there was a gun holstered at his side, a hell of a big one.

Suddenly dry-mouthed, Joe moved to the front door and awaited the policeman's coming. The guy mounted the front porch, saw Joe holding the door open for him, and entered the house without so much as a nod.

Joe told him he could sit anywhere. The cop took the armchair beside the couch. Joe didn't mind that so much – the only chair he really liked was in the basement anyway – but he detested sitting on their couch. It was an uncomfortable, flowery thing that reminded him of his mother-in-law, who'd helped Michelle pick it out.

The cop introduced himself as Police Chief Darrell Copeland. Joe gave his name, and Copeland nodded curtly. "I assume you know why I'm here, Mr. Crawford."

"Not really," Joe said and attempted a smile that didn't take. "I'm not accustomed to stuff like this. Thankfully."

Copeland eyed him steadily. "Well, you might as well get accustomed to it now. After all, you are at the center of it."

Now what the hell was that supposed to mean? Joe was about to point out he hadn't created this situation, but Copeland was going on.

"After a brief investigation," Copeland said, "the child and his mother were both taken into custody. We're not sure what to do about Grandma yet."

Joe felt a surge of emotions, but dominant among them was a sort of paralyzing nausea. "So what happens next?"

"Depends on who you're talkin' about. The girl or the little boy? Or Grandma?"

Joe didn't like the chief referring to Angie Waltz as *the girl*. It made her seem less like the vindictive harpy he'd encountered at the gas station and more like a kid who made a mistake.

Joe said, "Let's start with Angie."

"That one's pretty straightforward. She's charged with child abuse, so she's either gonna await trial or be let out on bail."

"Can they afford bail?"

"Don't see how. That old house of theirs is in such deplorable shape I'm surprised they can afford groceries."

"Where do they live?"

"About two blocks from the gas station. Big old home that probably looked nice about a hundred years ago. Now the whole neighborhood's low-rent."

Joe's belly was knotting up again, but dammit, how come? Was it his fault Angie was a child abuser? Was it his fault she chose to make her mistreatment of the little boy so public? And what if Joe hadn't done anything? What then? He didn't feel good now – hell no, he didn't – but he felt a damn sight better than he would've had he not intervened.

"You think she has a case?" Joe asked.

"Who, the girl?"

"Angie Waltz."

Copeland grunted, gave him a deadpan look. "There were a dozen witnesses, five of which have already given statements corroborating your account."

Joe sat forward on the couch. "She'll serve time, right?"

Copeland shrugged. "I'm not the judge, but yeah, I'd say there's a very good chance of it."

Joe mulled it over. "They usually go pretty strict on cases like these? Even if it's a person's first time getting reported?"

Copeland frowned, appeared to study the backs of his hands.

"It wasn't the first time."

"You've dealt with her before?"

Copeland was still staring at his hands, which Joe now noticed were the size of catchers' mitts. Dark brown, wide, veins wending their way up the salt-shaker knuckles. At length, Copeland said, "I've known Angie and her mom for going on four years now. Ever since they moved here, they've been bad news."

"Bad news how?"

Copeland looked up. "That happens to be none of your business."

Joe met Copeland's gaze with difficulty and told himself he wouldn't be the first to look away. When neither of them did, Joe said, "You told me it wasn't her first time being reported for abuse."

"That's none of your business either."

"I thought all that stuff was public record."

Copeland propped a forearm on his knee and leaned toward him. "Don't gimme that line of bullshit. The public has a right to know and all that. It's been a long day, and my patience has just about run out."

"Or maybe you don't have much of it to begin with."

The catchers' mitts balled into fists – *Jesus God, look at the size of those things*. Then Copeland's temperature seemed to lower a degree or two.

"I don't have to tell you anything, Crawford, so I'd back off if I were you. But because I feel like it – don't ask me why – I'll tell you one thing. When we looked at the kid, we saw bruises all over his cheeks, swollen lips, nose still crusty with blood—"

"That's what I've been telling you," Joe said. "She was beating the shit out of him."

"You mind shuttin' that mouth of yours for a minute?" Copeland said. "You'll let me, I'm tryin' to tell you something off the record."

"Sorry."

Copeland went on, not looking the slightest bit mollified. "The injuries we found weren't totally consistent with your story." When Joe opened his mouth to protest, Copeland overrode him. "Or at least your story doesn't account for *all* of them. Especially the age of the wounds."

Joe shook his head. "I don't get—"

"There were old bruises too, you understand?" Copeland said, his voice coming fast and fierce and low. "There were the new ones, sure.

The bloody nose, the blackened eye. Kid's bottom lip so swollen, you'd think…" Copeland broke off, voice suddenly thick. He cleared his throat. "But there were old bruises too. Those gray-green ones you sometimes see? The kid had 'em on his arms. Like he'd been grabbed, maybe shaken. He had yellowish contusions on his rear end, like he'd been smacked repeatedly there. And not just a spanking, either. The yellowish marks were long and thin. Like maybe she'd taken a stick or a fishing rod and whipped him with it."

"Oh hell."

"There were all kinds of colors on the boy. Even some faint bruising on either side of his neck."

Joe could scarcely breathe. "She choked him?"

"I'm not confirming anything," Copeland said, looking away. "I didn't even tell you the stuff you thought you just heard."

A voice from their left said, "And the boy?"

Joe turned and saw Michelle, a nearly empty wine glass held to her chest, standing atop the short flight of stairs leading to their bedroom.

Copeland looked up, surprised. Then he scowled at Joe as if Joe had beckoned his wife in to join them. His voice cheerless, Copeland said, "He's in state custody at the moment, Mrs. Crawford."

"That quickly?"

"You'd rather the kid stay in that house, ma'am?"

She took a deep breath, shivered a little. "It's not that…it's just…what will happen to the boy now?"

Copeland's gaze was steady. "God willing, he'll be remanded into foster care and eventually adopted."

Michelle took a step forward. "Isn't that a bit…extreme? Can't Angie go to classes? You know, become a better mom?"

Joe felt like he'd been socked in the gut. Somehow, hearing Angie referred to by her first name was even worse than hearing her called the girl. Because it created a link between Michelle and Angie Waltz, some bond forged by motherhood.

Copeland reached out, fingered the spines of the books on the built-ins. "I'd wager the boy's never gonna set foot in that house again."

Michelle and Joe exchanged a glance. He was hoping she'd be relieved by the news, but her expression was deeply troubled.

She said, "So that's it? They jail Angie and take her child away?"

"Don't forget Grandma," Copeland said. "She's as much a part of this as the girl."

That word again. Angie Waltz wasn't a girl, Joe thought. Girls didn't batter one-year-olds as they sat helpless in their car seats. Girls didn't flay the necks of men who tried to protect children. Joe realized he was gnashing his teeth and forced himself to stop.

Michelle moved down the steps, ran her fingers nervously around the rim of her wine glass. "Do you think it'll be permanent? The loss of custody?"

Joe saw something in Copeland's face. Joe said, "We're not just talking about what happened at the gas station, are we? You found something else in that house."

Copeland looked sharply at him, seemed to debate with himself. He pushed to his feet and continued his study of Joe's books.

"Angie Waltz is bad news. She's been jailed twice that we know of. Once for a DUI, another for manufacturing crystal meth with an ex-boyfriend."

My, my, Joe thought and glanced at Michelle. It was small of him, he knew, but he couldn't help it. *How's that motherhood kinship now, dear? Does it transcend drug-dealing too?*

Joe made a face, disgusted with himself. Christ, what an evening it had been. And it wasn't even ten o'clock yet.

When Joe looked up, he realized that Copeland had been watching him. The man's dead stare made it impossible to know what he was thinking.

"Listen," Copeland said, reaching into his shirt pocket and coming out with a pad of paper and a pen. "If you all need me, here's my cell phone. I don't like being disturbed when I'm off duty, but if it's something to do with this business, you can call me here."

He finished scratching out his number and handed it to Joe.

Michelle said, "You mentioned them finding more in the Waltzes' house?"

Copeland regarded her with what looked like bitterness, or maybe just distaste, but before he could answer, there came the ring tone of the cop's cell. Copeland took it out, said, "I'm here."

Joe heard the ghostly intonations of the voice on the other end and saw Copeland's brow furrow, the man looking indignant.

"But how could she?" Copeland asked.

More ghostly muttering.

Copeland's lips drew back, exposing straight white teeth. "Son of a motherf—Huh? Yeah, I'm still here."

He listened, nodded sourly, and hung up.

"What is it?" Michelle asked.

Copeland laughed humorlessly. "Well, you can forget what I said about Angie not making bail. Somebody already paid it."

★ ★ ★

Wind gusted outside their white bungalow home. The rain pattered against the windows, steady but not exactly an all-out assault. Joe did his best to concentrate on the book he was reading – *The Nightrunners*, by Joe R. Lansdale – but he couldn't keep to it. The *thunk*ing of the rain on the windowpanes kept intruding.

As did the face of Angie Waltz.

He kept seeing her not as she'd been yesterday at the gas station but as she might have been as a young, pregnant mother. Probably a scared, young, pregnant mother. He saw her lying propped up in bed because her back ached, saw her stroking the taut skin of her distended belly, pausing every now and then to feel for a kick or one of those breakdancing moves fetuses often performed.

He saw Angie Waltz in labor, watched her eyes whiten not in rage but in raw terror. He remembered when Michelle went into labor with Lily. God, they'd been through so much trouble and heartache trying to conceive that Joe had assumed the actual pregnancy would be a breeze.

But it wasn't. First, there was an ultrasound scare, the OB thinking Lily might have cystic fibrosis. Then, when that fear was quelled, it was the incapacitating morning sickness, which Michelle called morning, noon, and night sickness. Her back hurt like hell, her emotions went haywire. And on the day her water broke, it took twenty-seven hours of agonizing labor for their OB to suggest they try a C-section.

Had Angie Waltz gone through hell too? Had she experienced even a modicum of what Michelle was forced to endure? If she had, Joe couldn't help but feel—

"Why aren't you in bed?" Michelle asked, and Joe damn near shat himself.

He put a hand on his chest, felt his heart galloping. "I'm gonna put a bell around your neck, stop you from giving me a heart attack."

"It's one in the morning."

"You practice that or something? Sneaking up on people?"

She made her way over, knelt on the carpet, and placed a warm hand on his knee. "Come to bed, honey. Lily's gonna be up bright and early."

"No doubt."

She massaged his knee. "Want a backrub?"

He smiled wearily. "That's nice of you, sweetie, but you don't need to. No reason both of us should go without sleep."

She rested her chin on his knee, peered up at him. "You don't regret it, do you?"

"What? Helping the kid?"

She waited.

He threaded his fingers through her silky black hair, let his fingertips move gently over her scalp. They'd been married ten years, and he was more attracted to her now than he'd ever been. And those brown eyes of hers…they calmed Joe more than anything in the world.

"Joe?" she asked.

He said, "Only thing I regret is that there are people like Angie and her mother. I've never been much for the death penalty, but when it comes to hitting an innocent little kid…"

Michelle closed her eyes. "I know. I can still hear the sounds of her slapping him."

Joe continued stroking her hair. Outside, the wind had abated slightly, but the rain was coming down in sheets. "I keep thinking of Lily."

"Don't."

"I can't help it. She's not much older than that boy."

Michelle exhaled shuddering breath, leaned back. "Come to bed, Joe."

"I'll just lie there awake."

"Make love to me."

Unexpectedly, he felt a crooked smile forming on his lips. "Isn't it past your bed time?" And it was. Michelle often remarked how she'd go to bed at seven p.m. every evening if it weren't for Joe and Lily, both of whom were night owls.

"I'm awake now," Michelle said, pushing to her feet. "And the way you were fondling my hair made me horny."

"I'll be in directly."

She angled toward the stairs and smiled at him over her shoulder. "Thought that'd get you to come."

Joe chuckled. He reached over, fetched the paperback, and dog-eared the page he'd been reading. Placing the book on the nearest shelf, he twisted off the lamp on the end table and rose. He'd already brushed his teeth and washed his face, but he'd never eaten dinner. Of course, he thought as he passed through the dining room and into the dark kitchen, if he grabbed a bite now, his window of opportunity with Michelle might pass. She'd nod off soon, and there was no way she'd wake up just to have sex with him. The woman could sleep through a nuclear holocaust.

Going mostly by feel, Joe fished a glass out of the cabinet and filled it with tap water. The sensation of it washing over his desiccated throat was exquisite, and for the first time since pulling into the gas station, what might have been the start of some good spirits began to pierce the turmoil that had shaded his existence. He deposited the glass on the counter and made his way through the dark house.

Coming back into the living room, he noticed that the raindrops were intermittent now. They'd aired out the house earlier that day, and Joe was pretty sure they'd closed all the windows securely. Still, he couldn't stop himself from walking over and making sure. No sense in allowing the windowsills to warp out of carelessness. Joe had checked the first two windows and was reaching for the third when he became aware of a chill at the nape of his neck. There wasn't a draft – he could see well enough now that the third window was shut as securely as the other two had been. Suddenly sure Michelle had snuck up on him again, maybe as a joke or just feeling so frisky she couldn't wait for him to come to bed, Joe spun and stared into the darkness leading up the short flight of stairs.

Empty.

So Michelle was in bed waiting for him.

He blew out nervous breath, but for whatever reason that sense of being watched remained. Joe was moving away from the window when something in his periphery drew his attention. Something in the road out front of their house.

Joe froze.

Holy God, he thought.

Angie Waltz stood in the middle of the road, hair soaked and tangled. She was staring at Joe. Her head was tilted down, but he could just make out the hollows of her eyes, see how they were upturned and glaring. Searing into him through the veil of murk and rain. It couldn't be more than forty-five degrees out there now, even colder with the rain and the wind. Yet Angie wore only a sodden tank top and jeans. The rain glistened on her shoulders, drizzled down her slender arms and onto her balled fists.

Unhinged, Joe thought. The word was inescapable. *Unhinged.*

He didn't think he could move, but his feet obeyed his orders, carrying him away from the girl's cursed stare and toward the short flight of steps. Joe was about to ascend, but he paused, thinking of the depthless fury he'd glimpsed in the girl's oval moon of a face. Heart hammering, he rushed over and tested the locks on the front door. After a moment's deliberation, he hurried to the kitchen and checked the back door too.

It was locked, but what of the windows? God, of all the days for Michelle to have chosen to open every window in the house. Joe hated the notion of Angie Waltz seeing that she'd gotten to him, sent him scurrying to double-check every window they had. But he had to be certain.

He moved through the living room making sure not to look toward the street again. He didn't need to see Angie Waltz to know she was there. Hell, he could *feel* the malice baking out of her.

Joe crept into his bedroom, and it was as he suspected. His wife was asleep already.

Careful not to wake up Michelle, Joe tiptoed out of the bedroom, closed the door, and sat on the stairs. He thought it over for maybe ten seconds.

Then, he called Darrell Copeland.

CHAPTER THREE

"So what'd the cop say?" Kevin Gentry asked.

Joe shined his Maglite into the dank, cobwebbed basement and shook his head. "Not much of anything. Said it was a free country. Angie's out on bail, and the street is public property."

"Yeah, but that's your house, man. She can't just stalk you like that."

Gentry was standing too close to Joe, his breath like spoiled eggplant soaked in coffee. Joe had employed the guy for three years now, but Gentry still didn't grasp the concept of personal space. Or personal hygiene.

At least he was good with a circular saw.

They walked toward the eastern corner of the basement, which was even less promising than the other three corners had been. Here there were numerous cracks in the foundation, the brown stains of water damage and rot.

Joe sighed. "That's what I said to Copeland. But he said I'd have to file for a restraining order, go through all that rigmarole."

"I assume you're goin' to, aren't you?"

"Damn right," Joe said. "I don't want her around Lily. Or my wife."

Kevin was quiet a moment. Then he asked, "What'd Michelle say?"

"I didn't tell her."

"Come again?"

"You heard me." Joe knelt, ran his fingers over one of the largest cracks in the cinderblocks. It was almost as wide as his thumb. *Bad news*, he thought.

"But you're gonna tell her, aren't you?"

"Why scare her? She was upset enough as it was." Joe straightened, armed sweat off his brow. "There's no way they can do that second floormaster without shoring this up."

"The Johnsons have the budget for that?"

"I doubt it."

Joe started for the steps. Trailing after him, Kevin asked, "So what're we gonna do?"

"We're going to tell them their project can't go forward until they repair the foundation. Since that could cost twenty grand or more, they'll tell me to get lost and go with someone who'll do the job without the foundation work."

Kevin groaned as they began trudging up the steps. "Come on, Joe, it's not that dangerous. What's the worst that could happen?"

"Nothing much." Joe opened the door to the ground floor. "Other than the whole house coming down on their heads."

Gentry shook his head. "Stubborn."

"That's what Michelle always says."

"Maybe you should listen to her."

"Maybe you should stop humping goats."

Gentry chuckled as they passed through the kitchen en route to the mudroom. They went out the back door toward Joe's truck, the yard mucky from last night's rainfall.

"It's a shame," Gentry said. "I like this place."

"Enjoy it while it's still standing."

They got to Joe's black Tundra and climbed in.

Gentry said, "Well, I like it. You know, not all of us can live in the high-rent district like you."

Joe ignored that. "You know the place I'd really like to work on?"

"A titty bar?"

"The house next to mine."

Gentry rolled down the window, leaned on an elbow. "Seriously? You won't work on this one because of a few cracks, and you wanna go messin' around in a house that's one good storm away from fallin' down?"

"It's not that bad," Joe said, pulling out of the driveway.

"Place should be condemned," Gentry said. "Probably full of animals, water damage—"

"It isn't."

"How you know that?"

"I've been in it."

Gentry giggled. "What, you and Michelle go over there and tear one off?"

Joe arched an eyebrow at him. "What do you think we are, a couple of teenagers?"

Gentry shook his head. "It was me married to Michelle, I'd sure as hell take every opportunity I could."

Joe stiffened. "That's enough," he said as evenly as he could.

But he could see Gentry's leer from the corner of his eye. "Yeah, you *should* be worried, ol' hoss. She's what, eight years younger than you?"

"Six."

Gentry nodded. "Uh-huh. She might just get tired of you and your Viagra and decide to try out someone closer to her age one of these days."

Joe turned left at a four-way stop. "Keep talkin' and I'll chuck your sorry ass out that door."

Gentry chuckled at that, a little too loudly, Joe thought. He resisted an urge to make good on his threat.

Easy, he told himself. *Kevin's only a kid.*

He's almost thirty, a voice answered. *That's old enough to stop gawking at other men's wives.*

"So where to next?" Gentry asked.

"Your residence," Joe said. "It's your day off, remember?"

"Then why'd you ask me to inspect this house with you?"

Joe shrugged, motored slowly toward Gentry's modular home on the edge of town, where he lived with his wife and two young sons. "If that basement caved in, I wanted someone taller than me to take the brunt of the crash."

"That's awfully kind of you."

Don't mention it, Joe thought. *And I won't mention the real reason either. That after what happened yesterday and last night, I don't really want to be alone.*

The more witnesses, the better.

★ ★ ★

At least there was the Hawkins place. Though the water had been turned on again and he could've just drunk from the tap, Joe went out the back door and headed for the aged red pump back where the yard turned to forest. He'd grown up in a place similar to this, and being here, especially at midday, reminded him of his time with his parents and his kid brother. Reminded him of his dad most of all.

Joe realized his skin had gone cold.

Shivering, he raised the thick, cool handle of the pump, and water sluiced out over the grass. In time, if the Hawkinses' grandkids came out here often enough, the grass would turn to a bare, muddy patch again.

But the Hawkinses were elderly and seldom used the pump. Sadie said she operated it occasionally to grab a quick sip during her escapades in the garden, but most of the time the thing just remained there unused, like a neglected child left standing in the corner.

Joe bent, braced himself on the neck of the pump, and gulped long and lustily. God, it tasted good.

Joe enjoyed coming out here so much that Michelle had accused him of intentionally losing other bids so he could work on the Hawkins place. And while that wasn't true, he supposed he hadn't been in too much of a hurry to finish. After all, the Hawkinses only summered here and would be another two weeks in Punta Gorda, Florida. Joe and his crew would likely be done by then, and his afternoon respites at the pump would come to a permanent end.

Joe was straightening and drawing a forearm across his lips when Shaun Peterson came around the corner of the white farmhouse looking pale and shaken.

Son of a gun, Joe thought, because he knew what Shaun would say even before the tall blond kid pulled up about fifteen feet away, as though he was afraid to come any closer because what he was about to say would piss Joe off. But Joe didn't think he was going to be pissed off. He thought he was going to be sick. Because it was about the Waltz girl.

"I'm sorry, Joe," Shaun was saying, breathing heavy and stooped over as if he'd just run the 400-meter dash instead of walking from the front yard to the back. "I tried to tell her you weren't available, but…" He broke off, looking sheepishly at Joe. Then Joe saw her, slinking around the edge of the house.

Angie Waltz scarcely resembled the girl he'd tangled with at the gas station and looked even less like the rainswept specter who'd scared the living crap out of him last night by conducting her vigil in the middle of Hillcrest Road. But despite the fact that she now looked quite sultry – if a bit cheap – in her too-short white tank top and her skimpy Daisy Duke jean shorts, those dreadful feelings of the night before returned to Joe like symptoms of a terminal disease. Angie moved toward him like some inexorable force of nature, and though Joe had only been acquainted with her for less than twenty-four hours, he already felt like she was an albatross he was unable to escape.

Shaun took a few backward steps, the young guy's face showing plainly he wanted no part of Angie Waltz. Did Shaun know her already? Joe hadn't thought to ask him, mainly because he was trying to forget about her. But if he thought of it later, he would ask. The two couldn't be more than four or five years apart in age.

"Hi, Joe," Angie said, and the way she said it, with that white smile and languid complacence in her eyes, it was as though they were old friends rather than two people who'd needed to be physically separated yesterday. As though she weren't the reason he wore white tape and gauze pads on his throat and jaw.

Joe nodded and held his ground, but he'd be damned if he'd return that smile of hers.

Her eyebrows went up in mock bewilderment. "You told me he was busy, Shaun. All he's doin' is having himself a drink."

Shaun kept his eyes studiously trained on Joe. "I told her we were busy. I told her we had to be outta here by the end of the month so Harold and Sadie could enjoy their new addition."

Angie planted her hands on her shapely hips and nodded toward the back of the house. "Harold and Sadie must have a fair amount of money to build on like that."

Joe said, "What can we do for you, Angie?"

Angie cocked a hip. "That all you're gonna say, Joe? After you get my baby taken away from me?"

Here we go, Joe thought. "I told the police exactly what happened."

For just a moment, the yesterday Angie resurfaced. The tight lips. The flashing eyes. The tendons in her neck straining like some tethered mare.

Then her expression changed into one of hurt. "He's all I've got, Mr. Crawford. Little Stevie's my whole life."

Little Stevie, Joe mused. *Now where have I heard...*

Little Stevie Wonder, a familiar voice spoke up. *We used to listen to him all the time, Joey.*

With a start Joe realized who that voice belonged to – his dad, Joe Crawford Sr., who along with his mom and little brother were the only people who ever called him Joey. Joe's flesh began to crawl.

Angie took a step toward him, just out of arm's reach. Joe's hands hung at his sides, but if the woman drew any closer, he'd have them up and ready to fend her off. He'd seen how quickly Angie Waltz could strike.

"Mr. Crawford," she said, one hand massaging her throat, the other cupping her elbow, "can't you do something for us? I know what I did was wrong."

She must've seen Joe's expression change because a deeper desperation seeped into her voice. "I've got a temper. I know it's a problem, and I'm already calling around to get help for it. I saw what it could do yesterday. I saw—" Her eyes filled with tears, which looked genuine enough to Joe. She swallowed. "The last person in the world I'd ever want to hurt is Little Stevie. He's…he's everything to me, Mr. Crawford. Please don't let them take him away from me because of one mistake."

And listening to the tremor in her voice and seeing the heartache in her eyes, Joe was almost convinced.

Then a stern voice spoke up. *Remember what Copeland said last night. The bruises on that kid's body weren't just from the gas station. There were old ones and new ones, bruises of every shape and color.*

Joe shook his head. "I don't see what I can do, Miss Waltz."

She leaned forward a little, her eyes incredulous. "You don't *see*, Mr. Crawford? What do you mean you don't see?"

"I mean what's done is done. You beat the crap out of that child, and the authorities had to act."

"'*That child*'?" she demanded, the gas station Angie appearing again like some sort of deep-sea monster emerging from the depths. "You mean *my child*, Mr. Crawford. You mean Steven Patrick Waltz, the only child I have and the only thing in this shit stain of a town that means anything to me." As she spoke, her arms shook, and a little fleck of spit arced out of her mouth. But she didn't advance on Joe. Not yet.

He cast a glance at Shaun, who was watching the young woman with a look that reminded Joe of a child watching the coming of a bad storm through a basement window. Shaun was scared to death of Angie, and Joe couldn't blame him. Truthfully, Joe was too. He was still damned glad the kid was here. Who knew what kind of crazy story Angie Waltz might spread if she got Joe alone?

Joe took a steadying breath, met Angie's fierce glare, and said, "I didn't pull into that gas station with the intention of breaking up your family, Miss Waltz."

"But you sure did it, didn't you, Mr. Crawford? You sure as hell broke up my family. You took it right away." And now she did advance a step. All kinds of warning bells went off in Joe's head, and he saw that Shaun's expression had gone from trepidation to outright terror. Joe knew why. The tornado had come, and it was worse than Shaun could've imagined.

He had to get her away from this house, had to move them all three back toward the driveway, where he might stand a chance of talking her back into her van or broomstick or whatever she'd ridden here on. But something deep down in him, some primitive instinct, told him he'd have to stand his ground here in this shadowy backyard. Because if he didn't, if he showed any weakness at all, it would haunt him later on. Or cause her to attack right now.

Joe said, "What should I have done, Miss Waltz?"

"Quit calling me that," she said, and now Joe smelled something on her, something that reminded him of mouthwash, but almost certainly wasn't. It reeked of hard alcohol, Jagermeister or some such thing. And now that he'd noticed it, he couldn't believe he hadn't detected it earlier. She was swaying a little. That unsteady lilt to her gait, he'd taken that for a seductive saunter. But it wasn't. It was inebriation.

"Okay," Joe said. "What would you like me to call you?"

"I dunno," she said, her voice a little slurry. "How about Sweet Tits or Hot Buns? You keep lookin' me up and down enough, you might as well talk to me how you want to."

Get out of here, Joe, the voice in his head ordered, and though Joe knew this was sound advice, something held him back. Stubbornness? Gentry would've said so. But Gentry was off today. It was just Joe and Shaun, and Shaun wasn't going to be worth much in this situation. It was up to Joe to deal with it.

So deal with it, he told himself.

"You need to sober up, Miss Waltz. If you want your boy back, you're going to need to show them you're willing to change." He paused, then forced himself to add, "Drunk and angry won't cut it."

She laughed, but there was no humor in the sound. None at all. "You really think that'll make a difference? You really think some judge or that fucking social worker's gonna care if I stop drinking or take a few classes?"

"Look, I don't—"

"It's your *story* that has to change," she said, and all of a sudden she was grasping the front of his flannel shirt. "Can't you see that, Mr. Crawford? It's your *story.* You and your wife, you two were the main witnesses. If you guys change your story, they'll give me Stevie back."

The booze smell had enveloped him like a sinister aura. Beneath that he could smell the woman's body odor, a scent that was at turns beguiling and repugnant. Like sweat and sex and unwashed bedsheets.

And something else, he realized now. The reek of ashes. Unaccountably, the flesh of his arms began to tingle.

"Miss Waltz, you should probably go."

"Angie," she breathed. "Please call me Angie."

"Okay…Angie, I don't think what you're asking's possible. Besides, I only told the truth. Same with Michelle. Why would we lie about it? What could we possibly have to gain?"

It was as if Angie hadn't heard him. She continued to gaze up at him with that imploring look, her forearms hot against his chest, her alcohol breath puffing over him in steamshovel waves.

"Look," Joe said, "I wish yesterday had never happened. But—"

"*It didn't,*" Angie said, shaking her head vigorously, her eyes huge with hope and irrational faith. "It didn't happen, Mr. Crawford! We can just make it go away. We'll tell the cops and that bitch from CPS it was all a misunderstanding, and I can get Stevie back. They'll drop the charges and everything'll go back to the way it was before." He didn't think it was possible, but she drew even closer, standing on her toes now so their faces were only inches apart. "You didn't mean any harm, Mr. Crawford. I can see that in your eyes." She stared deeply into them. "They're kind eyes. Handsome eyes. You'd never do a woman wrong on purpose. Would you?" Her breath wafted over him, through him, insinuating its way up his nostrils, and making him a little dizzy. Her body had pressed against his, and her tight belly and the fabric of her jean shorts were melding into his midsection.

My God, Joe thought. *Does she actually think she can confound me with sex?*

He put his hands on her shoulders as gently – and platonically – as he could and moved her away. But she bit her lip and clung to him, a teardrop streaking down one cheek and more of them queuing up in her big blue eyes. "Please, Mr. Crawford," she whispered in a choked voice. "Please help me. I'll never touch Little Stevie again, except to love on him." She clutched his shirt harder, pulled their bodies together. "I'll do anything you want, Mr. Crawford. Anything at all."

Joe swallowed. "Please let go of me, Miss Waltz."

Angie watched him for a long moment.

She exhaled trembling breath, the embers of hope in her eyes guttering. She let go of him, took a couple swaying steps backward.

Her hands clasped in front of her mouth, she whispered, "You won't help me, Mr. Crawford? Please?"

Joe suppressed the urge to puke. "I'm sorry, Miss Waltz. I've done all I can."

Her hands dropped to her sides, her expression going dead. *Uncanny*, he thought. *Just like that. Just like a jack-o-lantern extinguished by a frigid October wind.*

Her dead eyes locked on his. She said, "So that's it?"

A tremor of fear passed through him. "I'm sorry."

She stared at him with such ancient hatred that he felt cold all over. "So am I, Mr. Crawford. I'm sorry too."

CHAPTER FOUR

Neither Angie Waltz nor her mother showed up at the worksite again that week, but the maroon van must've passed by Joe's house twenty times a day during that span. While Joe was lifting weights. When he and Lily were reading.

Now, as he sat across the kitchen table from Michelle, with Lily in her highchair flinging SpaghettiOs in every direction, Joe heard the rusty muffler buzzing up the street again.

Michelle dropped her fork on her plate. "Goddammit. That's the third time since we sat down."

Frowning, Joe glanced at Lily to see if she'd try to mimic the cuss word her mommy had just uttered. Thankfully, the girl was too busy slathering her cheeks with orange sauce.

Michelle said, "Can't you call Copeland?"

"And say what? That the Waltzes are using a public street again?"

"You don't have to make fun of me."

"I'm not," Joe said. He tried to enjoy a forkful of the Thai salad leftovers they were eating. The stuff still tasted good, though the lettuce was a bit slimy. "That's what he said the other night: 'Unless they set foot on your property, there's nothing we can do.'"

Michelle motioned toward the front of the house, where the rusty muffler was burring by. "So by that reasoning, I could go stand in front of their house and just stare at them?"

Joe chewed his salad. "I can't imagine why you'd want to do that."

"I'm just making a point."

Joe kept quiet.

"Couple white-trash rednecks," Michelle muttered. "Probably live in a trailer park."

"My parents and I lived in a trailer when I was little," Joe said. "Nothing wrong with it."

"Stop defending them."

"I'm not. Anyway, they don't live in a trailer. They're over there on Crosser Street."

Lily chattered about five little monkeys. It was currently her favorite book.

But Michelle was frowning at him. "How do you know where they live?"

Joe shrugged, sat back. "I followed them the other day."

Michelle gaped at him. "*Joe.* Are you *crazy*?"

He could not suppress a grin. "I love it when you say my name like that. Making it two or three syllables."

"This isn't funny! Those women are bad news."

Joe eyed Lily, noticed she was watching Michelle with trepidation. "Take it easy, hon."

"I won't take it easy. I'm scared. It's been a week already. How long do they plan on stalking us?"

Joe got up, wetted a washcloth from the drawer, and began the job of removing the patina of orange gloop from his daughter's face, hands, and hair. The clothes were a lost cause. When he'd gotten some of the SpaghettiOs off, he removed Lily from her highchair and patted her diapered behind. "Go play with your trains, honey. Daddy will be along in a minute."

Lily squealed and jogged to her room to play on her train table. Joe plopped down in his chair. "I imagine they'll keep on bothering us until they get tired of it."

Michelle's brow knitted. She was gazing out the kitchen window, maybe listening for a recurrence of the muffler. "Maybe if she gets her boy back she'll forget about us."

Joe sat forward, interlaced his fingers. "That's not gonna happen."

Michelle looked at him. "How do you know?"

"I talked to Copeland the other day. When you demanded we get a restraining order on the Waltzes?"

The seams in Michelle's forehead grew more pronounced.

Joe sighed. "Copeland said there's no way she's ever getting that boy back. In fact, she's lucky to be out of jail. He says the judge would have set bail higher if he actually thought there was a chance of Angie making it."

"How can they do that?"

"Do what?"

Michelle made a vague gesture. "Take her child away. Permanently, I mean."

Joe grunted. "You want Stevie back in that house?"

"How do you know his name?"

"Angie said it."

As soon as the words had left his mouth, he knew he'd made a mistake. He'd never told Michelle about Angie Waltz's visit to the Hawkins worksite.

"You talked to her?"

Joe knew he couldn't make up a passable story – he'd always been an abysmal liar and knew he'd never be able to fool Michelle – so he explained how Angie had shown up. He told her pretty much everything, minus the part about how Angie had pressed her supple, half-naked body up against him as part of her persuasion.

When Joe finished, Michelle shook her head. "I can't believe you didn't tell me."

"I didn't want to worry you."

"Well, I *am* worried. I'm worried those bimbos are going to do something violent."

"I haven't heard the word bimbo for probably ten years. I'm glad you're bringing it back."

"It's not funny, Joe."

"Sorry."

"What did Copeland say?"

"That between the bruises on the kid, the incident at the gas station, and the drug paraphernalia in the Waltzes' house, there was no way Little Stevie was going back to live there."

Michelle seemed to crumble, her arms dropping to her sides. "Do you have to call him that?"

"It's his name, isn't it? Besides, I feel sort of responsible for the little guy."

Something new seemed to creep into her eyes. "Don't say that."

He paused. "What are you worried about, Michelle?"

"I don't know," she said. "Everything?"

Outside, the ragged buzz of the van's muffler sounded again.

"Goddamn them," Michelle whispered.

Joe pushed away from the table. "Nothing we can do, honey. I'm gonna play trains with Lily."

★ ★ ★

"You own a gun, Joe?"

Joe stared at Darrell Copeland. The big cop had his forearms planted on the side of Joe's truck bed, which was parked in the graveyard. Joe was leaning against the rocker panel, arms folded, facing the woods. "Why would I need a gun?" Joe asked.

Copeland shrugged. "Might not hurt to have one."

Joe studied the cop's profile. "That doesn't sound encouraging."

"Don't read too much into it."

"Easy for you to say."

"You think so? You think Angie and her drug friends are big fans of mine? The cop who came and took her baby away?"

"Has her van been doing laps around your block?"

Copeland didn't answer. He looked around apprehensively. "You sure this was a good idea, Joe? Meetin' in a graveyard?"

"It seemed like it at the time," Joe said. "Now it feels a little macabre."

"I was thinking the same thing."

"Why do you think I need a gun?"

Copeland looked troubled. "I don't know."

"You must have an idea though."

"She and her mom are bad news," Copeland said. "People like that… there's no tellin' what they'll do."

Joe watched a rook wing toward the rim of the forest, then light on a broad oak bough. The leaves there were just beginning to bud. "This'll all be over soon, though, won't it? Isn't Angie's trial coming up?"

Darrell peered out over the cemetery, a speculative cast to his eyes. "Who knows? I'm not even sure she'll make it to trial."

"Now what's that supposed to mean?"

Copeland pushed up straight, tapped the side of the truck bed with his thick fingers. "I saw her the other day. Drove by her house over on Crosser Street? I went up the alley. You know, just to see what was going on. I saw her out there. There's a covered porch in back. She was just sittin' on the that porch, staring out at the alley."

"So?"

Copeland shrugged, stuffed his hands in his pockets. "I don't know. It's just the look she had that bothered me. Eyes all glassy. Looked like all she had on was an old nightgown she probably got from her mom. It was only eight in the morning, couldn't have been more than forty degrees. Yet she just sat there with only her spaghetti straps on her shoulders, her knees so far apart anyone could catch a glimpse of her privates."

"She wasn't wearing any…"

"No panties, no nothin'. Showin' anybody who drove by her crotch. Hell, she didn't even seem to notice me go by."

Joe imagined Angie Waltz sitting there in the cold, legs spread, eyes expressionless, and felt his skin break into gooseflesh, despite the fact that it was nearly sixty degrees.

CHAPTER FIVE

Kyle Everett, the attendant who'd helped Joe the afternoon Angie and Sharon Waltz had mauled him at the Marathon station, sat on the tall stool reading a tattered paperback novel and tried to block out the television playing in the corner of the small dining area. Presently, there were two customers seated at one of the four tables, both of them senior citizens who drank the brackish swill the Marathon station passed off as coffee every evening between six and ten and who frequently demanded Kyle turn up the television because neither one heard particularly well.

For the thousandth time, Kyle contemplated lobbing a rock at the old mounted television's screen so he wouldn't have to hear *Wheel of Fortune* or the evening news anymore.

"Turn it up a notch, would ya, Kyle?" Frank Gretencord called.

Lips compressed, Kyle scooped up the remote, pushed the volume button once, and placed it back under the counter. Man, he wished the hog plant hadn't laid him off. Compared to manning the desk at this gas station, toiling among hog carcasses didn't seem all that bad. At least he wouldn't have to listen to Pat Sajak every night.

Of course, it wasn't dark yet. The days were getting longer now, and though it was six-fifteen, twilight wouldn't end for another twenty minutes. Kyle scanned the pumps through the picture windows and saw they were empty. Everyone in town, it seemed, was eating supper. Everyone except Frank Gretencord and Elmore Hempel, widowers who both desperately longed for companionship and could only find it at a dreary gas station that specialized in leathery fried chicken and desiccated potato wedges.

Sighing, Kyle got up, went over to the coffee machine, and took down two Styrofoam cups. He filled them both, emptied a container of cream in one, and shook two packets of sugar into the other. He crossed to where Frank and Elmore sat commenting on Vanna White's boobs and deposited the two cups before the men.

Elmore glanced up at him in pleasure and surprise. "Hey, thanks, fella!"

"No problem," Kyle said. "I figured you two were getting a little low."

"He's a good boy," Frank said as Kyle returned to his post.

Feeling a little better about his dead-end job, Kyle assumed his perch on the stool and returned to the book he'd been reading. It was darned good so far, and diverting enough to make Kyle forget about—

"How much do I owe you?"

Kyle jumped and dropped his paperback.

Angie Waltz stared at him from the other side of the counter.

Kyle's heart thudded. "Jeez, I didn't even see you come in."

Angie said nothing, only stared at him in that same incurious way. Now that his heartbeat had begun to approximate a normal rhythm, Kyle noticed how dark the hollows of her eyes were, almost like she'd gotten the worst of a fistfight. Her clothes were awfully shabby too, just a dingy gray robe, untied and flapping open, and a nightgown that once might have been white. Kyle realized with some misgiving that the gown was made of some flimsy material, so that the dark circles of Angie's nipples were plainly visible beneath. Of their own accord his eyes traveled lower, and what he saw there made him feel a little queasy. Why Kyle should be repelled by the sight of an attractive young woman's shaved sex, he had no idea.

Maybe it's because there's something so obviously wrong with this girl, he thought. *And maybe because at this moment she's not attractive at all, despite her skimpy outfit.*

"Can I pay or not?" Angie said. Her voice held little rancor though. It was leaden, toneless.

Kyle nodded and stood up hastily. Leaning over, he peered out the window but didn't spot her maroon Dodge Caravan. "I'm not sure I—"

"I walked," she said. She lifted a two-gallon gas can. "Pump five."

"Ah," Kyle said and rang her up.

While she waited to pay, Kyle glanced askance to see if Frank or Elmore had noticed the girl. They'd both been present last week when Angie Waltz had abused first her son, then Joe Crawford, to say nothing of the damage Sharon Waltz had inflicted on Kyle. Frank Gretencord had been one of the sworn witnesses to the Waltzes' brutality.

But to his chagrin, neither man had marked Angie's coming.

Too transfixed by Vanna White, he thought.

Thankfully, the stupid cash register finally rang up. "That's seven dollars and forty-nine cents," he said.

Angie Waltz dropped a crumpled bill on the counter and walked silently toward the door. No, Kyle thought, the worm of uneasiness in his belly beginning to grow. Not *walked* toward the door. *Shambled* toward the door. Her gait reminded him of that television show, the one with the zombies. He never watched it, in fact he hated TV. But he'd seen a zombie walk – that hitching, shoulder-twitching stride that seemed somehow, well, *dead.* Angie pushed open the door and made a right turn, still shambling in that zombiefied manner.

Kyle watched until Angie disappeared, his fingers tapping the counter.

He didn't like it.

"Hey, Frank?" he called.

A long pause. The codger hadn't heard him.

"Frank? Elmore?"

"Just a minute, Kyle," Frank called. "We're tryin' to solve the puzzle. It's something about a wrench."

"Second word's only five letters," Elmore reminded him.

"Nude bitch!" Frank yelled.

"They wouldn't say *nude* on *Wheel of Fortune*, dumbass."

Kyle tapped his fingers, thinking. He glanced down, studied the crumpled bill. Flattening it out, he saw it was a fifty.

In the background, he heard a contestant say, "I'd like to solve, Pat."

"Rude bitch!" Frank called.

"Dude ranch," the contestant said. The audience applauded.

"Told you they wouldn't say nude on national TV," Elmore said.

Kyle moved around the edge of the counter with the greasy bill in his hand. "Watch the register for me, would you, fellas?"

Neither man looked up. Frank said to Elmore, "They had *Nude Beach* up there one time."

"You're senile," Elmore said as the front door wheezed shut behind Kyle.

Kyle hustled around the front of the station. Crosser Street was only a couple blocks away, but shambling along as she was and weighted down by a two-gallon gas can, he figured he could overtake Angie before she reached her back porch.

Truth be told – and Kyle was loath to admit this, even to himself – he'd more than once driven that alley behind Angie Waltz's house, hoping to catch a glimpse of her in her bedroom upstairs. Shadeland was a small town, and a young man's options were limited. If Angie weren't several years younger than he was and not always involved with some local druggie, Kyle would've gone ahead and asked her out on a legitimate date. Not that making slow cruises up and down her alley and peeping in her windows was legitimate, of course, but it was better than jerking off to internet porn.

He hurried past the unisex restroom – the Marathon station still kept its key attached to a Billy club, perhaps as a nod to a bygone era – and held his breath until he was well past the huge green dumpster. Ahead, he spied Angie, the rounded gas can bumping her leg with each awkward stride. If he hadn't seen her up close, he would've guessed she was high on some drug. But Kyle couldn't think of a drug that made a person look like an extra in a zombie film. Crystal meth did weird things to a body – some of Kyle's old high school buddies had turned into gaunt scarecrows after only a few months of taking the shit – but other than the purplish eye sockets and that dead look, Angie Waltz looked every bit as tan and nubile as she always had.

Maybe, he thought, jogging to catch up with her now, he could be the one to reform her. Sort of nurse her back to health. He knew she probably hated him – she had to know he was one of the ones who'd signed a statement about her abuse – and of course there was the matter of Kyle telling her and her mom to get the hell off the property after the incident…

Kyle slowed to a walk, realizing that his chances of dating Angie were somewhere between zero and the possibility of Frank and Elmore doubling up on Vanna White. And anyway, Angie was nearing her house now, the shuffling gait slowly but steadily delivering her to her covered back porch.

But still…something compelled him on, made him close the gap between them once again so that as she moved haltingly up the broken back sidewalk, he found himself less than thirty feet from her. She neared the wooden back porch, began the climb up the four rickety steps.

He spoke without thinking. "You left me a fifty!"

She stopped on the back porch, the overhang shadowing her slightly. The evening had darkened a little, but it was still plenty light enough to see how motionless her body was, how fixed her shoulders remained. As if she wasn't even breathing.

He tried again. "I owe you a little over forty bucks. You mind if I come back in a minute with your change?"

Her back still to him, Angie didn't move at all. It occurred to him she might be having some kind of medical episode. Weren't there conditions that made you zone out for short periods of time? Fugue states, he thought they were called. He remembered learning about them in Mr. Crabbe's sophomore health class. He thought they were associated with—

Angie Waltz turned to face him. In the sundown light, her blue eyes looked like polished onyx.

"Hey," he said, trying to smile, "is there anything I can—"

She reached down, unscrewed the gas cap.

Kyle swallowed. "I forgot to ask you. What did you get the gas for? You gonna mow the lawn tonight?"

Her eyes never leaving his, Angie lifted the can above her head.

The worm in Kyle's belly writhed.

Angie tilted the gas can, allowed the liquid to glug over her head, drenching her hair, her face, her half-open mouth. Her clothes turned dark with the stuff, her sheer nightgown plastered to the front of her body like a transparent bathing suit. A small breeze skittered across the backyard, carrying with it the pungent odor of gasoline.

There was no moisture in Kyle's mouth. His voice a croak, he said, "Angie, you need some help."

Angie reached into the pocket of the sodden robe.

She came out with something rectangular and silver.

Kyle sucked in horrified breath, took a couple unthinking steps forward. "Hey, Angie. Hey, you don't wanna—"

But she had flicked the lighter, was lifting it toward her face. For an endless moment, the warm orange glow from the lighter illuminated the pretty heart-shaped chin, the sensuous lines of her jaw and full lips. Above that, the onyx eyes only stared, their expression never changing. Only the glistening beads on her skin and the stench of gasoline indicated that anything out of the ordinary was happening.

Angie kept the flame a few inches from her face long enough for Kyle to hope she might just be playing a trick on him, frightening him because he talked to the police last week.

Then the flame licked her skin, and her face became a brilliant orange mask.

Kyle staggered backward and fell, his eyes fixed wide in horror.

Angie Waltz became a gleaming torch, the flames spreading around her in no time at all.

PART TWO
ASHES

CHAPTER SIX

Joe extended the train track with another wooden section, then began the curve that would eventually link up with the rest of the line. His daughter had her chain of seventeen trains and freight cars poised at the top of the big hill, clearly ready to let the whole thing rumble down the tracks.

"Just a second, honey," Joe said. "Daddy needs to finish this curve."

Lily let go of the lead engine.

The drag from the other sixteen train cars sent the whole thing reversing down the other side of the hill. The train derailed immediately.

Lily wailed.

Joe crawled over, began righting the toppled cars. "I told you, honey, if you make the train shorter, it'll be less likely to wreck."

Lily shouted, "I don't want them to wreck!" Only the way she said it, *wreck* sounded like *weck*.

From the doorway, Michelle said, "She's tired."

"Her nap's not for another three hours."

"Maybe she needs a snack."

Joe continued straightening the trains. "She ate a banana a few minutes ago. She just doesn't like it when her train goes off the tracks."

Joe knew it was coming, but the question still tore into him when Michelle asked it.

"Are you going today?"

"Didn't we have this discussion last night?"

Lily grabbed the lead train – a long blue one named Gordon – and started pulling it toward the hill even though Joe hadn't gotten all of the trains fixed yet.

"Don't you feel like you should?" Michelle asked.

"You know how I feel."

There were only two freight cars still overturned, but they were enough to upset the ones in front of them, causing a chain reaction that sent the whole line toppling off the hill.

Lily screamed, hurled Gordon across the room.

"Honey," Joe said, keeping the edge off his voice, "you need to pick that up."

Michelle said, "I can't imagine how Sharon must feel."

Lily kicked a pair of trains – Percy and a coal car – and they went tumbling under the couch.

"Honey, we don't throw and kick our trains," Joe said, knowing it wouldn't do a bit of good. Arguing with Lily when she threw a tantrum was like reasoning with a malfunctioning car alarm. "Now, let's pick up Gordon and Percy."

"No!" Lily shouted. Her face had gone a livid red, her eyes brimming with tears.

"Maybe I'll go," Michelle said, as if to herself.

"Come on, honey," Joe said. He got to his knees, grasped his daughter around the waist and attempted to pick her up.

"No!" Lily shrieked. "Leggo, Daddy! Leggo!"

His two-year-old reached back and grabbed at the only thing at her disposal, the hill Joe had assembled for her. She knocked one side of it over, latched onto the heavy center section.

"It's okay, sweetie," Joe said. "We'll pick up your trains, and then we'll—"

Lily raised the heavy center section with both hands and bonked Joe on the top of the head.

Joe sucked in air and clasped a hand to his skull. God, it felt like she'd smacked him with a brick. He clenched his jaws, waited for the shrieking pain to subside.

"Are you sure you won't go with me?" Michelle asked.

He checked his hand and saw a little blood on his fingers.

Michelle looked too, seemed to return from whatever far-off mental place she'd been. "What happened?"

"You didn't see Lily brain me with Sodor Mountain?"

"Uh-uh. Joe, you might need stitches."

Joe got up, rubbed his bloody fingers on the leg of his jeans. "I don't need stitches, and you don't need to go to Angie Waltz's funeral."

Michelle followed him up the carpeted basement steps. "But Sharon... she lost her daughter, her house. She probably won't get custody of her grandson. Don't you think one of us should go?"

"Why, so we can end up on the six o'clock news?"

"You don't really think she'll cause a scene, do you?"

Joe grunted humorless laughter. "Were you *at* the gas station?"

"But that's my point," she said as he moved to the kitchen. "We were involved in what happened. It just seems right that we should pay our respects."

"I don't have any respects." He snatched up his keys.

"You know it's the right thing to do."

"Michelle, I'll be damned if I'm going to her funeral," he said.

Michelle just looked at him.

★ ★ ★

Joe arrived at the funeral a half-hour before it was scheduled to begin. He could see the royal blue tent set up near the western edge of the cemetery, which was a goodly distance from where he was heading. The graveyard was hilly, which was a good thing. Joe curved away from the tent, did his best not to glance at the small columbarium, the place where...

He couldn't think about it.

Joe parked at the far eastern edge, just a few feet from the encroaching forest, in a dale low enough to prevent anyone at the ceremony from spotting him. Hell, even if someone did wander from the tent, Joe was a good hundred yards away. It'd take some very bad luck to be discovered down here in the oldest part of the cemetery.

A cynical voice in his head muttered, *Kinda like the bad luck you had pulling into the gas station that day?*

Ignore it, Joe, another voice spoke up. It was the voice of his dad, his poor, ineffectual dad who killed himself when Joe was away at college. Left by a cheating wife, plagued by bad luck in his business dealings, his father had shot himself in the temple with a Colt Mustang.

Joe's mom had decided to drop this particular bomb on him when he was away at college, during a time when Joe didn't have a girlfriend or any friends he particularly trusted. So he ended up dealing with it on his own, which was to say he cried about it a great deal and had endless nightmares about it. Until he learned to suppress it, which was what he'd done with traumatic events ever since.

The news of his mother's terminal breast cancer when he was twenty-three.

His mother's slow, awful death.

The morning Michelle suffered a miscarriage, only six weeks away from her due date. And now their little boy's remains were stored in the columbarium he'd just passed. He knew he should visit it more often, knew he should honor the memory of his son...but the pain was so deep, the images of Michelle on the bathroom floor, bleeding and wailing, were so soul shattering, that he'd buried the memory of it, entombed it in his mind.

But now he'd dredged it up, the sorrow and the rage and the hopelessness. The memory took him unawares, made him instantly short of breath and panic-stricken with claustrophobia. Scrabbling for the door handle, Joe gasped for breath until he stumbled clumsily out of the pickup and damn near blacked out from lack of oxygen.

Joe bent, hands on knees, as a maniacal carousel of images twirled through his mind: Angie Waltz grinning at him from her van, her face charred and lipless; his mother's yellowing face buried under a mound of morphine and strapped inside a fogged breathing mask; his father's closed casket, Joe's younger self staring at the cheap wooden exterior, imagining his dad's obliterated head within; Sharon Waltz's bared teeth in the gas station; blood gushing from Michelle's vagina as she sobbed on the bathroom floor; Angie that day in the Hawkinses' back yard, oozing malice and sexuality in equal measure; and finally, inexplicably, his own house on fire with Lily dozing innocently in her crib.

His breath came in great, sucking heaves, but soon the gray fog in his mind dissipated. Standing erect again, he inhaled another robust breath and surveyed the area around him. Downhill from where his truck sat in the weedy lane, there was perhaps an acre of grass and dandelions before the forest began. Though it was only April, many of the trees were beginning to bud, a trio of scattered magnolias starting to bloom. Another day or two and their pink blossoms would interrupt the brownness of the forest. Another couple weeks and the whole thing would be a riot of colors, green and pink and violet and yellow. Joe might return here then, he thought, not to visit Angie's grave – in fact, he was still unsure why he was here at all – but to read a book maybe. During one of Lily's naps. Michelle often lay with their daughter to coax her into sleep. And though Michelle spoke of their slumbering afternoons as a nuisance, Joe suspected his wife liked to nap with Lily as much as Lily enjoyed nestling under the comforter with Michelle.

Joe was thinking this when he became aware of mufflers rumbling, several cars apparently entering the graveyard at its western edge.

He pushed to his feet, rounded the truck, and pelted up the hill. The blue tent and its array of folding black chairs came into view. There were already a few older people seated there, their swirling white, gray, and bald heads reminding him of gooseberry marbles some child had arranged in an uneven line.

Joe frowned, thinking of the jar of marbles Michelle had insisted on placing on the shelf in the dining room. Twice they'd quarreled about the safety of letting Lily play with them. Michelle's argument was always about how much Lily loved the marbles, both the rolling of them along the wood floors and the smooth texture of them in her pink little hands. Joe had never disputed this, but he still cringed every time Michelle got them out because they were choking hazards. Yeah, they were pretty. Yeah, they were pleasing to the touch. But he couldn't wrest the image from his mind of little Lily swallowing one and getting it lodged in her throat, the soft pink flesh there closing over it like a giant pearl, the girl's face turning a gloomy plum color. Her airway closing off...

Joe shook his head, realizing he'd lost his breath again. He forced air into his lungs, though it cost him an effort. It felt as though some giant weight had been placed atop his chest. He felt like getting the hell out of this boneyard, but escape was now out of the question. All lanes led to a central paved thoroughfare, which meant Joe would pass within fifty yards or so of the gravesite. And anyway, the lane was now clogged with cars, each of them sporting a little orange flag indicating their inclusion in the funeral procession. Joe was stuck.

Joe glanced back at the forest, considered exploring for a while, the way he used to when he was a kid. They'd lived adjacent to a woods similar to this. Back then, Joe's dad used to take him exploring all the time. They'd slather themselves in insect repellent, take a bottle of water along, and spend hours on the paths. They'd both been prone to poison ivy rashes, and Joe's mother had often berated them for venturing into infested areas. But the itching and the discomfort and the endless applications of calamine lotion had been worth it just to have his dad to himself. Had Joe known his father would take his own life so soon after Joe went away to college, he would've gone walking in the woods with him every damned day.

The tears caught him off guard. He wiped his cheeks jerkily, amazed at his emotional volatility.

Joe clamped down on his emotions, turned and headed resolutely up the rise. He didn't need to brood about something that happened more than two decades ago; he needed to get a better view. Sure, it was probably a meaningless gesture coming here today. But at least *he'd* know he'd come.

On the opposite side of the lane, the graves began. Most of the markers were very old and very small. Crosses made from some white stone grown mossy and crooked from half a century or more of neglect. Low rectangular blocks so eroded by time and the elements that the inscriptions were scarcely legible. Joe took his time, scanning the dates and names as well as he could, and taking care to walk between the stones rather than treading on ground that had once been turned and reseeded after ceremonies just like the one occurring now.

Joe looked up and was surprised to note how swiftly he'd halved the distance between the truck and the blue tent. What was more, Joe realized he could now make out the faint murmur of a man he assumed to be the attending pastor. There'd come a couple lines in the man's deep bass voice – passages of scripture, Joe assumed – then there'd be an answering line from the crowd. Their backs were to Joe, so he remained fairly confident he could venture closer without being spotted, but it wouldn't hurt to exercise caution. He seriously doubted they'd form the lynch mob his imagination had conjured, but if he could avoid a scene of any kind, he would. The preacher wore a sable frock that was curiously open at the throat, but aside from this, the man looked like Joe supposed a preacher should – short, thinning brown hair combed over to one side, spectacles. Joe pegged him for about fifty-five.

Perhaps fifty yards away now, Joe stooped lower and moved with as much stealth as he could. He supposed he'd look ridiculous if someone noticed him tiptoeing through a cemetery in the middle of the day, but he didn't plan on being discovered. Thirty yards away now, Joe took refuge behind a marble angel mounted atop a four-foot-tall marble base. Since the epitaph was chiseled into the opposite side of the monument, he had no idea behind whose gravestone he'd hunkered, but Joe was grateful the unknown deceased's family had gone to such opulent lengths to bury their loved one. Aside from this monument, there wasn't a single stone big enough to conceal Joe's broad frame.

As he bent lower, both his knees went off like pistol shots. Joe winced and shook his head ruefully. He considered himself physically fit for being on the wrong side of forty, but it was as though his body liked to periodically remind him that he was indeed aging. Ignoring the damp grass beneath him, Joe rested on his knees and leaned against the marble base so he could better hear the ceremony.

He frowned. The preacher's resonant voice reached him easily despite the space between them, yet the words sounded like nonsense. Joe craned his head forward to better hear and realized after a moment the man was speaking Latin. Or at least it sounded like Latin. Joe had never studied the language in school, but he'd come across enough of it in his many years of reading to pick out a few words.

The preacher's voice rose.

"*Invidia,*" Joe heard him say. "*Ulciscor…spiritus…*"

Joe's frown deepened.

The preacher plowed on, his voice strengthening, the words taking on a sinister timbre.

This didn't sound like any kind of sermon Joe had ever heard before. He and his little family attended the Lutheran church a couple miles from where they lived, and though he didn't agree with everything said there, Joe reckoned he and Jesus understood each other pretty well. His only really negative experience had begun at a potluck lunch at which he and Pastor Walker had disagreed about Jesus and the Savior's views of homosexuals. Walker had claimed that Jesus would've condemned the gays to hell and proceeded to rail on about Sodom and Gomorrah and anal sex. Joe had disagreed and pointed out that Jesus's anger was directed at hypocrites – folks who made money off of worshippers, for example – but that had gone over like a lead balloon. The next week, Pastor Walker had recapitulated the same talking points in a sermon Joe was sure had been directed at him and his pagan views.

But even though the experience had soured Joe on Pastor Walker, he'd kept attending the Lutheran church. With Michelle's constant urging, Joe even managed to stay awake during Walker's sermons.

Yet in all the times he'd heard the man speak, Joe had never heard Pastor Walker reciting Latin.

"*Instruo*..." the man's deep voice said. "*Filia*..."

So the preacher's a priest, Joe's mind argued. *Why can't the Waltzes be Catholic?*

If this is a Catholic ceremony, Joe shot back, *where's the man's white collar? Why isn't there a cross anywhere?*

You're a goodly distance away, Joe. Maybe you just haven't spotted it yet.

Not the slightest bit reassured, Joe edged out from behind the marble block to better hear.

"*Mortuus*...*veritas*...*ignis*..."

Not only was the man's voice booming now, he was gesticulating wildly and pacing from one side of the casket to the other. The onlookers were nodding and muttering their approval. Joe made out the words "That's right," "Amen," and what he thought was a "Hell, yeah."

His disquiet grew.

The preacher, priest, whatever the hell he was, abruptly broke into English. "And those who would destroy the Chosen are everywhere, Brothers and Sisters. They conspired to bring down dear Angela, and they succeeded." He paused, stopping and surveying them slyly. "Or at least they believe they did."

Blaring shouts of approbation at this. Joe had a strong urge to hide himself again, but the preacher's voice held him spellbound.

"So we say goodbye to Angela today, but in doing so, we herald the coming of a glorious new age. A time of renewal. Brothers and Sisters, the heretics will not defeat us!" At which the preacher swept his arms over the group, the small man seeming to swell in stature, his voice reaching Klaxonlike power.

His eyes fastened on Joe. "They're out there, Brothers and Sisters! The reprobates, the conspirators! They are the ones who've taken dear Angela from us!"

Joe sucked in breath and lurched behind the monument. The preacher had seen him, of that he was certain. And in the moment before Joe reached cover, he was sure he'd seen other faces swivel around to discover him there, as well. Joe closed his eyes, but he could still make out their faces. A tall, cadaverous man with a brown crew cut and numerous facial scars. His opposite, a plump, pasty-faced man with sallow-hued skin and sagging jowls. A younger couple dressed far more affluently than the others. A biker with ropy muscles and greenish-blue tattoos festooning his arms. A deeply tanned bald man whose arms looked far bigger than the biker's, the bald guy's black jacket bulging so much it appeared ready to split.

And Sharon Waltz.

At least Joe thought it had been Sharon. She looked so different in the long black dress, black hat, and veil that he couldn't be completely sure. But the facial structure had been the same, as had been the peroxide blond hair peeking out from beneath the little hat. Yet instead of the snarling, unreasoning hatred he associated with Sharon Waltz, her expression today held none of the emotion it had at the gas station. This woman – what he'd glimpsed of her – had looked glazed, lifeless. A worn-out husk of a woman. Not someone rearing for a fight.

Joe listened, acutely aware of the silence pervading the cemetery. Were the onlookers, even now, stealing toward him, preparing to snatch him up and exact some sort of humiliating punishment on him? Or worse? Would they stuff him into the open grave and lower Angie's coffin down on top of him?

And why, he wondered, did Angie even need a coffin? How much of her could conceivably be left after burning herself alive?

Joe fought off the image. Even more, he fought off the urge to run.

Just stay hidden. This is a funeral, not some kind of satanic rally. They're no more going to come for you than Angie Waltz is going to climb out of her casket and do a pole dance on one of the tent supports.

Joe fought off an insane urge to laugh. There was still no sound from the tent. Not a Latin incantation, not a single "Hell yeah."

Joe held his breath, listened.

Finally, the bass voice murmured, "Let us bow our heads."

Joe waited until the prayer began before setting off for his truck. He only looked back a couple times, and each time he did he saw only the backs of heads, both the old and the young paying tribute to Angie, and presumably, praying for her soul.

Good luck with that, he thought.

When he reached the Tundra and climbed in, he remembered why he'd come in the first place.

Joe bowed his head and said, "God, please help Little Stevie to have a good life. Please forgive Angie and Sharon for anything they've done." He pulled out his phone, thinking to check his email, but before he powered it on, he paused.

"And, God," he added, "please forgive me for any mistakes I've made too."

Fifteen minutes later, Joe heard the engines on the western side of the cemetery fire up, the mourners gradually driving away.

While Joe waited, he ran through some of the words he remembered.

Veritas. That meant truth.

Mortuus. Something to do with death.

Spiritus. Spirit maybe? Or did that mean to breathe?

There was another one he recollected but couldn't immediately place.

Ignis. What was that one? Ignorance? Indignant, maybe? Anger?

Joe typed it into his phone, and moments later the translation came up.

Fire.

"Well, that's certainly fitting," he muttered.

It was after one o'clock. Michelle would be wondering about him. He missed Lily.

Without further delay, Joe started the Tundra and drove slowly up the weedy cemetery path.

CHAPTER SEVEN

"You did *what*?" Darrell Copeland demanded.

Joe sipped his beer. "I went to Angie's funeral."

"Now why the hell would you go and do something like that? And don't tell me it's because your conscience was bothering you."

Joe glowered at him across the table at Easter's Tavern. "Doesn't yours? The girl committed suicide, for God's sakes."

Copeland motioned to the waitress to bring him another beer. "It ain't my fault she decided to barbecue herself."

Joe almost choked on his beer. "Can we maybe find a nicer way to say it?"

"You're too sensitive," Copeland said. "How the hell'd you get to be a contractor? I thought those guys'd sell their own mothers to make money."

Joe sat back, draped an arm over the seat. "Michelle says that too. I'm not aggressive enough. That I lack a killer instinct."

Copeland took a swig of beer, wiped foam from his upper lip. "You sure were aggressive that day at the Marathon station."

Joe winced. "I wish things could've gone a different way."

Copeland tilted his head. "Meaning what?"

"I don't know. I guess I just feel bad."

Copeland pushed his glass aside, leaned forward. "You listen, Joe. There wasn't any other way things could've gone. You either let that little boy get the shit beaten out of him like everybody else did, or you intervene. By my estimation, you did the only sensible thing you could."

Joe looked at Copeland and felt a lump in the base of his throat. "Thanks," he said.

Copeland scowled at him. "Now don't get all mushy on me. We ain't gonna hug each other and share a heartwarming moment or anything, so don't you dare come over here to cuddle with me."

"That's just wishful thinking on your part."

Copeland chuckled softly, accepted the new mug of beer. "So no one saw you at the funeral. That's good, I guess. If they had, I'd have had to come down there for crowd control, make sure you didn't get drawn and quartered."

"Or have my eyes scratched out by Sharon."

"Ah, Sharon. Hey, what was she wearing? A black halter top? Maybe some stilettos to go with her mourning veil?"

"Man, that's cold. Can't we at least pretend to have some sympathy for her?"

Copeland's face betrayed no emotion. "She wanted sympathy, she should've raised her daughter better. Turned Angie into something respectable rather than a clone of herself."

Joe fell silent.

Copeland studied him. "You know, you wanna drink some more, I can drive you home. Your wife can bring you back tomorrow to get your truck."

Joe pushed his mostly full bottle toward the center of the table. He shivered.

"It isn't just guilt, is it?" Copeland said.

Joe shrugged, looking everywhere but at Copeland's eyes. There were a couple of unoccupied pool tables across the room, but he didn't feel like shooting pool either.

"What are you afraid of?" Copeland asked.

Joe did glance at Copeland then. "What makes you think that?"

Copeland only watched him.

Joe sighed, ran a trembling hand through his hair. "I don't know. Don't you get the feeling this isn't over? Like there's another shoe to drop?"

"She's dead."

Joe shook his head. "Sharon's not."

Copeland's eyebrows rose. "Sharon is treading an extremely perilous path. She's already got aggravated assault charges to answer to. There were drugs in a house she owns. The court date's coming up, which means she better not do anything to make her situation worse."

"Maybe she's incapable of behaving herself."

Copeland gave a derisive snort and stared down at his bottle of Budweiser. His expression grew thoughtful. "You wanna know what we found over there the night Angie beat the shit out of Little Stevie?"

Joe wasn't sure he wanted to, but he said, "Something bad?"

Copeland nodded. "If you consider all kinds of occult shit bad."

Joe felt a chill. "Occult?"

"Strange books, all sorts of weird knives and chalices, some of them with dried blood crusted on them."

"Whose was it?"

"How the hell should I know? All that crap was bagged and sent away. I haven't heard a thing about it since."

"You saying they used this stuff on Stevie?"

"I wouldn't put it past them."

Joe's throat was dry, but the thought of downing more beer made him slightly ill. "But you were there when they examined him. You saw the welts."

Copeland sat forward, spoke in a harsh whisper. "I was in the room, sure, but it's not like I wanted to sit there and stare at that poor kid's bare chest...all those goddamn burn marks—"

"Burn marks?"

"I told you these women were bad."

"Yeah, but you didn't say anything about—"

"Listen to me," Copeland said, "I don't know whether they cut on the kid or not, but they sure as hell did things to him no kid should have to suffer through."

Joe was about to follow up, but Copeland made a pained face and sighed. He said, "I already told you most of it. Hell, I might as well tell you the rest."

Joe waited, a curious thrumming in the flesh of his arms and neck.

Copeland said, "I've seen a lot of crazy shit in my years on the job, but I've never seen anything like that house. There were black rugs on most of the walls. Kind with designs on 'em?"

"Tapestries?"

"Yeah, tapestries. There were faces on some, but not the kind of faces you'd wanna see unless you were buying tickets to a theme park haunted house. Others had scenes displayed...people being roasted...what I assume were the souls floating above the bodies and screaming in agony. These blood red demons...goblins...some sort of menacing creatures were capering about the victims. Big cauldrons with babies being lowered into 'em. Men and women asleep with demons visiting them in bed. Big male demons with horns curling on the sides of their heads. Dicks as big as rolling pins. The women screaming underneath 'em, though some of 'em were clearly enjoying it. Men getting taken advantage of too, the she-demons all attractive and big-breasted, and looking at the expressions on the men beneath 'em you could have no doubt as to whether or not they were enjoyin' it."

"Wait a minute. All these things were displayed in the main room?"

"Main room? You kiddin', Joe? Damned things were all over the *house.* Living room, basement. The nursery."

Joe felt like he'd been slugged in the belly. "You're not serious."

Copeland smiled mirthlessly. "You think that's bad? Try this one. The ones in the nursery, they weren't tapestries. Looked like oil paintings instead. Those things were scenes from some black Mass or something. Figures in black-hooded robes. Some kind of satanic-looking church. More cauldrons, more scenes of torture, sacrifice. People rutting right there on the altar."

"Jesus."

"Jesus had nothing to do with what went on in that house. And if you ask me, it's a good thing it burnt down. Angie did everybody a favor."

Joe said, "Look, Darrell, I wasn't going to say anything about this, but something funny was up at the funeral today."

"Big fucking surprise."

"No really. I felt like some kind of sicko, but I snuck up on the ceremony."

"That's not sick, it's stupid. You're lucky they didn't find you."

"Someone might have seen me," Joe said. "I couldn't tell for sure."

"That's great. Get all her weird psychotic friends after you."

"I thought you said they were druggies."

"Sorry. Weird psychotic *druggie* friends."

"I'm not sure they spotted me." And Joe told him the story of the graveyard, this time leaving nothing out. He even included the part about nearly fainting when he first arrived there. Copeland listened patiently, only occasionally asking questions. When he was done, Joe asked, "What do you make of it?"

Copeland took a long swig of Budweiser, sat back. "I don't know, Joe. I hope they didn't see you."

"That doesn't help."

"You asked me, and I'm tellin' you. I'd say you stirred up a hornet's nest, but that doesn't really cover it. It's like you knocked down the nest, stomped on it, then stood there and waited for them to sting you."

Joe glared at Copeland. "I felt bad that a woman died and decided to go to her funeral. You act like that's a crime or something."

"You didn't go to her funeral, Joe. You spied on it from behind a marble angel. There's a serious difference there."

Joe slouched in his seat, enervated. "I better get home."

"That's the first intelligent thing you've said today."

Joe scooted toward the edge of the booth.

"You gonna stick me with the bill?"

Standing, Joe reached into his back pocket, retrieved his billfold, and dropped a ten on the table.

"That's too much," Copeland said, digging into his own pocket.

"It's fine," Joe said. "You have any more advice for me?"

"Seriously?"

"I asked, didn't I?"

"Lock your doors tonight."

Joe left without saying goodbye.

* * *

"You smell like beer," Michelle said as they kissed.

Standing next to Michelle's dresser, a few feet from the bed, Joe let his hands roam over the rump of her jeans. "That's because I drank a beer a little while ago."

"By yourself?"

"Darrell," Joe said, pressing his midsection into her.

She pulled away from him, gave him a quizzical look. "Darrell Copeland?"

"Yeah. Down at Easter's."

Joe leaned in to resume their kissing, but Michelle resisted. "Why did you do that?"

"I don't know. I figured he's been in on it since the beginning…"

"He wasn't there when those women attacked you – I was."

"Is that what this is about?"

"You could've talked to me about it."

"I was wrong not to. I'm sorry."

"It's okay," she said. "It was just a long day, wondering where you were. And we haven't exactly been getting along like usual lately."

He was nodding. "I know. That's my fault too."

She shook her head, rested her forehead against his chin. "You're just apologizing because you want sex."

"There a problem with that?" He kissed her hair, breathed deeply of it. Her shampoo always smelled to him like wildflowers.

She put a hand on his chest, her touch feathery on the thin fabric of his white dress shirt. "I've been meaning to tell you something, but I keep forgetting to."

"You've decided to get a sex change."

"Joe."

"You want *me* to get a sex change?"

She punched him lightly on the chest. "Would you be serious for once?"

"Okay, okay. Go ahead."

"What I've been wanting to tell you is…how proud of you I am."

"For what? Bein' such a good-looking guy?"

She traced a line along his jaw. "You're a damned good-looking guy, but that's not why I'm proud of you."

"It's because I'm hung like a grizzly bear, isn't it?"

"It's because," she said, clutching the front of his shirt with both hands and giving him a little tug, "of what you did last week."

"Oh."

She bit her lip, sighed. "I'm sorry for getting on you about that bid."

"Michelle…"

"It was selfish of me, and you didn't deserve it. And in all the confusion of the past week, I never even told you how proud of you I was for how you stuck up for that toddler."

He shook his head faintly. "I still can't believe it happened."

"At least it's over now."

"Is it?"

Her face clouded, but then, staring up at him, she said, "Kiss me."

He did. Her lips pushed against his, her tongue insistent this time. He kissed her with more energy, and then their hands were on each other, stroking, kneading. He slipped a hand inside her underwear, let his fingers rove over the contours of her sex. They moved toward the bed, her hands plunging inside the waistband of his dress pants and squeezing his buttocks.

"What about Lily?" he whispered through their kisses.

She clawed at his back, her tongue licking his lips. "She won't bother us."

"How much longer" – he kissed her – "will her show last?"

"Shut up," she said, her voice throaty with longing. She fumbled open his belt buckle, the button on his khaki pants. She yanked his zipper down, her fingers squeezing his cock through his underwear.

Joe moaned, moved down to suck on her breasts.

The doorbell rang.

"They'll go away," Joe said and proceeded to push down one cup of her bra.

"Who is it?" Michelle said.

"Doesn't matter." He licked her nipple. "Probably selling magazines."

"What if it's a client?"

"They can wait."

The doorbell rang again, followed by a loud knocking.

"Joe?"

"Fuck," he said.

"Language, honey."

Joe slumped on Michelle's bare chest. "I know, but every time I'm about to make love to my wife, somebody interrupts us."

Michelle's hands on his shoulders were firm. "Check on it, honey. Before Lily goes to the door to see who it is."

That got him moving. They'd told Lily not to answer the door under any circumstances, but she usually did anyway. Zipping up his pants as fast as he could without getting his junk caught in the zipper, Joe shrugged his shirt back on and set about buttoning a few of the buttons. Coming down the steps to the front room he could see that Lily hadn't left her post in front of the den television. That was good. Maybe she wouldn't hear him telling whatever salesman or Jehovah's Witness this was to get the hell off his property.

Joe tore open the door, ready to snap at whoever it was that had interrupted his long-overdue session of lovemaking, but sight of the couple staring back at him pleasantly from the other side of the glass door so stunned him that the truculent words died on his lips. They were in their thirties, well-dressed but not haughty-looking. The woman had a Burberry coat on, the man an Armani suit. Could they be prospective clients?

Joe ran a hand through his hair, buttoned another button on his untucked dress shirt. He opened the glass door. "Can I help you two?"

"We're the Martins," the woman said, offering a gloved hand. "Bridget and Mitch."

When Joe went to shake, Bridget Martin looked down, saw the glove covering her hand, uttered an embarrassed little laugh, and peeled it off. Joe shook her hand, which was very warm and soft.

The man extended his hand and said, "I'm the Mitch."

Joe nodded. "I sort of guessed that."

Mitch Martin laughed, gave Joe's hand a squeeze. Bridget bent at the knees and made an apologetic face. "We're so sorry to bother you like this, but we were wondering if you know who owns that beautiful old house next door."

Joe had been just about ready to tell these people to get lost despite their fancy clothes, but the woman calling the Baxter house beautiful stopped him.

"I know the guy," Joe said. "I actually offered to buy it from him a couple years ago, but he wanted too much."

"How much?" Mitch asked. When Joe hesitated, he said, "Only if you're comfortable telling us, of course."

Joe scratched the back of his neck and wondered if Michelle was still half-naked and waiting for him. He said, "I can't promise the price is the same as it was then, but he told me he wouldn't part with it for less than four-seventy-five."

Mitch whistled. "That's an awful lot for a place that needs that much work."

Joe nodded. "It's salty, but the house has a ton of potential."

Mitch didn't look convinced. "I don't know."

His wife gave him a pleading look.

Joe thought of Michelle in the bedroom, waiting. "Well, that's all I know. I was working on a project when you guys rang, so I need to—"

"You're a contractor, aren't you?" Bridget said.

Joe paused and regarded the Martins warily. "How do you know that?"

Bridget gave him a sheepish grin. "I saw your truck at the top of the driveway. It says *Joe Crawford Construction* on the door."

Joe opened his mouth, uttered a soundless little laugh. "I guess that would give me away, huh?"

"Would you mind," Mitch said and hooked a thumb at the house next door, "you know, walking through it with us?"

Joe's erection had sunk to half-mast, but he knew once he saw Michelle's nude body again, he'd recover in a millisecond.

"I'm really sorry," he said. "But I promised my wife I'd finish this project right away."

"What's going on?" Michelle's voice called.

Joe turned to see her making her way toward the door, fully dressed and looking completely normal. Only the slight blush around her cheekbones suggested she'd been aroused, but he figured only he would notice that.

"Hello, Mrs. Crawford," Bridget said and introduced herself and her husband.

Dourly, Joe introduced Michelle.

"Are you two thinking of moving to Shadeland?" Michelle asked.

"We're up from Indianapolis," Bridget said. "Actually, we were just seeing if we could borrow your husband for a minute."

"Of course you can," Michelle said. "Go on over there, Joe."

Joe gave her a strained, closed-lipped smile. "Thanks, honey. I guess you and I are gonna reschedule, huh?"

He could see from her expression she was enjoying his frustration.

"Take your time, honey," she said and winked.

* * *

A half-hour later, Joe came back inside. Michelle was giving Lily a bath.

"How'd it go?" she asked over her shoulder.

"Fine," he said. "I would've rather been in bed wrestling with you, though."

"*Joe*," she said and nodded at Lily, who was making raspberry sounds on the surface of the water.

He came in, knelt beside his wife and immediately felt water drench his knees. Lily was like a hurricane in the tub. It was a wonder all the floorboards under the bathroom hadn't rotted through.

"Hi, Daddy," Lily said.

"Hey, sweetie." He rubbed a scrim of shampoo suds off her forehead before it got in her eyes.

"Watch my boat," she said and made her raspberry sound as she pushed an empty shampoo container around the bath. Water lapped over the edge and doused both his and Michelle's knees.

"So what were they like?" Michelle asked.

"Rich."

"Yeah? How do you know?"

"Just a hunch. New Mercedes. A Rolex for him, a heck of a big rock on her finger."

Michelle began the job of rinsing Lily's hair. For a two-year-old, she had a lot of it. "Maybe they just like to look affluent," she said. "Plenty of people are that way."

"Could be," he said noncommittally. The truth was, he was almost certain the Martins did have money, but he didn't want to get Michelle's hopes up.

She said, "Did they like the house?"

"Yep." He stood, took a pair of towels off the door hooks, one for Lily to stand on, the other to dry her off with.

"They like it enough to buy it?"

"Maybe," he said and resisted the urge to add that he'd be surprised if they didn't buy it. He reached down, hoisted Lily out of the tub and placed her wet feet on the towel. He began the job of drying her off.

Michelle reached out, levered open the drain. "You think they'll want you to do the work?"

"How should I know, honey? I barely know them."

"Yeah, but surely you got a sense of how interested they were?"

Joe didn't answer, focused on getting Lily's long black hair dry, and resisted the urge to say, *Yes, honey, I got a sense. They all but hired me on the spot.*

He could see she wanted more details, so he gave her a few more after he'd read Lily to sleep. He told Michelle that something about the people struck him as familiar, but he couldn't say why. Maybe they'd been introduced before, a long time ago.

It wasn't until after he and Michelle finally made love and she was fast asleep that Joe, lying on his side and close to drifting off himself, recalled where he'd seen the couple.

The funeral. They'd been at Angie Waltz's funeral. Joe remembered them now but understood why he hadn't before. It was because they'd been so incongruous among the other mourners by the graveside. Instead of tattooed flesh, blue jeans, and piercings, they'd been Burberry coats and tailored suits.

So what's the problem? he thought, coming wide awake. *They stopped at the cemetery to pay their respects. Was that a crime?*

Not really, except for the timing. Why come here the same day as Angie's funeral and inquire about a house that had been untenanted for at least a decade?

Joe didn't have an answer for that, nor did he sleep for nearly two more hours. And when he did drift off, his dreams were horrifying, grotesque. He dreamed of Angie lighting herself on fire. Only this time the house that burned up around her wasn't empty. There were voices screaming inside as people were roasted alive. The voices belonged to Michelle and Lily.

And when Joe finally did break through the flaming front door, the whole damned house came down on top of them.

CHAPTER EIGHT

It took some prodding, but in the end, Darrell Copeland agreed to let him know the names of the emergency foster parents: Bruce and Louise Morrison. Copeland then instructed Joe not to bother the foster parents, promising he'd kick Joe's lily-white ass if he so much as drove past the Morrisons' house. But judging from the resignation in Copeland's voice, he already knew Joe would go over there.

Joe did, right after work.

Louise Morrison wouldn't unchain the door at first, opting instead to peer at Joe through a crevice less than an inch wide.

Apparently, Joe thought to himself, she'd been warned about Sharon Waltz.

"I'm sorry to drop in unannounced," he said, "but I was wondering if I could talk for a minute."

A single hazel-colored eye watched him through the narrow aperture.

"I'm a friend of Darrell Copeland," Joe ventured and wondered whether or not it had been prudent to mention the policeman. It was a dead giveaway that he was here regarding Little Stevie. As if to confirm Joe's folly, the hazel eye narrowed to almost a slit.

Joe shifted from foot to foot and did his best to make himself look unthreatening. "I can wait until your husband comes home if you like?"

"Why, so you can talk man-to-man rather than deal with me?"

Joe frowned. "It's not that at all, Mrs. Morrison. I was just trying to put you at ease."

"I don't like the sound of that."

Joe's mouth was dry. "No, I don't suppose you would."

The door closed. Joe stood there a long moment wishing he could start over. Then he heard the muffled snick of the chain being slid out of its housing. The door opened, and Joe was faced with a tall, broad-shouldered woman in her fifties. Steel wool hair down to her shoulders. Very pale skin. Outfit that was clean, ironed, and very much in style thirty years ago, the button-down shirt ivory with green pinstripes. The jeans were stonewashed or whitewashed or some other kind of washed. Regardless, Louise obviously didn't put a lot of effort into her appearance.

Her expression bland, Louise said, "You don't approve?"

Joe stared stupidly at her for a moment, then found his voice. "I didn't mean to stare. I just—"

"Expected someone younger."

"I didn't say—"

"You didn't have to. CPS didn't pick me because I'm a bombshell. You want that, you can go have a snuggle with your wife."

Joe could only stare.

Louise gave him a shrewd look. "General contractor, married, one child. A daughter. Of course I know about you. Copeland told me. He's the worst gossip I know. You came to see Stevie, I suppose."

Joe nodded, feeling very much like a prizefighter dazed by a flurry of vicious jabs.

"Get in here then. It's too chilly to keep the door open."

Mutely, Joe stepped inside. The house looked like Louise did. Nondescript, though if there was a style here it was Outdated Country. The walls were beige with dark green trim up top. The tables and dressers were lined with knickknacks and cheap curios. Ceramic statuettes of country kids fishing and frolicking. Assorted gnomes and angels. A black rotary phone that Joe suspected the Morrisons still used.

"Stevie's in the next room," Louise said, throwing a nod to Joe's left. "He's playing with Jessica's old Weeble Wobbles."

"Is Jessica your daughter?"

Louise eyed him expressionlessly. "You should've been a detective rather than a contractor."

"That's what they tell me."

"Jessica's twenty-six now. They're expecting their second child this fall."

"Congratulations."

"I have three grandbabies already."

"Jessica has an older sibling?"

"Regular Sherlock Holmes, aren't you?"

"I don't play the violin."

"You did the right thing for Stevie."

Joe took in the woman's changeless expression and discerned the merest hint of emotion there. So tucked away in the corners of her gray eyes, you wouldn't notice it unless you looked.

"I really appreciate that, Mrs. Morrison."

"Watch him for a few minutes while I cook his supper."

Wordlessly, she left Joe standing in the front room. He watched after her, smiling a little. Then he followed the sound of Little Stevie's babbling.

When Joe entered the starkly decorated living room, he noticed two things aside from the toddler sitting on the thick beige carpet, a pacifier in his mouth and a navy blue jogging suit covering his pale skin: the room was very clean, and there were three white bookcases, each of them crammed with books.

He fought off the urge to wander toward one of them to peruse the titles and forced himself to approach the child. It wasn't that he wasn't interested in Little Stevie. No, he realized as he came to a halt before him. It was something far simpler than that.

Joe felt guilty.

Here was a child who'd been orphaned, and it was at least partially due to Joe's intervention. He'd been over it too many times in his head to believe he'd done the wrong thing, but as he peered down at the little blond-haired toddler in his velour jogging suit, he couldn't help but rue the way things had turned out. Why had the kid's dad evidently been such a deadbeat, and why, of all the potential moms in the world, had this innocent little boy incubated in the womb of such a wretched creature?

Wincing a little, Joe lowered himself to sit crosslegged on the floor in front of Stevie. The boy, apparently not noticing him, continued to manipulate the eight or so Weeble Wobbles lying before him on the carpet. Stevie would knock a pair of them together with a sturdy clunk. Then he'd line them up and examine them, their bottom halves buried in the deep shag of the carpet. Joe noticed that the boy's hair was combed to one side, giving him the look of a junior executive. Or maybe a future banker. Stevie sucked on the pacifier steadily, his blue eyes riveted on the Weeble Wobbles as though he were engaged in a serious game of chess.

Joe reached out, fiddled with a Weeble Wobble. Little Stevie grunted, shoved Joe's hand away.

Joe chuckled. "Sorry about that, Stevie. Didn't mean to mess up your arrangement."

Silently, Stevie returned the Weeble Wobble to its former position.

"I want you to know I'll help you," Joe said. "I don't know what my role's gonna be, or even if I'm gonna have one. In your life, I mean." He bit the inside of his cheek. "It's not like I have any claim to you. Some might argue I have less right to be here than anybody. But—" Joe reached out, tousled Stevie's hair "—I feel really crummy about what happened, and if you ever need help, I'll give it to you."

If Stevie understood, he gave no sign.

Joe reached out, did his best to finger-comb Stevie's blond hair back into place. "My wife and I are done having children. It took us a long time to get pregnant. Took Michelle a long time, I mean. Not that it was her fault or anything." He scratched his jaw. "I just mean we tried for quite a while before Lily came along. I've been thinking that maybe..." Joe sighed, rubbed his eyes with the heels of his hands. "Maybe it's a dumb idea. Who the hell knows?"

"Don't use that word in front of him."

He turned and saw Louise leaning in the doorway, her hands tucked in the front pockets of a blue apron. Her expression was the same, but something about the set of her mouth gave the impression she wasn't annoyed with him. Her eyes were on Little Stevie.

Joe turned and saw that Stevie was gazing up at her.

Joe said, "Do you think you and your husband...do you think the arrangement might be permanent?"

"It can't be," she said. "I'm fifty-nine this December. I'll be in my seventies by the time he's in junior high."

"That's not so old."

"Says the guy not old enough to run for president."

"I'm over forty. And I've got too many skeletons to run for president."

"We all have skeletons, Mr. Crawford."

"It's Joe."

Louise said nothing, only continued to watch Little Stevie, who'd returned to his Weeble Wobbles.

"It's very good of you and your husband to look after him, Mrs. Morrison."

"They call us when they don't have a suitable foster home ready," Louise said. She came over, pulled up an orange vinyl footstool, and sat on it. "Longest we've ever sponsored one is two years."

"Sponsored."

"CPS's word, not mine."

Joe reached out, rubbed Little Stevie's shoulder. The velour material was soft and warm. "Two years," Joe said in a quiet voice. "Must've been hard to say goodbye."

He glanced up at Louise, who for the first time was really looking at him. Her gaze was a little misty. "It's usually not that long."

"What if they don't find some place for Stevie here?"

"I could ask you the same thing."

Joe let his fingers glide down the boy's sleeve until they touched the back of Stevie's hand, the flesh there so soft the kid might as well be a newborn.

"You have the space," Louise said. "You make a good enough living."

"How do you know so much about me?"

"You're not the only one Copeland talks to."

Joe frowned. "Premature to talk about that now."

He could feel Louise's gaze on him. "Or maybe you just don't want to get your hopes up?"

Joe's voice wouldn't work for a long time. When he finally found it, he said, "You mind if I come back to visit him?"

"If you have to ask that, you'd make the worst detective in the world."

And with that, Louise rose and returned to the kitchen.

Joe sat playing with Little Stevie for ten more minutes before Louise reentered and fastened a Cookie Monster bib around the boy's neck. Joe mussed Stevie's hair, kissed his forehead, and said his goodbyes. The sky had cleared, leaving behind a silken orange twilight shot through with lavender-colored clouds. Across the street from the Morrisons' house was a mostly empty park. The sight of the unused playground equipment made Joe a little bit wistful. Or maybe it was Little Stevie who'd done that.

He was nearly to his truck when he saw the woman angling in his direction.

Oh hell, Joe thought.

And waited for Sharon Waltz to unload on him.

★ ★ ★

"How'd you know he was here?" Sharon asked.

Joe swallowed. He knew it was pointless to play dumb, but he did anyway. "I was just visiting a friend."

"*Stevie's not your friend,*" Sharon hissed. "He's an orphan whose mother was murdered by a bunch of lying snakes."

Oh man, Joe thought. This was worse than he'd anticipated. He'd imagined this scenario several times in the past few days. Hell, this confrontation had nearly come to pass that day in the cemetery. But now that it was upon him, he found he had no earthly idea what to say. *Sorry your daughter incinerated herself?*

As casually as he could, Joe looked over at the Morrisons' house and was grateful to note the front door was shut. With any luck, they wouldn't even know this scene had taken place. As for whether or not they and Little Stevie were safe from Sharon, that would be a matter for Copeland and the social workers to decide.

Sharon stalked closer, effectively ensuring he couldn't open the door of his truck. At least, not without knocking her out of the way. Accentuating every word with a poking forefinger, she said, "*You* did it. You fucking *did* it."

When Joe didn't answer, she bared her teeth. "Say something, you coward. You at least owe me that after stealing my daughter from me."

Joe realized Sharon had been drinking. *From bad to worse,* he thought. He was pretty sure she'd been sober that day at the gas station. How much more ghastly would she be after a few drinks?

"*Say something,*" she demanded.

"Okay, take it easy," he said and made the mistake of putting a hand on her shoulder.

She jerked it away as though his hand were on fire. "How *dare* you lay hands on me, you son of a bitch. You're trying to rape me, aren't you? You're trying to bang me right here against your truck!"

My God, was she on drugs too? Joe put up his hands, palms outward, and took a step back. "Hey, I'm sorry about your daughter, but—"

"Oh, you're *sorry* are you?" she asked, her eyes like bloodshot moons. "Well, that just changes everything, doesn't it? Being sorry's gonna bring her right back. Being sorry's gonna make it all like it never happened."

And as she advanced on him, Joe noticed something else, something that worried him even more than the swaying and the flaring nostrils. Sharon's sweater – a couple sizes too tight and short enough to expose her pierced belly button – was on inside out. The tag stuck out in back and waggled like a tail every time she brandished her index finger at him. Joe glanced to his right, saw the public park spread out there with a couple little kids and their young mothers playing on the playground, and wondered if he should head in that direction. Oh, he was sure Sharon would follow him, but at least there'd be witnesses. For whatever reason, despite the fact that it was only early evening, there was nobody else outside on this street.

"Nothing to say?" she snapped. "And here I thought talking was your specialty. You didn't have a problem telling your lies to the cops, didja? Didn't have any trouble getting my grandson taken away from me."

"I know you won't believe me, but I didn't want any of this to happen."

"Bullshit!"

"I didn't want your daughter to die any more than I wanted to witness her abusing her son."

Whatever the right thing to say was, this wasn't it. Joe knew that the moment the words left his lips. Sharon actually grabbed twin handfuls of her bleach-blond hair and tore at it. "*She did not abuse Little Stevie!*"

Joe was standing next to the truck bed; he wondered if he'd be able to scurry around to the passenger's side and sneak in that way before she harrowed his face with those talons of hers.

Joe had actually backpedaled another step to attempt his escape when her expression changed to one of dawning amazement. "You have a daughter of your own, don't you, Joe Crawford?"

Joe froze. "My daughter's none of your business."

Sharon's face twisted into a hideous mask, like a caricature of a fairy-tale troll. "I'll decide what she is, you puling coward." She poked a long nail into his face, actually abrading his cheek this time. "I'll decide what she is."

Joe took another step back, drawing even with the tailgate now, but she moved with him, muttering obscenities and flashing those pale talons at his face. She jabbed him hard this time, drawing blood along his cheekbone.

"I'll bet that girl's not even yours," Sharon rasped.

Joe kept his eyes trained on the ground. "That's enough, Sharon."

"'*That's enough, Sharon,*'" she mimicked in a hateful, childish falsetto. "Not sure you're her daddy, are you?"

Joe reached out, squeezed the top of his tailgate, and told himself to get control. He knew a rise was exactly what Sharon was seeking from him, but knowing it and preventing it were two very different things.

Sharon giggled. "Maybe that wife of yours has been bangin' the help.

You got a couple young bucks on your crew. Maybe she spread her legs for one of them."

Joe glared at Sharon in disbelief. In the space of thirty seconds she'd transformed from a grieving mother into a vicious, taunting crone.

Get out of here, he told himself. *Get out now before you really screw up.*

Joe clenched his jaw, gave the tailgate a smart pat, and made for the passenger's side of the truck. He hated the feeling he was fleeing from her, but it seemed the only sensible course of action. Stay here and she'd either claw his eyes out or goad him into violence. Walk away and she'd simply follow, hurling her taunts after him and cackling like a witch.

"That Gentry boy seems to fancy Michelle most of all," Sharon called.

Joe stopped, his whole body gone rigid.

"That's right, Joey," she said. "You've suspected it all along, haven't you? That Lily doesn't really belong to you? One of your workers shot his load in your wife, and out popped that daughter of yours!"

Joe whirled, his face centimeters from Sharon's. "*Shut your fucking mouth*," he hissed.

"Yeeesss," Sharon breathed into his face, the stench of stale alcohol and rancid cheese washing over him. "Yeeesss, Joey. You wanna have a go at me? Do it right here against your truck?" She reached down, ripped open the fly of her jeans. "Go ahead and jam that little prick of yours in here and see if you can make me scream."

He pulled away, passed a disgusted hand over his mouth. "You really are crazy."

He reached the passenger's door, tugged it open, and ducked inside. She lunged for it, but he slammed it and triggered the lock before she could get it open.

"You're a fraud, Joe Crawford!" she raved through the closed window. "You aren't man enough for me! You aren't man enough for Michelle!"

"Psycho," Joe muttered, sliding behind the wheel and firing the engine.

"That little bitch isn't even yours, Joe. Check the blood test, it'll tell you!"

Joe shoved the Tundra into gear, sure Sharon Waltz would caper out in front of the truck before he could pull away. The worst part was, if she did jump in front of the Tundra, he wasn't sure he'd want to stop.

But she didn't. Joe drove away, his hands trembling on the wheel.

CHAPTER NINE

Joe and Mitch Martin were side by side in the second-story hallway of the Baxter house. Kevin Gentry was supposed to meet them here ten minutes ago, but thus far he was a no-show.

"Hey, I meant to ask you," Joe said as casually as he could.

Mitch's eyebrows rose. "Yes?"

Joe smiled to show how embarrassed he was. "This'll probably seem like a weird question, but did you go to a funeral the other day?"

Mitch nodded. "A girl named Angela Waltz. My wife's a distant relation of hers."

"Is your wife close to Sharon Waltz?"

"She's not close to any of them, from what I gather. She went more out of duty than anything else."

The matter apparently resolved, Mitch entered the first bedroom they came to and looked at the cobwebbed ceiling with trepidation. "So, which one of these do you figure will be the master suite?"

Joe contemplated pressing the matter of the Martins' association with the dead woman, but decided to leave it. For now.

"That all depends," Joe said. "Are you talking about the room that'll be cheapest to fix up, the one that's biggest, or are there other considerations?"

"What other considerations would there be?" Mitch asked.

Joe nodded at a window, went over to it. The panes were smudged and cloudy, as though a hundred small children had taken turns smearing their hands all over them. "Some people favor an eastern-facing bedroom because they like to wake up with the sunrise."

Mitch laughed. "Not Bridg. She'd sleep in till noon every day if she could."

"So we can either choose a west-facing room, or you can use light-blocking curtains."

"Seems logical."

Joe nodded, was about to speak, but noticed Shaun Peterson hovering in the doorway. Joe went over, crouched beside an old radiant heater, which had been painted ivory but over the years had begun to rust badly. It would need to go unless Mitch and Bridget wanted the heaters to stay for historical flavor.

Running his fingers over the cool iron, Joe said, "Shaun, would you mind heading downstairs and waiting for Kevin?"

Shaun hesitated as Joe knew he would. The kid was a good worker, but he was lazy when it came to climbing stairs. "Can't he let himself in?"

"He can, Shaun, but I prefer he receive a warmer welcome."

Shaun's forehead crinkled in puzzlement. "Huh?"

Joe gave him a look. "I'd like to speak to Mr. Martin without you in the room."

Comprehension dawned on Shaun's slack face. "Ahh, gotcha. Just holler for me when you want me."

Joe smiled and continued studying the heater. He liked its white-brown ridges and the way its slender iron spinal cord pierced the floor. "Sorry about that, Mr. Martin. Shaun sometimes doesn't take a hint."

"I gathered."

Joe stood up, moved across the room so that he and Mitch were eye-to-eye, the slightly younger man seeming a little uncomfortable in the thick silence. Joe grinned easily, hoping to relax his potential client. "There's no way to ask you this without it sounding awkward, Mr. Martin, but—"

"Mitch, please."

Joe nodded. "Mitch, then. This is really none of my business, but I need to ask you a couple questions before we get too far into this thing."

Mitch crossed his arms. "Sure, Joe. Fire away."

"One, what kind of project are we talking about here? Are you mainly interested in cosmetic changes, making this place functional? Or are we talking about knocking down walls, building on, that sort of thing?

Mitch shrugged, eyed the ceiling as if the answers would be written there. "I'll do whatever it takes to make Bridg happy. It's her money, anyway."

"Ah." Joe paused, searching for the least indelicate way to phrase his question. "I got the impression you did pretty well for yourself."

Mitch nodded. "I do. I'm one of the top producers in the Indianapolis area."

"Investments?" Joe asked.

"Mostly," Mitch agreed, turning toward the hallway. "I occasionally dabble in other areas."

Joe followed. "Sounds like you two can do pretty much what you want to this place."

When Mitch stopped and shot him a look over his shoulder, Joe added, "Monetarily, I mean."

"You are direct, aren't you, Mr. Crawford?"

Joe noted the return to formality, but took it in stride. "I've just never seen the need for obliqueness. If we end up working together, I don't want there to be any surprises – on either end. I tell you everything, and you tell me everything. Experience has taught me it's the best way."

Mitch studied him a moment longer. Then, apparently satisfied with Joe's answer, continued to the next room, which was on the right. This one, being on the western side of the building and it still being morning, was dimmer than the first bedroom they'd entered. But it was bigger, more like a master suite. Or some lucky kid's bedroom.

"Ask your next question, Mr. Crawford."

"Sorry if it sounds like an interrogation. I'd just rather be up front about things. It can save an awful lot of heartache later on."

"I suppose," Mitch muttered.

Joe moved deeper into the room, noticing as he did the torn skeins of wallpaper, the ceiling stained and drooping from water damage. Probably the roof, but he hoped it was merely a burst pipe. There was another story above this one, and if a roof leak had caused this much damage to the second floor, how much would it have done to the third? That the roof would have to be replaced went without saying. But a bad leak could mean a complete gutting of the third story, and that would raise Joe's estimated project cost exponentially. He felt the familiar sinking sensation in his belly of a bid getting away from him.

He cleared his throat. "When I mentioned other considerations earlier, I was mainly talking about children."

Mitch scowled, but Joe plunged on. "I know it's none of my business, but if you're planning on starting a family, we really should plan for it in the blueprints."

"Do we have to decide that all today?"

"No, but the earlier we figure it out, the better."

"I don't get you."

"Let's say you're going to keep things just you and Bridget. If that's the case, we'd figure out the best functions for each room to decide where we want to spend your money, how you want things laid out."

Mitch's forehead unfurrowed a little. "Go on."

"Let's say you're gonna have one kid and stop there. Well, you'll want him – or her – to have his own bathroom."

"I guess so," Mitch allowed.

"But if you plan on having two, three, four kids—"

"We're not having four children."

Joe smiled. "If you don't mind my asking, how old are you and Bridget?"

"I'm thirty-four," Mitch said. "Bridg is a year younger."

"So there's a good chance you all might have multiple kids."

Mitch tilted his head this way and that, considering. "There's a chance."

"Then we'll want to connect two of these rooms so you can have a nursery."

Mitch was watching him closely now, most of his surliness drained away. "What happens when the child grows up?"

"You convert the nursery to a study, or maybe a reading room."

"We're not much into reading," Mitch said.

Joe didn't let his disappointment show.

Mitch said, "I still don't know what the number of kids we have has to do with anything."

"I don't want my clients to spend a big chunk of their hard-earned money only to have to up and tear out the renovation five years later."

They moved into the hallway, saw the next room on the left was a small bathroom. Poking his head inside, Joe saw how the tile floor was ominously buckled, and spotted a diagonal crack through the vanity mirror that reminded him of a cartoon lightning bolt.

"We'll keep this room as-is in case your kids ever misbehave," Joe said.

Mitch chuckled at that, and some of the tension between them dissipated.

"If I'm not mistaken," Joe said, moving briskly down the hallway to the room next door to the nightmarish bathroom, "this one's gonna be…" He went inside. "Yep, there's another bathroom adjoining the bad one."

Mitch followed him into the second bathroom, which wasn't nearly as torn up. Joe patted the antique basin. "This could be preserved, if you wanted to do that. If not, I could buy it from you."

"Bridg likes old things. She's a freak for antiques. Anything that reminds her of Ireland. We've got an antique bedstead, a rocking chair, even a pair of Celtic swords."

Joe nodded. "You could renovate both bathrooms, or you could turn them into a Jack-and-Jill. But these rooms look like they'd be great for your kids."

Mitch began to grin.

Joe went on, nodding toward the stairs. "You might think about adding another stairwell in the rear of the house."

"Is that expensive?"

"Very. But it bears considering. Most houses this size, they have two ways up and down. But your stairway is centrally located, and to be honest, that's not the safest arrangement in case there's ever a fire."

Mitch tilted his head at Joe. "You really do think things through, don't you?"

"In my business, you have to."

Mitch nodded. "I respect that."

As they exited the bedroom, Shaun joined them with Kevin Gentry in tow. Together, the four of them toured the rest of the house, with Shaun taking measurements and Kevin jotting them down. By the time they were finished, it was nearly noon, and the day had grown balmy and not nearly as overcast. On the lawn of the Baxter house, Mitch shook Joe's hand and told him how much he appreciated his guidance. That word – guidance – boded very well, Joe decided. As Mitch went to his black Mercedes, Shaun and Kevin exchanged a look and grinned their excited grins at Joe. He told them he'd see them tomorrow, and as they walked away, Joe cut through the small copse of pine trees separating the two properties.

And saw Sharon Waltz coming around the side of his house.

Joe's first response was to freeze, an atavistic fear of the woman enkindling in him a fleeting hope that he could recede into the darkness of the pine trees and thus avoid detection. *But what kind of crap was that?* he chided himself. His first responsibility was to Michelle and Lily. The figure moving around the corner of his house – she now had her back to Joe and seemed not to have spotted him – was a madwoman. Sharon was capable of anything.

Perhaps thirty feet away, Joe took a step in her direction, meaning to shout at her.

Then he remembered that Michelle and Lily were out this morning, would be out until well past noon. Lily had a play date with one of Michelle's friend's kids, which meant the four of them would be at a park playing or eating lunch right now.

And what was Sharon doing?

For the first time, Joe really focused in on the woman, realized that she was clutching something at waist level. Plagued by a growing sense of dread, Joe watched her reach into whatever she held, then make little tossing motions toward the house. The façade of Joe's home was white aluminum siding with a low brick base. It was toward the eighteen-inch strip of bricks and mortar that Sharon was casting something.

She turned slightly, and Joe caught a glimpse of what it was.

Jesus, Mary, and Joseph, he thought.

An urn.

"Hey!" Joe yelled, striding down the short hill into his yard.

Sharon spun around, wide-eyed, looking for all the world like a naughty toddler just busted for smearing shit over the nursery walls. Then a look of such devious cunning twisted her features that Joe feared she would rush him and claw at his face the way she had on the prior two occasions they'd been in each other's company.

He had time to hope that Kevin or Shaun or even Mitch Martin was still parked out by the road. Then he reminded himself to grow a pair. This lunatic was on *his* property, not the other way around. And what she appeared to be doing was not only bizarre – it was incredibly morbid and unsanitary.

Joe found his voice, now ten feet or so from where Sharon stood, that crafty look still darkening her features. "If that's what I think it is, you've got worse problems than I thought. Now get your ass off my property before I call Copeland."

"You'll call Copeland anyway," Sharon said. "So you just do that, Joey. Call up your butt buddy so you two can cozy up again at the bar."

Joe stopped, off balance again. It shouldn't have bothered him that Sharon knew about him and Copeland having a beer together, but the knowledge made her seem omniscient.

"That's right," Sharon crooned in that weird hag's voice she sometimes used. "You and Copeland. And the bitch from the CPS. All three of you are in on it together, aren't you? You three and your wife and the witnesses and all the other assholes."

As she spoke, she reached into the urn – some plain-looking pewter thing – and gathered another handful of ashes.

"Sharon, don't," he said, his heart thumping. "Just—" His eyes flicked to the urn. "—just think about what the hell you're doing. Think about what that is in your hand."

Sharon's eyes flashed with pleasure. "I know what's in my hand, Joey. Believe me, I know." And with that, she sifted it over the bricks.

Mouth dry, Joe said, "I'm calling the police now. They were going to grant me a restraining order anyway, after the other night..."

Sharon's hand stole into the urn again.

"...but now that you've actually trespassed – Sharon, don't do that," he said in a tight voice.

The hand came out, white with ashes. Her whole fist was clutched full of powder.

Joe said, "Please keep that stuff away from my house."

"*Stuff*?" Sharon said, and the smile slipped a bit. For a moment, he saw the same crazed hellcat Sharon had been that night outside Stevie's foster home. "You mean my child's cremated remains?"

Joe licked his lips. "I thought they buried her."

Sharon nodded sagely. "They did."

Joe didn't dare think about that. "Just go, Sharon. Please."

"Oh, I'll go, Joey. I'll go."

Sharon turned, and for the briefest of moments Joe clung to a vestige of hope that this might all be over, that she'd go away and leave him alone.

And then she spun and enveloped him in a cloud of ashes. Joe stumbled backward, coughing and spluttering. He landed against a dwarf juniper tree and smacked his head against the gas meter. My God, it was painful, but the pain was eclipsed by the revulsion undulating through his body. She'd gotten the ashes in his mouth, his eyes. He could feel the powder clinging to the oil of his face, collected in the creases of his forehead and the hollows of his ears. He wiped his eyes thinking to spot Sharon before she followed up her terrible desecration with further violence. Perhaps she'd beat him with the urn, or maybe just attack him again with those razorlike fingernails. But when he got his eyes open, he could see her bleary figure crossing the yard, moving toward her van.

Joe leaned on an elbow and spat. He tried not to think about the smoky grit on his tongue, the sensation like chalk dust in his windpipe. He looked again and saw Sharon stepping off the curb into the street, her tight butt sashaying as she descended Hillcrest Road. Yes, she reminded him very much of a hooker. A washed-up, violent, depraved hooker. With an urn dangling from one hand.

If there were still witches in the world, he decided, Sharon Waltz was one.

His gorge threatening to unleash, Joe pushed to his feet, went inside, and twisted on the shower.

He'd call Darrell Copeland after he got Angie Waltz's cremated body out of his ears.

* * *

The good news, Copeland told him over the phone, was that any good will or grace period Sharon might have had in the minds of the authorities would be erased by this latest assault. If Joe would be willing to preserve some of the ashes Sharon had tossed on his house – or on Joe – Copeland would see to it that they were bagged and analyzed. Of course, if Sharon refused to admit what she'd done, it would cost a great deal of money to analyze the ashes, maybe more than the county sheriff's office would be willing to dole out.

Joe nodded, thinking that the only solution was to somehow make Sharon go away entirely. If they couldn't incarcerate her – and he was pretty sure a woman couldn't be jailed for tossing ashes in a man's face – he wished they could relocate her. She was, after all, homeless, at least to Joe's knowledge. Probably shacking up with one of her druggie friends, some hard-drinking man no doubt. Joe couldn't imagine Sharon with a doctor or a librarian.

When Copeland was done, Joe asked him for the bad news.

"The bad news," Copeland told him, "is that you need to tell Michelle."

Joe cringed at the thought. He drummed on the desk in his upstairs study.

Copeland said, "You haven't told her yet, have you?"

"Uh-uh," Joe said, rubbing his temples.

"I know you better than you know yourself, Joe. It's like we're an old married couple."

"Why should I tell her?"

"For one, she's in the house now, right?"

"Maybe."

"So unless you want her to think you're on the phone with your mistress, you better let her know we talked."

"Yeah, but I don't need to tell her about—"

"The hell you don't. Don't you think she's got a right to know about what went on today? It's her house too, isn't it?"

"You don't know Michelle."

"I know you're avoiding the issue."

Joe eyed the door, wondered if Michelle might be on the other side listening.

"Hey, Copeland?" Joe said slowly. "I really don't like you sometimes."

"Real friends tell each other the truth even when it's painful."

"Is that what you think? That you're my friend?"

"Only one you got," Copeland said.

"There's Kevin and Shaun."

"Hell. They only like you because you pay them. They'd never take you out for drinks the way I did."

"I paid for my own."

"That's cuz I don't want you feeling guilty about taking advantage of my generous nature."

Joe stood. "Anybody ever tell you you're full of shit, Copeland?"

"People never appreciate honesty. Oh, and you ever see *The Big Lebowski*?"

"Of course," Joe said.

Copeland chuckled. "You remember the scene at the end? When Jeff Bridges and John Goodman scattered their friend's ashes?"

Scowling, Joe hung up.

He went downstairs. Michelle was bouncing Lily on a hip and dancing her around the room. The Emotions' 'Best of My Love' was blasting on the little Bose sound system he'd bought Michelle last Christmas. Lily was squealing with delight and making jerky dance movements with her arms. When Michelle saw him in the big mirror over the fireplace, she turned. "Who were you talking to?"

"Can't believe you heard me over The Emotions."

Michelle's face clouded. She moved to the Bose, turned it way down. "What's wrong, Joe?"

Joe took in Lily's crestfallen expression. "At least let her finish the song."

"After," Michelle said. "What's happened now?"

Joe eyed his wife a moment. "Maybe you better have a seat."

It didn't take long to tell. Joe considered leaving out the last part, the ashes in his hair that took a doubly long shower to wash completely out, but in the end he decided on full disclosure. Michelle listened to him with a growing look of dismay, and though Joe had expected this, he still didn't relish the inevitable aftermath. The reassurance. The arguing. The lingering atmosphere of worry in his once peaceful home.

"So is Darrell going to arrest her?"

Joe reached for Lily, who was eating a blue crayon. "He'll do what he can. I'm heading outside now to collect some of the stuff Sharon scattered around the foundation."

Michelle stared at him. "Angie's ashes?"

"That was a Pulitzer Prize-winner."

"Please don't joke about this."

Joe took the crayon from Lily's mouth, told her to spit out the rest. After she'd decorated his hand with slobber and crayon fragments, Joe set to tickling her.

"Joe?" Michelle said.

Joe gave Lily a kiss on the forehead, sobered. "I know it's not ideal, honey, but it's the only way to prove what happened."

Michelle shivered. "How will you collect it?"

"I don't know. A spoon and a plastic baggy, I guess."

"You're not using my silverware for that."

"Then I'll use a paper plate or something. It's not like I've done this sort of thing before."

"And don't track her remains into the house."

"I'll wash off my shoes when I'm done. Hell, I'll power-wash the whole foundation. I don't want that crap there any more than you do."

Michelle grimaced. "Maybe we shouldn't call it crap."

Joe gave her a dour look on the way out. "I'm too pissed off to be politically correct."

★ ★ ★

Collecting the ashes didn't take long. There was some dirt and some leaf particles mixed into the baggie, but Joe figured the folks at the lab could use a strainer or something to separate the good material from the bad. The power-washing took a little longer. There'd been a good deal of rain lately, and the ground was already soggy. As a result, when Joe aimed the spray gun too low, a lot of mud and dead leaves spattered the brick and the white siding near the ground. And when Joe stood too close to the siding, he actually peeled off flecks of paint, revealing a dingier ivory beneath. When he finally got the house looking halfway decent and had at least mixed the ashes with the rest of the mud and mulch, he took care to rinse off his work boots.

After grabbing a quick bite, Joe headed off to a smaller project at a house downtown, taking care not to pass by the scorched remains of the Waltz house. He and his crew worked on the basement they were finishing while an electrician Joe often subcontracted put in new wiring. The day moved briskly, and though Joe wanted to be home with Michelle and Lily, he knew he'd missed too much work lately and wanted to make sure his crew knew he was still focused. It was therefore after eight o'clock when Joe arrived home.

Michelle was waiting for him in the kitchen.

"Sorry, honey," he said.

She cocked an eyebrow at him. "For what? Working your ass off to support your family?"

Joe noticed the wine glass in Michelle's hand. "I take it Lily's gone to bed?"

"I put her down twenty minutes ago. You can bathe her tomorrow."

"Shoot. It was my night, wasn't it?" Joe dropped his keys on the counter, went over to get himself a glass.

"I already poured yours," Michelle said, nodding toward a tall glass of Merlot. "And don't worry about missing bath night. She'll need one again tomorrow. Especially if she keeps rubbing her spit all over her face."

Joe eased down across from her, sampled the wine. "Mm. You buy this?"

She shook her head. "The Martins. They said it was to thank you for being their new contractor."

The wine glass halfway to his mouth, Joe paused, stared at her. "You serious?"

Michelle smiled. "Mitch said he wants to do a major renovation. He was talking about the master suite, something about a Jack-and-Jill bathroom. Converting the third story into a bonus room for their future children."

"The Martins were here?"

"They stopped by this afternoon. I like the woman a lot."

Joe sat back, processing all of it. "Wow."

"Congratulations, honey."

Joe sat forward, took her hand. "This is amazing."

"It is," she said. "Would you like to fuck?"

Joe choked on his wine, reached out and grabbed a handful of napkins. When he'd mopped off his face and the table, he looked at her. "You're a real tomcat, you know it?"

She nodded. "Go kiss Lily good night. I'll be in the bedroom."

★ ★ ★

Joe opened the door to the nursery as gently as he could, but it still creaked slightly. He told himself for the hundredth time he'd oil it soon, but it was one of those things he never remembered afterward. In a house this old, there were always those kinds of issues. Things you resolved to fix but ended up learning to live with.

Lily didn't awaken. Michelle had cowled the top of the crib with a pair of blankets – what Lily called her tent – and left a foot or so of open space for Lily to poke her head out if she wanted to. Because the blankets were so small, the slatted walls of the crib were left mostly uncovered, so there was plenty of air for Lily to breathe. Michelle said it made their daughter feel secure. Joe still worried about suffocation, but he knew he was just being fretful.

He knelt beside the crib and attempted to touch Lily's face through one of the gaps, but his arm was too thick. That was good, he supposed. If the rails were too wide-set, Lily might get her head caught between them, and that really could be trouble. Joe stood, leaned into the gap between the two blankets and had just spotted his daughter's sweet, slumbering face when it hit him.

The smell.

The acrid odor of smoke, heavy and sharp, made his nostrils tingle, his eyes water.

"What the hell?" he muttered.

He wanted it to be imagination, wanted to believe it was just a remnant of his experience earlier. But he'd washed his face vigorously enough to turn it bright pink, and his boots were downstairs. He knew he wasn't smelling himself.

Was it possible Lily had gotten into the ashes earlier on?

He supposed it was. He hadn't told Michelle what had happened immediately, which meant there'd been a twenty-minute window in which Lily could've discovered the ashes and—

No, that made no sense. Michelle kept a close watch on their daughter, and anyway, once she heard about the incident with Sharon and the ashes, she would've recalled any exposure Lily might've had.

Not necessarily, he thought, his heart pounding harder. Lily didn't get a bath tonight. Michelle watched Lily, sure, but it wasn't like she never let the kid touch the ground. What if, while Joe was on the phone with Copeland, Michelle had gone outside to water the window boxes?

Joe's breathing thinned, his pulse throbbing in his neck. He reached down, opened the blankets that formed Lily's tent, but it was too dark to see anything other than his daughter's slumbering form.

This is insane, he thought.

But...hadn't the scent of smoke, of a dead campfire, grown stronger when he'd parted the blankets that roofed Lily's crib?

He didn't have a flashlight on him or his cell phone, but beside his daughter lay her Glo Worm, one of her favorite bedtime toys. Joe reached down, grasped it, and pushed on its belly. The interior of the crib promptly lit up, and though the melody it played made him worry his daughter would awaken, he could at least see that there were no ashes on Lily's face. He examined her hair, her hands.... No, it was apparent she was clean. Or at least cleaner than she would be had she smeared Angela's remains all over herself.

Breathing a little easier, Joe placed the Glo Worm next to Lily and returned her tent to the way it had been. He had no idea where the smell was coming from, but at least he was sure it wasn't from Lily. Joe made to leave the nursery.

Soft laughter emanated from the crib.

He froze, the sound like a lullaby played off-key.

One of Lily's dolls. It had to be. It was a rare thing now to find a toy that didn't talk or squawk or play the William Tell Overture. Joe bent over, peered into the darkness to spot the offending doll.

All of Lily's normal toys were here – her Thomas the Tank Engine, her seahorse, her maniacally meowing cat, her Dora doll. And of course the Glo Worm. None of them had made the sound.

So the laughter had been his imagination, he thought.

Except it hadn't. Unless he was cracking up – which wouldn't be all that surprising given the insanity of the past few weeks – he'd heard laughter. Low, female laughter. There had been something unsettling about it. Something...well, *beguiling*. Like the sultry voice had known something very private about Joe and was poised to use the information against him. It was an absurd thought, one he should have dismissed out of hand, but it festered, replaying in his memory like the idiot refrain of a mindless pop song.

Joe had taken a step away from the crib when his shoe bumped against something, and he bent over to retrieve whatever it was so Michelle or Lily wouldn't trip on it tomorrow morning.

At first he thought it was a naked Barbie doll. The smoothness of the appendages and the stringbean frame certainly suggested it. But stepping into the semidarkness of the hallway, he saw it was Lily's favorite doll, Belle from *Beauty and the Beast*. Joe secretly approved of this particular princess because she had a brain and spent more time improving her mind than brushing her hair. But Lily had apparently stripped Belle of her accustomed yellow gown for some purpose only logical to her two-year-old's mind.

He carried the doll downstairs and was about to ask Michelle about it, but when he opened the door and saw his wife lying on her stomach, her body gloriously, deliriously nude, he forgot all about Disney movies and Glo Worms and creepy laughter that made his flesh crawl.

All he could think about was Michelle. And soon they were lost in a warm world of flesh and light and the afterglow of their lovemaking.

CHAPTER TEN

Joe was sitting at the dining room table sketching out the master bath configuration for the Baxter house when Michelle walked in. "Any word from the Martins yet?" she asked.

"Uh-uh," he said. He jotted down the dimensions of the shower stall, realized they were wrong, then scribbled them out.

"How long will it be until they sign?"

His tongue poking from the side of his mouth, Joe recorded the proper measurements. It would be wide for a shower, but some people liked that.

"I don't know," he said. "It's possible they're still talking to other contractors, getting other bids."

"But they said they'd go with you though." Michelle leaned against the antique buffet, and though he didn't look up, he knew she was frowning. "And you're going to match any bid, right?"

Joe kept his tone noncommittal. "If I can."

"What do you mean 'If you can'? Joe, you don't have any other jobs lined up."

"I know that."

"Sure doesn't seem like it."

He sighed, dropped the pencil on his notepad. "Sounds like you want to talk about something."

"It would be nice if you showed some urgency."

Now he did turn in his chair. "You think I'm lazy, Michelle? Because if you do, that stings worse than just about anything you could say to me."

"You know I don't think that."

"Then I'd appreciate a clarification."

"You don't have to be mad."

"Well, I am. You would be too, if you were sittin' here."

Michelle seemed to deflate. She moved over to the window, pretended to stare at the backyard. "I just wish you'd be willing to compromise a little."

"There're a million ways to take that."

"You always have to be such a horse's ass?"

"You're the one criticizing. At the very least, I think I deserve the courtesy of a clear message rather than this passive-aggressive bullshit."

"Keep your voice down."

"Lily's not wakin' up. Kid's like you. She'd sleep through a tsunami."

"So you're just going to let the Wilson Brothers step in and take this bid?"

"Been looking at your crystal ball again?"

Michelle rounded on him. "I don't need a crystal ball to see a pattern. People ask for your bid, you give it to them, then someone else comes up with a lowball figure, and you lose the client."

"And then the lowball figure balloons to double what it was supposed to be, and the client gets screwed."

"And the builder's family has enough money."

Joe drew back. "You really think we're hurting, Michelle? Living in a nice house. In this neighborhood. Both our vehicles paid for?"

"Not now, we're not hurting, but what about next year and the year after that? College is expensive."

"So I'm told."

"So tell the Martins what they want to hear."

"And when the price tag doesn't match my bid?"

Michelle crossed her arms, shrugged. "You'll already have the signed contract."

Joe grunted. "The joke's on them, huh?"

"Better them than us."

"Why don't you think about what you just said, honey. Let it sink in a little bit."

Michelle gave a shuddering sigh. "Let's just forget it, all right? This PMS and everything, I'm really emotional right now."

Joe grunted. "Sometimes I wish I was a woman. Any time I acted like an asshole, I could just blame it on hormones. Or cramps."

"Go to hell."

Joe went toward the kitchen. "I think I'll go for a drive instead."

* * *

Joe got the call a couple minutes after leaving the house. Some guy named Patrick said he wanted Joe to come out to his place in the country for an estimate. Joe didn't particularly feel like talking to anybody at the moment, but he figured he might as well meet the guy, hear him out. Maybe it would take his mind off his fight with Michelle.

But as Joe motored down the country road, he found himself unable to let it go. The Tundra hurtled around the corner, his knuckles white on the wheel. He wasn't really going that fast – no more than forty – but the road was composed of loose gravel, the turn sharper than he remembered. The back end of the Tundra slued toward the grassy shoulder, hopped the lip of the road before gaining traction and lurching ahead. Well, that was something anyway. At least he hadn't overturned the truck, tumbled end over end like some crazed NASCAR driver. He settled into a more comfortable speed and told himself to be safe.

Yeah, his conscience spoke up, *you're safe, but you're still an asshole.*

Joe's lips became a thin white line. *She wanted me to lie to my customers. What was I supposed to say?*

The crack about hormones was a low blow, and you know it.

He sighed. Yeah, he knew it.

So call her, tell her you're sorry.

"I will," he muttered. "Just as soon as I stop being mad at her."

Another curve appeared ahead, this one trending left and away from the valley that bordered Deer Creek, and as Joe decelerated he happened to glance in his overhead mirror.

There was a car back there. Not that far, about fifty yards or so, but something about it made him uneasy. Hadn't he passed a car just like it before turning off the highway onto the winding country road, the car parked alongside I-25 like a police cruiser trawling for speeders? Only this was an old white Buick, a beast of a car, probably from the mid-seventies. Joe was pretty sure it was the same car tailing him now. If it hadn't been so old it wouldn't have even registered, but...yes. He was fairly certain this car had pulled out and followed him.

Okay, so it pulled out and happens to be behind you, he thought. *That doesn't mean it's* following *you.*

True enough, he conceded, but it did seem strange. Especially when this area was so secluded, so cut off from the rest of civilization. If Joe remembered correctly, there were a few scattered dwellings out here, Amish mostly, with a few ramshackle cottages sprinkled into the countryside like old bird droppings.

Joe looked up in time to see the curve was upon him, and though he hadn't slowed down enough, he was able to navigate it without plunging over the shoulder and, like an inept villain in *The Dukes of Hazzard*, go freefalling into the valley.

He accelerated around the turn, the Tundra's tires grabbing the road without difficulty, and entered another straightaway, this one shaded by the forest that tracked the creek. Joe glanced in the mirror expecting the Buick to be right on his tail, but it was another second or two before it drifted lazily around the bend Joe had just completed. If anything, he was putting distance between himself and the Buick, and though this should have made him feel better, for some reason it made him livid. He'd had enough mystery in his life lately and didn't need anything else to worry about.

Joe's iPhone phone vibrated in his pocket. Keeping his eyes on the road, he fished it out. He half-expected it to be his pursuer, ringing him up to tell him he was about to die. Or to rendezvous at some remote location. But it was Michelle, God bless her. Joe went to answer it, but the buzzing stopped abruptly, the symbol in the upper-right corner of the phone informing him he'd gone beyond signal range.

Crud, he thought, and set the phone on the dash.

Without further deliberation, Joe slowed to a crawl. In his mirror the Buick swam closer, but did so only gradually, the driver apparently as wary as Joe was.

"Come on," Joe murmured. "Let's sort this out now. I need to tell my wife what a prick I was and hope she doesn't make me sleep in the garage."

Even though Joe was now inching along at about ten miles an hour, the Buick remained a goodly distance back. Perhaps forty yards.

Joe felt his irritation level rise. Ahead, there was a dip in the road, a curve to the left, then a stop sign preceding a one-lane bridge. Tomlinson Bridge, it was called, and it was one of the oldest iron bridges in the state. A study had been done on it by a nearby college, and it was found to be unstable. It might not fall apart right away, but soon, the study proclaimed, the bridge would need to be repaired or replaced.

That was fifteen years ago.

In the meantime the bridge had deteriorated further, the whole thing a riot of rust and flaking bolts. It hadn't been closed yet because it was the only means of crossing Deer Creek for a ten-mile stretch. Joe didn't like to drive over it, especially when the girls were with him, but when he was alone, the risk didn't seem quite so extreme.

He reached the stop sign preceding the bridge and gazed across its thirty-yard expanse. Beneath it, he saw Deer Creek bubbling and churning, the turbid water at a level four feet above normal because of all the rains. Joe glanced at the far end of the bridge again, decided it was safe to cross, and rumbled forward.

At which point a black car swung around the corner and bounced toward him at the opposite end of the bridge.

"Son of a bitch," he muttered. He'd only gone about fifteen yards, but it was still a pain to have to stop, shift it into reverse, and back up all the way down the single lane to the road. He had begun to do just that when he glanced in the overhead mirror and saw the white Buick enter the bridge behind him.

Shit, he thought. He was trapped.

Joe shifted the Tundra into park and snatched his cell phone from the passenger's seat. He powered it on and gazed into its glowing face.

Still no service.

Well, fuck a duck, he thought.

Behind him the Buick was close enough to hump his truck if it felt frisky enough. Before him, the other vehicle, an older black Ford Taurus, was damn near nose to nose with his front bumper. For a crazy instant Joe considered driving forward and attempting to steamroll his way over the smaller vehicle. It would kill the driver without a doubt, but wasn't it fairly obvious both of these drivers had planned this, had plotted to trap him out here on this rickety old bridge? He seriously doubted they intended to serenade him or surprise him with roses.

As the driver behind him got out of his vehicle, Joe realized with a nasty shock that one of them had almost certainly been 'Patrick.'

And Joe had fallen for it.

In front of him the driver of the Taurus climbed out, and as the man straightened to his full height – which looked to be about six-and-a-half feet – Joe realized the man's face was familiar. It was gaunt and crosshatched with numerous scars.

One of the men from the funeral, one of Sharon Waltz's friends. And that would make the other...

Yep, Joe thought as the long-haired driver of the Buick came into view through the driver's side window. The tattooed guy with ropy muscles. The one Joe had thought of as a biker.

Joe thumbed the automatic door locks. For some reason, their muted clicks weren't particularly reassuring.

Tattoo Man tapped on his window.

Joe cast a glance to his right, saw Scarface leaning toward the glass, the man's pale-blue eyes leering at him. Scarface's teeth were yellower than sweet corn and terribly uneven.

Joe took a deep, steadying breath and thumbed down the window two or three inches. "Help you?" he asked Tattoo Man.

"Turn off your engine," the man said in a voice that surprised Joe. The guy had what sounded like a thick Irish accent. His hair was gunmetal gray, the bags under his eyes purple and sagging. Yet he sounded like the spry leprechaun from the Lucky Charms commercials.

"Got a dick in your ear?" the man demanded.

Joe grinned at him. "Did you really just say that? I haven't heard that one since junior high, and even then it was out of style."

Tattoo Man opened his hand and slapped it hard on the window. Joe jumped a little. The blow had been hard enough he worried the window would shatter, but it didn't. To his right, Scarface rapped smartly on the passenger's window four or five times.

Joe knew he could sit here waiting for help to come, but the chances of someone happening by were slim. This was mostly German Baptist country, which meant it'd be someone in a horse and buggy, and Joe was pretty sure those folks were pacifists. At least they had been in that old Harrison Ford movie.

He swallowed, thinking fast.

No phone. No other cars or houses nearby. No gun in the truck. No gun anywhere, for that matter. Michelle abhorred them, and though Joe didn't harbor any strong opinions either way, he was suddenly regretful he'd never invested in one for protection.

Of course, he'd never thought he'd needed protection.

Joe mentally riffled through the contents of his silver toolbox, the one in the truck bed where he kept all his equipment. There was a power drill there, but that was of no practical use. In a horror movie, maybe, but not here. There was a hammer, which he knew could do some serious damage, but how the hell was he supposed to retrieve it with these guys blocking both doors?

Tattoo Man beat on the glass with a closed fist. "Open up!" he shouted, only his Irish accent made the command sound more like a suggestion.

But there was nothing suggestive about the rock Scarface slammed against the passenger's window. The whole thing spiderwebbed, and though it didn't implode, Joe figured it would only take a good breeze to finish the job.

"Open the fucking door!" Tattoo Man roared, and Joe held up his hands. "All right, all right! Just take it the hell easy."

Sighing, Joe reached out to unlock the doors. He knew he'd have to be fast. It all depended on what Tattoo Man did. If he stepped well away from the Tundra, Joe might have a chance. If he crowded Joe, grabbed hold of him as soon as the door swung open, Joe might very well receive a serious beating.

Or worse.

He figured the men had come to coerce him into doing what Angie Waltz hadn't been able to do before she killed herself: change his story. Though Joe knew it was fruitless – what were they going to do, intimidate every single one of the witnesses from the gas station? – he also knew that these men were not the kind to listen to reason. They figured Joe was the troublemaker, and if they could scare him badly enough, Sharon could get her mitts back on Little Stevie.

It was the thought of the boy that did it, endowed him with the courage he needed.

Joe depressed the unlock button, thrust the door outward hoping to knock Tattoo Man back a few paces.

It worked. The man stumbled against the rusty guardrail and spat curses.

"Sorry," Joe called as he climbed out. He turned as he did it, so that he was facing the seat. In his periphery he saw Scarface coming around the front of the Tundra, the tall man having to sidle slowly because he'd left so little room between the Taurus and the pickup. Taking care to be casual about it, Joe reached under the seat, felt the hardness of the crowbar through its vinyl sleeve.

"You're a stupid guy, Crawford," Tattoo Man said.

"Grab him, Shannon," Scarface called.

Joe stored the name away, though he didn't think Tattoo Man looked at all like a Shannon. More like a Road Rash or a Crazy Train. Not Shannon.

Joe grasped the crowbar by the chisel end. He only wanted to protect himself, not kill these men.

Not unless he had to.

A hand dropped on his shoulder, the fingers hard and fraught with vicious strength. "Have some of this," the one named Shannon growled.

Joe whirled, the crowbar clutched in his right hand. He whipped the curved end of the bar at Shannon's face just as the man's fist arced toward Joe. The bar caught Shannon flush in the side of the head, the sound like a boot crunching down on a glass bottle. Joe cringed even as Shannon dropped bonelessly to the ground. Jesus, he'd gotten the guy good. He sent up a feeble mental wish that he hadn't killed the man, but by that time Scarface was clawing around the open truck door and cocking back the big rock to retaliate.

Joe was a little off balance from the force of his backhanded swing at Shannon – holy shit, the guy was barely moving, unless you counted the way one of his legs was twitching; maybe Joe really had killed him – so he was barely able to thrust the crowbar up in time to block Scarface, whose right arm was hammering down at him, apparently meaning to stave his head in with the rock, which was larger, harder, and more jagged than a good-sized grapefruit. The crowbar smacked Scarface's wrist and the rock jarred loose from the man's long fingers. The rock continued its descent, however, and caught Joe right in the middle of the sternum. His breath instantly gone, Joe stumbled back, realizing as he fell against the seat that Scarface had gotten hold of the crowbar and was in the process of wresting it from his grip.

Joe scrambled to yank the crowbar out of the man's fingers, but Scarface was as strong as he was skinny. With seemingly no effort, the guy ripped the crowbar away and cocked it high in the air. Joe spun toward the truck bed like a running back evading an aggressive lineman and narrowly missed being brained by the crowbar, which whistled down like a scythe and pounded the cloth seat with an audible thump. Joe nearly tripped over Shannon's twitching form, recovered, and scrambled along the rocker panel until he was a couple arm lengths away from Scarface. Joe flung an arm over the side of the truck, pushed off as hard as he could, and vaulted into the truck bed. He tumbled onto the plastic liner and pushed to his feet. Scarface had recovered and looked ready to strike again. What Joe needed was on the driver's side of the pickup, which was regrettable. Joe couldn't very well open up that side of the toolbox without serving himself on a platter for Scarface and the crowbar. But the long silver toolbox spanned the width of the truck bed, and it wasn't compartmentalized. Thankfully, Joe seldom kept it locked, and he hadn't locked it today. On the side opposite to where Scarface now stood, Joe threw open the toolbox so the door stood up almost at a right angle. He heard a clatter from Scarface's side of the truck and looked up in time to see the man's long, spidery form scuttling into the truck bed.

Joe thrust his arm into the open toolbox, groping for his weapon. Scarface had nearly made it into the bed. Joe debated briefly overpowering the man and ripping the crowbar out of his hands, but he'd seen how crisp Scarface's reflexes were. If Joe got brained by one of those long-armed blows, it'd all be over in an instant. Something told him Scarface wanted to do more than throw a scare into him.

With a final push, Scarface thumped down in the truck bed.

Joe's fingers closed on the hammer.

The crowbar came whistling down just as Joe tugged on the toolbox door. Though Joe himself lay in the opening and the door slammed down on his shoulders, it also deflected the crowbar, which glanced off the steel surface with a teeth-rattling clang. Hoping Scarface had been thrown off balance by the thwarted attempt, Joe elbowed the toolbox door open and pushed to his feet.

Scarface's eyes were wild with hate and confusion. He'd already begun cocking the crowbar back to strike again. So when Joe came up with the hammer and struck Scarface with a rib-crunching blow just under the armpit, the tall man squealed in pain and let loose of the crowbar. Scarface seemed to dance sideways toward the tailgate, both arms covering his side protectively. The crowbar clattered to the floor of the truck bed.

Joe moved forward grimly, the hammer raised again. Scarface halted a foot from the tailgate and tossed up an arm to fend off the hammer blow. But instead of striking with the hammer again, Joe took a step and kicked the man as hard as he could in the side of the knee. Scarface buckled, his butt hitting the tailgate and his long body toppling over the edge. A meaty thud told Joe that Scarface had banged his head on the rear bumper, and then a softer thump sounded as the tall man collapsed on the pavement.

Joe vaulted over the tailgate and landed a couple feet from where Scarface lay grasping his knee and yowling like a lovelorn cat.

"You're a real asshole," Joe said, "but I'm not gonna kill you." He grasped Scarface by the hair, began towing him toward the side of the bridge.

The one named Shannon had come to, but he was doing little more than gazing about with a drugged expression. Joe reached into the Buick, shifted it into neutral, and made sure the wheel was straight. Then, with hardly a glance at either of his assailants, Joe climbed into the Tundra, put it in reverse, and drove until his back bumper kissed the Buick's grill. He depressed the gas and began the job of moving the big white car backward. He hoped the damned thing would cooperate. He didn't relish the idea of getting out to straighten the Buick's wheel again, and he harbored no illusions about Scarface or Shannon moving their cars for him.

But the Buick rolled in a straight line, and within moments, the Tundra had cleared the edge of the bridge. Joe didn't bother climbing out to throw the Buick into park. In truth he sort of hoped the big white car would keep rolling until it tumbled into the river valley. As Joe pulled a U-turn, he glimpsed Scarface lying on his side, both hands still clutching his knee. Beyond him, Joe spied Shannon stumbling sideways into the guardrail, the guy too woozy to stand upright. He reminded Joe of a newborn deer. Or a bad drunk.

The U-turn completed, Joe moved the Tundra steadily back toward the highway. He didn't floor it because he didn't want the two bastards back there on the bridge to know how badly they'd scared him. Because they had. And he knew just how fortunate he was to still be in one piece.

He was thinking this when a car swerved around the bend and headed straight for him. Joe thought for a moment the driver would simply ram him head-on. If that happened, Joe knew, the other guy would have it worse than he would, though they both might die. He saw in the moments before the green car bore down on him that it was only a Camaro, and a rusted one at that. The driver's face – there was something familiar about it – stretched in a look of horror. Then the man jerked the wheel to the right, and the Camaro veered into its own lane. Joe saw, as his Tundra nearly clipped the rear of the Camaro, the faces of both the driver and the passenger, and in that instant he recalled exactly where he'd seen them before. Like Shannon and the one he thought of as Scarface, he'd seen these bastards the day they'd interred Angie Waltz. Or had a ceremony for her. What they'd lowered into the ground, he had no idea. But the men had been there, that he knew.

Joe checked the rearview mirror to see if the Camaro was going to give chase, but apparently the men had decided to save it for another day.

Joe concentrated on his driving. He suspected he'd be okay as long as he kept the truck on the road and didn't make a move out of panic. He was rattled, sure. Who wouldn't be rattled after being attacked by a bunch of freaks?

As the pickup emerged from a dense thicket of country road, Joe thought of the faces in the Camaro.

One of them, the driver, was a plump man, very pale. He didn't look dangerous, but then again, you put a gun in someone's hand and he could get dangerous pretty fast.

The other one...he was the one who spooked Joe worse than the others. The bald guy with the leathery skin. The one whose muscles were abnormally large and whose square-jawed stare was abnormally hostile. The bastard looked like he'd kill you as soon as look at you, and when he killed you he'd make it nice and slow so he could exult in your anguish.

Gritting his teeth, Joe guided the pickup around a corner. The road straightened out, and when he was sure there weren't any more crazed drivers ahead of him, he checked the rearview mirror to see if he was being followed.

So far, he wasn't.

★ ★ ★

Michelle met him in the driveway. It wasn't until she pointed it out to him that he realized he'd been gone for three hours, a good bit of that time explaining to Copeland what had happened on Tomlinson Bridge. She could see he was still rattled from the experience, and of course she could see the starred passenger's window, and perhaps that was why she was so solicitous of his wellbeing. Or maybe she just felt bad about their argument. Joe sure as hell felt bad about it.

She moved with him up their long sidewalk, a hand on his lower back. Her touch felt good, though his muscles ached from the skirmish.

"And what did Copeland say?" she asked him as he finished the story and told her he'd gone straight to the chief to file a complaint.

"Lots of things, actually. Where's Lily?"

"Watching *Thomas*," Michelle said, nodding toward the illuminated basement window. *Kid loves her trains*, Joe thought. He felt a pang in his chest at the thought of his daughter. It'd only been hours since he'd last seen her, but man did he miss the kid. "What did Copeland tell you?" Michelle asked.

"For us to invest in a gun, for one thing."

Michelle furrowed her brow, and Joe couldn't blame her. By mutual consent they'd decided on not having a gun in the house on the off chance Lily ever found it and had an accident. Plus, Joe had always suspected he'd do more harm than good with a gun. He had visions of mistaking a friend for a home intruder, of killing someone he cared about, or even harming his wife or daughter.

Michelle looked up at him. "Are we?"

Joe stopped on the front porch but didn't go in. "We should make that call together, don't you think?"

Michelle moved past him, leaned on the black porch rail. "Darrell can't arrest them?"

"There are a couple problems with that," Joe said, pocketing his hands and staring out across Hillcrest Road. "For one, it's my story against theirs, and I seriously doubt they'll tell the same story I will."

"But Darrell knows you."

"That doesn't make my testimony any better than anyone else's. And in some folks' opinions, it might make mine worse."

Michelle shook her head. "It's just like when Sharon Waltz was here."

"At least Sharon didn't try to kill me."

"Yet."

"Now that's a cheerful thought."

She hung her head, scuffed the porch with a tennis shoe. "I'm sorry, Joe. I feel like all of this is my fault. Like it wouldn't have happened if I hadn't forced you out of the house today."

"You didn't force me anywhere. And I'm sorry about the hormone comment."

"Don't forget the part about the cramps."

Joe winced. "Don't remind me." When he saw the look on Michelle's face, he said, "Okay, you can remind me. I wish I could take it back."

Her eyes rose to meet his. "Thanks."

"Darrell said because they were the ones who got injured, as well as the fact there were no other witnesses it means that it'd be tough to make any kind of charges stick. Plus, he doesn't know if they'll even find the guys."

She glanced down the hill at the truck. "Will insurance at least take care of the window?"

Joe shook his head. "Deductible's too high."

"Even if we say it was an act of God? Like a rock flung by an oncoming car?"

Joe grinned. "That wouldn't be honest."

She rolled her eyes, but she was smiling too. She wrapped her arms around his waist, pushed into him. "You're obstinate as hell, but I do respect you."

He wrapped her up, stared down at her brown eyes. "That's about the nicest thing you could say to me right now."

She rocked up on her toes and kissed him. It lingered, and Joe eased her down, moved her gently to rest against the porch railing. As he kissed her, he felt a good deal of his worry and frustration melt away.

When she finally broke the kiss, she said, "Lily's been waiting for you."

"Yeah?"

"She says I don't do the train voices right."

He reached back, opened the front door for his wife. "I am good at the voices. Gordon, Salty…you should hear my Harold the Helicopter. I'm great at a British accent."

"She's two, Joe. She has low standards."

"That's jealousy talking."

As they moved through the house and down the basement steps, Joe heard the sounds of Alec Baldwin narrating one of Lily's favorite episodes. He imagined his daughter sitting in the middle of the couch, her favorite blanket in her lap, her green pacifier bobbing ruminatively. *God, I miss that girl,* he thought as he came round the corner, and when he saw her it hit him again, his debilitating love for her. It knocked his wind out, made him weave a little as he crossed the room and knelt beside her bare, soft legs. Joe wrapped his arms around her waist and rested the side of his head on her plump thigh.

"Hi, Daddy," she said and put a hand on top of his head. Her little paw, it was so tiny.

Please, God. Let me protect this little girl. Please let me be the dad she deserves.

Lily was absently stroking his ear and the hair above there, which oddly enough didn't tickle. It just felt nice. Joe inhaled deeply, caught the powdery scent of her skin, the slightly oily smell of her blanket. It'd need washing soon, but the problem was there was never a good time to do it. You couldn't wrestle that blanket away from Lily when she slept, and you sure as hell weren't going to take it from her when she was awake.

"Can we play *Thomas*, Daddy?" she asked.

Joe grinned up at her. "Right after I find the woogedy-boogedy."

He lunged toward her neck, and she squealed with laughter. The woogedy-boogedy was an object of indeterminate size that grew on her neck or arms and could only be removed by Joe pretending to eat it. It was one of Lily's favorite games.

When the woogedy-boogedy was tended to, Joe shut off the TV and started pulling Lily's trains, tracks, and assorted railway paraphernalia out of the big wooden trunk.

Standing at the foot of the stairs, where she'd apparently been watching for a few minutes now, Michelle said, "Can I play too?"

"Let Daddy do the voices," Lily cautioned.

Michelle looked at Joe, who shrugged and commenced setting up the big hill for Lily.

They played on the floor for the next hour, and when it was time for bed, Lily allowed Joe to read to her. Their daughter usually preferred to be put to bed by Michelle, so Joe was especially glad to get to read Lily to sleep.

It gave him something to think about when everything went to hell.

CHAPTER ELEVEN

Joe and Copeland were striding along Hillcrest Road. There weren't sidewalks to tread on, but as usual the traffic here was very infrequent. They passed through the intersection at the bottom of the hill and began trudging up the long rise.

"I don't know why we had to go for a walk like some old married couple," Copeland said. "Neighborhood's so hilly we might as well be in the Swiss Alps."

"Better here than Easter's Tavern."

"What's wrong with Easter's?"

"Don't you worry people will get the wrong impression, the police chief slumming at the local dive?"

Copeland's breathing sounded labored. "First of all, I find Easter's decor to be really cosmopolitan. Secondly, it's not like I'm dancing all over the tables and passing out on the floor."

Joe slid his hands into his hip pockets. "So you don't think there's anything peculiar about the Martins being connected to Sharon Waltz?"

"It's a small town," Copeland said. "Go back far enough, and damn near everybody's probably related in some way."

"If it's such a small place, why don't you know more about the people?"

"I'm not the town historian," Copeland said, scowling. "You act like I'm some guy with a long white beard sittin' in a rocking chair down at the barber shop telling stories about how Calvin Coolidge once rode through the courthouse square in a horse and buggy."

"He would've ridden in a Model-T."

"Man, don't challenge me on historical stuff. Guy like Coolidge, he would've ridden in a Duesenburg. Let me rest for a minute."

Joe regarded Copeland, the plump beads of sweat on his smooth brown forehead. "You ever find those guys that cornered me on the bridge?"

"Still looking," Copeland said. "Like I told you, they're not from around here, else I'd have heard of them before. Guy stands six-foot-six, got a face with so many scars it looks like he's been raising feral cats in his spare time, he's not easy to miss. And the other guy, Shannon? He sounds like he'd stand out too. There are plenty of men with tattoos around here, but very few of 'em have their whole arms covered with 'em."

"So we just sit around, hope they don't show up?"

"You take my advice yet?"

Joe scuffed the ground. "I picked it up yesterday."

"What kind?"

"A Ruger."

"Caliber?"

".38."

"Good boy. That's the kind I favor, only mine's a Smith & Wesson."

"I haven't fired the thing yet. Michelle, though, she already signed up at the shooting range."

Copeland grinned. "You better behave yourself, Joe."

"She doesn't need a gun. Michelle gets angry, she's scary enough."

They were halfway up the hill. Though overcast, the day had warmed up considerably. It was sixty-five at least, the sweat making Joe's long-sleeved red flannel shirt cling to his arms.

He glanced across the valley. "I better be getting back."

"You need to hire better workers."

Joe frowned at Copeland, who was now grimacing from the exertion, runnels of sweat streaming down his neck and darkening his brown collar. "What's wrong with my guys?"

"There aren't enough of them, first of all. A job that size, you need at least six or seven workers."

"That's not what you meant."

Copeland blew out breath, started back down the hill.

Joe caught up with him. "Darrell?"

Without looking up, Copeland said, "It's that Gentry dude. I don't trust him."

Joe tried to look affronted, but found it too difficult. "He's a little coarse, sure, but he's a skilled worker."

Copeland raised an eyebrow. "He looks at every woman like she's a succulent cut of steak."

"What, did he eyeball your ladyfriend or something?"

"I don't have a ladyfriend," Copeland said. "And it was yours."

Joe stopped. "Darrell, what the hell are you talking about?"

Copeland halted, hands on hips. "I wasn't gonna say anything, but sometimes a guy needs to, you know?"

"Louise Morrison says you're the biggest gossip in town."

"Louise can suck it. What I'm tellin' you, I'm tellin' you as a friend, all right?"

Joe waited, a restless snake of dread slithering in his guts.

"Couple days ago, I was driving by your house. I don't trust that bitch Sharon Waltz any more than you do. And I still worry about the assholes who tried to hurt you on the bridge. I was going real slow, moving up the hill and watching your house. Seein' if there was anybody scattering ashes on your doorstep."

"I still don't see why you can't arrest her for that."

Copeland went on as though Joe hadn't spoken. "I'm so focused on your house, I almost miss it, the guy standin' outside the Baxter place, at the northwest corner of the property. Back in the little pine grove?"

Joe found he was holding his breath.

"And there's Gentry, nestled between two pine trees, tucked away like. Where he thinks nobody can see him."

"Darrell, I don't think—"

"He's back there with his hand down his trousers, strokin' himself. His dick ain't out, probably because he's afraid of getting caught. You being right inside the Baxter house and all."

Joe turned away from Copeland, as if in doing so he could evade the rest of it.

But Copeland shuffled with him, his big eyes so riveted on Joe's that Joe found it impossible to look away. "He was lookin' up at your office, Joe."

"That doesn't mean—"

"I didn't wanna look," Copeland overrode him, "but I needed to be sure, so don't go getting all pissy with me because of this. When Gentry saw the cruiser, his hand shot out of his drawers like his dick had caught on fire and he'd just been burned. Bastard scurried around the corner and didn't come out. I know because I parked outside and waited, thinking maybe the moron would show his face again. I was so nettled, I was ready to knock those shiny teeth of his out."

Joe stood mulling it over, not wanting to ask the question but knowing he needed to anyway. "Was Michelle..."

"She was near the window," Copeland said. "A little ways in. She was sitting there in her bra, looking at something."

Joe's voice was barely a croak. "That's where the computer is."

"Well, I didn't take the time to figure out what websites she was on. It was embarrassing enough seeing her there wearing hardly any clothes."

"You don't think she knew Gentry was there?"

Copeland took a step back from him, his expression aghast and more than a little irate. "Man, don't you have any faith in your wife? Of course she didn't know she was being gawked at. The hell kind of question is that?"

Joe blew out disgusted breath, took a couple steps into the road. "Man, I'm an idiot. I don't know what the hell's wrong with me."

But Copeland's voice was not unkind. "What's wrong with you is you've been through a terrible ordeal, and you need some time to get your head on straight."

"I feel so damned paranoid. I mean, to think Michelle…"

"It is stupid, but at least you know it's stupid, right? I'd be worried if you got all angry at her, started going through her things to make sure she wasn't cheating."

Joe chuckled softly.

Copeland tilted his head. "You aren't going through her things, are you?"

"Man, shut up."

Copeland put his palms up. "Just checking."

They moved in silence down the hill, then up the long rise toward Joe's house, outside of which sat Copeland's cruiser.

Opening his door, Copeland said, "Guess I don't have to do my twenty minutes on the treadmill today."

"Hold on," Joe said. He came closer to where Copeland stood, his hand on the top of the open cruiser door. "Thanks for telling me. It's just not what a man wants to hear, you know? That someone who works for him… someone he considers a friend is…"

"Ogling his wife?"

"Yeah."

"No problem," Copeland said.

"But you still haven't explained the connection between Sharon Waltz and the house."

Copeland shrugged. "Why does there have to be a connection?"

"The timing is too convenient. That place has been vacant for decades, and less than a week after Sharon's daughter dies, someone who attended the funeral buys the place and hires me to renovate it?"

"Like I said, Joe. Small town. Not too many people. They're bound to be connected."

"The Martins are from Indy."

"Which is only an hour away."

"You don't think the Martins have anything to do with it?"

"With Sharon Waltz?"

Joe waited.

Copeland shook his head. "They're not exactly cut from the same cloth, you know?"

Joe glanced up at the Baxter house. There was no sign of Kevin or Shaun.

The big cop plopped down in his seat, pulled shut the door, and rolled down his window. "Good luck."

Without taking his eyes off the three-story house, Joe said, "Darrell?"

"Yeah?"

"Thanks again."

"Don't worry about it," Copeland said, keying the engine. "But I'd deal with Gentry, if I were you. That's bullshit, looking at Michelle like that."

"I know it's bullshit."

"You firing him? You want, you can tell him what I saw. In fact, I'd sorta like to watch you shitcan the idiot."

"I'll do it later," Joe said.

"Why later?"

"Because I need to see my wife first."

★ ★ ★

Joe went upstairs and gave his wife a good long kiss. She seemed impatient to get back to her eBay selling, so he left her alone and crept past Lily's room. She'd be napping for another hour or so. He returned to the Baxter house with Copeland's words banging around in his head.

Shaun was in the downstairs hallway repairing the wainscoting. They'd been able to restore the original, which had been fashioned with a deep, gorgeous cherry. Shaun was surprisingly good at that sort of work, and rather than disturb him, Joe merely said hello and went upstairs to find Gentry.

Once on the second floor, Joe crept silently to the door of the bedroom in which Gentry was supposed to be scraping wallpaper. Joe leaned forward, listening, but he didn't hear any scraping. He turned the knob and opened the door.

Gentry was on his iPhone.

"Break time, Kevin?"

Gentry gasped, bobbled the black iPhone a moment, then stood glowering at Joe. "Jesus, man, you damn near gave me a coronary."

"That would've been a shame."

Joe went in, shutting the door behind him.

He nodded at the scraper, which lay on the windowsill. The wallpaper around the window frame, Joe noticed, had barely been touched.

Gentry glanced at the scraper, then at Joe. "Where the hell've you been?"

"I went outside to get a little air."

"Been gone damn near an hour."

Joe eyed the untouched wallpaper. "I stopped in to see Michelle."

Gentry's voice altered. "Just say hello, did you?"

Joe turned and looked at him, at the flush of scarlet on his cheeks, at the horny glaze in his eyes. "When's the last time you did something nice for your wife?"

Gentry recoiled, his chin half-swallowed by his neck. "What's that got to do with anything?"

"You talk about pussy, about licking whipped cream off of women's asses… How often you do something nice for your wife? You know, the one you're married to?"

Gentry's eyes narrowed to slits. "Like you never talk like that."

"Not all the time I don't."

"Fine. You want me to stop making dirty jokes, I will. Jesus, it's no reason to get your panties in a bundle."

"It's not just the dirty jokes, Kevin."

Something wary seeped into Gentry's face. "Wait a minute. Who were you talking to just now? Couldn't have been Michelle. She thinks I'm a great guy."

"There you go again."

Gentry chuckled and set the iPhone on the sill. Picking up the scraper, he said, "Jealous, Joe? Sounds to me like you're in the doghouse. You piss off the little woman?"

"Kevin?"

"What?"

"You're fired."

Gentry had turned to scrape wallpaper, but at Joe's words he froze, the red-handled scraper clutched in fingers that had turned white from the pressure. Gentry shook his head a little and commenced scraping. "Whatever's wrong, you don't have to take it out on me."

"You leave now, I won't press charges."

Gentry rounded on him, bewilderment and indignation at war on his face. "What in the hell are you talking about?"

"You were staring at my wife and jacking off in your pants."

Whatever color had come into Gentry's face seemed to drain. "It's that cop, isn't it? That's who you were talking to."

"Thanks for admitting it. It's more than I expected from you."

Gentry chucked the scraper across the room. It clattered against the wall and came to rest. "I'm gonna give you more than you expected."

Joe reached into his pocket, retrieved his cell phone. He began to dial.

"Go ahead and call that fatass. Tell him you need protection from your own workers."

"You're not my worker anymore, Kevin." Joe brought the phone to his ear, waited.

Gentry stepped nearer, rolling his shoulders. "You tell Copeland I'll take him on too when he's off-duty, see if he's man enough—"

"Hey, Shaun," Joe said into the phone. "I need you to come up here right away. Thanks."

As Joe hung up, Gentry's face twisted into a smirk. "I can't believe you brought Shaun into this. You really think that moron's gonna do you any good? You know I could whip both of you in my sleep."

Joe eyed Gentry a moment, then laughed softly. "I remember back when I was in junior high. We used to talk about which girls had the biggest jugs, which ones we'd like to see naked. I was a horny little bastard. In fact, I thought of little else."

"That supposed to make us friends?"

"No, Kevin, it isn't. It's to tell you I know how your mind works. Because I once thought the same way. I thought with my pecker instead of my brain. But what happened was I grew out of it. I realized that there was more to a girl than a vagina and a pair of breasts. Most guys come to the same realization."

Gentry's jaw was flexing, his upper lip twitching into a sneer. There were footsteps in the hallway.

"But you," Joe continued, "you still treat women like slabs of meat. You've been eyeballing my wife for a good while now, and I've dropped more than enough hints for you to know you need to knock it off."

"Listen, I don't give a shit—"

"I know you don't," Joe said, "and that's why we're here now."

The door opened behind Joe. "You needed me?" Shaun asked.

"I need a witness," Joe said.

He could sense Shaun hesitate. "A witness for what?"

Under his breath, Joe said to Gentry, "Bet your wife and kids'd be proud if they knew their daddy was a Peeping Tom."

Gentry swung at him.

Prepared as he was, the blow still nearly caught Joe on the jaw. But he was fast enough, and Gentry, thrown off balance by the force of his own punch, stumbled forward. Joe pumped a knee into his gut, sidestepped Gentry's blundering body, and shoved the man hard toward the doorway. He landed prostrate at Shaun's feet, as though he'd decided to worship his blond co-worker, then scrambled to his hands and knees.

Gentry came up swinging, a wild right whooshing an inch from Joe's nose. Again Gentry stumbled – the guy fought like a Tasmanian devil – and this time Joe helped him complete his spin with a left-handed shove to the hip. The moment Gentry came around to face him again, Joe let loose with a bone-crunching fist straight from the shoulder.

Gentry flew back like he'd been shot out of a cannon.

He landed in a tangled heap, holding his left cheek and muttering curses. Joe couldn't make out most of what Gentry was saying, but he did hear both "Michelle" and "bitch" in there somewhere, and that was enough. Joe stepped over and kicked him in the ribs. As his work boot connected with Gentry's side, he heard a dull crack. Gentry collapsed on the ground, arching his back as though he'd been shot with a rifle. Shaun was asking what the hell was going on and Gentry was groaning out a stream of expletives. Joe watched him scrabble around on the floor like a deranged crab for a few moments, then crouched beside him.

"I gave you the chance to leave and you didn't. Instead, you took a swing at me." He nodded toward the tall blond kid, who was still gaping at Gentry's squirming body. "Shaun here's a witness. You attacked me, I defended myself, and now you've got the choice again. Get your sorry ass off this property, or get up and fight."

Lying on his side, Gentry glowered up at him. Seeing the look on his face, Joe was sure the guy would come at him again. But instead, Gentry said, "You deserve it, you know."

Joe stared back at him, thought, *Play along. This'll be over soon.*

"What do I deserve, Kevin?"

"They told me it was fate, all this stuff happening."

"Who told you?" Joe asked, his voice tight. He realized his heart was thudding, and it wasn't from the exertion of kicking Gentry's ass.

And Joe realized something else: Gentry was grinning. And not just the salacious kind of grin or the cruel, teasing one to which Joe was accustomed. No, the look on Gentry's face now was almost triumphant, like he possessed some secret tactic for which Joe would have no defense. "I didn't believe it at first," Gentry went on, "but lately I've started to wonder…everything coming together so fast…you going right along with it."

Joe reached down, grasped Gentry by the collar, and dragged him toward the door. "I told you to get the hell out of this house, and I meant it."

Shaun backpedaled into the hallway. "Seriously, Joe, what the heck's going on?"

Gentry said, "I thought they'd leave the kid out of it, but they said it was necessary."

That stopped him. Joe let Gentry drop and stood glaring down at him, his breath coming in great, molten heaves. "What kid?"

"I ain't telling you shit," Gentry said, climbing to his feet. He dusted himself off, smiling. "And I'm glad you fired me. Makes what's about to happen even better."

And with a grin of depthless malice, Gentry turned and strode away.

Joe watched after him, his heart whamming in his chest.

Shaun moved up next to him. In a small voice, he asked, "You really fire him, Joe?"

Joe didn't answer. He couldn't. Because the only thought in his mind, for reasons he didn't care to ponder, was of Little Stevie.

I thought they'd leave the kid out of it, but they said it was necessary.

Joe swallowed and winced at the dusty feel of his throat. He'd need to call the Morrisons later, make sure Stevie was okay.

Shaun stood watching him. "I think you should rethink it, Joe. You shouldn't have fired Kevin."

Wordlessly, Joe moved down the hallway, down the stairs, and let himself into the burnished gold sunlight. It was a pretty May afternoon and the air was rife with pollen and the fragrance of lilacs in bloom. Yet beneath it Joe sensed something acrid, something bitter.

Something like ashes.

PART THREE
SERPENTS

CHAPTER TWELVE

The rest of May passed in a blur of eleven-hour workdays, gloomy weather, and time indoors with Michelle and Lily. Had the renovation of the Baxter house involved more exterior work, their progress would have been sluggish. But since Mitch and Bridget were adamant that the interior should be completely finished before the façade was touched, Joe and his workers were able to make rapid progress in transforming the old Queen Anne from something out of a Gothic horror movie to a place that looked as if it might someday be inhabitable.

Partially out of necessity and partially due to Michelle's constant harping, Joe hired three new workers to replace Kevin Gentry. It wasn't that Gentry had been so valuable – in fact, as the tasks got knocked out at a fairly astonishing pace it became increasingly obvious that Gentry had been as much of a hindrance as a help. Granted, the guy had possessed skills that the new workers hadn't yet developed, but his utilization of said skills had been fitful to say the least. And besides, Joe reasoned, each of the new workers was still in his twenties, which meant there would be ample time to learn the trade if they became permanent fixtures on his crew.

Joe suspected they would.

After quitting time one afternoon, Joe was pushing Lily's stroller through the neighborhood when Michelle looked at him and said, "How're the new guys working out?"

Joe told her.

She nodded. "You should've hired more men a long time ago."

"Honey, it's not like we do all the sub-work. The heating, the electrical, concrete…they all bring in their own guys. We're mostly there for the carpentry."

"You still used to take on too much."

"Nothing I couldn't handle."

"You know, you could admit I was right for once."

He gave her a lopsided grin. "You're always right, dear."

"You're full of sh—" She glanced over at Lily, who was eating goldfish crackers out of the stroller tray. "You're full of ka-ka, Joe Crawford."

"Part of my charm."

Lily started screaming.

Joe glanced down at her, saw she was arched over her tray, groping for something that had tumbled to the asphalt. Joe engaged the wheel brakes, rounded the stroller, and spotted what had fallen. Her green pacifier. He plucked it off the road and examined it. There was a scrim of dirt on one side of the translucent nipple and a tiny black ant crawling along the perimeter of the handle. Joe flicked the ant off.

Lily shrieked louder.

Michelle wrinkled her nose in distaste. "It's okay, honey," she said to Joe. "I'll wash it when we get home."

Joe rubbed the pacifier on his sleeve, saw he'd gotten most of the dirt off. Then, he popped it into his mouth, removed it, and spat on the asphalt.

Michelle watched, appalled, as he returned it to Lily's mouth. "*Honey*."

"What? She stopped crying, right?"

"There were bugs on it."

"Just an ant. I got rid of it."

"But the germs—"

"Aren't going to hurt her. I'm the one with dirt in my mouth."

"Are all men as disgusting as you?"

He disengaged the brakes, recommenced pushing the stroller. "Worse."

"I can't imagine. Leaving the seat up, peeing on the floor…"

"You'd miss too sometimes if you were trying to wield such a big, powerful instrument."

"It's not that big and powerful."

"Hey now, you don't wanna go hurting my confidence. That could lead to psychological issues, insecurity. Maybe even erectile dysfunction."

"I think that's the least of your worries. You get more hard-ons than a stud horse at breeding time."

Joe grinned. "That's more like it."

"I didn't say you were hung like one."

"Ouch."

They were quiet a few moments, taking in the beauty of the neighborhood. Not all the houses were big, but there were trees everywhere, lots of rises and dales. Several of the houses had windowboxes, and nearly all of them had flowerbeds somewhere. Joe inhaled the sweet purple fragrance of the lilac bushes, the undercurrents of honeysuckle and mowed grass. Dogwoods and cherry trees bloomed in several of the yards they passed, and though most of the magnolia blossoms had fallen by now, there were still enough of the lovely pink petals to add contrast to the greening trees.

"Kiss break!" Lily said, though the way she pronounced it, the words sounded more like *kif bwake.*

"Kiss break," Joe agreed and moved around the stroller to kiss his daughter several times on the forehead and cheeks.

"Take it easy, Joe," his wife said, though she and Lily were both laughing.

Joe buried his nose in his daughter's hair and pretended to gobble her neck. Lily squealed with delight.

Straightening, he looked at his wife and said, "What about you? I'm on a roll."

"Your kisses are too wet. It's like being slobbered on by a German shepherd."

"Know a lot about that, do you?"

"Shut up."

They moved on, the gray skies beginning to break up overhead. *About time,* Joe thought. *It's damn near June, but it still looks like February.*

"Should we have another child?" Michelle said.

Joe stopped and stared at her. "You mean get pregnant the old-fashioned way or do it in vitro?"

"In vitro's too expensive."

"Agreed. Plus, I'm a whole lot better than a turkey baster."

Michelle made a face. "Gross."

"So does this mean we can ditch the condoms for a while?"

"*Honey.*" Michelle nodded toward Lily. "Don't say that in front of her."

"She doesn't know what a condom is. She ever finds one, I'll blow it up and make a wiener dog out of it."

"Are you ever serious?"

"When I'm making love."

She smiled ruefully, took hold of the stroller, and pushed it ahead.

He hustled up next to her, laughing. "Okay, I'm sorry. Of course I'd like to start trying again."

"I didn't say I wanted to."

"I thought—"

"I asked you if we should have another child, not if we should get pregnant."

"Hey, I always wondered that. Why do they say 'we' when it's the woman gets pregnant?"

"Because you share the experience."

"The insemination, sure. But I'm not the one gets morning sickness, has to lug around a thirty-pound sack of flour in my belly."

"What if we adopted?"

Joe stopped. "What?"

"You heard me."

"Your pregnancy with Lily went pretty well."

"But it took us *years*, Joe."

"That's the fun of it. The trying."

"Wasn't fun for me."

Joe saw tears in her eyes and felt his smile fade. "Hey, honey, I'm sorry. I was just..." He sighed, bent down to caress one of Lily's hands. The one that wasn't tossing goldfish crackers into the road. "I shouldn't have joked about it. I didn't mean to make you sad."

Michelle passed a trembling hand over her eyes. "I know you didn't. I just don't want to go through that again."

The memory was plain in her face, and Joe could see she didn't want to go down that road any more than he did. Not a day had gone by when he hadn't thought of their boy, of Ben Crawford, the child who'd never even gotten the chance to live. Who should have been outside playing with his friends today rather than sitting on a shelf in some fucking columbarium.

"I'm sorry, honey."

She forced a smile. "It's not your fault. It just..." She inhaled shuddering breath, looked away. "...it just sneaks up on me, you know?"

And he did know. Or he knew to a degree. Then again, how the hell could he fathom the pain Michelle must've felt that day, the pain she still must be feeling? To feel that child growing in her womb, to talk to Ben and sing him songs and stroke her belly and dream of holding him…to go through all of that only to have him stolen from her only six weeks before his birth. Michelle was a strong woman, but that didn't mean she didn't feel as deeply as the average person. On the contrary, he'd always thought his wife felt things more deeply than just about anyone else he knew. Which was one of the things he loved most about her.

He put his arms around her waist. "Tell me what you're thinking," he said.

She looked up at him. "What about adoption?"

"Doesn't that process take a long time?"

"Even if we know the child?"

Joe frowned at her a moment before cottoning to her meaning. "You're talking about Little Stevie."

Michelle looked at him. "Why not?"

"I don't know," he said. "That seems pretty complicated. I mean, the Morrisons—"

"Are only temporary foster parents, you said that yourself."

"That's true," he allowed. "But—"

"Has a permanent home been found yet?"

Joe hesitated. In truth, he'd stopped by the Morrisons the day before to check in on Stevie. And while the boy seemed healthy and happy stumbling around in the Morrisons' fenced-in backyard, Louise told Joe she was worried that if the CPS didn't find a family soon, the boy might miss out on crucial bonding time with whatever parents eventually adopted him. Joe had asked what would happen if no one else came forward to claim Stevie. Louise hadn't answered for a long while, and just when he thought she'd ignore the question altogether, she said, "I'll be sixty soon, Mr. Crawford. It's not fair to me or my husband – or to Stevie here – for us to adopt him."

Stevie had been on Joe's mind all through the month, and though he himself had toyed with the notion of broaching adoption with his wife, now that he was faced with the reality of it – the possibility that Michelle would actually want to raise the child of Angie Waltz – he felt very little excitement and more than a little terror.

"Joe?" she said. "Stop brooding and talk to me."

"I would if I knew what to say."

"Kiss break!" Lily yelled.

Joe bent to kiss his daughter.

"Tickle me, Daddy!"

Joe tickled her. But he could feel Michelle's stare on his back. Eventually, he straightened and turned to his wife. "I'll tell you how I feel, but you have to promise not to get mad at me."

"How can I promise that? What if you say something offensive?"

"I might," he said evenly. "I don't even know how I feel yet."

"Why do you always have to complicate things?"

"Because it's complicated. If this were just another kid, I'd be all for it. But Stevie isn't. He's the son of a woman who cremated herself because of something I did."

Michelle shook her head. "It wasn't because of—"

"But that's how it feels, okay? You're always telling me it can't be wrong if it's how you feel. Why's this any different?"

"Fine. What else?"

"I'm not saying it if you're gonna get aggravated."

"But that's how I feel."

"Exactly!" he said. "And how I feel is guilty. I feel responsible, Michelle, for the fact that that poor kid doesn't have a mommy."

"He's better off without her."

"You're probably right about that."

"Damn right I am."

"But I still feel responsible."

Michelle spread her arms. "So be responsible for him. It'll take away your guilt and give the child a loving home. It'll be more stable than the Waltzes' ever would've been."

"Yeah, and what about Sharon? Are we gonna let her see Little Stevie? Give her visitation rights?"

Michelle's face hardened. "Not a chance in hell."

"Language. But you see how complicated it is already, right? We'd not only have to go through adoption proceedings, but we'd have to get a judge to declare Sharon doesn't have any legal right to see Stevie."

"Maybe she won't want to see him."

Joe grunted. "The woman's profession is being a pain in the ass. Of course she's gonna want to see him."

Michelle flailed her hands in exasperation. "Isn't she…I don't know, in trouble or something for having all those drugs?"

"Copeland said she claims they were all her daughter's, that she had no idea Angie had a drug problem."

"Nice mom."

"She might be the worst person I've ever met," Joe said. "But I don't see any way to keep her from Stevie forever. Hell, I'm surprised she hasn't tried to get custody of him already."

"Maybe she has. Maybe they've already turned her down."

Joe sighed, started pushing the stroller again. "Maybe."

Michelle's eyes were large with hope. "Will you ask Copeland? Maybe that's already been settled. If it has, it'll make everything easier, won't it?"

"It would," Joe said, "for whoever adopts Stevie."

Michelle stopped. "Why can't it be us, Joe?"

He turned and regarded Michelle, who was standing a few feet downhill from him and Lily. Framed that way, with the dark asphalt and the high angle, Michelle looked very small, very vulnerable. She looked like something easily broken.

He sighed. "I'll talk to Copeland. I can't make any promises, but I'll check it out. Okay?"

She smiled, and at the sight of it, Joe's heart hurt a little.

"Come on," he said, turning the stroller around. "Lily's sippy cup is empty, and she's gonna be parched from all those goldfish."

They walked home in silence, Michelle smiling quietly to herself, Joe pausing every fifty feet or so to give his daughter kisses.

★ ★ ★

"You want to do *what*?"

Joe didn't turn away from the radiator pipe he was shearing with the Sawzall. He lay on his side, concentrating on his task. Fitting the blade into the cut he'd started, Joe said, "You heard me, Darrell, I don't need to repeat myself."

"Aw, listen to you, callin' me by my first name. Almost makes me feel like we're buddies now. Next thing you know, we're gonna be going on fishing trips, sitting around a campfire sipping Old Milwaukee."

Smiling, Joe sawed through the stout iron pipe. He knew he should be wearing safety goggles, but the Hodge twins each needed a pair, and Joe hadn't gotten around to buying more since he expanded his crew to five.

As the jagged teeth pumped up and down, shredding through rusty iron and scattering dust and brownish flecks all over the place, Joe squinted his eyes to make the smallest possible targets for errant debris. The last thing he needed was a visit to the emergency room to extract a sliver of rust from one of his corneas.

The cut finished, Joe set the Sawzall on the floor and passed his fingertips over the severed pipe. It was good, flush with the floor and easily covered over with caulking and wood putty. Once they'd refinished the floors, no one would ever know there'd been a radiator here.

Copeland leaned over. "Say, you're not too bad with that thing. How about you come over to my house and help me finish my basement?"

"Sure," Joe said, climbing to his feet. "I'll even give you a ten per cent discount if you take care of cleaning up at the end of the day."

Copeland looked aghast. "Ten per cent? That's the only deal you'd give me? Guy who's a dear friend, who's gotten you out of more trouble than anybody else?"

Joe crossed to the southern wall of the master suite, where his glass of ice water sat bleeding on an old newspaper. "'Dear friend' is stretching things a bit. And Michelle's the one who keeps me out of trouble." Joe took a long drag from the glass and then regretted it when he got a painful brain freeze. He grimaced. "I told Michelle not to put so much ice in it. I like cool water better than cold."

"That's a character flaw," Copeland said. "So's taking a friend for granted."

Joe took a smaller swig this time. Swallowing, he said, "Fine, I'll give you fifteen per cent, and I'll help you clean up. But I'm not gonna give you piggyback rides up and down the basement steps."

"Shit, you're not man enough to lug my ass around. We'd both be in traction, you tried to do that."

Joe replaced the glass on the sodden circle of newspaper. "So you don't think it's a good idea, huh?"

"What, adopting Stevie Waltz?"

Joe's arm muscles tensed. "That's not his name."

"It's gonna be his name until someone legally changes it. And if you think you're gonna be the one to do it, you've been inhaling too much asbestos."

"How'd you know this house had asbestos?"

"How many houses this old don't?"

"Good point."

"Gentry pressed charges against you this morning."

Joe's mouth fell open.

Copeland grinned. "Now that's a priceless expression. Hold on while I get my phone out. I gotta get a picture of that. You look like a big ol' lake trout."

"What kind of charges?"

"Assault. Wrongful termination of employment."

"Wrongful termin— Is that even a real crime?"

"Gentry thought it was. Of course Gentry thought it was legal to diddle himself on a job site too."

"Am I gonna be in any trouble?"

Copeland scowled at him. "Hell no, you're not in trouble. Don't you have any faith in me?"

"But—"

"Gentry came by when I was off-duty. You know, thinkin' he could get one of my people to arrest you when I wasn't around?"

Joe listened, his butt cheeks slowly unclenching.

"But I happened to drop by the station just a couple minutes after Gentry showed up. It was total happenstance – I forgot the book I was reading on my desk the night before – but when I came in, I saw him sitting with Alyssa."

"Who's Alyssa?"

"Alyssa Jakes. One of my officers. You've never met her. Anyway, Gentry's in there with his back to me, not even noticing I've come in. I can tell from the look on Alyssa's face that she's not buyin' anything he's selling. I hear him saying things like, 'And then he fires me without giving a good reason, doesn't even give me two weeks' notice.' Stuff like that."

"Employees who masturbate to their bosses' wives forfeit their right to two weeks' notice."

Copeland held up a palm. "Hold on. I'm comin' to that."

Joe listened. In the background he heard the Hodge twins sawing through pipes.

"Alyssa, she doesn't look up at me even though I know she sees me standin' there in the doorway. I'm about five feet behind Gentry, but the guy's got no clue I'm there. Alyssa, she says, her expression totally deadpan, 'Why didn't you bring this to the attention of Chief Copeland?'

"Gentry, he makes this scoffing sound, like Alyssa's just suggested he should slather himself in honey and roll around on some anthills. He says, 'Copeland and Crawford are bosom buddies.'"

"I used to watch that show," Joe said. "I knew Tom Hanks would be a star even back then."

Copeland went on as though Joe hadn't spoken. "Alyssa, I can tell she's enjoyin' herself, but if you didn't know her as well as I do, you'd think she was just doing her job. She says, 'Are you implying Chief Copeland wouldn't give your complaint the proper attention?'

"Gentry, he makes that sour scoffing sound again, like I'm some corrupt small-town cop on the take. He says, 'Copeland's too busy bein' drinking buddies with Joe to arrest him.'"

"See," Joe said, "I told you word of our affair would get around."

"Alyssa, she looks at Gentry with that same expression, but I know her well enough to see the impish gleam in her eyes."

Joe smiled. "She's setting him up."

"Like an FBI sting. Alyssa says, 'Chief Copeland always has been like that.'" Copeland grinned. "Gentry, I can tell he's really interested now. He leans forward, says, 'Like what?'

"'Drinking on the job,' Alyssa says. 'Associating with undesirables.'"

"What the hell?" Joe said. "Now I'm an undesirable?"

"That's the one part she got right. Anyhow, Gentry's gettin' into it. Like he's some kind of muckraking investigative reporter or something. He says to Alyssa, all conspiratorial-like, 'Have you thought of bringing this to the attention of Copeland's supervisors?'

"'Of course I've thought of it,' Alyssa says, and gives a little shiver. 'But Copeland's a scary guy. Last officer tried to bust him for his lawlessness, he disappeared and was never seen again.'"

Joe started to chuckle. "She really use that word? Lawlessness?"

"She said it."

"Sounds like a good actress."

Copeland was laughing too. "Goddamn Oscar-winner is what she is. I couldn't believe it. But Gentry, he's sittin' on the very edge of his chair, just eatin' that shit up. Like he's gonna bust my syndicate of corruption wide open."

"So what happens?"

"Gentry says, 'If you put yourself out there, I'll protect you. I'll see to it neither Darrell Copeland nor Joe Crawford lays a finger on you.'"

"He didn't say that."

"Swear to God. And then Alyssa – I mention she's sort of gorgeous?"

"Of course she is," Joe said. "Why else would Kevin want to protect her?"

"Bingo. Alyssa put on her best damsel-in-distress look, says to Gentry, 'I'm frightened of him, Kevin. I don't want him to hurt me.'"

"No!"

"Yes. As God as my witness. Gentry says, 'I'll kick his black ass before he can look at you crossways.'"

"Bet you liked that."

"I'll be honest, Joe. I thought it was all pretty funny until he said that. But once he brought my black ass into it, he crossed some kind of unspoken line."

"Never talk about a man's ass."

"Exactly. So I decided to speak up. In my biggest voice, I said, 'You threatening me, boy?'

"Gentry, he jumps so high off that chair, I thought he'd been zapped in the nether regions with an invisible cattle prod. He cranes his head around at me and I swear to God whatever pigment he had in his skin had disappeared. The bastard was whiter than fresh snow.

"Gentry says, 'How long you been standing there?'

"I said, 'Long enough to know you talked about assaulting a police officer.'

"Gentry, his mouth opens and shuts so many times without making a sound I thought I might've taken away his power of speech permanently. You know, like Jonathan Harker's hair turning white in *Dracula*? Only this was a loss of speech."

"I understood the analogy."

"Way you stared at me, I wasn't sure. Anyway, after about an hour of that voiceless mouth movement, he's able to say, 'Joe hasn't been fair to me, Chief Copeland.'"

"Real respectful now, huh?"

Copeland nodded. "Like I was the Pope. I said, 'You've been jerkin' your little carrot too hard, Gentry. I think you jarred that little pea brain of yours loose.'"

Joe resisted an urge to hug Copeland. "What'd he say?"

"He got some of that pigment back, only this time it was all red. He said, 'I don't know what you're talkin' about.'

"That pissed me off somethin' fierce, him callin' me a liar. So I bent down, got right in his face and said, 'We corrupt alcoholic cops still have video cameras in our cruisers, you know? I decided to turn mine on you while you were whackin' off to Crawford's wife.'

"That got rid of his pigment again. I see over Gentry's shoulder that Alyssa's coverin' her mouth to stifle laughter. I had to block her out so I wouldn't laugh too."

"What then?"

"Then I said, 'If you say another word about me, about Joe, or even drive by his house again, I'll post that clip of you flogging your bishop all over YouTube.'"

"You didn't."

"Hell if I didn't. Gentry, he's looking at me with more horror than I thought a human face could contain. It was sort of cruel of me, but the dipshit had me so irate, I couldn't help myself. I drove it in further. 'What'll your wife say when she sees you've gotten a hundred thousand hits for choking your chicken in broad daylight?'"

"You've got a lot of euphemisms for masturbation, you know that?"

"One of my many talents."

"So what happened after that?"

Copeland shrugged. "We talked for a while. Nothing much of interest was said. I think he was too terrified to form a coherent sentence."

Joe pondered it for a few moments. He was about to let it go when he remembered something Gentry had said the day Joe fired him. "Did Gentry mention anything else?"

"Like what? His thoughts on the Middle East?"

Joe shrugged. "I don't know. Stuff about children or getting revenge on me or anything like that?"

Copeland gazed at him closely. "Whose children?"

"No one's in particular. He just said some things the day we had our fight."

"I thought you said he attacked you."

"He did. But when he was leaving…ah, never mind."

Copeland glanced at his watch. "I better go. I'm supposed to watch for speeders on Carrolton. I swear, the people in your neighborhood think I've got nothing else to do all day but sit by the side of the road with my radar gun."

He ambled toward the door.

"Hey, Copeland?"

Copeland turned in the doorway.

"What book was it? The one you came back to the station for?"

Copeland's look went stony. He shifted uneasily on his big brown loafers. "Just some light reading. I'm between biographies right now."

"You didn't answer the question."

"That's because you'll be an asshole about it."

"Try me."

Copeland's eyes widened. "I'll have you know I'm currently reading a book by Nicholas Sparks."

"Oh yeah?" The corners of Joe's mouth twitched.

"*Message in a Bottle*," Copeland said.

Joe's stomach began to shake.

Copeland nodded. "And you can go fuck yourself."

Joe couldn't suppress it any longer. "Hey, man, don't go. It's okay."

"Dickhead," Copeland muttered on his way out.

Joe followed, laughing harder. "Seriously, Darrell, there's nothing wrong with Nicholas Sparks. You want, we can watch *A Walk to Remember* together, do each other's nails, swap recipes…"

"Shut your dumb ass up," Copeland growled as he stalked toward the stairwell. "I take care of that idiot Gentry for you, and how do you repay me? By makin' fun of my book choice."

"Aw, man, don't leave like that. There's nothing wrong with a heartfelt love story."

Copeland raised a middle finger and disappeared down the stairs.

Joe watched after him, smiling. Maybe he'd give Copeland twenty percent off on his basement.

CHAPTER THIRTEEN

Joe decided to knock off early so he and Lily could play with trains. Now their basement carpet was crisscrossed with wooden tracks, hills, and various other Thomas the Tank Engine paraphernalia. Michelle had been trying to get Lily interested in Barbies and other girly toys, but thus far, trains and Matchbox cars were her obsessions.

Joe was lying on his side, reflecting on what an asshole Kevin Gentry was when Lily thrust a big blue train in his face. "Talk to Gordon, Daddy."

That was Lily-speak for *become* Gordon the Train. Joe switched over to his arrogant Gordon voice. "I'm the fastest train on Sodor. Everyone should bow to my greatness."

Lily grabbed a green train and situated it nose-to-nose with Gordon. "Talk to Henry, Daddy."

Joe put on his easy country drawl. "You might be the fastest, Gordon, but I care more about being useful."

"Uh-oh!" Lily said. "Here comes Cranky!" Only the way she said it, the *R*s became *W*s.

Joe helped her crank the magnet down and attach it to Gordon's front end.

"They're buffering up!" Lily said.

"My chain aches," Joe said, shifting into his surly Cranky the Crane voice.

Lily was up and bouncing on her knees. "Oh no, the wind!" And she pushed Cranky over.

Joe leaned in, tickled his daughter's sides. She squealed with laughter and tumbled toward him. Smiling, Joe wrapped her up and wrestled her amidst the wrecked tracks and the overturned trains. They were both laughing when something made his muscles tense, an unexpected texture on his fingertips. Lily continued to thrash in his arms and squeal with delight, but Joe's good spirits had vanished. He was staring down at his fingertips with dread.

Gray dust.

Ashes.

"Lily?"

"Tickle me, Daddy!" she said.

"What have you been into?" he asked. Drawing away from her, he saw the hair around her shoulders was dusted with the stuff. And now that he noticed the ashes on his fingers and in her hair, the acrid scent of it became overwhelming. Hissing between clenched teeth, Joe spun his daughter around and inspected the back of her hair. It was as though someone had turned her upside down and dragged her head through an extinguished campfire.

"Daddy? What's wrong?"

"What have you been— How did you get this stuff in your hair?" Joe realized his voice had risen several notches – apparently loud enough to attract Michelle's attention, judging from the rapid thump of footsteps down the carpeted basement steps – but he couldn't quell his escalating terror.

"Daddy…" Lily said, pushing away from him, "…*don't!*"

Without realizing it, Joe had clutched her slender arms harder than he'd intended. "I'm sorry, honey, but where—"

"What's happening down here?" Michelle asked, her eyes fierce.

Joe tamped down the flare of anger her expression enkindled in him. Christ, like he was abusing their daughter or something. "She has ashes all over her hair," he said, as Lily broke away. "What were you two doing earlier?"

Michelle swept their toddler into her arms. "What do you mean, 'What were we doing?' What do we always do in the afternoon, Joe. Lily napped and I worked on the computer."

"That sounds rough."

Michelle's mouth fell open. "What does that mean?"

Just shut up, a voice in Joe's head commanded. *You're already in a hole. Don't dig any deeper.* "I'm sorry, honey. I didn't mean to insult you."

"How else can I take a statement like that? 'Sounds rough.' You act like I do nothing all day. I'm selling clothes on eBay, and that's after I've done all the dishes, cleaned the—"

"I know honey, I shouldn't have—"

"—house, done all your laundry. Gone to the grocery store, changed Lily's—"

"—I'm an idiot, honey. I really don't know what I was—"

"—diapers. Why do you—" She broke off, and Joe saw with horror that her eyes were brimming.

"God, honey, I don't know what to say. I'm so sorry. But would you look at her hair?"

He took a step toward his wife, but she shrank from him, her lips thin.

Joe felt his shoulders slump. "I have no idea what came over me. I just— Would you please look at her hair for me?"

Michelle's brow furrowed. "What do you mean—"

"There're ashes in it," he explained. "In the back part."

Michelle examined Lily's long black hair, her fingers combing the glossy locks. "It's fine," she said. "A little oily maybe, but tonight's a bath night." Her expression hardened. "Or is every other night not good enough for you now? Maybe I've been slacking again."

"Honey, you never slack. That was the dumbest thing I've ever said."

"Damn right it was."

He took a step toward them. "But you're sure...you mean you don't even smell any—"

"Ashes? Why on earth would she have ashes in her hair, Joe? You think I let her play in the fireplace when I want to surf the computer?"

Joe massaged his forehead. "What can I say, honey? I wish I could take it back."

"I wish you could too." She turned away, Lily clinging to her and watching Joe with big, frightened eyes.

"Please, honey."

Without turning, Michelle said, "No sex for you this week."

"All week?"

She mounted the steps. "Maybe a month. Depends on how mad I decide to be."

"I want Cranky!" Lily called.

"Let Daddy bring him upstairs," Michelle said. "He needs to dig himself out of the hole he's in."

Joe watched after them, his stomach roiling and his throat aflame. He was about to follow them up the stairs, maybe do a little damage control, when the memory of the ashes returned to him. He'd smelled them – of that he was certain. Hell, he'd *seen* them, felt the fine grit between his thumb and fingertips. It wasn't his imagination.

But where would Lily have gotten into ashes? Theirs was a gas log fireplace, not a wood-burning one. At least not since he'd converted it three years ago. He supposed Lily could've gotten into the little fire pit he'd made on the back hill, but that didn't seem likely either. Michelle watched her too closely for her to play around with that, and Joe sure as hell wasn't going to quiz her about it now. She might not have sex with him for a year.

So where did that leave him?

Cracking up, a voice in his head muttered.

No, I'm not, he thought. But if Michelle hadn't seen or smelled the ashes, how could he account for them?

Scowling, Joe bent and began the job of disassembling the railway network he and Lily had created. If he did some extra cleaning, maybe even threw in a couple loads of laundry, Michelle just might take some time off his sentence for good behavior.

★ ★ ★

But Michelle was true to her word. Six nights later, she still hadn't let him touch her, though the rest of their interactions had slowly returned to normal. Joe made it a point to knock off by four o'clock so he could spend extra time with Michelle and Lily, and because of his new workers the renovation of the Baxter house was going smoothly. The Hodge twins, Duane Mincel, and Shaun Peterson made a reliable, if somewhat inexperienced crew. All four worked vigorously and steadily, and if they did ask Joe a heck of a lot of questions, the trade-off was worth it. Where Gentry had been more knowledgeable than his current workers, they all surpassed Gentry in sheer elbow grease. Astoundingly, the renovation was a week ahead of schedule.

It was a pretty June night, and Michelle had gone to bed early with a headache. Lily had ceased kicking her crib a half-hour ago, and full dark had fallen. Joe contemplated giving Copeland a call, seeing if he felt like sitting out on the back porch and drinking a beer or two, but he worried they'd get loud enough to awaken Michelle, and Joe had no desire to undo the good will he'd built up since hurting her feelings that afternoon in the basement. He didn't particularly feel like reading, and his back ached too much to lift weights in the basement. Besides, he'd already worked out three days in a row and was feeling stronger than he ever had.

So he decided to drink a beer and check out the ESPN website, see if the Cubs might be worth a shit sometime this century.

He'd been sitting in the dark of the upstairs office when movement in his periphery caught his eye. He glanced to his left and saw that someone had flicked on a light in the Baxter house. The room was on the second floor, which because of the hill, was slightly higher than his vantage point. A quick calculation suggested it was one of the bathrooms. Of course it was, he realized. He could see the showerhead poking down. They'd need to order a frosted glass window, he reminded himself, so whoever took a shower there had some privacy.

Joe frowned. At first he thought one of the guys had left the light on, and that Joe just hadn't noticed it until now. Then he realized that, no, the light hadn't been on next door when Joe had entered the office. He'd have almost certainly noticed something like that by now. The Baxter house had been lightless as long as they'd lived here; Joe would've had to be the most unobservant neighbor in the world to miss a change so profound.

Bridget Martin stepped into view.

Joe watched her and wondered why she was there. At the Martins' request, they'd gotten the rest of the utilities hooked up last week, and while he supposed he couldn't blame Bridget for wanting to check on their progress, there was a territorial part of him that bristled at her intrusion on his work site.

Relax, he told himself. *She's not intruding. She's just up from Indianapolis to see her future home. She is the owner, after all.*

That was true enough, he guessed, but why had she come at night? Why not during the day when he could guide her through the house, show her what they'd done and what they hadn't gotten to yet? It could be dangerous for her, walking around at night like that.

Bridget twisted on the shower.

He drummed his fingers, wondering if he should go over there, let her know that without a shower curtain she could soak the exposed sub-floor, do a hell of a lot of damage. As he watched, Bridget extended a hand, let the spray wash over her fingers.

Joe's throat constricted. Certainly she wasn't going to…

For the first time he wondered if Mitch was with her. Just because Joe hadn't seen him yet didn't mean Bridget's husband wasn't there. In fact, the more Joe pondered it, Mitch probably *was* there. He was just in a different part of the house. Goodness knew the place was big enough for Joe not to have spotted him. Nearly six thousand square feet, and that was without the basement. Now that Joe thought about it, it wasn't a good idea at all for either Bridget or Mitch to go poking around the house at night. Even with all the lights burning – which they weren't; as far as Joe could tell the bathroom light was the only one on – the place was a hazard. There were power tools, sharp pieces of metal pipe they'd sawed but hadn't yet removed, holes in the floor they needed to repair. Joe was assaulted with a nightmare vision of Bridget stepping into a hole unwittingly, her foot plunging through the jagged opening, the exposed nails harrowing her flesh—

He'd just risen to hurry over there when Bridget began unbuttoning her red shirt.

Joe's mouth went dry. He stood there beside the office chair and watched in dim surprise as Bridget peeled the shirt off her shoulders and let it drop. She wore a satiny green bra.

Of course, Joe thought.

Looking up at her as he was, Joe was afforded a view all the way to her thighs, and he saw, as she unbuttoned the top of her jeans, that while she was a full-bodied woman, her tummy was firm, her build voluptuous and achingly attractive. Before he knew it, she'd shimmied out of her blue jeans and now stood before the mirror in only her green panties and matching bra.

Get out of here, Joe, a voice declared.

He knew this was sage advice, but he found his legs wouldn't cooperate. Granted, there was a part of him – a very specific part of him – that had responded to the sight of Bridget Martin in her skivvies, but the majority of his brain was flooded with guilt.

But still…he watched her hands reach toward the back of her bra, undo the clasp. The shoulder straps went slack, the confined breasts sagging a little, but not much at all. She reached up, dragged one strap down a creamy arm. She half-turned in his direction, started to take down the other strap.

You're no better than Kevin Gentry.

Joe jarred to his senses. That had done it. He forced his legs to move this time, compelled his body to stride toward the door, his hand to clutch the knob. He willed his eyes to remain studiously forward, to not glance back over his shoulder. He didn't need to see Bridget Martin take a shower. Maybe his inner fourteen-year-old wanted to do that, but the part of him that mattered, the husband and father part, reminded him what a terrible idea it was, what an awful thing to do to his family, not to mention Bridget.

His movements more assured now, Joe opened the door.

To stare at Michelle.

His mouth unhinged.

"What's the matter?" she asked. "I heard the floorboards creaking up here, thought you might have taken a fall or something."

Oh shit oh shit oh shit, he thought. Could she see around him? Joe was broadly built, but he didn't know if he could blot out the illuminated window behind him.

"Joe?" Michelle took a hesitant step forward. "Are you sweating?"

Swallowing, Joe stepped through the doorway and pulled the door shut behind him.

"What were you doing in there?" Michelle asked. Her voice was hushed because the nursery was only about ten feet behind her, but her eyes were large and suspicious.

"Nothing," he said, but his voice was so thick and froggy he sounded like he'd just done something reprehensible.

Michelle drew back to scrutinize his face. It was dark in the hallway, but not so dark she wouldn't notice the way his forehead was dotted with perspiration, the way his breath was coming in feverish heaves.

"Were you… Joe, were you in there watching porn?"

He let out a high-pitched laugh. He couldn't help it.

Her eyebrows drew in. "You were, weren't you?"

He began to chuckle – he saw the way it made Michelle glare, but dammit he couldn't help it. He'd always been like that, giggling like an idiot whenever he absolutely needed to be serious. Growing up, sitting in church with his brother, they'd cracked up at the silliest things. Someone singing off-key. A kid saying something inappropriate during the sermon…

Michelle sighed, shook her head. "I guess it's not the worst thing you could do, but I do have to say I'm a little annoyed. I mean, it's only been a few days—"

"I wasn't watching porn, honey."

Her eyes narrowed. "Then why are you sweating?"

Shit, he thought. Maybe he should've gone with the porn story.

"I guess I was just feeling nervous. This Martin renovation and all…"

"I thought you guys were ahead of schedule."

"We are," he said, doing his best to subtly move away from the closed office door. He prayed she'd follow his lead. "The job's going well, but it's the only thing we've got going right now. If we mess something up…" He gestured vaguely.

"Why would you mess up? Are you afraid you're suddenly going to forget how to drive a nail?"

"It's not that, honey, it's juggling all the subs, making sure they show up on time." She was moving with him toward Lily's room and the stairwell. Joe felt his anxiety lessen a notch. "You know, it's like dominoes. You can't do it out of order. We can't get the drywall guys in before the electrical and plumbing are done, and the painters can't do their work until the drywall is completed."

"Someone dragging their feet?"

Joe rounded the banister, started down the stairs. "No one specifically."

"You think she knew you were watching her?"

Joe froze. He glanced up at Michelle in the meager light of the hallway. Standing there as she was, on a level five feet above him, it was like his mom had come back to life and was chiding him for some juvenile transgression. Eating too much candy or maybe peeing the bed.

Michelle's hands were on her hips. "I'm not blind, you know."

"Honey, I—"

"You got a good look, felt guilty, then you decided you better stop peeping."

"I wasn't—"

"It's fine, Joe. Reason I came up, I saw Bridget from our bedroom window. Good thing I decided to let in some fresh air, huh?"

Joe swallowed, licked his lips. "Honey, I really wasn't watching her. I mean, I saw her, but I wasn't *staring* at her. I—what the hell are you laughing about?"

"It's fun watching you squirm."

"You're not mad?"

"That depends. Were you doing something about it?"

"You mean was I…"

Michelle's eyebrows rose.

"No way. I did look for a few seconds – I'll admit that."

"Don't give me that 'I'm a man and I can't help it' crap."

"I didn't say that."

"But you looked."

"I *stopped* looking, that's the point."

"Is it?"

"You saw her out the window, then you came upstairs, right?"

She shrugged, obviously unwilling to concede the point.

Joe gestured in the direction of the Baxter house. "And when you got up here, I was coming through the door. I felt guilty for what little looking I did do and decided to get out of there."

"You act like you were fleeing a forest fire."

"I sort of was."

"Her breasts that nice?"

"Better than I expected."

"That was the wrong answer."

Joe winced.

"Get downstairs," Michelle said. "Let's see if you can still perform after your brush with that wildfire next door."

CHAPTER FOURTEEN

Harold Hawkins came out as Joe approached the farmhouse. "Cubs are getting ready to start. Want a beer?"

Joe smiled. Harold had turned eighty only a few months ago, but he was still ornery. His sparse salt-and-pepper hair was plastered to his shiny scalp, and as he stood there he kept rucking up the front of his brown sweatpants. To Joe he looked like a man very comfortable in his element.

"No thanks, Harold. I've got to get back to Michelle and Lily in a little while."

"That's a wise decision," Harold said. "The Cubs are gonna get walloped again." When Joe only nodded, Harold explained, "It's an interleague game with the Yankees."

"What do you think?" Sadie asked as she ambled down the front porch.

Apparently seeing an opportunity to return to his game, Harold turned and trundled past his wife and disappeared into the house.

Coming up the narrow strip of sidewalk, Joe nodded at the new landscaping, the boxwood bushes, the rhododendrons, and the hydrangeas, their green all made more striking by the dark umber mulch beds from which they poked. "Looks fantastic. You have it done professionally?"

Sadie planted her hands on her hips and gave him a disappointed look. "Now, just because I'm old doesn't mean I'm incapable of gardening, Joe Crawford."

Joe made a sheepish little bow. "I should've known, Sadie. The place looks great."

"Darn right it does. I even got Harold to weed whip around the north side of the house so it won't look like an eyesore."

He glanced in that direction. "Anyone ever go over there?"

"*I* do," she said, "and I don't want it to look overgrown."

Joe took a deep breath of the warm May air, which was redolent with the fragrance of flowers and the subtler smell of the evergreens in the forest ringing the yard. He shook his head, taking it all in. "I come out here, it makes me wanna sell the house and move to the country."

"Living in the country can be very inconvenient."

"Sure it can," he conceded. "It's longer to get places. Groceries can be a pain."

"That's not what I mean," Sadie said, and her tone made him look at her. Though in her seventies, she was still an attractive woman. But the careworn expression on her face now made her appear ten years older.

"Something happen?"

She pursed her lips, some of the stubbornness bleeding back into her features. "Oh, you'll probably be like Harold and claim it's nothing. It's ironic, don't you think, that men are always dismissing things and chalking them up to female hysteria, when it's the men who are actually in denial?"

"Um…"

"You use it as a coping mechanism. But it's actually more hysterical than a woman's fretfulness. You men won't even admit when there's a problem."

Joe grunted softly. "You sound like my wife."

"And don't forget, your daughter will grow up and have friends soon. You won't feel like being her taxi service back and forth from town five times a day."

"What is it that has you distraught, Sadie?"

Her face clouded again. She sighed. "Oh. That." She looked like she was about to speak, then glanced up at him, visoring her eyes from the sun. "You said you needed a favor from me on the phone?"

"I did," Joe agreed. And he told her. Told her all about how he and Michelle had begun to consider adopting Little Stevie, about how they figured they'd need character witnesses, letters, that sort of thing.

To his surprise, Sadie reacted warmly to the idea. He wasn't sure, but he thought he saw latent tears forming in her blue eyes.

"So you don't think it's a bad idea?" he asked her.

"It's the first good idea I've heard in a long time."

He smiled, put a hand on Sadie's shoulder, which was so bony he felt a moment's apprehension. Thrusting it from his mind, he said, "No hurry or anything. I'm sure it'll be a long process. And that's if we decide to do it."

"I'll drop the letters by your house tomorrow."

He smiled. "I know better than to argue with you."

"Men are slow, but on occasion they can be taught."

He studied her haggard face, her imperfectly pinned hair. "Tell me what's on your mind. I can tell something's got you riled."

Sadie didn't answer straightaway, so Joe waited. Under the soft susurrus of the breeze, which worried the leaves of the cherry trees and the Cleveland pears, he could just detect the sounds of a baseball game on the radio. He pictured Harold in there, their dog Louie at his feet, and a beer bleeding on the end table beside his faded brown recliner. The image restored some of Joe's good spirits.

Then Sadie began to speak, and his good spirits were bulldozed into rubble.

"I've been sleeping poorly, Joe. At first I thought it was moving back up from Florida...the chaos of the renovation...getting used to the new rooms." She paused, chewing her bottom lip. "I've been having terrible nightmares. It's gotten so I don't want to sleep anymore. Because when I do..."

Joe listened, a chill whispering over his bare forearms.

Sadie exhaled loudly. "I wake up sweating. Sometimes gasping. And when I rise, Louie is curled up in a ball at the foot of our bed, trembling so badly it's like we're having a thunderstorm. Only most nights there isn't a cloud in the sky. And I fancy I can hear—" She broke off, her expression troubled.

"You need to sit down, Sadie?"

"Oh, don't treat me like I'm a decrepit old woman. I'm fine, Joe. It's just these damned nightmares." She gave him a sidelong glance. "Sorry about the profanity."

"I've heard worse."

"I'm sure you have. But it's these dreams. These dreams are the most vivid, the most disconcerting things."

Joe waited, suspecting it was difficult enough for a proud woman like Sadie Hawkins to admit to weakness of any kind. The only problem was that Joe sort of hoped she wouldn't verbalize her dreams. Something deeper than intuition told him it would end up affecting his own sleep, which had been spotty enough since the Angie Waltz business.

Sadie looked up at him. "It's fire, Joe. Fire everywhere."

Of course it is, he thought.

"But you and your family are in it. You're...oh, I don't know how else to say it. You're *burning*."

His voice a dry croak, Joe said, "All three of us?"

"I don't like saying it, but yes. You, Michelle...even the baby."

"She's two now," he said and paused. "Where does the dream take place?"

"The Baxter house," she said.

Joe drew back, frowning. It was too much like his own dreams, his own unformed fears. "You know something about it, don't you?"

"Of course I do. You don't live in a place your whole life and not know something about its history."

"What happened there?"

Sadie uttered a mirthless little laugh, shrugged one shoulder. "Oh, nothing much, just a mad woman burning her family alive."

Joe felt as though he'd been slugged in the gut.

"You want to hear something even better?" she said.

Not really, Joe thought, but hadn't the strength to say it.

Sadie went on. "The woman – her name was Antonia Baxter, but she was originally Anna Blake – was first-generation Irish. She was an extraordinarily beautiful woman. Had this blazing red hair, striking green eyes. I was a little girl when she was alive, but I still remember her."

Joe thought of another redhead he knew.

"Antonia, Anna, whatever you want to call her, she was a fierce woman, very eccentric. Most men thought of her as free and easy, but they were afraid of her. There were all sorts of rumors about what went on in that big house of hers."

"What sort of rumors?"

"Oh, you know, the usual. Murder. Pagan rituals. Orgies that ended in torture."

"Good wholesome fun."

"Her husband was a local lawyer, but he made his money traveling to various places taking on cases no one else wanted. He had an interest in the occult, which you'd have never guessed by looking at him. Poor Edwin was as bloodless as a turnip. Anyway, word had it he'd defended Antonia down in Indianapolis when she was accused of some unsavory crime. He fell for her, but Edwin Baxter wasn't exactly known for his passion and virility. He took her in, tried to make her respectable, but she had little interest in that."

"Skip to the part where she kills her family."

She glared at him. "Don't rush an old woman. It's not only impolite, it's not very smart. There might be something in the story that'll help you."

Joe listened, his dread growing by degrees.

"Antonia bore Edwin three children. She also got pregnant one summer when Edwin was back East defending an accused murderer. When he returned and saw how swollen her belly was, he took it pretty manfully. Told her she could stay as long as she gave the baby up, which she did. Gladly. Antonia liked to screw, but she wasn't sentimental about her children, as was to be proven." Sadie paused, glanced up at him. "Does it surprise you, my talking like that?"

"I'm not offended, if that's what you mean. Though I do have to admit it's a change from our normal vein of conversation."

"We can only talk plumbing and insulation so much, Joe. A relationship has to evolve."

"You've got a point."

"The child was given to the state, and life went on. Antonia got pregnant again, and that brought their family up to seven."

"Wouldn't it be six?"

"Edwin already had a son. I forgot to mention it. Young Byron was from a prior marriage."

"Did Edwin's first wife die under mysterious circumstances?"

"Only if you consider a ruptured appendix mysterious."

"Oh."

"So the seven of them lived in that big house on Hillcrest for another year or so, and if Antonia's reputation wasn't the greatest – she was known to cat around the bars for some supplemental physical entertainment—"

"That's nicely put."

"Thank you. But other than the fact that everyone knew Antonia was a nymphomaniac, the Baxter clan lived a semi-normal existence. Until her friends started coming around."

Disquiet moved over him like a winter shadow.

"They'd rent from the local landlords or live in shacks or trailer courts in the poorer parts of town. But they'd show up at the Baxter house and be treated like royalty."

"Any of them have tattoos?"

"Now what kind of question is that?"

"Never mind. Go on."

"You're an odd one, Joe. Need to read something other than horror novels."

Joe gave her a bemused smile.

"Oh, I always see those old paperbacks sitting on the passenger seat of your truck. At least you had the good sense not to bring them into my house during work."

"Why? That kind of stuff offend you?"

She rolled her eyes. "Don't make me out as some prude, Joe. I just wouldn't want you to sit there staring at a book when you're on the clock."

"Ah."

"Let's go to the backyard," she said. "There's something I want to show you."

They started around that way, keeping to the south side of the house. The landscaping here was as impressive as it was in the front.

Sadie paused to snap off a dead rhododendron branch, which gave with a brittle crunch. "Word began to spread that the newcomers were part of a cult, that Edwin had actually been a part of it all along, and that Antonia was their leader."

"Was she?"

Sadie cast the rhododendron branch into the forest. "She fancied herself that, I suppose, though most of the townsfolk just thought of her as addled. And morally compromised, of course."

They'd come to the corner of the house, and as they did Joe allowed himself a long look at the addition he and his men had put on. Other than the Pella stickers still adhered to the inside of the new windows, the back rooms looked like they'd been built at the same time as the main structure. It was a point of pride for Joe to blend the old and the new as seamlessly as possible. He'd even found a place that sold aluminum siding that would match the façade put on back in the 1940s.

"We couldn't be happier," Sadie said, following his gaze.

Joe permitted himself a small grin.

Sadie nodded. "What I want to show you is back here in the woods."

Joe followed Sadie through the backyard, and though he would have much rather basked in the glow of a job well done, he knew whatever Sadie was about to show him was important.

"Where was I?" Sadie asked.

"You were saying how Antonia was worshipping the devil and banging half the town."

"You shouldn't joke about it. Antonia Baxter was a frightening woman. She did what she wanted and dared people to speak against her."

"Did anyone?"

"A few," Sadie said. "My father was one of them. The other two who did, they died."

"Do I even need to guess how?"

"House fires," she said. "Them and their families."

"How'd you guys escape her wrath?"

"I don't think she knew my dad was one of them."

"You said he spoke against—"

"My dad was on the town council and was one of three who decided to approach the sheriff about putting a stop to what they considered morally reprehensible conduct. The sheriff...well, after it all happened it was rumored he was part of Antonia's cabal, but no one knew for sure. But when the letter was delivered to the sheriff outlining the litany of Antonia's offenses, my dad happened to be taken ill. It was pneumonia. He was never the same after that.

"So the other two selectmen, the ones who delivered the letter, they and their families are incinerated, and word goes out that Antonia and her people were behind it. But even though she was a pariah in the town, no one dared cross her publicly after that."

"I can't blame them."

Sadie gave him a queer look, one that made him feel as if he'd committed some blunder. But before he could muse on it further, she said, "The Summer Solstice was approaching, and that made everyone nervous. It was well-known that Antonia's debauchery was always worst around that time, but after the death of the selectmen and their families, people feared the Solstice would be worse than ever."

They'd reached the pump. "Have some water," Sadie said. "You'll need it."

Joe looked at her.

She fluttered an impatient hand at him. "Oh, don't question it, just drink."

Joe drank.

When he stood and wiped his mouth with the back of a wrist, she said, "The whole throng came to the Baxter house the night of June twenty-third."

"The Summer Solstice is on the twenty-first."

"I know that. And St. John's Eve is the twenty-third. It's the night of bonfires."

Joe lapsed into silence, and Sadie continued. "Edwin Baxter was gone, of course. Not that it would have made a difference anyway. Man was as ineffectual as a castrated bull, and like I said, folks had begun to think he was part of it. That his litigation was what kept the cult members out of jail."

She started toward the declivity at the rear of the yard, the place where the grass first became sparse, then gave way entirely to underbrush, bare soil, and the exposed roots of old-growth trees. "But they all came. And they conducted their ceremony."

"What sort of ceremony?"

Sadie shook her head distractedly. "Who knows? Most of the ones who were there were never subpoenaed. The ones who were wouldn't say a word about it. But that morning Antonia's kids were seen in town with their mother. By the next morning, the only thing left of them was ashes."

"That's horrible."

Sadie didn't answer, nor did she chide him for the obviousness of his statement. They proceeded through the increasingly overgrown yard in silence. Joe worried Sadie would trip and injure herself. But the older woman moved as easily through the brambles as she had through the mown grass, exhibiting a grace he couldn't help but admire.

"Was Antonia arrested?" he asked.

Sadie shook her head.

Joe heard his voice rise. "How is that possible? Even if the sheriff was part of her group...one of her lovers...how could she get away with that?"

"I didn't say she got away with it. I just said she wasn't arrested. Watch your step here," she said when they came to a small washout. Stepping down over the foot-high dropoff gingerly, she said, "There were several complaints that night about the collection of strange individuals who'd shown up at the Baxter house. Remember that even then your neighborhood was one of the prettiest in the northern half of Indiana. So word did eventually reach the state police, who sent an officer over to investigate.

"The man – I've long since forgotten the officer's name – he knocked on the door and was met by one of the cult members. This person, whoever he was, apparently got irate with the officer and started threatening him. The state policeman called for backup. There were three cars parked out front of Antonia's house when Antonia herself appeared on the front stoop."

Sadie stopped, only a little bit winded, and gazed down the gradually falling valley. "I wasn't there, of course. After all, I was only ten, and I didn't live in that neighborhood. And I wasn't in their sect. But several neighbors had come out to witness the scene, and their accounts dovetailed enough for me to believe the story isn't apocryphal.

"Antonia was soaking wet. She was nude, too. I suppose I should mention that. The men, they sort of shifted on their feet and averted their eyes like shamefaced schoolchildren, but Antonia just beamed at them like being wet and naked was the most natural thing in the world."

"It is natural, I suppose."

"Not when you're covered in gasoline."

Joe's face went slack.

Sadie nodded. "The odor hit them after just a few seconds. By the time they realized what was happening, Antonia was striking a match – don't ask me where she'd hidden it – and holding the flame to one breast."

"Oh hell."

Sadie sighed. "She went up like a goddamned candle."

Joe swallowed, was speechless for a long moment. Then he said, "Holy crap."

"That sums it up pretty nicely."

"What happened after that?"

"Bedlam. They tried to put her out, but they were state troopers, not firemen. The neighbors said whatever people were still at the Baxter House emptied out the back door and made off while the cops tried to put Antonia out."

There was a sour, corrosive taste in Joe's mouth. "Did they?"

"Not before she was roasted down to an unrecognizable twist of charred flesh and smoking gristle."

"That's awful."

"Familiar too, huh?"

Joe could feel his heart slamming in his chest, like some poorly calibrated machine that was on the brink of tearing loose and spinning out of control. "What do you think the connection is?"

She eyed him with grim humor. "I'm surprised you haven't figured it out."

"Sadie, it'd be nice if you'd just tell me what—"

"Antonia Baxter was Angie Waltz's great-grandmother."

It was as though someone had doused him with ice water.

"Which makes Sharon Waltz," she said, "Antonia's granddaughter."

"Hell," he said.

"I thought you'd feel that way. Katherine Waltz was the child Antonia gave up."

"Do you think Angie—"

"Got the idea to burn herself up from her great-grandma?"

Joe waited.

Sadie frowned. "The similarities are too great to pass off as coincidence. As for the reasons behind the connection… I guess we'll never know now that Angie barbecued herself."

"What do you think?"

Sadie glanced toward the valley, her features tough to read from Joe's angle. "I think she heard the story as a child and probably wondered about her great-grandma's motives. Antonia was a lot of things, but she was also a strong woman. I wouldn't have been surprised if she was a role model of sorts for Angie."

"But wouldn't Sharon… I mean, her grandma abandoned her mother. You wouldn't think she'd paint Antonia in a positive light."

Sadie turned to him. "You wouldn't think a lot of things, but that doesn't mean they're not so."

Joe thought it over. "Were there any other details about Antonia?"

"Uh-uh," Sadie said. "Just that she had a glorious body. And that she was a real redhead."

Joe fell silent. He tried not to picture Antonia Baxter's glistening body going up in flames, but found the image crystalizing in his mind like a news replay on loop. But something was gnawing at him, something Sadie had mentioned earlier…

"Sadie," Joe said, peering deeply at her, though she now seemed unwilling to meet his gaze. "There's more you're not telling me, isn't there?"

Her lips twisted in frustration. "Oh, it's all so damned silly. I'm not like this. Never have been. Superstition is for simpletons, and I have enough to think about without worrying about these dreams."

"Tell me the rest of it."

Sadie half-turned toward the house, as if eager for sanctuary.

"You said there was a sound when you woke up," Joe prompted.

"I was hoping you'd forget that."

"My wife says I have a long memory."

"That's seldom a good thing."

"So she tells me."

Sadie crossed her arms and massaged her sticklike biceps. She shivered despite the humidity of the day, the closeness of the forest. "Like I told you, I wake up a lot now. Constantly, actually, and that takes some doing considering how hard it is for me to sleep in the first place. But I wake up sometimes and I can tell that Louie hears it too. Harold, he sleeps like a dead thing, but Louie's getting old like me, and that dog hears everything at night. He—"

She broke off, pressed a fist to her lips. Joe thought she was stifling a cough, but then realized that Sadie Hawkins was weeping.

He moved closer, put a hand on her back. Through the white cotton of her shirt, her knobby backbone felt vaguely reptilian. "Sadie..."

"Don't take pity on me, Joe. That'll only make it worse."

Joe asked in a soft voice, "What do you hear when you wake up?"

Sadie's voice became harsh. "Laughter. It's always the same. Just this teasing, mocking laughter. It comes from the woods."

Joe found himself looking around, then felt a rush of foolishness. It was midday, after all, and it wasn't as though Sadie had claimed there was a serial killer roaming these woods. Still...the shadows and the trees and the deep silence made him feel like getting back to civilization, and in a hurry.

"Have you seen anybody poking around back here?"

She shook her head.

"Anyone tried to break in?"

"No," she said.

He opened his mouth to question her further, but judging from the look on her face, her thoughts had turned inward.

Joe sighed. "Sadie, I appreciate you telling me all this—" At her testy look, he said, "I'm not claiming it's pleasant or anything. In fact, if I'm able to work in that house anymore without jumping at shadows it'll be a miracle. But at the risk of sounding rude, I'd really like to cut short this hike and get back to my wife and daughter."

"It doesn't matter, Joe. We're here now anyway."

She threw a wordless nod down at the carpet of pine needles and moist humus. Joe felt his windpipe squeeze closed.

On the ground, at the base of a hawthorn tree, lay a small, primitive-looking doll, the kind made from cornhusks.

"It's a corn dolly," Sadie said in a toneless voice. "I used to have one when I was a girl. Those clothes look familiar, Joe?"

Joe didn't answer, didn't do anything but stare at the diminutive yellow dress draped over the cornstalks. He remembered his daughter claiming someone had stolen Belle's dress.

Sadie said, "I thought you'd recognize it. How would someone have gotten into your house?"

"You tell me."

"I can't. I can't any more than I can explain what was in the Waltz girl's mind when she drenched herself in gasoline and flicked that lighter."

"It has to be Sharon," he said, more to himself. "She's the only one still alive, she's the one who hates me."

Sadie's eyes widened, the raw fear in the woman's expression terrible to behold. "But why does she keep coming out here to torment *me*? I haven't done anything to her."

"But you know me. You employed me and my men. Maybe that's enough. Maybe Sharon wants to spread bad word of mouth about my work."

"Seems a pretty extravagant way to do it."

"I was thinking the same thing. But...what other way of getting at me is there?"

"She could leave a doll in your backyard, terrorize you and your family."

"Thanks a lot."

Sadie's face crumpled. She drew in quivering breath, composing herself. "That was a cruel, vicious thing to say. I'm sorry."

"Sadie—"

"It's just this wretched sleeplessness. I've never had it this bad before. I feel like I'm cracking up."

Joe picked up the corn dolly and regarded it with distaste. Though the silky yellow dress had been on his daughter's doll until very recently, the fabric now felt oily to the touch. Tainted.

"You going to take that to Copeland?" Sadie asked.

"I suppose so, though I don't know what he can do about it."

"Jail that witch on breaking and entering is what he can do." When Joe looked up at her, she said, "I mean it, Joe. She's got to let this go. I know what happened to her daughter was a dreadful thing, but it was never anyone's fault but Angie's. Or Sharon's. Or even Antonia's for giving Sharon's mother up. But it's sure as hell not ours."

They walked back in silence and had just reached Joe's truck when he stopped and said, "Back there in the woods."

"Yes?"

"You called Sharon a witch."

Sadie's chin rose, her eyes unblinking. "I did, didn't I?"

CHAPTER FIFTEEN

Several days later, Joe was working in the Baxter house when he remembered Sadie's story about Antonia Baxter and her children. Joe was in the living room, which was so big a guy could just about get lost in it. He judged it to be about twenty-by-thirty, the kind of room in which you'd hold a recital. Or a pagan ritual.

Brushing away the thought, Joe moved to the immense hearth and stooped to peer inside. The fireplace was as high as his chest and was easily eight feet wide. As he examined the scorched concrete walls, he told himself he'd find nothing, that the tale of Antonia Baxter incinerating her own kids was the stuff of legends, one of those chain stories that gets wilder and wilder with every retelling.

Then he spotted the screw holes.

Oh hell, he thought. There were several pairs of them, each set spaced about three inches apart. If he hadn't been spooked by the old house before now, gazing at the holes that might have been used for manacles chilled him to the marrow. Jesus God, what kind of a sick person would do that? And what kind of a religion, cult, whatever, would condone the ritualistic burning of innocent children?

A voice behind him said, "I'm surprised you fit in there."

Joe gasped, tried to stand, and smacked the base of his skull against the overhanging hearth. Cursing, he shuffled back a few paces and rubbed his smarting head. A wooden clock that sat atop the mantel wobbled for a moment, then came to rest. Man, he'd knocked his head hard.

A hand was on his back, soothing him. "I'm sorry, Joe. I didn't mean to hurt you."

This time he recognized the voice.

Bridget.

"It's fine, Mrs. Martin. I was just lost in my thoughts, I guess."

"You do an excellent job," she said. "I was admiring the grout work in the shower last night."

Joe took in her meaningful gaze and looked away, sure he'd turned all kinds of red. He told himself she couldn't possibly know anything, but her look had been so intent, so playful.

She's just flirting with you, he told himself.

Then he thought, *That's not a whole lot better.*

"It's in good shape," he said, nodding toward the fireplace. "None of the cracks are severe. Just the house showing its age."

"How old are you, Joe?"

He looked at her again, saw that same demure look in her eyes. *Too old – and too married – for you*, he thought.

"I'm forty-one, Mrs. Martin."

"Stop being so formal," she said, grasping his bicep and giving him a little squeeze. He did his best to ignore the scalding bolts of electricity her touch sent through him, but they registered all the same.

"Sorry," he said, forcing a laugh. "Just habit, I guess."

When she continued to stare at him in that same penetrating way, he said, "We got the windows installed, but you probably noticed that."

"I did. They'll dampen the sound?"

He nodded. "They're top of the line. You'll hear a few loud noises. Car horns, violent crashes of thunder. But I doubt you'll hear dogs barking or people talking on the street."

"Good. Did you see the bed that arrived last night?"

Careful, he told himself. "I did. It's an interesting frame."

Her finger traced the plunging neckline of her tight red shirt. "It's made from hawthorn trees. They're sacred in some religions."

Joe glanced up at the swords that had also shown up since yesterday. They crisscrossed over the mantel, both of them long and apparently razor-sharp. "Those religious artifacts too?"

"Spiritual might be the better way of phrasing it, but yes. They have a great deal of significance."

"They Celtic?"

"Very good, Mr. Crawford."

Joe eyed the swords. "Hope your husband moored them to the walls well enough. I'd hate for one to fall down and decapitate somebody."

"Mitch is very careful," she said. "Sometimes I wish he'd loosen up a little."

Joe decided not to touch that one. "What about the floors, Mrs. Martin? You never told me what color of stain you all want."

"I'm not worried about the floors yet," she said. "Particularly in here. They'll just get messed up anyway."

Joe frowned, wondering if she was talking about him and his men. He took pride in a neat work site and considered saying so. But instead he said, "Have you and your husband decided on any other finishes?"

"Actually, yes," she said and paced toward the center of the room. "I was wondering. Do you think it would be hard to put an eyebolt up there?"

Joe glanced at the ceiling, which was ten feet high. "I don't see why not."

"It would need to support plenty of weight."

Joe scratched his cheek. "Why would you put an eyebolt there?"

In answer, Bridget's face broke into a lewd grin.

Oh man, Joe thought. He cleared his throat. "Well, we can certainly install what you need..."

"We'll take care of getting the materials," she said. "Do you think you'll be able to put it together for us?"

Joe eyed her for a moment, a fine sheen of sweat breaking out on his forehead. Then he thought, *To hell with it.*

"Bridget, are you asking me to install a sex swing for you and your husband?"

She returned his gaze, unabashed. "Or whoever else wants to try it out."

Get out, a voice in his head declared. *Get out now, while you're still ahead. This lady is trouble.*

He said, "Can you get the materials here? Or is there a factory outlet that sells that sort of thing?"

She started toward him, laughing softly. "You have a good sense of humor, Joe. I have fun with you."

Joe took a couple steps toward the fireplace, contrived to examine the mantel he'd installed.

Bridget followed. Her voice went a little husky, the smell of her – like tangerines and fir trees – surrounded him. "Marriage doesn't equal death, you know." Fingertips caressing his shoulder through his denim work shirt. "We're still adults."

He wouldn't meet her gaze. "Adults should know how to behave themselves, Bridget."

Her voice was closer. "I like how you say my name."

Footsteps sounded behind them. Joe half-turned and saw Mitch Martin regarding them from across the room. If he was perturbed at discovering his wife breathing down Joe's neck, he gave no sign.

"How's it going?" Mitch asked.

Joe sidestepped Bridget, shoved his trembling hands in his jeans pockets. "Still ahead of schedule. I think we'll have a good bit of it done by the end of June."

Mitch nodded at the ceiling. "Did Bridget tell you about her contraption?"

"She told me about *a* contraption," Joe said. "Did you have a timeframe in mind for it?"

"No sense in waiting. It'll arrive here tomorrow."

Joe did his best to keep it professional, to talk about the kinky object the way he'd discuss a screen door or a showerhead. "Whenever you'd like us to install it is fine by me."

Bridget chewed a nail girlishly. "Are you sure you'll be able to manage it?"

"I'll have Shaun put it together tomorrow afternoon."

Bridget looked aggrieved. "Joe, this is a specialty item. It was very expensive, and I'd rather you be the one to handle it. It's not your normal swing. It's very large, with several vital modifications."

Joe made to protest, but Mitch cut in. "You can be here to help him, can't you, honey?"

Bridget beamed. "That's right. I can show you how it fits together."

Jesus. "I'm sure I can figure it out."

She held his gaze a beat too long.

"Then it's settled," Mitch said, clapping his hands. "I've got to get back to work. Bridget, you'll help Joe with the swing?"

"My pleasure."

Mitch was about to go, but stopped halfway to the door and stared at Joe. "Is there something wrong?" he asked.

Where do I start? Joe thought. *Your wife wants to jump my bones, and you're either on board with it or too dumb to see it. Either way, I wish both of you would get the hell off my job site so I can turn my back without fear of being groped.*

"Everything's great, Mitch. I've just got a lot on my mind."

Apparently satisfied, Mitch went out.

Leaving him with Bridget.

"If I don't answer the doorbell, you can come in," she said. "Tomorrow afternoon, I mean."

"Why wouldn't you answer your door?"

She shrugged. "I might be in the shower."

"That reminds me."

Her smile was eager. "Yes?"

"I need to see my wife."

And he left her standing in the living room.

★ ★ ★

But Michelle was gone, and of course Lily was too. Afraid Bridget would follow him over, he left his house and started up the Tundra, hoping by the time he got back Bridget would have left the work site. Or taken a cold shower.

He thought about seeing Little Stevie, but he'd been to the Morrison's twice already that week. He hadn't told Michelle about it, feeling strangely as though he were having an affair behind her back. There were still no leads for permanent foster parents, though Copeland said Sharon Waltz was as intent as ever on gaining custody of the boy. Joe hadn't broached the topic of adoption again with Michelle because he knew how gung ho she'd be. It'd cease to be a discussion about *if* and would become a matter of *how* and *when*. And though Joe's emotional attachment to the child was growing, he knew how complicated the situation would be, how problematic his own history with Angie and Sharon would become. *Yes, Judge*, he imagined himself saying, *I get kids kicked out of their parents' homes so I can raise them myself. It's actually very logical if you turn your head sideways and squint a little.*

Joe rolled down his window, felt the warm kiss of the summer air on his forearm.

Joe passed through the business district and motored past the police station, outside of which Copeland's cruiser was parked. He didn't really feel like seeing Copeland at the moment, he realized. For that matter, he didn't feel like seeing anybody.

Yet ten minutes later he found himself rolling down the Hawkinses' winding gravel lane. Part of it, no doubt, was the growing affection he felt for the old couple. It also probably had to do with the fact that he was naturally drawn to the country. This place, particularly, appealed to him. The way the trees seemed to lean over the road, the lane itself infrequently dappled with sunlight. The aroma of green leaves and tough bark.

The house came into view.

Joe let his foot off the gas, the hackles of his neck unaccountably rising. He reached up to turn off the stereo with nerveless fingers, but he regretted it instantly. The silence was so profound and palpable that it was almost like driving into a different dimension, one where the air hung gravid as a threat and sound was totally nonexistent. Joe had no idea exactly why the sight of the two-story farmhouse was so foreboding to him, nor were there any physical details heralding trouble. The garage doors were closed; the yard was as meticulously kept as ever. The front door was closed too, the interior wooden one as well as the glass storm door, and he realized as he brought his pickup to a halt that this was precisely why he was so uneasy. The interior door could be closed for many reasons, and the fact that he'd never known the door to be closed when the Hawkinses were home should have simply indicated the obvious – they'd gone to town for something.

Yet Joe sensed there was life within the house right now, and further, he sensed that whoever was here was not Harold or Sadie Hawkins.

Wishing he hadn't left his gun back at the house, Joe cut the engine and climbed out of the pickup. Feeling like a man in a dream, Joe drifted up the front walk.

It's nothing, he told himself. *Quit being such an alarmist.*

Joe looked around, wondered, *Where are the bugs, the birds?*

It's a quiet day, the voice reassured. *It's not like there's been some sort of mass extermination out here.*

Joe shivered. He didn't like that word. Not a bit.

He mounted the front porch. Depressed the doorbell with a sweaty fingertip.

It's fine, he thought. *Sadie will answer and have you drinking iced tea within five minutes. Maybe you can listen to some of the ballgame with Harold.*

It's not fine, he thought, the sweat now trickling down his temples. *It's not fine at all. And Harold's not listening to the ball game. You'd hear it by now.*

Check the garage windows! the voice challenged. *One of the cars will be gone, I guarantee it. Then you'll know everything is normal and you can get your butt back to work.*

Joe reached out, grasped the handle of the glass door, and drew it open. As he did he fancied he caught a whiff of something unpleasant.

But it could be anything, he reasoned. A dead mouse left rotting in a trap. A flyblown raccoon carcass, its belly wriggling with maggots somewhere in the woods nearby.

Or your paranoid, hyperactive imagination?

Joe grasped the inner knob and pushed open the door.

The smell was like a hammer blow to the face. Not only because it was so putrid, but because it was so damned hot in the entryway. Someone had cranked up the heat to eighty at least, so that whatever fetid stench had mushroomed in here had pretty much had its run of the place. *My God*, Joe thought, grinding his shirtsleeve into his nostrils, the odor had bored its way into his *bones*.

Joe told himself to take it easy, to breathe. But that was a tall order when he was sucking in short sips of oxygen through a sweaty denim filter. His whole body was slicked with perspiration now, and Joe decided that turning down the heat was the first job that needed tending. He'd be able to think better without that stuffy air blowing on him from every vent in the house. Joe went over to the thermostat – the HVAC subcontractor had installed a new one with a digital readout – and Joe was shocked to see the display claiming it was functioning properly. According to the readout, it was a comfortable seventy degrees in here. And what was more, the heat wasn't even running. Supposedly, the system had been turned off.

The sweat pouring off him, his shirt turning dark and clammy on his skin, Joe strode over to the floor vent and let his hand hover over the grate.

Nothing.

Nothing was blowing from the vent, but the air in here was definitely stirring. No, more than stirring. It was roiling, churning, swirling through the entryway like a low pressure storm system, the kind that spawned tornados and a urine-colored haze. Joe glanced left and right and noted the windows were shut, and furthermore, the door leading to the living room in front of him was closed as well.

Which was troubling. He'd never seen that door closed, never known the Hawkinses to keep their house shuttered up this way.

Get out of the house, the voice in his head urged.

Ridiculous, he thought.

"Sadie?" he called, and winced at the eruption of his own voice in the eerily silent house. "Harold?" he said in a voice slightly less resonant.

No answer.

Of course there's no answer! he thought. *Harold and Sadie took a little trip, and they somehow screwed up the settings on the heat pump. Or the pump itself is malfunctioning. It could be the way they installed it. More likely it's the unit itself.*

And what about the smell? he wondered as he started tiptoeing toward the living room door.

That's easy, he thought. *The Hawkinses are old, especially Harold, who's over eighty. They left some food out – maybe an open gallon of milk – and now it's spoiled. Or they left the fridge open. Hell, you've nearly done that yourself.*

Joe allowed himself a sniff. His eyes began to water.

That isn't spoiled milk.

Then what is it? he wondered.

It doesn't matter, the voice in his head answered. *You're about to find out.*

And that was true enough. Joe's fingers closed on the knob, twisted, and pushed.

The stench in here was worse.

His forearm to his face, Joe moved through the living room, into the four-seasons room, and spied no sign of Harold. The television and radio were both silent, the rooms themselves glum and musty with disuse.

Can't be, he thought. *I was here last week.*

A lot can happen in a week.

Right, he thought as he moved into the kitchen. *A guy can lose his mind and start jumping at shadows.*

"Sadie?" he asked. "You in here?"

Empty too. What was more, there were no packages or milk containers on the table or the counters. The place was as neat and tidy as always. Sadie kept a clean house, and despite his age, Harold was faithful with the vacuuming and dusting.

So where were they? And what about their dog Louie?

Would you check the damned garage? the voice within him shouted.

Moving swiftly, he passed through the dining room, into the mudroom, and opened the door to the garage.

Which contained both cars.

"Crap," he muttered.

A shaky, sullen voice within him spoke up. *Doesn't mean anything. They could've been picked up by friends. Hell, they could be upstairs.*

Sure, he thought. *Upstairs and dead.*

Joe passed a hand over his forehead and was amazed at the amount of sweat he'd generated. If he didn't get out of the house soon, he'd combust.

He returned to the living room, grasped the banister, and started up the stairs. He called their names a couple times, but his heart wasn't in it.

He'd begun to hate the sound of his own voice, and not only because he sounded like a terrified grade schooler. Mainly, he hated the idea of making his presence known in the house. Known to *what* wasn't a matter he was in the mood to speculate about.

Joe gained the second floor and turned left, not because he wanted to, but because he knew it was chickenshit to turn right. The only rooms in that direction were the bedrooms the Hawkins children had used many years ago. The only things he'd find down there were old toys and artwork Sadie couldn't bear to throw away. At least if Sadie was anything like Joe's own mother. And she was, he realized now. Which might've explained why he'd taken such a shine to her, and she to him. Which might've also explained why he felt so goddamned scared right now as he neared the bedroom. He'd definitely located the source of the odor. The bedroom doorway was ajar, and it smelled like a landfill at this end of the hallway. Only worse. And he knew, with a sense much deeper than smell, that it wasn't garbage he was scenting. It was…it was…

Joe shoved the door open.

And gagged. The room was dark, but not dark enough to conceal what was on the bed, what was bloated and buzzing with flies.

Harold's corpse lay like some ancient grizzly bear decaying in a secret forest glade. The stench was withering, a sickening goulash of rancid pig blood and spoiled vegetables. Joe felt his gorge elevator into his throat, a sizzle of bile as hot as a cutting torch on the soft flesh of his palate. He knew he should go away now, call Copeland. Hell, he *wanted* to go away, wanted it more than he wanted anything. Yet there was something about the bloated corpse that drew him onward, that called to him in spite of the odor, in spite of the furtive sounds he heard coming from the bed.

Joe drew nearer, breathing through his mouth even though it was a futile measure. The stench still insinuated itself into him, still clung to his nostrils like a pestilence. Five feet from the bed Joe saw the bizarre shapes wending their way down Harold's bare arms, shapes that rose from the skin like childish decorations yet were clearly part of Harold's body.

Joe's eyes had adjusted pretty well to the dimness of the bedroom, and though he knew it was only a matter of flipping a switch or releasing the roller blinds with a tug, he couldn't bring himself to wash the room in daylight. Not yet. Something about the idea seemed blasphemous to him, as if he'd be committing a further degradation on Harold's rotting corpse.

Joe took another step, leaned down, and screwed up his eyes. Harold's arms were threaded with what looked like branches from some sort of evergreen tree. The thin strands of wood pierced Harold's flesh beneath the sleeves of his white T-shirt and serpentined their way down to his knuckles as though someone had decided to use his arms as a cross stitch pattern. Joe reached out, let his fingertips whisper over the needles of the evergreen branches and realized they were from a yew tree, likely one on the Hawkinses' property. The effect was hideous.

But not as hideous as the sight of Harold's face.

Whoever had worked on the old man had been at it for a good while. His mouth had been stuffed with yew branches – in fact, there were so many that Joe could see sharp tips poking out of the cheeks and tenting the already distended flesh of his throat. Tiny black ants crawled lazily over the branches and along the purpled skin of Harold's puffy neck.

A filament of burnished afternoon light spanned the right side of Harold's face from ear to bald crown, and though the eye was a half-inch beyond the daylight's reach, the glow was strong enough to reveal another horror.

Sable feathers protruded from the empty sockets, whoever had committed this atrocity having taken Harold's eyeballs with them. Joe was no ornithologist, but he suspected the feathers had belonged to a raven. In addition to the bluebottle flies buzzing drowsily over the corpse, there were ants teeming in and out of the gory eye sockets, the blood having long since congealed.

Something else drew Joe's gaze. He didn't want to venture any nearer – the smell was already making him lightheaded – but he did anyway. He got as close as he dared to and peered through the murk at Harold's face.

Someone had tattooed the old man from mouth to forehead. The design was crudely done, but Joe could make it out well enough. The upper lip was festooned with navy blue roots and what was supposed to represent the wide base of a large tree. The trunk encompassed Harold's nose, the flesh between his eyes, and then spread into a vast network of branches on his forehead and bald pate. It looked like a crudely scrawled oak tree, whoever having done it either in a hurry or not particularly skilled with a tattoo needle. Yet Joe could discern the shape well enough. In the tree there appeared to be faces, or perhaps they were skulls. Too curious to just let it go, Joe moved over and tugged one of the roller blinds. The room flooded with light. Joe turned away, blinking like a mole, and regarded Harold.

And bellowed in terror at what lay beyond the man's corpse.

Sadie Hawkins lay huddled in the corner, clearly dead, and clearly having suffered some unspeakable shock. Her mouth was hinged wide in a permanent shriek, her eyes staring moons that had filmed over from having baked in this suffocating heat for God knew how long. But it was her hands that stunned Joe the most, the arms somehow having frozen in a warding off gesture, the fingertips roasted by some incredible heat. The fingertips were nothing more than white powder, the flesh of her knuckles charred and blistered. Joe regarded her pathetic sticklike form and felt nothing more than a desolate sense of shock, a feeling that he'd torn through some protective veil and glimpsed something so monstrous and unnatural that his emotional equilibrium could never again return to normal. Sadie had worn a simple blue nightgown, but the gown had browned and scorched in several places, the hem having ridden up and revealed underwear that was soiled and crawling with ants. Numbly, Joe slumped down on the edge of the bed and felt something move beneath him. Gasping, he stumbled away and beheld a long black snake slithering out of the downhanging blanket like some insidious afterbirth. The snake's tongue flicked, the sinuous body writhing slowly toward Sadie's corpse. Joe wanted to trample it, to squish its virulent body before it crawled over the dead woman, but a faint sound made him freeze, a new terror washing over him.

There were footsteps from the first floor.

* * *

Joe reached down, patted his hip pocket for his cell phone, but it was gone. Dammit, he'd left the thing in the truck. He deplored the feel of it on his thigh while he worked, but couldn't he have just this once kept it with him?

The footsteps sounded once more, and something about them made his fears intensify, something even beyond the mere fact of them. His mind raced. He was in the same room with two corpses, and though whoever was downstairs could hardly believe he was the one who'd done it – the bodies were already decomposing, after all – the person might think he *had* committed the crimes and had simply returned to the scene to marvel at his handiwork.

Joe swallowed.

"Oh fuck," he whispered. The idea was so obvious, so grisly that he couldn't believe he hadn't thought of it immediately. Whoever was downstairs was the killer! Or kil*lers*, he amended. The ones who'd done this to Harold and Sadie had taken their time, had reveled in their abhorrent artwork. Of course they'd want to see Joe's reaction to it. Right before they butchered him.

Joe cast feverish glances about the bedroom, praying he'd happen upon an object with which to defend himself. He spotted a lamp, several picture frames on the wall. A wooden cross hung over the Hawkinses' bed.

If I wanted to perform an exorcism, that might come in handy.

Sweat dripped off his chin, poured in runnels beneath his sodden shirt. His ass felt like it'd been dipped in cooking oil.

He cast a glance toward the double closet doors, considered for a moment rummaging through them. But what did he think he'd find in there? Nothing but nightgowns and trousers and scrapbooks. Harold didn't strike him as the kind of guy who owned a gun, and Joe strongly doubted Sadie had amassed much of an arsenal. He could borrow one of her large knives from downstairs, but downstairs was where the footsteps were.

Where the killers were.

The images flashed through his mind: the tattooed man, the one named Shannon, clawing to get into Joe's truck that day on the bridge… Scarface, the rangy one, smashing Joe's window with a rock…. The look of hatred on their—

Something brushed the heel of his work boot. With a startled yelp, Joe spun away from the snake, the damned thing flicking its tongue and veering toward him like a faithful mutt. Joe backed through the open doorway, scarcely registering how seething the temperature was out here, the way the air churned and skirled around him. Joe wheeled toward the stairs, for a moment completely unmindful of everything else, his mind concentrated wholly on escaping the snake. It was at least five feet long, coal black and as broad as Joe's wrist. He had no idea what species it was, but the thing looked as poisonous as could be. Joe hustled down the steps, his movements so frantic that his work boots slipped several times. He reached the bottom, looped toward the foyer, but as he moved through the living room, he realized that something was amiss, even beyond the murdered man and woman upstairs, even beyond the snake and the inexplicable heat.

By the time Joe had reached the foyer, he'd finally realized what it was.

The entryway was as black as pitch.

Which made no sense at all. Because it was the middle of the day, and unless someone had tarpapered the windows or he'd missed mention of some rare solar eclipse, there was no earthly reason for it to be so dark this early.

And the door. Joe had left it open. He knew he had. Despite all he'd seen upstairs, despite his throbbing heartbeat and the sneaking suspicion he'd voided his bladder somewhere between the top of the stairs and the bottom, despite the mind-shattering guilt brought on by the idea that all of this was somehow his fault...despite everything, he was still certain he'd left that door open. The air now so smoldering he was afraid he'd lose consciousness, Joe swayed toward the door. Grasped the handle.

Hissed in surprise and pain at the way the knob seared his flesh. With a cry he jerked his hand away, stared through the gloom at the knob, half-expecting the brass to be glowing red. But it wasn't. It was just appallingly hot. And his hand – he was certain he'd need medical treatment for it. He thought of Sadie's outstretched fingers, looking for all the world like they'd been cremated. He thought of the scorch marks all over her nightgown, the blisters on her pallid skin. Joe turned away from the door, thinking vaguely of escaping out the back, when he discovered the figure watching him from the hallway.

Backlighted as it was by the windows at the rear of the house, Joe could only make out the shape of the person and not the features. The figure stood a mere ten feet away, motionless, the head tilted slightly forward, which threw the face into deeper shadow. But God help him, Joe didn't need to see the face to know who this was. He could see the roasted flesh of the shoulders, the way the skin had separated from the dermis and curled up like strips of bacon. The smell hit him then, and it reminded him disgustingly of hog roasts, of something spitted and rotating, something licked by eager tongues of flame. Joe cast a desperate glance at the door to his right, which he knew led to the kitchen. It was surely unlocked. There was surely a way to evade this apparition, to escape into the blessed coolness of the day. Joe stepped over and grasped the knob, forgetting his experience of only a moment before. Grimacing, he pulled away and glanced at his hand. The blisters that had begun to form on his palm popped open, the clear liquid splattering all over his fingers, his wrist, dripping from his quivering hand into the pooled darkness of the foyer.

And it grew hotter. The heat swarmed over him, choking him, like boiling hot oil funneled down his throat. He'd been in a sauna once, had managed to remain inside the thing for nearly twenty minutes. And when he'd felt the sweet kiss of the air outside that wooden sepulcher, he'd vowed to never repeat the experience. Only this was a thousand times worse. Because there was no glass door promising him release. There was no light at all. Only there had to be, because he could still make out the ruin of his hand, could still see a string of his saliva drooling down toward the palsied, quaking fingers.

Joe's breath caught in his throat. The bacon smell, it had—

Joe turned and looked into the staring white eyes of Angie Waltz.

He shrank away, his mouth stretched in a soundless shriek. His shoulder blades cracked the rigid door, his legs failing. Joe slid down, the unspeakable heat searing his skin, the white eyes of the figure tracking him all the way to the floor. It staggered forward, loomed over him. Its movements were jerky, unnatural, but the white gaze never wavered, never left the slightest doubt as to the thing's intent. It was Angie, he knew, Angie who'd scared Sadie Hawkins to death, who'd transformed Harold into the gnarled abomination up there on the bed. Angie who'd brought with her the serpent now slithering toward him, the one he heard but could only barely distinguish in the deepening murk. The air continued to beat against him, assaulting him like the oily wings of ravens, and he could no longer breathe, could no longer do anything but avert his eyes. He'd been trapped. He knew that now. Angie had somehow lured him out here and arranged this macabre torment, this nightmarish demise. Joe realized he was weeping, but he no longer cared. He only wished he were home, wished he could hold Michelle and Lily one more time.

Joe lay there in a trembling ball, his eyes squeezed shut, whispering his wife's and daughter's names over and over, like an incantation. He expected at any moment to feel the ruthless fingers of Angie Waltz close over his throat. Or the muscular length of the snake to coil around his body. Either way it came to the same thing – an ending. Of everything. Of life, of his dreams of being the kind of man his family deserved, of undoing his father's failure.

Joe waited. His breath still came in short bursts, but he realized his throat no longer burned with every inhalation. Yes, it was definitely cooler now than it had been moments earlier, but what did that mean? That he was dead? That Angie had sewn branches into his arms or burned his fingers to ashes?

Reluctantly, Joe opened his eyes.

The foyer was as it had been when he'd arrived. Further, the temperature felt positively frigid, though he suspected it was merely normal. Joe turned and saw with surprise that the front door was open. He got totteringly to his feet and had to steady himself against the wall while a wave of dizziness gusted through him. Joe sucked in deep lungsful of air, his sweat-soaked clothes clinging to him like icy parasites.

As soon as the room stopped cartwheeling, Joe trudged to the door and let himself out. He expected at any moment for the door to slam shut, for Angie to reappear and shatter the peaceful illusion, but he reached the porch unscathed. What was more, the day had brightened outside, the overcast gray having given way to a muted amber.

Joe didn't take time to admire the weather. Moving as fast as his body would allow, he hurried down the walk, grimly intent on retrieving his cell phone and calling Copeland. He'd make sure to tell Copeland to bring an officer or two out here with him. Even if what Joe had just witnessed had been a hallucination, whoever had done this to the Hawkinses were bad news. In fact, Joe decided, fifteen feet from his truck now, maybe he should wait until he'd driven safely away before calling. The killers could still be prowling the woods.

Joe slowed as he reached the truck.

It *had* been real, hadn't it? He was certain it had been real, but then again he'd been sure that Angie Waltz and her staring white eyes were about to murder him two minutes ago. Yet even if what he'd witnessed in the foyer wasn't true, surely what he'd seen upstairs had been.

Hadn't it?

He thought so, and he sure as hell wasn't going to return to the murder scene to confirm it wasn't a hallucination. No, he'd call Copeland. Joe would leave out the part about Angie Waltz, the equatorial heat, everything except the dead bodies.

And the snake. He didn't want Copeland to discover the snake on accident. Even if the thing didn't bite the police chief, Copeland would never forgive him for leaving out that little detail.

Joe took a deep breath, reached out, and yanked open the Tundra's front door.

And saw what lay on the seat.

For a long moment all Joe could do was stare. Then he bent over with his hands on his knees.

Oh Christ, he thought. *Oh my holy Christ.*

The triangle of yew branches framed Joe's cell phone, which he'd left on the dash but had somehow moved to the gray felt of the seat. Whoever had moved the phone had turned it on too. Had gone into Joe's pictures.

The faces of his wife and daughter smiled up at him.

PART FOUR
BLAZE

CHAPTER SIXTEEN

Copeland stared at him from the driver's seat of the cruiser. "That's the craziest goddamned story I've ever heard."

Joe had expected that, so the response didn't elicit any anger in him. Hell, he'd have responded the same way had Copeland come to him with a similar tale. Not to mention the fact that the big cop had spent the past seven hours investigating a double homicide, being bullied by a mayor who seemed to regard the murders as somehow Copeland's fault, being usurped by the county sheriff, and knocking on the doors of the Hawkinses' neighbors in what Copeland no doubt knew were futile attempts to get to the bottom of the mystery.

Parked at the top of Joe's driveway, they had a great view of the white garage doors and little else. Joe wished Copeland would turn off the engine and roll down the windows, but the big cop apparently wanted privacy in case any of the neighbors were eavesdropping. At least Copeland had the air going.

Copeland was still glaring at Joe. "You gonna add anything to that account, because I know you're not sadistic enough to leave me with nothin' but snakes and ghosts and houses turning into ovens."

"It's what happened."

"Bullshit."

"I don't blame you."

"I don't care, you don't blame me. I care about the fact that the closest thing I've got to a witness is sounding like a patient in a sanitarium."

Joe stared back at him evenly. "Absent of the fact that I'm the one who found them and might be incriminated in the crime, why would I make a story like that up?"

"You make it sound like that first part's no big deal. The incriminating thing."

"Hey, I liked Harold and Sadie. A lot."

"I know you did. And you know where that gets us?"

Joe turned all the way in his seat to face Copeland. "How long do you suppose they were dead before I found them?"

"Better part of a week," Copeland said. "The only thing that proves is you didn't kill them today. Who's to say you didn't do it several days ago and come back to bask in the glory of your accomplishments?"

"Who's to say I did?"

"Can you account for your whereabouts this entire week?"

"You saying I need to?"

"You might."

Joe's cheeks burned. "You're telling me you think I did it?"

Copeland made a face, flapped an angry hand. "Hell no, I don't. I'm just wanting to eliminate you from the list of suspects so I don't have to worry about any charges of bias toward my office."

"I told you it was a bad idea having beers together."

"Yeah, and I didn't know you were gonna start finding dead septuagenarians."

"Good word, but Harold was in his eighties."

"I was talking about Sadie, asshole. We both know this wasn't a random killing. There's no way someone would drive all the way out to the boonies, take all that time to perform pine tree cross-stitch—"

"Yew tree."

"—on Harold Hawkins's arms, tattoo his face, if there weren't some serious motive beneath all of it. And it's not like the old couple had any real enemies. Unless, that is, they pissed off someone down at the bingo parlor, and one of Sadie's blue-haired friends decided to exact some retribution."

"Sadie didn't play bingo."

"How the hell you know? You two had something going, maybe after Harold went to bed?"

"That's not very funny."

"And you can just cut me some fucking slack. I got up at five-thirty this morning, and it's going on eleven at night. I had a plain salad for lunch, skipped supper, and am pretty goddamned pissed off about the way my day has gone. I'm not even officially on the case anymore. Those pricks from the county act like I'm the black Barney Fife."

"Nobody found the dog?" Joe asked.

"Not a sign of him."

Joe held up the yew branch he'd found on the seat of his pickup. "What do you make of this?"

"Not a hell of a lot, other than the fact that I'm glad you didn't tell anyone but me about it – you didn't, did you?"

"Uh-uh."

"You're not as dumb as I thought then. For a moment there I wondered if maybe you posted about it on Facebook, put it on your blog."

"I don't get into that stuff."

"One of the few things I like about you."

"It ever occur to you that if I'm telling the truth, my day has been pretty shitty too?"

Copeland gave him a dead look. "You ever had to roll a corpse over so the coroner can examine his shit-smeared ass?"

"I don't do it often."

"And I thought the smell in there couldn't get worse. You shoulda seen those sheets. Maggots and diarrhea and—"

"Can we just skip that part?"

"Hell no, we can't skip it. You only have to hear about it, I had to be there at ground zero, the guy's cold; rotten flesh splitting around my fingers..."

"Didn't you wear gloves?"

"Man, you have any idea how thin those things are? I might as well have used Saran wrap." Copeland shivered. "I can still feel that stuff on my fingers."

"So what did Sharon say?"

"What do you think she said? She didn't say anything because I haven't talked to her."

"I told you—"

"I know what you told me. You told me her and her buddies from the graveyard are the ones who did it and they're gonna do the same thing to everyone who's nice to you."

"It's the truth."

"You need to lay off the horror novels."

"What, and read Nicholas Sparks instead?"

"Piss off."

Joe chuckled softly. It felt good. It was the first time he'd laughed all day.

Copeland's eyes shifted to something behind Joe. "She doesn't look happy."

For an insane moment Joe was sure it was Angie Waltz, her huge white eyes and charred face shoved right against the passenger window. He whirled, a little moan escaping from his open mouth.

Michelle stared back at him, one eyebrow raised.

Joe sagged in his seat, a hand pressed to his chest. Beside him, Copeland was laughing so hard his belly jiggled. Joe reached out, thumbed down the window.

"You two all right?" Michelle asked.

"I'm fine," Copeland said through his laughter. "That husband of yours, he might need a change of underwear."

"Shut up," Joe muttered. He looked at Michelle. "Having trouble sleeping?"

"What do you think?"

Copeland leaned toward her. "Joe tell you the same story he told me? Snakes and dead women?"

"I believe him."

Joe looked at Michelle in surprise.

Copeland said, "You believe Angie Waltz clawed her way out of her grave, killed Harold and Sadie, made a solar eclipse in their entryway, then decided to let Joe off the hook?"

Michelle pursed her lips. "I amend my original statement. I believe that Joe believes it."

Joe's surprise faded.

"Thank God there's another rational person in this town," Copeland said.

Michelle saw the way Joe was looking at her. She sighed, bit her lip. "How about you two come in and drink a beer? You guys look like a couple of teenagers out here about to start necking."

★ ★ ★

Joe actually had three beers, and it wasn't until he'd begun to feel a pleasant buzz that he realized he'd never had supper either.

Sitting at the kitchen table with Copeland and Michelle, Joe said, "You want something to eat?"

"About time you asked me," Copeland said. "I've been staring at those Nutter Butters in your pantry for forty-five minutes now, hoping you'd offer me some."

Michelle got up, went to the pantry. "Why didn't you just ask?"

Copeland shrugged. "It seemed impolite."

Joe said, "It's impolite to scratch your balls in front of a woman, too, but you've been doing that since you sat down at the table."

Copeland looked sheepish. "Can I use the excuse about not having supper again?"

"Uh-uh."

"Joe's got a point," Michelle said as she placed the Nutter Butters before Copeland. "Way you've been digging down there, I thought you were scratching off lottery tickets under the table."

Copeland bit into a cookie, looked at her. "You're as much of a smartass as your husband."

She smiled. "More so, actually."

"She's right," Joe agreed.

"That why you married her?"

"I took pity on him," she said.

Copeland chewed his cookie. "That I can believe."

"So, what are we gonna do about the murders?" Joe asked.

Copeland stopped chewing. "What's this 'we' stuff? Only 'we' in this is me and my people. And the county sheriff, who has more to do with it than anyone."

"You've got cookie on the side of your mouth. They killed her because of what happened with Angie. And because Harold and Sadie wrote letters explaining why we'd be good parents for Little Stevie."

"Do you have to call him that?" Copeland asked. "Every time you say it I imagine the little boy in his diaper sitting in front of a piano singing 'My Cherie Amour.'"

Michelle leaned forward on her elbows. "You do have to admit the timing is pretty suspicious. The Hawkinses, who don't have any enemies—"

"That we know of," Copeland cut in.

"—write letters of testimony about the child coming to live with us, and around that same time, someone comes in and murders them in a ritualistic way?"

"How did you know it was ritualistic?" Copeland asked. He glanced at Joe. "Man, you told her all that gory shit? I thought you had better judgment than that."

"I trust her enough to be honest with her," Joe said.

Copeland narrowed his eyes. "And I suppose you told her about the picture on your cell phone too?"

Joe cringed.

Michelle stared at Copeland. "What picture?"

Copeland bit into another cookie. "So much for trust."

Joe shifted in his chair. "You didn't have to—"

"What picture is he talking about, Joe?"

Joe told her. And though he knew there was no real way around it, his heart still hurt a little at the way Michelle blanched.

He forced a smile. "I probably just left it on, honey."

"Your phone doesn't stay on that long," she said in a small voice. "You said you were in the house for twenty minutes."

"Yeah, Joe," Copeland said. "What about it?"

Joe glared at him. "You don't have to pile on."

Copeland put up his palms. "Hey, I'm just glad it's not my ass being reamed for once. I've been barked at so many times today I started to feel like I was the one who'd scared Sadie to death."

Michelle looked at Copeland. "You think that part is true?"

"I didn't say that."

"But it's pretty hard to ignore the look on Sadie's face," Joe said. "Wouldn't you agree?"

Copeland eyed him. "If someone held a lighter to your fingers, wouldn't you be scared too?"

"How'd her arms and hands get frozen in the air like that?" Joe said. "Poor woman looked like she was doing the 'Thriller' dance."

"Rigor mortis does some weird stuff," Copeland said, but Joe could tell his heart wasn't in it. Copeland swallowed, massaged the base of his throat. "Could I trouble you for some milk, Mrs. Crawford?"

"We're all out," Michelle said. "Unless you want some of my breast milk."

"I don't think our relationship is at that stage yet."

"I meant from a bottle."

"I still don't think we're there."

"How about water?"

"I can make do with that," he said, looking crestfallen. "It ain't the same as milk, but it'll do."

Joe gave him a wry look. "You're pretty particular for a guest eating someone else's cookies."

"I spent the day with two dead people. I think I'm entitled to a few amenities, don't you?"

Joe couldn't argue with that.

Michelle came back with the water, placed the glass in front of the big cop. Sitting down next to Joe, she said, "So what's the plan now?"

"I've been thinkin' about that," Copeland said after gulping half the glass. "I think it's time to take a proactive approach."

Joe watched him. "You mean spend your time solving the murders?"

"No, asshead, I mean preventing others."

Joe exchanged a glance with his wife. She looked like she was about to speak, but Copeland went on. "There were enough ominous events before today to make me think bad times were coming. But slaughtering two old people in cold blood—"

"Two good people," Joe added.

"I don't know I'd go as far as that."

"What the hell's that supposed to mean? Harold and Sadie were—"

"Sadie was a neat old gal," Copeland broke in. "I'll grant you that much."

Joe paused. "What is it you're not telling us, Darrell?"

Copeland leaned back, munching another peanut-shaped cookie. "Well, hell. I guess I've told you too much to hold back now, Joe. You look at me with those puppy dog eyes, and I can't keep secrets from you."

Michelle said, "You two want some time alone?"

"We went through Harold's things," Copeland said, "and we found some interesting stuff. It turns out Harold had a different kind of life before he met Sadie…kind you'd never have expected just by lookin' at him."

Something tickled at Joe's memory, but he couldn't quite grab hold of it, drag it into the light.

"When you were out there the other day with Sadie," Copeland said, "did she say anything about an Antonia Baxter?"

Joe drummed his fingers. "As a matter of fact, she did."

"And you didn't tell me about it because…?"

"I guess I thought it was ancient history."

"How 'bout you fill me in now?"

So Joe did. Copeland and Michelle listened with what looked like mingled dread and consternation as Joe recounted the tale of the red-haired woman who incinerated her kids before burning herself alive. More than once Copeland or Michelle interrupted him by asking why he hadn't mentioned it to them. Joe didn't have a good answer because he didn't know himself. Maybe he'd been so creeped out by it all that he didn't want to think about it any more than he had to.

When Joe finished, Copeland sighed and said, "Well, that certainly fills in a lot of blanks."

"Like what?" Joe asked.

"Like why Sadie hated Antonia so much."

Joe shrugged. "I don't see how that answers anything."

Copeland said, "How 'bout we let your better half answer that one?"

"How would she know?"

In a distant voice, Michelle said, "Harold Hawkins was Sharon Waltz's grandfather."

"Bingo," Copeland said.

Joe stared at her. "How the hell did you know that?"

"There's a lot I know that you don't."

"Like where you've been going when Lily's home with a sitter?"

Michelle didn't answer, but she didn't look displeased either. Joe stared at her, waiting, but Copeland was going on.

"So I propose a change in our approach. I've been feeling like that little Dutch boy, one that put his finger in the dike?"

"If either of you turns that into a joke," Michelle said, "I'll kick you in the nuts."

Copeland continued, "See, I've been like that boy, only instead of plugging one hole and then plugging up the next one that springs open, I've been staring up at that dam and just hoping and praying it doesn't give way."

"I guess the dam broke today," Michelle said.

Copeland shook his head grimly. "That wasn't the dam, Mrs. Crawford. It was a mighty big leak – that I'll admit. But it wasn't the dam. No, what's coming is gonna make what happened today look like nothing. Unless we put a stop to it."

Joe sat forward. "What's on your mind?"

"We find someone to tail and let him lead us to the killers."

"Makes sense," Joe agreed.

"There's only one issue," Copeland said.

"And that is?"

"We don't have anybody to tail."

"Sharon?" Michelle asked.

"She's a candidate," Copeland allowed. "But she's got too much sense to let herself be followed."

Michelle looked incredulous. "Sharon Waltz has the brain of a mentally challenged squirrel."

"I'm not talking about brains," Copeland said. "I'm talking about jungle instincts. Radar. A woman that nasty, she's gonna expect others to act as horribly as she does."

"You've got a point," Joe said.

"I know I do," Copeland said. "What we need is somebody who doesn't expect to be followed. Someone a lot dumber than Sharon. Or at least with less-developed survival instincts."

"I know who," Joe said.

Copeland and Michelle looked at him.

"Kevin Gentry."

"I thought he was just a pervert," Copeland said.

"So did I," Joe answered. "At first. But when I fired him, he said some stuff that has me reconsidering my assessment."

"What kind of stuff?"

Joe told them. When he'd recounted all he could remember, he said, "So I figure we tail Gentry until he takes us to more of them."

Michelle looked at Joe. "Shouldn't you let Darrell take care of this?"

"Not if he lets me be a part of it."

Michelle glanced at Copeland, but his expression was impassive. She said, "Why take any chances, Joe?"

"Because I've been feeling the same way Darrell has. Only I haven't been standing under a dam, I've been out on my lawn watching a violent storm approach. I've been trying to protect you and Lily, but the storm just keeps getting closer and closer."

"We're fine, Joe. No one's going to come near us."

"Someone already has."

Her face darkened with fear. "What do you mean?"

And Joe told her about the corn dolly in Sadie's woods, told her all about how he'd found Belle's dress gone from Lily's room and the same dress on that accursed cornhusk doll. Michelle's eyes grew more and more frightened, and though Joe hated himself for it, he decided to make it sound just as bad as it was.

"Oh my God," she said when he'd finished.

"So the storm's already been here," Joe said.

Copeland shifted uneasily. "I think you can drop that whole storm metaphor, Joe. You've got the missus good and scared."

"And that's why," Joe went on, "you and Lily are going to stay with your parents in Indy for the next several days."

Michelle folded her arms. "We're not leaving."

"I hate to sound like one of those guys who expects his woman to behave like the hired help, but I'm sorry, honey – yes, you are."

Michelle's nostrils flared. "Where the hell do you get off—"

"Where I get off is I'm the one who loves you and who loves Lily and who doesn't want either of you to get hurt. I can't do anything about this if I've gotta constantly worry about something happening to my two favorite people."

Michelle looked slightly mollified, but her frown told him there was still work to be done.

He said, "Darrell and I've got a good plan, but we're outnumbered. Even with his officers, it's at least, what? Thirty ghouls to five sane people?"

"Where do you get thirty?" Michelle asked. "There's Sharon, the guys from the bridge, whoever murdered Sadie and—"

"There were thirty or so at the funeral," Joe said, "and I'm going to assume that every one of them is a psychotic cult member."

Copeland said, "Would that include your current employers?"

Joe's stare was level. "The jury's still out on the Martins. I think they're all right, but Bridget's starting to worry me a little."

"How come?"

"Because," Michelle cut in, "she's been flashing her nude breasts at my husband."

Copeland glared at him. "Hey, why haven't I heard about this? That's some juicy stuff, Joe." When he saw Michelle's look, he added, "Sorry, Mrs. Crawford."

Joe put his hand over his wife's. "I'm asking you respectfully, honey,

I'm not telling you. But will you please go to Indy? So I'll know you and Lily are safe?"

Michelle exhaled pent-up air. "I suppose so. But only for a few days."

"A week?" Joe asked.

"Don't push it."

Joe lowered his head in surrender.

"Hot damn," Copeland said. "I finally feel okay about life."

Michelle gave him a rueful look. "Why, because you've eaten half a bag of cookies?"

"Uh-uh," Copeland answered. "It's because I don't feel aimless anymore." He looked at Joe. "Six a.m. good for you?"

"Better make it seven," Joe said. "Gentry's a late riser."

Copeland left soon after that, and Joe followed Michelle toward their bedroom. But before he went in he decided he better check in on Lily. He moved up the steps fearing he'd smell ashes, but he made it all the way into her room without smelling anything other than the normal odors. Baby powder and a vague tinge of urine from her nighttime diaper.

Standing over her crib, he thought about their plan, such as it was, and wondered if they were doing the right thing. Surely Michelle and Lily would be safe in Indianapolis, wouldn't they? Surely the members of Sharon's cult wouldn't follow Michelle's car all the way down to the big city.

Uneasily, Joe peered down at his daughter. She was evidently dreaming, her little eyeballs twitching under closed lids. He longed to comfort her, but if he touched her now, he might wake her all the way up, and then it could be hours getting her back to sleep again.

He'd crept halfway to the door when she suddenly sat bolt upright in her crib and said, "Daddy?"

He came back to her, cursing his inability to move stealthily. He hadn't thought he'd been loud, but apparently the noise he'd made had been enough to rouse her from whatever scary dream realm she'd been inhabiting.

He put on a smile. "Hey, sweetie. You okay?"

In the light from the hallway he saw her face crumple, her eyes gleaming with tears. "They were hurting me, Daddy!"

Her words took his breath away. He wrapped her up and lifted her out of the crib. "Shhhh," he said. "You're safe, sweetie. You're safe."

She sobbed into his shoulder and gibbered about bad people and scary faces and someone hurting her, and though her words imbued Joe with a dread so profound it made his bones ache, he concentrated on soothing her, on being strong enough to thwart her terror. "It's okay, sweetie. You're safe. We're safe. Nothing's going to hurt you."

It took a while, but after perhaps twenty minutes of carrying her around the room and whispering calming words, her body resumed its drowsy, boneless state. He lowered her into her crib and told her how much he loved her. He told her she was safe. He hovered over her crib, caressing her and speaking to her, until she was soundly asleep.

"You're safe," he whispered as he moved through the doorway and started down the stairs. "We're safe."

He wished he believed it.

CHAPTER SEVENTEEN

A quarter-mile down from Kevin Gentry's gray modular home, Joe and Copeland sat in Copeland's white Acura sipping coffee from Styrofoam cups.

Joe grimaced. "How the hell you drink this swill, Darrell? This is so bad I bet the prisoners complain."

Copeland sipped his cup. "I don't pay much attention to the taste."

"I gathered. It's like vinegar and motor oil."

Copeland ignored that. "I just like the caffeine rush. In fact, I think I'd die without it. Or at least be like one of those movie zombies for the better part of the morning."

"You have something against zombies?"

"Oh, that's right. I forgot. You like that gory bullshit. Probably watch that TV show too. One with the crossbow guy, squints all the time?"

"Not all of us can read Nicholas Sparks novels and have a good cry every day."

"Keep talking, I'll come over there and show you a good cry."

Joe grinned and sipped his swill. Man, it really did taste awful.

At length, Joe asked, "So what happens when we follow Gentry and find one of his confederates?"

"This ain't the Civil War."

"It means his—"

"I know what it means, dickweed. It just sounded funny, that's all." Copeland drank his coffee. "To answer your question, when we find out where he goes, we talk to both him and whoever he's associating with. See if they know anything about the Hawkins murders."

"What if they lawyer up?"

Copeland's eyebrows rose. "'Lawyer up'? Man, how many cop shows you been watching? Confederates. Lawyering up. It's like I'm sitting here with Perry Mason."

"That show was before my time."

"Before my time too, asshole. How old you think I am?"

Gentry's car was pulling out of his drive.

"I didn't even see him come out," Joe said.

"That's because you were too busy dazzling me with your cop show lingo."

"Shut up."

"Here we go," Copeland said and guided the Acura onto the country road.

They stayed a good ways back, knowing that in a town the size of Shadeland, they ran little risk of losing Gentry's red Chevy Cobalt. Especially since the guy had added a spoiler and gold rims to the thing. Joe wondered if Gentry ever spent money on his wife and kids.

The Chevy didn't take the left turn into Shadeland, however, moving north instead in the direction of the next town over, a little hamlet called Ravana. Joe didn't like that. He'd heard disturbing stories about the place. Stories about cults and other unsavory practices. There was even a wild rumor about vampires.

He supposed it was only fitting that Gentry would be heading there.

They hung back about a hundred yards or so, never venturing much closer. There was even less need for close pursuit out here in the country. Granted, it was possible that Gentry could clue into their presence and take a quick turn into one of the many forests or fields that framed the road, but Joe strongly suspected that Gentry had no idea they were back here, the guy probably listening to his music too loud and fantasizing about some woman. Maybe Joe's wife.

They followed for perhaps twenty minutes, neither one of them saying much. Joe felt his stomach coiling into a tense ball, but he felt excitement too. He badly wanted to attach Gentry to the rest of Sharon's group. It would give him more reason to hate the guy.

Not that he needed more reason.

When the Chevy neared the right turn that would take him into Ravana, it instead hooked a left onto a densely wooded gravel road.

"Careful," Joe said.

"Of what? Rocks hitting my exhaust pipe?"

"Of him seeing us."

"That's right," Copeland said, preparing for the turn, "we gotta watch for all those confederates."

"You're not gonna let that go, are you?"

But rather than answering, Copeland nodded ahead. Joe turned and saw that the Chevy was slowing in front of what looked like a plain but rather large white farmhouse. There were several outbuildings behind it, what Joe first mistook for chicken coops and farrowing houses.

"Well, hell," Copeland said in a wondering voice.

"What? It's just a farm."

Copeland gave a faint shake of the head. "It isn't a farm. I think it's a commune."

Joe opened his mouth to respond, but he realized it was as Copeland said. The buildings weren't in immaculate shape, but they were better taken care of than chicken coops would be. They were bigger too.

The ball of nervous tension in his gut calcified.

No sooner had Gentry's Cobalt pulled into the driveway than a short man stepped onto the front porch of the farmhouse. Even from a distance of more than a hundred yards there was something familiar about the guy.

"That doesn't look like the men you described," Copeland said. "Ones on the bridge."

"That's because it's someone else."

Copeland looked at him. "You know the guy?"

"I don't know him, but I know who he is," Joe said in a thin voice. "He's the preacher who did Angie Waltz's funeral."

Copeland let his little Acura crawl forward.

"You gonna call for reinforcements?" Joe asked.

"There you go again."

"What if the bastards are all there?"

"Drink your coffee."

"I'm telling you," Joe said, trying and failing to keep the panic out of his voice, "that tall bastard and the tattoo guy, they weren't messing around on the bridge."

"You handled 'em all right."

"That was luck and adrenaline. I still can't believe I got out of there alive."

Copeland rolled forward, the Acura moving inexorably closer to the farmhouse. Fifty yards away, and apparently neither Gentry nor the preacher had noticed them.

"Can I at least have a gun?" Joe asked.

"That's the last thing you need."

Joe looked at him incredulously. "You told me to buy one."

"For home protection," Copeland said, "not to take on Charlie Manson and his crew."

Shit, Joe thought, sinking back into the seat. "You really think they're like Manson's people?"

"Who knows what they're like?" Copeland said. "But for now we gotta assume these are some seriously dangerous confederates."

"You're a dick."

Copeland just chuckled.

At thirty yards away, the preacher finally spotted them.

It was another several moments before Gentry turned also. As usual, Joe's former right-hand man appeared too wrapped up in whatever he was talking about to take notice of others' social cues, Gentry gesturing frenetically about something or other, probably some married woman he had just masturbated to. Eventually, though, Gentry also saw them approaching, and his expression slipped from plain curiosity to extreme trepidation. When Copeland parked the Acura and climbed out, Gentry – likely taking in the police chief's imposing girth – actually moved a couple steps toward the far end of the covered porch, as if seeking refuge. A moment after that, Joe got out and trailed Copeland up the flagstone walk.

"Morning," Copeland called.

"Good morning, Chief," the preacher said in the deep, resonant voice Joe remembered from the graveyard. The sound of it gave him chills. It was powerful, rumbling, full-throated. Yet something about it was oddly penetrating, like a sonic blade. The sound of the preacher's voice seemed to vibrate in Joe's head long after the man's words had died.

Copeland moved straight toward the preacher, who wore a short-sleeved black shirt and black trousers. Copeland grinned at the preacher, ignoring Gentry altogether. At least so far.

"You know me, apparently, but I don't know you."

"Grayman," the short man said, a disconcerting smile splitting his face. "Patrick Grayman."

Patrick, Joe thought, remembering the name he'd been given the day those assholes had lured him to the bridge. It fit too well to be coincidence.

Copeland's manner changed. Had Joe remembered to give Darrell that detail? Yes, he realized, he had told Copeland about the nonexistent Patrick. Or the *seemingly* nonexistent Patrick. Because evidently Patrick did exist.

He was looking at Joe now.

"Why don't you two come inside?" Grayman said. "I've just made some coffee."

Copeland put up a hand. "I'm afraid I've already had some, Reverend. I'm too fond of the coffee at the station to drink anything else."

Grayman's smile didn't falter. "I'm not a reverend, Chief Copeland. I'm not sure what gave you that idea."

Copeland shrugged. "Oh, it's just something I heard."

Grayman fixed Joe with his sludgy brown eyes. "Your friend shouldn't haunt funerals, Chief Copeland. He should at least have the decency to join those who appreciate what Angela did."

Joe's chest tightened. Copeland, too, seemed to hesitate.

Gentry's face stretched in a savage grin. "Thought you were smarter than us, didn't you?" He shook his head. "Jesus, I'm glad I don't work for you anymore."

Copeland nodded. "You kept your willy in your pants, you might still have a job."

Gentry glared at Copeland murderously.

But Grayman's smile remained serene. Perhaps, Joe mused, that was precisely what was so troubling about it. The utter placidity of the man's expression. He was clearly older than Joe. At least twenty years older. Yet there were very few wrinkles around the man's eyes, few signs at all he had lived for six decades or more. So why, Joe wondered, did he put the man at sixty?

Because, he now realized, if he examined his own impressions honestly, the conclusions made even less sense. Grayman had the skin of a man Joe's age or younger, yet he couldn't be that young. There was the hair loss, for one thing, and the knowing cast to the man's muddy eyes. That kind of experience didn't come to a man early in life. It was the kind of look, Joe thought, an extraordinarily sharp nursing home resident might wear, one whose body has broken down but whose intellect remains intact. Yet Grayman might not be that old. He might be…he might be…

"Hey, Joe, you okay?" Copeland asked.

Joe listed backwards, and was only prevented from tumbling off the porch by Copeland's iron grip, which was cinched around the crook of Joe's elbow. But it was still no good. His legs were liquefying and somewhere far off, Gentry was laughing. Copeland was saying something, sounding half nettled and half concerned, and Joe had time to think, *Not what I came out here to do*, and it was this thought that centered him, that brought him back to himself.

He was stooped over, Copeland supporting him. He realized very little time had passed, ten seconds at the most, and Grayman hadn't moved at all.

Gentry, however, was staring down at him without pity. "Heat get to you, Joey?"

"I'm fine," Joe said and made himself stand upright. Copeland was eyeing him uncertainly, but Grayman looked on as though nothing much had happened. But Joe knew it had, knew Grayman had somehow...what? Bewitched him? Hypnotized him? It didn't make any sense – the man hadn't *done* anything – but Joe couldn't shake the notion that Grayman had somehow inflicted the dizzy spell on him.

Grayman asked, "Are you sure you don't need to come in out of the heat, Mr. Crawford?"

"It isn't hot," Joe muttered.

Copeland was frowning at Joe. "We came out here to ask you some questions, Mr. Grayman."

"Is this about that poor old Hawkins couple?"

Copeland stared at Grayman for a moment, perhaps detecting the same gloating undertone Joe had in the man's deep voice.

"That's right," Copeland said. "You wanna tell me how you knew that?"

"Shadeland is a small town," Grayman said. "And our home isn't far away."

"Or maybe Mr. Gentry here had firsthand knowledge of the crimes," Copeland said.

Joe glanced at Copeland in surprise. He hadn't expected such a direct approach. He certainly hadn't expected Copeland to accuse Kevin Gentry of murder.

"What a bunch of crap," Gentry said. He addressed Grayman but gestured at Copeland. "This guy's got it in for me. He and Joe here are buddies, and Joe's still pissed off because his wife has the hots for me."

Joe tilted his head at Gentry. "You're scared of them," Joe said.

Gentry's expression went sullen. "The hell you talking about?"

"You're right to be scared," Joe persisted. "You're in over your head."

For the first time, Grayman's composure seemed to slip a little. Nothing overt, just a slight crease between the eyes, but it was enough to tell Joe he'd hit close to the mark.

"Kevin hasn't the slightest reason to fear us, Mr. Crawford."

Joe grunted. "That's because he follows your orders."

Grayman favored him with an indulgent smile. "I'm afraid you and Chief Copeland are too enamored with conspiracy theories. What is it precisely you think I've done?"

"Not you," Copeland said. "Your followers."

Grayman gave him a bemused smile and interlaced his fingers before him. "Followers? But Chief Copeland, you make me out like some sort of religious leader."

"You led the funeral ceremony," Joe said. "You read that black Mass."

Grayman looked pained. "Please, Mr. Crawford. You should hear yourself. Black Mass? We are not Satanists, Zionists, Jehovah's Witnesses. We're least of all Christians."

"No kiddin'?" Copeland said. "I'd have thought those tattoos you all engraved on Harold's forehead were straight out of Leviticus."

"We did no such thing, Chief Copeland. You sound to me like a man who's desperate for a scapegoat."

Copeland nodded. "Or maybe you've got a persecution complex, Pastor Grayman. You sure you're not the leader of this here cult?"

Grayman's lips thinned. Joe eyed Gentry, wondered if the guy was smart enough to follow the conversation. Probably not. Either way, he wouldn't do anything until Grayman gave the go-ahead. It was the same way when he worked for Joe. Gentry had enough knowhow, yet he'd stand around with his thumb up his butt until you drew him a picture and ordered him to move.

"Mr. Copeland," Grayman said, "I've already corrected you, so I must assume your continued reference to our family as a cult is an attempt to make me angry."

"Call me Chief Copeland if you want," Copeland said with a wintry grin. "Unless of course you're trying to make *me* angry."

Grayman drew in shuddering breath. "Why don't you just get to the point?"

"That'd be great with me, pastor. Honestly, I don't much like being in your presence. Or Gentry's. I keep thinking he's going to drop his drawers and take a little personal time."

Grayman sighed. "What do you want?"

"Information," Copeland said, peering about the yard. There were numerous oaks, maples, sycamores, and ash trees about, so that very little of the yard actually got the sun. Here and there, patches of grass were mottled with the pale orange of early morning, but mostly there was just gloom.

Grayman looked from Copeland to Joe and back to Copeland. "I'm waiting. You said you had questions..."

"Mind if we look around?" Copeland said.

Joe was sure Grayman would order them off his land then, but the short man surprised him by smiling and spreading his arms. "Of course! We'd love for you to see the property."

And Grayman was splitting them and trotting down the porch steps into the grass. Joe and Copeland exchanged a glance, and Gentry muttered, "Assholes" as he followed Grayman's lead. When Gentry passed between Joe and Copeland, the big police chief threw out a shoulder, and Gentry was suddenly sprawled on the grass below the porch, staring up at Copeland with wounded surprise.

"Sorry about that, Kevin," Copeland said, smiling jovially and dismounting the porch to proffer a hand. "This darned shoulder has a mind of its own." He rolled it around to demonstrate.

Gentry's face twisted in anger as he shoved to his feet and followed Grayman. Moving after him, Joe said, "You're really pushing it, you know?"

"They're killers," Copeland said in a low voice. "They deserve to be pushed."

★ ★ ★

They came around the house and saw the structures Joe had first mistaken for livestock buildings. There were three of them lined up in a neat row. There were maybe thirty feet between them, the buildings themselves about sixty feet long and half as wide. The roofs were peaked in the middle, giving them the appearance of pole barns, the kind in which farmers often kept their machinery. Only these buildings weren't constructed of sheet metal; the facades looked like good, solid wood. The white paint was weathered, but the structures didn't look like they'd blow down any time soon. Joe wondered how long the commune had existed.

Grayman was standing before the first building. He gestured toward it as Joe approached. "This is the Dagda, the oldest of the three cottages."

Copeland eyed the long building. "Cottage, huh? Looks more like a barracks to me."

Grayman looked embarrassed. "Please, Chief Copeland, you make us sound like a militia."

Copeland didn't answer, but his noncommittal grunt made it plain he thought Grayman's group might be exactly that.

"Would you like to see the inside?" Grayman asked.

"I wouldn't do that," Gentry said, but when Grayman gave him a freezing look, Gentry shut up fast.

"No need yet," Copeland said. He indicated the second building. "What about those other two?"

"The same," Grayman said. "With a few variations."

"Like what?" Joe asked.

"The floor plans differ slightly," Grayman explained. "In the Dagda, for instance, the sleeping area is in the rear of the building. In the Morrigan, it's in the front."

"Those Irish words?" Joe asked.

In answer, Grayman favored him with a peculiar smile.

Copeland was nodding thoughtfully. "So all three of these places are living quarters."

"That's right."

"You sleep out here or in the main house?"

"The house," Grayman answered. But was there the slightest hesitation in his answer?

"Are these co-ed?"

Grayman chuckled, regarded his shiny black loafers. "Now you're making us sound like a college dormitory, Chief Copeland."

"Okay," Copeland said. "I'll rephrase. The guys and gals here shack up in the same rooms? A lot of fucking go on among your family members?"

But Grayman didn't seem abashed. He held Copeland's gaze for a beat, then said, "You'll find that our attitudes involving sexual congress are very different than the rest of society's."

Copeland swatted Joe on the chest with the back of his hand. "Hear that, Joe? 'Sexual congress.' I always got a kick out of that phrase. Makes me imagine senators gettin' blow jobs from their assistants."

Grayman nodded. "I also find it ironic how puritanical American politicians pretend to be, when their behavior runs so counter to their platitudes."

Copeland grinned broadly. "Well, look at us, Pastor Grayman. Sharing our views like two old pals. Maybe we should bump chests, show our solidarity."

Grayman's answering smile was patient. "No, thank you, Chief Copeland."

"So where's your church?"

Grayman's smile faded.

Copeland's eyebrows rose. "You don't call it that? I apologize, Pastor. Your temple then? Or synagogue?"

Grayman's eyes had gone fierce.

"Mosque?" Copeland persisted. "Nah, y'all don't look like you'd worship Allah here. More like the Satanic Cathedral of the Goat, something along those lines."

Grayman's words were low, clipped. "When you're quite through mocking our beliefs, I'd like you to finish your questioning."

"Sure," Copeland said. "I know you guys got stuff to do, chickens to sacrifice and all. Just show us where your place of worship is, and we'll be on our way."

Grayman said nothing, but Gentry's eyes flicked toward the woods beyond the outbuildings.

Copeland noticed it too. "Out there, huh? Thank you, Kevin! You're a hell of a good man. I wondered why Joe kept you on so long, but now I know. When a guy's as helpful as you, a boss can put up with a certain amount of public indecency."

"You fucker," Gentry said, teeth clenched.

"You wanna take out your anger on me," Copeland said, stepping forward, "you go right ahead. Sounds to me like Joe whupped your ass good and proper, and I know I could take Joe. He's strong, but he ain't as nasty as I am. I used to get into bar fights every weekend when I was a younger man. Figured the ladies weren't gonna go for me because of my devilish good looks, so I had to impress 'em somehow. Kicking their boyfriends' asses seemed the best way to go about it."

"Did it work?" Joe asked.

"Occasionally," Copeland said. "Most of the time, the bouncers called the police before I could see the effect my barbaric behavior had on the lady. Once or twice I got arrested."

Joe smiled. "That's how you got interested in becoming a cop."

"You got it."

Grayman said, "I'd like you both to leave."

Gentry took Copeland by the bicep. "You heard the man."

Copeland didn't budge. "You don't want me to tear your arm off, bitch slap you with it, you better let go of me now."

Gentry did.

Copeland turned to Grayman. "You wanna do this the hard way, that's fine with me. The judge and I, we've gone on fishing trips together. It'll take me about a half-hour to get my people over here with a search warrant. Meanwhile, Joe and I'll stay right out there on that country road, watch your activities. We see you and your little stoolie here scurrying back to those woods, we'll know you're destroying evidence."

Grayman seemed to consider. He tilted his head. "You really believe we're violent people, Chief Copeland?"

"Depends on what you call violent," Copeland said. "You consider mutilating a helpless old man and sewing up his skin with branches violent, then yeah, I'd say you guys fit that bill."

"That's an ugly thing to say."

"It is indeed," Copeland said. "It is indeed."

Grayman exhaled wearily. "It's obvious you're not going to treat us with dignity, Chief Copeland. I shouldn't allow you to investigate our property – frankly, I doubt you have just cause to procure your search warrant – but I'm sick of listening to your insults and am eager to be rid of you and your lying friend. You may search on one condition."

"I'm listening."

"You take Mr. Gentry with you."

"That's it?" Copeland asked, grinning. "Well, hell. I was hoping old Kevin here would go with us anyway. He'll make a great tour guide. 'Less of course he spots a woman in a brassiere on the way past one of those dorms and succumbs to an ungovernable urge to spank his monkey."

Joe bit the inside of his mouth to stifle laughter. Gentry looked like he might strangle Copeland.

But Grayman moved toward the house without a word.

Copeland called out, "Oh, and Pastor Grayman?"

Grayman froze about ten feet from his back door, but the small man didn't turn. "What?" he asked.

"Joe's not a liar. Oh, he's got a lot of bad habits. Peeing on the seat, forgetting to say please and thank you. But he's not dishonest. You'd be smart not to insult my friend again."

Grayman headed for the house, his stiff-limbed movements indicating plainly just how indignant he was.

Joe watched him disappear into the house and said to Copeland, "You're a real instigator, you know that?"

"Bet your wife thinks I'm charming."

"Why'd she marry me then?"

"You're right," Copeland said, starting toward the woods. "She must have questionable taste to marry a sad sack like you."

CHAPTER EIGHTEEN

They'd trudged through the winding forest trail for perhaps ten minutes when Joe first spied a large, hulking shape through the branches and leaves.

"That our destination?" Joe asked.

But Gentry didn't answer, only continued leading them down the tortuous path. Whoever had chosen this spot hadn't done so for its accessibility, Joe decided. He wondered how far away the nearest neighbors were, how vast Grayman's land was. He thought of asking, but figured Gentry either wouldn't know, would make something up, or wouldn't answer at all.

A minute or so later they emerged into a clearing and stared up at a pitch-black structure. It wasn't immense, but it was as big as most small town churches. Joe figured it would hold at least a hundred people, probably a few more. The roof was shingled with black shakers, the shakers either having been painted that color or perhaps even treated to look that way. The wood façade was the same scorched hue. Joe assumed the boards were pine or cedar, but it was hard to tell when they were so dark. The black building took up most of the clearing, the boughs of various old-growth trees extending over the roof protectively.

"What is this place?" Copeland said.

"The Black Chapel," Gentry answered.

Joe eyed the ebony exterior but didn't speak.

"You going in or not?" Gentry said.

Copeland glanced at their guide. "You sound agitated, Kevin. Something supposed to happen to us in there?"

"Like what?" Gentry asked.

Joe stared at his profile. His words had sounded easy enough, but his expression was tight.

Copeland studied Gentry. "You know not to do anything stupid, don't you?"

"No one's as smart as you," Gentry said, looking like someone had just whispered the world's greatest joke in his ear. Except there was no one else out here, not that Joe could see. Unless you counted the blackbirds sheltering under the chapel entryway.

"Enough screwin' around, Gentry," Copeland said. "What's waiting for us in there?"

Gentry finally looked at them. His smile was somehow both cowardly and aggressive. "Now who's afraid?"

Copeland glanced at Joe. "See what he's doing? Like we're ten years old again. Standing outside some supposedly haunted house."

Joe nodded. "Daring us to go first."

"Door's unlocked," Gentry said with a grand gesture.

"Shit," Copeland muttered. Eyeing the black door ruefully, he made his way to the chapel.

They were met with a room so large and murky Joe had the sensation they'd discovered some sprawling underground military bunker. Only this one, he saw from the scant light washing in through the doorway, had two rows of church pews, an aisle down the middle.

Joe and Copeland waded into the murk.

"Why the hell's it so dark in here?" Copeland asked, and Joe detected the faintest hint of panic in his voice. He was pretty sure Gentry wouldn't notice, but if you knew Copeland well enough, you could hear it. Joe couldn't blame the chief for feeling tense. The skin of Joe's arms had broken out in goose flesh.

Gentry didn't answer, only stood there in the doorway.

Copeland looked around. "Why don't you flip on some lights, Gentry?"

"No electricity out here," Gentry answered. "Or didn't you notice the lack of wires?"

"I've got a Maglite," Joe said, fishing it out of his pocket. "It's not much, but…" He shrugged and clicked it on, flicked it about the tenebrous space. He saw a raised area straight ahead. It seemed like the kind you'd see in a church, only there was no altar there, and there certainly wasn't a big cross. Joe suspected the kind of worshipping they did here had as little connection to Jesus as Sharon Waltz had to Harvard or Yale. There did appear to be a piece of furniture up front, but Joe didn't linger on it long enough to surmise its purpose.

"What do you think?" Gentry asked.

"I think this place needs airing out," Copeland said. Joe noticed with a rush of misgiving that Copeland's right hand had drifted to the handle of his .38. "Why aren't there any windows?"

"There *are* windows," Gentry said. "All over the place."

And as Joe leveled the flashlight to their left, he saw that this was indeed the truth. Only the windows weren't letting in any sunlight.

"Wait a minute," Joe said. He took a couple steps behind the back row of pews. The whole eastern wall of the chapel was lined with windows, but he saw as he moved closer that his Maglite beam was penetrating not only the glass, but several feet beyond. There was a space there, a long, narrow room bordering the main chapel.

A face stared at him through the glass.

"Jesus," he hissed, fumbling the flashlight.

By the time he got the Maglite under control and aimed it, the spot was empty. He'd almost begun to believe he'd imagined the whole thing when Copeland said, "Was that Shannon?"

Joe swallowed, blinked at Copeland in the darkness. "What do you—"

"The tattoos," Copeland broke in angrily. "The tattoos, dammit. Didn't you see 'em?"

"Huh-uh," Joe answered, and his voice was a raspy croak. He wanted out of this place, and he wanted out now.

"All right, Gentry," Copeland said, "I think we've seen—"

But Copeland didn't finish, and when Joe swung the light in his direction, he saw why.

Gentry was gone.

"Well, hell," Copeland said. "I've had enough of this."

The door banged shut. There was the rattle of a lock. Joe's belly tightened into a knot.

Copeland started in that direction. "That little weasel. He thinks he's gonna lock us in here, trap us like some kind of—"

"You came willingly," a voice interrupted from the front of the chapel.

Joe whirled, the flashlight dancing over the front wall, over what looked like a series of red and black tapestries, until he finally picked out a shape in the foreground.

Someone was sitting in the front pew.

"That you, Gentry?" Copeland asked, but Joe knew right away it wasn't. Not only because he was certain it had been Gentry who'd shut the door on them, but because of the shape of the figure's shoulders, its slender neck and head.

Joe recognized that figure.

Scarface rose to his full height, the man like a pale human walking stick.

Scarface was totally naked.

Copeland's voice was thick with fear. "Hey, man, we didn't mean to interrupt anything. You want, you can go back to doing whatever it was you were doing."

But there was something wrong with Scarface. His eyes, Joe saw, were completely white. And there was something glinting on his chest, some dark gruel Joe wanted to believe was ketchup or barbecue sauce or something other than what he knew it was, knew it even before he saw what was clutched in Scarface's left hand.

"Oh hell," Copeland said, drawing his weapon.

Scarface, his white eyes agleam with lunatic rapture, took one step in their direction and heaved the human arm at them. In the split second before he lost track of it in the gloom, Joe saw where the flesh had been gnawed, saw that the arm had belonged to a woman, or a man with hairless skin.

Joe thought Copeland would open up on the crazed cannibal, but the man darted behind the pews before the chief could nail him.

"We love to watch the hunters at work," a voice from their right said. But it was weirdly muffled, as if overheard from another room. Joe swung the flashlight around, realized the voice *had* come from another room – or rather another section of the chapel. The windowed partition between the pews and the exterior wall was crammed with faces, some of them familiar, most of them not. Joe assumed that the majority had been present the day Angie Waltz was buried, but in the end it mattered very little. They were all on the wrong side – Grayman's side. Sharon Waltz's side. Hell, maybe some of them had belonged to Antonia Baxter's clutch of ghouls, though none of the faces looked old enough to go back that far.

Grayman spoke again. "It's long been part of our tradition, Mr. Crawford. The hunting. It has protected our way of life when threatened and provided us with a suitable diversion while we've waited."

"Waited for what?" Copeland said, but his question was half-hearted. He was busy scanning the chapel, the nose of his .38 probing the darkness like a frightened bloodhound.

Joe moved the flashlight to their left and saw with little surprise that the eastern wall was now full of faces as well.

One of them was Sharon Waltz's.

He knew he shouldn't have been surprised, but seeing her ravenous stare was still a kick in the belly.

At least, Joe thought grimly, the fact that the entire cult was here made it likelier that Michelle and Lily had gotten cleanly away. With any luck they were secure at Joe's in-laws. He gritted his teeth, wondering if maybe he should've sent them to a hotel instead, told them to stay there under an alias. Because Michelle's parents could be tracked and found. What if someone had been dispatched to drive down to Indianapolis? What if—

Copeland tapped him on the arm. "Hey, Joe, you mind shinin' that light somewhere other than those folks' faces? I mean, they're pretty and all, but I'm a trifle more concerned with the bastards that're in here with us."

"The hunters," Grayman said from behind the glass.

"You're a shitty preacher," Copeland muttered.

The big cop backed up against Joe. Copeland's body heat was intense, the man's polo shirt soaked through with perspiration. Joe was sweating too, but he felt colder than January frost.

"Anything you can use as a weapon?" Copeland whispered.

Joe thought a moment. He stuffed a shaking hand into his hip pocket. "I've got this pocketknife." He pulled it out, opened the little blade. He glanced down at it. The thing looked like a fingernail cleaner.

Copeland bent down.

"What are you—" Joe began to ask, then jumped as something was shoved against his hip. He realized it was Copeland's hand. Taking care not to stab his friend with the pocketknife, he grasped what Copeland held.

A gun.

"This your .38?" Joe asked, examining it.

"Hell no, numbnuts, it's not my .38. I carry more than one."

"Is the safety on?"

"Keep your voice down," Copeland hissed. "I'd rather them not know you're armed. It'll give us better odds."

"What are our odds?"

"Terrible," Copeland said and swung the Smith & Wesson toward a shadow behind them. As Joe speared the shadow with the flashlight, Copeland opened up, the two rounds exploding in the silence of the chapel, yellow tongues of fire licking from the end of the black barrel.

"You get him?" Joe asked in the silence that followed.

The sounds of someone scrambling along the rear of the chapel told him Copeland hadn't.

"The safety's on the left side," Copeland said. "Get ready."

"For what?"

"Shoot anything that moves. Just don't hit me."

"Hell," Joe said. He pinned the Maglite in his armpit while he switched off the safety. Then he grasped the flashlight, aimed it into the murk, and tracked the narrow beam with the barrel of the gun.

"Be ready," Copeland said.

Joe shone the Maglite around the chapel, but other than the staring faces of the spectators, he spotted nothing.

Yet the chapel now seemed alive with rustlings.

Joe swallowed. "Let's just head for the door."

"Best idea I've heard today," Copeland said, beginning to creep in that direction.

Movement to their left drew Joe's flashlight beam. For a moment there was what appeared to be an elbow, maybe someone's blue-jeaned hip. Then it was gone, presumably scuttling under the pews.

Unaccountably, Joe had an image of gigantic sewer rats scurrying toward him. Jesus. He was gripped by a wild, body-racking shiver.

Copeland seemed to pick up on it. "Almost there, Joe. Stay with me."

Okay, Joe thought. He'd stay with Copeland. He'd stay with him all the way until the door, and then they'd blow the damned thing open if they had to. After that he'd set the world land-speed record getting back to Copeland's car.

"Don't you want to know whose arm that was?" Grayman called from the glassed room.

"Not particularly," Copeland answered in a tight voice.

But Joe did want to know. He *had* to know. Because there was a ghastly image crystalizing in the darkest recesses of his mind, his own black chapel. Inside it, Michelle was shrieking as Grayman's followers worked on her. Lily was shrieking in the background, but in the foreground there was Michelle and there was Scarface and there was the one named Shannon with a hacksaw. The pasty-faced man was there too, the one with the sagging jowls. And the bald man, the muscular one Joe had seen in the passenger's seat of the Camaro on the day of the bridge attack, he was the one cradling Lily. And laughing.

"Who'd you kill?" Joe called out.

"Don't," Copeland said.

The humor in Grayman's voice was too horrid to stomach. "Anyone in particular you're worried about, Mr. Crawford?"

Joe swallowed, his throat clicking like an empty chamber. "You better not hurt them." He'd meant for his voice to come out gruff and commanding, but it had sounded like a plea. A desperate, ineffectual one.

"Say their names, Mr. Crawford."

"Hey, fuck you!" Copeland shouted.

"Still discourteous," Grayman said.

"That son of a bitch," Copeland growled. "Gimme some light."

Joe obliged, shining the Maglite in the direction Copeland was facing, the rear of the chapel immediately to their left. As he did he beheld a wide-eyed figure whose mouth was all wrong. The man was gliding rapidly forward, approaching as if borne along on a moving sidewalk. Copeland fired on the man, the shots slamming the body in the chest, the throat. Red ponds of blood splurted out of the man's twitching body. The man thumped down at their feet just as another figure revealed itself behind the man. Before Copeland could recover, the figure dove out of the way, disappearing behind a pew and scrambling for better cover.

Joe knew even before his flashlight picked out the dead, staring eyes of Copeland's victim what had happened. Whoever it was – probably some random person Grayman's henchman had snatched from the street – had been unable to make much noise because his lips had been sewn shut. The stitches reminded Joe of the job done on Harold Hawkins. Joe saw without surprise that the man's hands had been bound with rope behind his back.

"Ah Jesus," Copeland said. "Ah Jesus God."

"It wasn't your fault," Joe said. "You didn't know."

Hideous laughter echoed through the chapel.

"I thought it was one of them…I thought—"

"Let's go," Joe urged. "We're almost to the door."

But Copeland didn't move. "I know this guy," he said in a choked voice. "It's Bruce Morrison. He's a pharmacist."

Which meant, Joe thought with a sickening jolt, that the bastards had likely gotten Louise too. Which meant they'd kidnapped Little Stevie. Or done God knew what to him. Joe thought again of the arm Scarface had lobbed at them. The flashlight beam quivered in his hand.

Joe spoke through clenched teeth. "Darrell, we've gotta go now. We—"

A high-pitched, ululating shriek sounded behind them. Joe leveled the flashlight down the center aisle in time to spot a headless body jarring toward them, the thing without arms or a head but somehow moving anyway.

"Mother of God," Copeland murmured, and he stepped in front of Joe.

Joe realized a second too late what was happening, spotted the figure behind the headless corpse bearing it along. The tattoos festooning the forearms, the gray-black mane of hair.

Shannon heaved the body at them, but Copeland's big left arm reached up and batted it aside as though it was nothing more than a misguided sparrow. Copeland brought the barrel of his .38 to rest six feet from Shannon's chest. The tattooed man's eyes bugged out in an expression of comic fright. Except before Copeland squeezed the trigger there was a movement to their right, a terrible whistling noise, and the stomach-churning sound of a blade cleaving flesh and bone.

The unfired gun slapped the floor still clutched in Copeland's right hand. Copeland sank to his knees and gaped at his severed arm. An appalling amount of blood gushed out of Copeland's shoulder.

Before Scarface scuttled into the darkness, Joe caught a glimpse of the scarlet machete blade, saw the way the man was grinning. Joe wanted to shoot Scarface, wanted to kill him worse than he wanted anything in the world. But Scarface was gone, eaten by the dark.

Shannon, however, was still standing there admiring Scarface's handiwork.

The Maglite twitched in Joe's hand and lit up the tattooed man.

His gorge clenching, Joe brought up the gun and fired at Shannon. The first slug hit the tattooed man in the right shoulder and spun him sideways. The second vaporized his left ear, the gruesome hole that opened there large enough to jam a fist through.

Shannon dropped to his knees as Joe turned to Copeland, who was grasping his hemorrhaging wound with his remaining hand. Blood was spraying through the police chief's stout fingers, his friend's eyes already taking on a distant glaze. Joe was about to undo his belt to make a tourniquet when the machete whipped down again. Gasping, Joe shrank away from it, but not before the sharp blade had split him from nipple to abdomen. The white-hot blast of pain was so intense that the gun slipped from his fingers. Falling backward against the edge of a pew, he patted the slit in his flesh, decided it was fairly shallow.

Joe shot a frenzied glance toward the gun he'd dropped, but it was already gone. He'd thought it had fallen beside Copeland, but evidently it had tumbled away or been knocked beneath a pew.

He looked up in time to see a new attacker bearing down on him, this one swinging a machete too.

Joe just had time to throw up his arms when the chapel erupted in a fusillade of gunshots. The wielder of the machete – Joe realized it was the Camaro's driver, the pale-faced man with the saggy jowls – jittered in place, his head whipping up and down as if he were fervently agreeing with something Joe had said, and then the man slumped forward onto Joe, the machete clunking to the ground. Joe let the man bang headfirst onto the floor, and though he was screaming now, Joe didn't think the man would scream for too much longer.

The guy's blue-jeaned buttocks were a horrorshow of what looked like ground chuck. Copeland had shot the man in the ass at least five times.

Copeland lowered the gun – the one Joe had dropped – to his side. He'd shot the man left-handed, but Joe supposed it was tough to miss at point-blank range. Joe reached out to support Copeland, but Copeland slouched sideways against a pew. Joe noticed as he knelt next to his friend how the floor around them had become a viscous crimson lake.

Joe fumbled for his belt, but he saw it was useless. Copeland mumbled something, but his face had gone a sick ashen color, the lips a pale mauve. Still, Joe tried to encircle the bleeding stump with his belt. But the goddamned thing kept slipping on the slick shoulder, and there wasn't enough of Copeland's arm left for the belt to snag hold of. With tears stinging his eyes, Joe finally got enough of the remaining limb to draw the belt tight, but of course there were no holes in that part of the belt for him to keep the thing cinched. Moaning, he wrapped the belt double around the stump, and as he did he heard several sets of footsteps approaching. *Not the whole congregation,* he thought. Not yet. But four or five people at least. Too many for him to defeat by himself.

Still, he got the belt fastened and made a grab for the gun Copeland had fired. His fingers had just brushed the grip when a booted heel descended and crunched down on Joe's fingers. Joe yelped and attempted to jerk his hand away, but the heel ground deeper, bouncing a little, and Joe did the only thing he could do, which was paw at the big boot. Someone seized his hair from behind and hauled back on it. Joe howled in pain, the roots of his hair tearing free and his hand still pinioned under the heavy, grinding boot.

The light in the chapel shifted, reformed. Someone had retrieved his Maglite, and evidently, Joe saw through bleary eyes, the main door had been opened. Joe reached back, slapped at the hand grasping his hair, but then a granite fist appeared from nowhere and crashed into his nose. Joe let out a garbled moan and fell, only distantly aware that the boot had been removed from his hand. He lay on his side, writhing and pressing his good hand to his face. He lay like that for a time, and when he opened his eyes again, he saw that the chapel was brighter now, or at least relatively so. He could now see the raised area at the front of the chapel, the tapestries dangling over what Joe now recognized as a bed.

It was larger than a normal bed, which might have been why Joe hadn't identified it earlier. Big enough for several people to fit onto at once. Joe didn't want to dwell on the idea, but it was difficult not to when there were naked people striding toward it, men and women of various ages and sizes. Joe recognized a couple of them from the graveyard, but he didn't linger on their nude forms for long.

Because Sharon Waltz was slinking toward him down the center aisle.

Sharon wore a skimpy black dress, the most revealing outfit Joe had seen her in yet. And that was saying a lot. He already felt like he knew her anatomy better than he knew his own.

The translucent dress swished an inch or so below her crotch. The neckline began in the general area of her ribcage, her nipples peeking at him over the fabric like the pink eyes of a cornered possum.

To Joe, she had never looked more revolting.

Yet she vamped down the aisle, moving for all the world like men were chucking tens and twenties onto a stage and begging her to disrobe. Her eyes were fixed on Joe, her look telling him she'd won, she'd gotten her revenge.

It was too much, so he glanced down at Copeland, then wished he hadn't. His friend was hardly breathing, the big body moving only a little bit more than the pews next to which it lay.

The lump in his throat choking him, Joe looked up, saw that Sharon had produced a long carving knife. She hadn't had it a moment ago, and Joe didn't care to speculate where she'd been hiding it. Next to her were two of the men who'd assaulted Joe: the bronze, muscular bald man whose boot had mangled Joe's right hand, and Scarface, his frame just scrawny enough to avoid being shot by Copeland. Joe's scalp was still screaming from the job Scarface had done on him a moment ago. He reached up and fingered the hair there, and when he inspected his fingers he saw they were bloody. Scarface had ripped a good-sized clump of hair from his head. Jesus, like a divot of sod chunked out by a hack golfer.

Scarface and Baldy flanked Sharon now, the men polar opposites physically. Scarface looked even taller and uglier than he had that day on the bridge, but that might have something to do with the blood riming his mouth. Baldy, his dark skin gleaming like polished leather, was even more muscular than Joe had previously thought. The guy had squiggled veins in his biceps as thick as garden hoses, and the scowl on his face told Joe how much he'd enjoy using those biceps to squeeze Joe's head until it popped off like a bottle cap.

Of course, if Sharon reached him with the carving knife first, Baldy wouldn't have that opportunity.

Sharon brandished the knife, its wicked blade catching the orange light that now seemed to engulf them. Joe glanced about and saw that several of the cult members were bearing lanterns, the kind that ran on kerosene. To Joe, with the black décor and the swaying orange lights, it felt like some kind of Halloween celebration gone bad. All they needed were some masks and some pumpkins, and they'd be all set. Sharon sure looked ready to carve something up.

Joe remembered his puny pocketknife, but he had no idea where it had gone. Probably lost in the scrum. Not that it would've done him much good anyway.

Copeland suddenly convulsed, then set to coughing. The sound of it hurt Joe's heart, and though he knew it meant his friend was still alive, he knew Copeland wasn't long for the world. How much blood could a body lose and still draw breath?

The one Joe thought of as Baldy bent down and inspected Copeland's face. Baldy pinched one of Copeland's eyelids, and yanked it roughly up. Joe caught a glimpse of Copeland's eyeball, which seemed not to register anything, much less the vicious weightlifter giving him an impromptu eye exam.

"Gimme the knife," Baldy said. His Irish accent was even thicker than Shannon's had been. There was a slur to his words too, though Joe didn't believe it was from drinking. No, he was sure it was the man's normal voice.

It reminded Joe of the tapestries hung over the stage. There was darkness and sadism and carnality in the sound, the type of voice you imagined in your nightmares.

"Let's see what's inside here," Baldy said, and before Joe could react, Baldy reached down and ripped open Copeland's shirt.

"Don't touch him," Joe said and made a grab for Baldy.

But it was apparently what the man had been hoping for. The moment Joe's good left hand groped for the knife, Baldy flicked it toward him. The blade plunged between Joe's pinky and ring finger and sliced him halfway down the length of his hand. Joe groaned as the blade tugged free, and before he could pull away, Baldy whickered the knife at him again, this time slashing him from one side of the chest to the other, so that as Joe collapsed and took stock of himself, he saw that the two rips in his clothing and flesh formed a jagged burgundy cross. The blood from the vertical slit, the one meted out by the saggy-jowled man and his machete, had begun to congeal, but the new wound bubbled and trickled like a jubilant forest creek.

"Where was I?" Baldy murmured. "Oh yeah..." And he sliced into Copeland's undershirt.

Joe rolled over with a mind to intervene – Baldy could cut him again for all he cared, but he'd be damned if he allowed the son of a bitch to increase Copeland's agony in these last moments – but something hammered him in the lower back. Christ, right in the kidneys. Joe landed on his side, the tears streaming from his eyes. The black chapel had looked hellish enough upon entering, but now it seemed as if it really was hell on earth. With an effort, he turned and gazed up at whoever had kicked him.

At first he thought he was seeing double, but upon further consideration, he realized there really were two women there. They both had long, frizzy hair, gray for the most part, but with enough brown for Joe to imagine how the women had looked when they were younger. They were identical twins, from their weirdly shining faces to their grungy bohemian dresses, which reminded Joe of the quilts his grandma used to sew. He had no idea which of the women had kicked him, but it was the one on his right to which his attention was drawn.

Maybe because she was grasping a decapitated head.

And not just any head, Joe realized with a new lurch of sorrow. Louise Morisson's. As sad as that was, Joe recognized that most of his feelings centered on what it meant for Little Stevie. Even with Bruce Morrison dead, Joe had clung to the hope that Louise and Stevie had gotten safely away. But now that he knew for sure it had been Louise's headless body out of which Shannon had fashioned a human shield, there could be no doubt that the little boy was either held captive by these monstrous people or worse.

But Joe didn't want to think about that possibility. Not yet.

There were wet, squelching sounds emanating from the direction of Baldy and Copeland. The chief was still making noises, but they were scarcely human, strange ragged snuffling sounds that reminded Joe of when his daughter had suffered from the croup. But Lily had recovered.

Baldy may as well be operating on a corpse.

Joe looked up, saw Sharon leering down at him.

"You don't like that, do you?" Sharon asked.

Joe said nothing.

Baldy straightened, his bronze arms gory up to the elbows. He slapped something onto the floor in front of Sharon.

Her grin broadened. "Our police chief had a big heart."

This was met by scattered peals of laughter. Joe closed his eyes and choked back a sob.

"Hey," Sharon snapped. "Hey—" She smacked him in the face. "Come on, open your goddamned eyes!"

Someone seized Joe's face and squeezed, someone much stronger than Sharon Waltz – unless Sharon had suddenly taken up steroids.

Joe opened his eyes. Baldy's face was inches from his. "Listen to the woman," he demanded in his guttural Irish voice. "It's the least you can do after taking her little girl."

Joe stared up at Baldy. "Her little girl did it to herself."

Sharon elbowed Baldy out of the way. She reached down and shook Copeland's heart in Joe's face, spattering him with blood. "I should make you eat this."

Joe closed his eyes. The grin on Sharon's face was too much to take. If the devil was real, Joe decided, the bastard had nothing on Sharon Waltz.

"Look at me," she growled. "Open your eyes, you daughter-killing motherfucker."

Joe didn't respond.

"Look at me!" Sharon screamed.

Joe opened his eyes. As his vision swam into focus, he saw how her nails had been filed into wicked points. As if they'd needed any sharpening.

Sharon nodded at him. "Not so uppity now, are you, Crawford? Not so superior."

Joe's voice was almost a whisper. "I never said I was."

"*The hell you didn't!*" Sharon screeched, her voice breaking a little. "You set out to destroy my life that day at the gas station! You got into our business, you went where you didn't belong. And my poor girl paid the price. My poor…" She faltered, her face convulsed with anguish.

"It was for the best," someone said quietly.

Sharon's eyes flared into excess lunacy. She whirled on the speaker, her fists clenched with rage, the tip of the knife trembling like a dowsing rod. "It didn't have to be my Angie!" she yelled. "It didn't have to be my little girl!"

Joe saw the man facing Sharon, a surprisingly distinguished-looking man. Like Grayman, the guy's face was only slightly marred by age, yet the white hair and liver-spotted hands gave the impression he was in his late seventies or early eighties.

"More than fifty years had passed," the man said, his voice almost gentle. "Had your daughter not undertaken the rite, our sect might have died out."

"That's a lie," Sharon said. "Someone would have done it."

"Who?" the man asked.

"It doesn't matter, does it?" Sharon answered, her voice rising hysterically. "Because this bastard—" pointing the carving knife at Joe's face "—decided to make the decision for us. He decided my baby would be the one to die."

The man nodded. "And he will suffer for it."

"Not enough," she said. "It won't be enough."

Sharon spun toward Joe, jabbed the knife into his shoulder. Joe jerked away, but not before the tip punctured his flesh.

"Don't like that, do you?" Sharon said, eyes gleaming. She jabbed the knife again, this time nicking him just under the jaw.

"That's enough," someone said.

But Sharon loomed closer, the bloody knife hovering nearer and nearer Joe's throat.

"*SHARON!*" a voice thundered from behind them.

Her eyes narrowed to slits, her mouth twisted momentarily into a snarl. Then the look went away and she bowed her head like some obsequious cur. Somehow, this expression was more ghastly than her previous one had been, because at least the hatred in her face had been authentic. This...this expression was practiced and calculating. The look of a cunning monster biding its time until the best opportunity for the kill presented itself.

Sharon receded, and in her place Grayman appeared. To Sharon, he said, "We will not do it here. We must maximize its power."

"He doesn't deserve to live another second," she answered in a low, quavering voice.

"That isn't for you to decide," Grayman said. "The Mother has spoken, and we must obey her wishes."

Joe again caught that look of naked loathing on Sharon's face, but this time it was even more fleeting. Apparently remembering her place, she bowed her head and said no more.

"We have much to do," Grayman said, circling Joe to stand between him and Sharon. "The chief's car must be taken far away. His body must be hidden."

Joe couldn't resist a glance down at Copeland's motionless body.

Grayman was looking at Joe, but Joe knew it was the entire congregation the man was addressing. "Tonight will be the greatest St. John's Eve since Antonia's passing. Our restoration will be complete."

Enthusiastic voices echoed their assent. Joe realized the whole chapel was now clogged with lunatics. The temperature in here, muggy to begin with, was now sweltering.

Grayman continued, "Kevin will ensure the site is ready. Won't you, Kevin?"

Joe heard his former employee, though he couldn't see him with the cult members so tightly massed, answer, "Yes." Joe couldn't tell if Gentry was just being respectful or if he was sick to his stomach; either way, the enthusiasm in his voice was several ticks below that of the other ghouls.

If Grayman noticed or was bothered by this, he didn't let on. He smiled down at Joe. "Have you figured it out yet, Mr. Crawford?"

Joe grasped his bleeding hand. "I've figured out that you all are sick sons of bitches who are a blight on humanity."

"But don't you see?" Grayman said in a wondering voice. "Don't you see how close you came to reaping the delights of our way of life?"

"You mean chopping off heads? Cutting people's hearts out?"

"Our people have been awaiting the sacrifice," Grayman said. He favored Joe with a mordant smile. "After three centuries, one becomes rather fond of living."

Joe glanced from face to face. The twin sisters. The distinguished older man. Scarface. Baldy. "You're saying all these assholes have been alive that long?"

Grayman laughed softly. "Not everyone, no. Sharon is new to our family. But she is a member of one of the oldest bloodlines in—"

"I know all about Antonia Baxter," Joe interrupted. "The crazy bitch who burned up her own children."

Grayman's face went tight with fury. "Don't you dare speak of her that way. She was a goddess. An ethereal being who purchased the lives of her followers with her love."

"Ethereal being, huh? Then why'd she murder her kids?"

Grayman looked amazed. "What an absurd idea, Mr. Crawford. She didn't murder them. They sacrificed themselves willingly."

Joe only stared at him.

"That's right, Mr. Crawford. Those kids were special. They climbed into the fireplace on their own. They doused themselves with gasoline. And the oldest child struck the match."

"Why the holes in the fireplace wall then?" Joe demanded. "Why were they cuffed?"

Grayman spread his hands as though the answer were self-evident. "Because they knew they'd be tempted to extinguish the flames."

"That's the most horrible thing I've ever heard."

Grayman shook his head. "It's simple, really. There are two requirements for renewal. The willing sacrifice and the culling of the heathens."

"Culling," Joe said, the word tasting bitter in his mouth. "You mean slaughtering."

Grayman's face remained serene. "Ask your questions, Mr. Crawford."

"Who are the heathens? Fifty years ago it was the city council members and their families. Who's it gonna be this time? The Morrisons? Harold and Sadie Hawkins? Me and Copeland?

Grayman merely watched him.

Joe's breath caught in his throat.

Grayman nodded. "You're right to be frightened, Mr. Crawford. Because tonight, you, young Steven…perhaps even your wife and daughter will be sacrificed to ensure we live on."

Joe fought back the surge of panic. "You can't touch Lily."

"She's been prepared, Joe."

"What the hell are you—"

"We had to use ashes from someone related to Lily. We probably should have burned you, but that wouldn't have been as enjoyable."

"You're not making sense."

"It was easy, Mr. Crawford. We visited the cemetery. Where your son's ashes were stored?"

Joe remembered the columbarium then, the small building in which loved ones stored their urns. He realized why the urn Sharon Waltz had carried that day looked so familiar. And then it all came crashing back on him. Michelle's miscarriage. Their baby boy only six weeks away from birth. And then the blood and the horror, and eventually the cremation. His son – Ben, they were going to name him – would have been five years old had he lived. But he hadn't. And these ghouls...these *monsters* had...

"You son of a bitch," Joe said.

"But it was necessary, Mr. Crawford. Someday your daughter will take her own life. If, of course, she lives that long."

Joe was screaming then, tearing at Grayman, but there were a multitude of hands on him. Battering him, bashing his head on the floor. Joe resisted for as long as he could, swearing to Grayman he'd kill them all. But soon his resistance waned.

The last thing Joe saw before losing consciousness was Copeland's face staring sightlessly at him, the chief's mouth open like a dark red cave.

CHAPTER NINETEEN

Joe awoke slowly, and as he did he realized several facts in rapid succession. One, he was moving, albeit gradually. *It must be vertigo*, he thought, dizziness brought on by the beating he'd sustained from the mob of cult members. Secondly, he became aware of several terrible pains. His left hand. His right. The cruciform gashes on his torso. The puncture wound in his shoulder. But his head ached worst of all. He wondered how many knocks he'd endured before he'd finally gone under. Had they disfigured him in their assault? Did it matter?

The third revelation that Joe experienced was even more disconcerting. He'd been stripped of clothing.

Joe opened his eyes and blinked at the faint amber glow. He didn't know where he was, but the ornate trim girdling the ceiling looked familiar. There were chains hanging down around him, all of them fastened to something directly above his navel. He had no idea where they'd taken him, but it sure as hell wasn't the black chapel. Joe's hearing was muzzy, but he distinguished several voices, people engaged in casual conversation.

No, he thought, that wasn't quite right. People were talking, but their voices were louder than normal. As if they were excited about something or nervous or both.

Groggily, Joe raised his head and saw people seated around a large room. Joe saw, beyond a middle-aged couple in black robes, an immense stone fireplace. Joe realized where he was.

The Baxter house.

Unbelievable, Joe thought. They'd driven him all the way from that accursed chapel in the woods and deposited him in the house next door to his, the place he'd been renovating for the past two months.

Joe made to sit up, but as he did he realized his hands were bound. No, not bound, he saw with a sidelong look – manacled. Each wrist, he saw, was restrained by a metal clasp. And the clasps, he realized as his chest began to tighten, were grafted to a metal platform, one that distended from the ceiling by chains.

What had Bridget Martin said? *This is a specialty item.*

You gotta be kidding me, Joe thought.

He was caged in the sex swing.

He closed his eyes and forced himself to remain still. If anyone had noticed he was awake yet, they weren't letting on. Which was fine by Joe. Despite the fact that he was naked, he didn't expect they wanted to use the swing for anything erotic. Not if the way they'd treated him earlier was any indication.

Okay, he thought, doing his best to control his breathing. *Okay. They have you tied down on some specialized swing, and they've told you they plan to sacrifice you. They must be batshit crazy, but deep down you're starting to believe Grayman's story. Or, at the very least, you're certain* they *believe it, which comes to the same thing.*

You're in a world of trouble.

Joe suppressed a terrified moan.

I don't want to die, he thought. *It comes down to that. I don't want to die. Of course, I don't want Michelle or Lily or Little Stevie to die either, but the fact remains, I don't want to die tonight.*

Joe clenched his aching fists. *So do something!*

Incredible suggestion, he thought. *Like what?*

As subtly as he could, Joe tested the manacles.

The clasps held firm, the edges sharp enough to split his skin if he pulled any harder. He tried his legs, but the effect was the same. The steel only permitted him a centimeter or so of movement. There was no chance of slipping free of his fetters.

Joe felt the onset of panic. He'd always been a trifle claustrophobic, which sometimes made his profession challenging. He hated wriggling into crawlspaces or even cramped attics. He'd always made Shaun or Gentry complete those tasks.

At thought of Kevin Gentry a fresh wave of fury swept over him. Gentry had led them out to the commune like a Judas cow. Only Gentry was still living, and Copeland was dead. The memory of Baldy mutilating Darrell's dying body came back to him, made him grit his teeth and tremble with rage.

"He's awake!" someone called.

That's right, Joe thought grimly. *I'm awake. Now let me out of this cage so I can go down fighting.*

Joe opened his eyes and stared up at the eyehook he'd installed. He wished he'd done a sloppier job. But even if he could get the swing moving, there was no way it would tear free of its mooring.

"Tell her it's time," someone said.

"Should I get Grayman?" a male voice asked. This one was familiar. Joe craned his head around to identify the speaker and saw with a new surge of betrayal that it was Shaun Peterson.

Shaun turned and saw Joe staring at him. Shaun flushed and looked away.

"Why?" Joe croaked.

"Don't talk to me," Shaun said. "We've got nothing to say to each other."

"Speak for yourself," Joe said, his voice rasping like sandpaper. "I wanna know how long you've been with them."

"It doesn't matter," Shaun said, sounding near tears now. "What matters is I figured out the way things were."

"You listened to that moron Gentry, in other words."

Gentry stalked forward and stood between Shaun and the swing. "This is gonna be a pleasure," he said. "I hope she lets me do the honors."

"You know she can't," someone answered. "She has to be the one."

Gentry opened his mouth, shut it. Perhaps to save face he said, "I can't wait," before rejoining the milling people.

Joe lifted his head to examine the Martins' expansive living room and was struck by how normal it all looked. Other than the black tapestries now hung on the walls and, of course, the man lying suspended in the middle of the room on some souped-up sex swing, the event could have been a dinner party or some kid's high school graduation open house.

But then he saw Bridget Martin, and all thoughts of normalcy vanished. She was draped in a satiny black gown, the thing opaque but the material so malleable that every detail of her figure was outlined with breathtaking clarity. And though Joe had already seen the woman naked in the shower – a sight that remained emblazoned in his mind no matter how he tried to purge himself of it – she was somehow even more alluring now. In her stunning red hair was threaded a laurel wreath, giving her a look both youthful and ancient. It made Joe feel as though he'd time-traveled to an era when pagan rituals sustained entire communities, a time when people were held in thrall by superstition and magic.

The crowd moved away from Bridget as though she were a goddess.

"All bow," Grayman said.

And to Joe's amazement, everyone in the room genuflected before her, even Shaun and Gentry.

Good Lord, he thought. *They've been converted. Converted utterly.*

Joe's neck ached from lifting it for so long, but the spectacle around him was so captivating that he forced himself to keep watching a few moments longer.

Bridget stood before the great fireplace now, the four-foot-high blaze seeming to surround her and dance around her sinuous form. She spread her arms, taking in the entire assembly, and smiled a sphinxlike smile.

"We serve only you, Holy Mother," Grayman said.

Looking pleased, Bridget nodded. Then she approached the swing and gazed down at Joe. Her green eyes seemed to shine in the firelight. "Hello, Mr. Crawford."

"You're the one," he said.

She raised her eyebrows.

"The one they've been talking about," he explained. "The one they worship, the new Antonia Baxter."

"She was more eccentric than I am," Bridget said, looking flattered but a little abashed. "I don't have the same taste for blood."

"That mean you're gonna let me go?"

Something somber and perhaps even regretful flitted through her face. "You know I can't do that."

"So you're gonna kill me," Joe said. "That about the size of it?"

She opened her mouth, seemed about to speak, then let out a soft sigh instead. "Joe..."

"How will you do it? With a knife? Or maybe a machete, like those psychos in the chapel?"

She looked away. The faces of the onlookers stared stonily back at her. Her gaze returned to Joe. "Will you complete the rites of coalescence with me?"

Joe didn't like the sound of that, but he said, "Depends on what you mean."

She smiled, looking less like an ageless goddess and more like a coy young maiden. "It means we make love."

Joe opened his mouth to tell her to go to hell, but he paused, his mind racing. He looked around at the clasps shackling his wrists, the chains surrounding the metal platform. "You propose to use this device as something other than a prison?"

She smiled. "Not on that, Joe. A bed has been prepared upstairs."

Beyond Bridget, Joe spotted Mitch Martin. He looked supremely uncomfortable in his starched dress shirt and navy blue sports coat, like he'd just arrived home from the office to find his wife the center of some satanic ceremony, one that culminated in her copulating with another man.

Bridget leaned her elbows on the swing, interlaced her fingers, and supported her chin on them. She smiled, awaiting his answer.

"I'm not saying I agree to it," Joe said cautiously, "but if I did fulfill my…well, duties, I guess, what would happen afterwards?"

Bridget shrugged. "We would still kill you."

"I see."

She leaned forward, the swing rocking a little with the weight of her elbows.

"Will you do it?" she asked.

Joe looked around at the cult members. They'd never let him escape this place alive. Dying upstairs was the same as dying in this cage. "Thanks for asking, Bridget, but I'd rather my last act on earth not be adultery."

Her grin evaporated. In its place came a look forged of cold steel, of agonized screams and pitiless laughter. Gazing into that face, he could understand why the maniacs here regarded her as something supernatural. She looked very much like a goddess with her flaming red hair and her supple, pearlescent flesh. The curves, the firm muscles of her thighs…most of all that unnerving emerald stare. Yes, Bridget Martin played the role of goddess exceedingly well. He couldn't imagine anyone – not even Antonia Baxter – playing it any better.

Bridget reached back, untied the strings holding up her gown. The black garment pooled around her feet, leaving her completely nude. Around them the crowd seemed to crackle with energy and what might have been adoration.

"You won't make love to me?" she said. "Not even now?"

He swallowed. "I'm a married man."

Her green eyes flared, then narrowed. Her lips twitched together, her jaw flexing. She said, "Mr. Grayman?"

Grayman detached from the crowd and hurried over to the fireplace. There was a bundle of twigs on the mantel Joe hadn't noticed before. They looked like they'd been wrapped with twine. Grayman plucked the twig bundle off the mantel and poked it into the fire. When he stood erect he was holding a blazing torch. Without pause he moved up next to Bridget, who extended an arm. Without taking her eyes off Joe, she accepted the torch and held it two-handed before her, like some nudist pyromaniac about to say her wedding vows.

"We honor Angela Waltz tonight," Bridget said. "She undertook the darker of the two rites, the sacrifice of innocent blood."

Several cult members nodded at this or bowed their heads, but very few actually spoke. The only sound Joe could hear was the pop and crackle of the twigs as they were consumed. Several orange embers singed the flesh of Bridget's fingers, but she didn't seem to mind.

"Now, all that is left is the consumption of the heathens."

"Yes," Grayman said, and several cult members looked up at this, the contagion of the moment showing in their bared teeth, their heaving chests.

Joe heard footsteps from the back hallway and wondered how many more people could fit in here. The room was vast, but there were already two dozen or more people packed shoulder to shoulder. But the crowd parted for the new arrival, and when he spied Baldy and what the man held, Joe began to shake his head.

It was Little Stevie. The boy was naked, though Baldy's beefy forearm covered most of the child's bare rear end. In his other hand Baldy clutched a machete. The burly man strode over to the fireplace.

"Wait!" Joe shouted.

Grayman nodded reassuringly. "The child is too young to know any better."

"You can't do this," Joe said, though his voice came out a harsh sob. "You can't hurt that boy."

"It is all for the renewal," Bridget explained. "Neither of you will have died in vain."

"It's all a waste of life," Joe cried. "Can't you see that? Me, Little Stevie, Copeland? Even Angie…she didn't have to do it to herself."

Sharon Waltz burst loose from the crowd. She wore a sleeveless white dress tied around the waist with hemp rope. The dress, of course, was cut very short, and there were flowers in her hair. She was no doubt going for the flower child look, but to Joe she still resembled a porn star with too much mileage.

"Don't you talk about Angie!" she shrieked. "Don't you talk about—" She broke off, seized Bridget's wrist, and thrust the torch under the swing.

All at once Joe realized what was happening.

The heat on the metal base was instantaneous, the flames so high beneath the swing they actually licked up over the edge. Joe moaned and began to thrash. He realized why the Martins had wanted double-paned windows and as much sound damping as Joe could provide.

It was to muffle his screams.

But he still screamed, screamed almost as much as Little Stevie was screaming. Baldy had turned with the boy and was extending him toward the fire. Beneath Joe the metal base began to burn his naked flesh. Joe smelled sizzling bacon and shrieked until his throat went raw.

No! he thought. This was beyond his worst nightmares. *Please help Lily to be safe*, he thought, the tears streaming down his cheeks. *Please help Michelle—*

There was a collective gasp and outraged cries as something happened behind Joe, some commotion he couldn't see from his angle. He supported himself on his elbows and heels because they didn't hurt as badly as his shoulder blades and his ass did on the molten surface. He couldn't help but let the back of his head touch the searing base, however. Soon his hair would ignite.

His body contorted that way, he could just swivel his head enough to spot, upside down, two women, both of them with guns extended. One of them wore a police uniform…Alyssa, he thought. That's what Copeland had called his fellow officer. Alyssa Jakes.

The other woman was Michelle.

★ ★ ★

"Let them go!" Joe's wife shouted.

"Now, ladies," Grayman said, raising a hand and stepping toward them. "You don't want to—"

His forehead disintegrated.

The crowd, which had been moving forward, stopped as one and watched Grayman drop to his knees, his eyes hinged wide in shock, and then slump forward face first onto the floor.

Joe glanced back and saw it had been Michelle who had shot him.

A man entered behind Michelle and Alyssa, and for a moment Joe thought one of the cult members had ambushed his saviors, would add them to the list of sacrifices. But the man wore a dark blue cop's outfit like Alyssa's, and he immediately rushed forward and pushed against the swing.

Joe hung sideways, nearly perpendicular to the floor, but he saw the way the flames surrounded the officer's ankles, the way they were already licking up his pant legs.

"*Shoot the chain*," the officer grunted.

Alyssa Jakes strode forward, but a cult member darted out of the crowd, and Alyssa was forced to swing the gun sideways and fire at the man from point-blank range. A gout of pulpy matter exploded out the back of the cult member's head, the man falling very much like Grayman had moments earlier. The rest of the cult members froze. Joe was coughing, retching, his mind beyond rational thought. He knew it was too late, but somewhere, buried deep beneath the strata of horror and panic, he marveled at Michelle, at his wife who'd returned to save him. She was aiming at the eyehook from which the swing distended.

A shot sounded and the swing gave way. The drop wasn't far, but the impact was bone-rattling. The heat was unbearable, the whole room a maelstrom of smoke and scorched flesh. Joe was dimly aware of his own shrieking, but he couldn't do a thing about it, couldn't do anything but thrash and kick and bellow in agony. The metal disk was still roasting him.

The whole world tilted, and Joe was suddenly face down on the floor. But at least it was cool wood, not the bonfire on which he'd been barbecued a moment ago. The cops and Michelle were trying to loosen Joe's bonds. Joe's left cheek was pressed flat with the weight of the swing bearing down on top of him, and from his vantage point he was able to see what had been beneath him moments before.

It was a copper fire pit, a large, circular one. The kind you'd buy at a hardware store or even Walmart. It had been kicked over, the burning logs starting several smaller fires in the living room. Joe wondered if maybe his imagination hadn't made things worse than they'd really been. Hell, he'd been envisioning the climactic scene from an old Christopher Lee movie he'd once watched, but though he knew his back was burned, it might not be as bad as he'd thought.

Joe's right hand popped free of its manacle, then his left. The circular disk of metal was lifted away from him, allowing blessedly cool air to swarm over his bare ass, his blistered back. His ankles popped free a moment later, and then the swing was removed, leaving Joe with his agony and gratitude. He pushed up on his elbows and felt Michelle's arms around him. She helped Joe to his knees, and though he was aware of his own nudity, his dick out in the open for the whole congregation of freaks to behold, he didn't much mind the exposure.

Anything was preferable to being burned alive.

Of course, if they all didn't get out of this house soon, they might still perish. One of the curtains on the right side of the room was glowing with flames, and several pieces of furniture had begun to flicker. The room was growing hazy with smoke.

Joe tried to say something but found his voice wouldn't work. All he could manage was another coughing fit.

Michelle was in his face, her eyes concerned moons. "What, honey?" she asked.

"Stevie," he managed to say.

Alyssa, her gun leveled at the crowd, glanced down at him. "That's the little boy, right?" She looked at Bridget and Sharon, who stood before the group. "Where is he?" Alyssa asked.

"The boy," Bridget said, "is none of your concern. Now get out of my house."

The male cop – he had a bushy mustache and was slightly overweight – chuckled, but he didn't lower his gun. "You're kidding, right? You guys try to burn these people alive in some sick ritual, and you think you're not going to jail?"

"I'm never going to jail," a voice from their left said, and Joe saw the distinguished old man from the chapel step through the crowd.

With a gun.

The cop with the bushy mustache just had time to shift his gun, but the old man opened up on him too quickly for the cop to even fire a shot. The slugs slammed the cop in the belly and chest, the man jagging like he was being electrocuted, and then the room devolved into pandemonium.

No sooner had the old man opened fire on the officer than the entire throng of cult members darted in different directions. Several of them started for the back hallway, but the flames had spread to the doorway, the ivory paint seeming to breathe with shimmering heat. Seeing one escape route blocked, most of them scampered up the steps. One of the many who took refuge upstairs, Joe saw, was Baldy, who still carried the sobbing little boy in his arms.

Bridget, Joe saw, was ushering her congregation up the steps, shouting, "Don't be afraid! Don't be afraid!" And despite the lunacy of the sentiment, almost all of them followed her command. But two cult members ignored her and instead headed straight for Alyssa.

She fired on one, then the other. They both dropped and clutched the middle of their chests.

At the same moment, the old man turned his gun on Joe.

Then the old man was flailing backward, his shot going wild, both Michelle and Alyssa pumping rounds into him. One of the cult members, a giant shaggy-haired man, sprang at Michelle, but Joe's wife was too quick. Her pistol fired just as the man's ursine body crashed into hers. The man came down on Michelle, the gun sent skittering across the floor and Michelle's head cracking the wood with appalling force, but then her attacker was scrabbling at his throat, the huge hole there spraying blood everywhere.

As he finally got to his feet, Joe saw another cult member had produced a knife, and though Alyssa Jakes had already impressed Joe as a serious ass-kicker, she wasn't fast enough to stop the man from slamming the blade straight into her belly. She fired her gun as the man stabbed her, but the shot hit the ceiling and the man pumped the knife into her gut four more times before Joe could grasp a log of firewood by the end that wasn't burning, pivot, and bash him in the head. Sparks burst from the man's skull as he stumbled back. Joe made to follow, but three more cult members – one of them a curly-haired twin – had regained their courage and doubled back to renew their attack.

Joe reached down, pried the gun from Alyssa's dying fingers, and brought it up just in time to shoot a boy no older than twenty who came at him with a fireplace poker. The slug punched the kid in the belly, and the boy went down screaming. Another cult member, this one a young woman – perhaps she was the gut-shot kid's girlfriend – swooped toward Joe and began clawing at his face. Joe kneed her in the gut and hoped that would do it, but the girl, stooped over that way, spotted her boyfriend's weapon, retrieved it, and came at Joe again with the fireplace poker, so Joe shot her in the face. She collapsed sideways and lay without moving.

"You...*coward*," the twin woman said to him.

Joe glared at her and saw murder in her eyes. He raised the gun, squeezed the trigger.

And heard a click.

The twin sprang at him, moving with the agility of a jungle cat. Joe swung a foot up and caught her in the chest. Her breath whooshed out, and she dropped like a sack of meal. He brought his foot up and stomped on her chest. The woman squealed and clutched herself. Joe glanced down at Michelle, who was pushing up to her hands and knees. In the melee her gun had apparently been lost. The cop with the bushy mustache, his gun was gone too, probably pinned under one of the corpses. Joe threw a pained glance at the mantel, and above that, the crisscrossing Celtic swords displayed there. If he couldn't locate a gun, he might have to use one of those.

But the smoke was thickening, the flames climbing a wall now. The old-fashioned settee the Martins had arranged under one of the eastern windows was ablaze, as were the tapestries dangling over it. Joe got his hands under his wife's armpits and hoisted her up. She moaned, muttered something unintelligible, but allowed him to lift her and carry her toward the doorway and the foyer beyond.

They moved onto the newly laid tile, and Joe was just reaching for the knob when a strident battle cry erupted behind them. He turned in time to see the twin he'd stomped on moments ago hurtle toward them, something grasped above her head.

The woman had noticed the swords too.

The silver blade whished down at them and damn near chopped Joe's head in half. He was just able to wrench Michelle sideways a millisecond before the heavy blade chunked into the front door. Fueled by a nauseated rage, Joe seized the twin by her curly hair and bashed her face into the door. He knew he'd likely immobilized her, but his arm moved without volition. He cocked her head back and then, as if swinging an axe, smashed her head into the door again. When it caroomed away, he saw a red spot on the ivory paint, but just to be thorough he smacked her head on the door three more times with as much force as he could muster. On the last strike he heard a sickening crunch and figured he'd just about obliterated the woman's skull. So he pivoted and heaved her limp body back through the foyer.

His whole body numb and trembling, Joe bent and shouldered his wife.

Michelle hardly moved as he carried her out of the Baxter house. He knew he should get her to a hospital – she'd sustained a concussion at the very least – but at the moment all he cared about was getting her somewhere safe. Joe was about to carry her to their house when he spotted the neighbors on the lawn across the street. They were the Murphys, he remembered. John and Jenny. Two kids, both teenagers, were gawking on the lawn with their parents.

With his wife slung over his shoulder, Joe strode toward them.

"We heard a commotion," Jenny said.

Her husband didn't speak, nor did the two teenagers, perhaps because they were struck dumb by the sight of a naked man, his body blistered and bleeding, approaching them with his unconscious wife draped over his shoulder.

"Take her inside and lock your doors," Joe said, pushing Michelle into John Murphy's arms. Murphy accepted the load, but looked to Joe like a largemouth bass that had inadvertently leapt inside a fishing boat.

"You have a gun?" Joe asked.

When Murphy only continued to gape, Murphy's teenage son said, "Dad has a twenty-two. He bought it to keep the raccoons out of our trash."

"Get it," Joe said. "Take Michelle down to the basement, turn off all the lights, and stand guard." He nodded across the street. "The people over there are the nastiest kind." He started toward the Baxter house. "Call the fire department too."

Jenny gaped at the house. Wisps of smoke were beginning to curl from the first-story windows. "There are people in there?"

"That's the thing about zealots," Joe said, moving away. "They don't have enough sense to save themselves."

Joe was crossing the street when the teenage girl finally found her voice. "Where are you going?"

Without turning, Joe said, "To get my son."

CHAPTER TWENTY

He was fervently hoping the sword would still be wedged in the front door when he reentered the Baxter house, and it was. He was also hoping the fire hadn't spread too much, and while it seemed this wish had been granted as well, the smoke still made breathing difficult. Joe's eyes began to water as he reached up for the sword handle, braced a foot on the door to give himself some leverage.

Something cracked the base of his skull. Joe sucked in startled breath and whirled to face his attacker.

Scarface.

The son of a bitch.

The wraithlike man still gripped the stout wooden block with which he'd brained Joe. Upon further review, Joe realized it was the small clock from the mantel. The clock looked undamaged from its collision with Joe's skull, but Joe's head ached.

He balled a fist and swung at Scarface, but the man danced away, smiling.

"We'll find your daughter," Scarface said. "We'll dine on her flesh."

Joe knew the bastard's words were good news, that Lily was alive and at least for now was beyond their reach. But the rage inside him swelled so fast he could hardly think. He swung again at Scarface, but missed wildly this time, and Scarface brought the sharp-edged clock down on the top of Joe's head.

He sank to his knees, half-dazed, and saw that he'd backed Scarface into the wall. Before the man could strike again, Joe grasped him by the legs and lifted. Though Scarface was tall and surprisingly strong, he was as light as a mannequin. Joe squatted him easily into the air. He expected the man to bludgeon him with the clock again, but Scarface astonished him by letting loose with a witchlike cackle, the man delighted by Joe's attempt at retaliation.

Keep laughing, Joe thought.

"I ate your friend," Scarface said through his laughter. "The cop. I ate his heart this afternoon."

Joe pivoted toward the door.

"I'll eat your daughter's heart t—" Scarface said but broke off when Joe let him straddle the sword. There was a neat slicing sound as the sword edge sank into the man's perineum. From the sound of Scarface's bellow of pain, the blade had cleaved his scrotum too. The man's weight unseated the sword from the door, but not before it had done enough damage to send Scarface to the tile in the fetal position, the man gibbering in agony and pawing at his bleeding undercarriage. Joe reached down, grabbed the sword hilt, and though he yearned to make Scarface suffer more for his treatment of Darrell Copeland, he knew the time he had before the Baxter house became uninhabitable was short. So he inverted the sword, grasping the hilt with both hands, and drove the point straight down into the side of Scarface's head. The keen blade entered through the man's ear, shot through skull and brain, and cracked the tile floor beneath. Joe wrenched the sword out and was about to move to the living room when a heartbroken wail filled the foyer.

At first he thought, irrationally, that it was Scarface doing the wailing. But the ugly bastard wasn't doing anything but convulsing and dying. Joe stepped forward and saw, in the short hallway between the foyer and the living room, a huddled shape near the floor.

The living twin had found her dead sister.

Through a swirling caul of smoke, Joe saw her face come slowly up, her eyes riveting on his. Her lips stretched back in a rictus of hatred.

"You miserable fucker," she growled and started to rise.

Joe stepped forward and kicked her in the chest.

The twin went tumbling backward and landed in an ungainly tangle of quiltlike fabric and bony limbs. But she was back up in an instant, leveling a knobby forefinger at him and cursing him like some witch in a cheap production of *Macbeth*. "You won't touch me, you coward! You won't dare kill both of—"

Joe swung the sword and lopped off her head.

There was a fountain of blood and a meaty thump as her head smacked the floor. It didn't roll or anything, the way heads did in movies, but the eyelids did flutter a little, like one last futile mating call from a barfly who'd never mastered the art of picking up men, even desperate ones.

The body crumpled, a maroon geyser spewing out over the floor.

Sidestepping the head and the body, Joe entered the living room, the whole area foggy now from smoke. He should've grabbed some piece of clothing off of one of the twins to breathe through, but it was too late for that now. Because he could see someone standing in the center of the room, a tall figure he first mistook for Scarface, despite the fact he knew Scarface wouldn't be getting up again. At least not in this life.

The smoke shifted, and Joe saw it was Shaun Peterson.

Shaun was whimpering.

"I didn't want to come down here," Shaun said, and from where Joe now stood, about eight feet away, he could see something at the young man's side, something bulky and incongruous at this particular moment.

"That a lamp?" Joe asked.

"It was all they had," Shaun explained. "They didn't think there'd be resistance. Said there wouldn't be much fighting."

"What you get for trusting a bunch of idiots."

Shaun sniffed, but the twin worms of snot dangling from his nostrils only quivered. To Joe they looked like diseased grubs. "They sent me down here to kill you, Joe."

"With a lamp."

Shaun's face contorted in a violent sob. "I don't wanna kill you."

"Then don't."

Joe continued on by the young man, leaving him in the center of the room clutching his pitiful weapon.

"I'm sorry!" Shaun moaned.

"Get out before you die," Joe said, nearly to the stairs.

"Okay."

"And Shaun?"

"Yeah, Joe?"

"Fuck off."

Joe mounted the stairwell, the sword resting on his shoulder like a baseball bat. In fact, he thought, rounding the first turn, the weight of the sword reminded him a lot of the bat he used to use in high school, a size 36 Adirondack. He wished he could go back and tell himself to use a lighter bat, but it wasn't until he was an adult that he realized that bat speed was far more important than size. Sort of like the penis rule. Michelle told him it was less about a man's size than his skill and endurance. Or maybe she just thought he had a little pecker and was making him feel better.

Joe was nearly to the top of the staircase when the first cult member appeared.

Joe cocked the sword, planted, and swung. The sword scythed through the cult member's leg just below the knee. The screaming person – Joe thought it was a man, but it was too damned dark to tell for sure – blundered down the steps caterwauling like a horny panther. Joe was splashed with a brief jet of blood from the man's hemorrhaging leg, but other than that he got past unscathed. A sentimental impulse in Joe suggested he double back and put the screaming man out of his misery, but then he remembered Copeland and decided there was poetic justice in letting the asshole bleed out.

Joe trudged up the stairs.

And was immediately beset by a pair of psychopaths. This time Joe had no time to react, so he merely thrust the sword straight out ahead of him. The first cult member impaled himself like an energetic hors d'oeuvre, but the force of the impact drove Joe back. Before he could recover, he was canting backward, hitting the stairs with his blistered back, the cult member having sunk all the way to the hilt atop Joe's sword. For a brief moment they came to rest like that, diagonal on the stairs with their feet higher than their heads, the cult member fixed on top of Joe like a lover too impatient to wait for a more suitable place to screw. Only this cult member, Joe now saw, was a middle-aged man with eye-watering halitosis, several missing teeth, and a wart the size of a swollen tick on his upper lip. And that wasn't even taking into account the gurgling cry issuing from the man's mouth or the rills of blood now streaming from his belly onto Joe's hands.

Joe bucked beneath the dying man's weight and heaved him up with his knees. The guy's body yawed down the steps, described a slow somersault, and the sword unsheathed from his flabby midsection like some lurid version of Excalibur. When the flabby guy's body tumbled down the stairs, Joe felt like celebrating, but he realized what a bad idea that was when he heard the power drill.

Shit, he thought. *That's what I get for leaving my tools at a work site.*

The drill bit darted at him like a screeching cobra. Joe forearmed the drill aside, but not before the edge of the bit tore into the meat of his elbow. It had only grazed him, but it had the effect of waking him up to just how lethal the drill could be. Lying on his back that way, he could no more use the sword than he could dance the foxtrot, so he did the only thing he could do, which was to seize the cult member's pant leg and yank. There was a wildly gesticulating shadow for a moment, then the cult member – it was either a woman or a long-haired dude – began to fall. Joe had hoped he or she would tumble down the stairs the way the guy with the wart had, but instead the assailant tilted sideways and landed on Joe's belly. The breath whooshed out of him, but he knew he had no time to feel sorry for himself. The man – he saw it was a man now, with hair like one of those eighties glam-rock bands – had kept hold of the drill. And despite the weird angle – the back of the dude's head was resting on Joe's belly like they were picnicking in a meadow and gazing at clouds – the man still managed to manipulate the drill in Joe's direction.

Relinquishing his hold on the sword, Joe gripped the shrieking drill with both hands and guided it away from his face. The cult member, who in the semidarkness reminded him a bit of Axl Rose, gasped in fear and began to fight Joe for control of the drill. But Joe was stronger than Axl, and goddammit, this drill belonged to him. He'd be damned if this scrawny psychopath would put a hole in his head with something Joe had purchased at Sears.

The whirling bit hovered nearer and nearer Axl's face. Evidently realizing the peril he was in, Axl made a shrill mewling sound. Joe's hands, wrapped on top of Axl's, depressed the trigger harder. Then the drill bit was entering the man's forehead.

The bit was a good one, a thick silver masonry bit, either a 5/8 or 3/4, and though its tip was wide and blunt, it bored into Axl's forehead without problem. The skin began to swirl into bloody ribbons, the curls spinning around the bit like May Day streamers, and though Axl thrashed to be free of the drill, Joe had both the leverage and the brute strength to drive it relentlessly downward. In short time the bit met the man's skull, and though the going became slightly more difficult, the drill scarcely hesitated. Joe used the bit for drilling plaster walls, and he figured a skull was spongier than plaster. The man's legs fluttered in a paroxysm of agony. Axl gave off fighting Joe for the drill and began trying to pinch the revolving bit, which only tore up his fingers too. But then the drill was piercing the dude's brain, ripping and tearing the gray matter in there, or whatever kind of matter Axl possessed. Gray mush, Joe figured.

When the drill sank all the way in, the man ceased struggling.

Joe shoved Axl off, the man's convulsing body slithering down the stairs like a sack of garbage. Joe rose and grasped the sword. He'd wasted too much time, and the smoke was growing thicker. Within ten minutes, maybe less, the house would be a chamber of roasted flesh and caving walls. He had to find Little Stevie.

He made it to the second floor without being attacked again, but he knew it wouldn't be long before a new wave of psychos arrived. He thought of Jonestown, of Waco. When a gang of extremists got their hive mind fixated on an idea, they never relented. They'd drink their Kool-Aid and defend their wrong-headed beliefs until the bitter end, which meant he had to be ready for anything.

But that didn't make it any easier to swallow the sight of the huge black snakes that slithered out of the room ahead.

The snakes reminded him of some nature show about the Amazon rain forests. Only these three creatures weren't slithering over palm fronds and swallowing hapless squirrel monkeys – they were writhing toward him over an unfinished wood floor in a historical home.

But they still looked hungry. Joe retreated a couple steps before he remembered the sword. His weapon didn't seem ideally suited to vanquishing the snakes, but it was better than a power drill. Or a lamp.

Joe had raised the sword to lop off the head of the nearest snake when something rustled behind him.

Diversion, Joe thought, but realized even as the cult member crashed into him that he was giving these assholes too much credit. They'd no more know how to stage a diversion like the snakes than they'd know how to solve advanced trigonometry problems.

But that didn't make it any less painful when he was driven into the wall.

The force of the tackle had moved him forward and to his left, so that the lead snake was now right under his bare feet. From the corner of his eyes he saw the thing dart at him, and an atavistic terror of the slimy creature made him hop backwards. His attacker had him clutched in a bear hug from behind, but the person was apparently too weak to hold Joe in place. Both of them went stumbling away from the snakes, who proceeded toward them serenely, as if they'd expected a pursuit like this. Joe and his attacker pitched backward, and as Joe's weight slammed down on the bear-hugger, the person grunted and broke wind. The arms lost their grip on his torso, and Joe scrambled around until he had the attacker pinned. It was a woman, he saw, and a fairly old woman at that. Her puckered mouth was tight in anticipation of Joe's next move, but he was so damned scared of the approaching snakes that he didn't have any idea what his next move would be. So he raised the hilt of the sword and brought the base of it down on the woman's face, her nose breaking like an egg. She screamed and covered her face. Joe pushed to his feet, saw the snakes were already slithering over her legs. The woman's shrieks doubled in strength, her limbs a sudden whir of terror. Joe sidestepped the long black snakes and managed to reach the next room, the room from which the snakes had issued.

Joe had an inkling of who was in here before he stepped through the door, but it was still a surprise seeing Bridget Martin lying naked on the king-sized bed.

Perhaps that had something to do with the four decapitated heads adorning the bedposts.

The room glowed with candlelight, and it was by this shifting auburn light that he made out Copeland's face, Louise Morrison's. Over each of Bridget's shoulders he spied another head, one Bruce Morrison's, the other belonging to the erstwhile Shannon, the tattooed man who'd chopped off Copeland's arm with a machete.

"Lie with me," Bridget said, and so insane was the request and so unexpected at that moment that Joe found himself starting to laugh.

But Bridget's languid smile never wavered. She traced the mounds of her breasts with delicate fingernails, her strong pale legs spreading wider. "We're both going to be consumed, Joe. We should make the most of our time."

Joe stepped into the room. There was very little smoke in here, but before long there would be plenty of it. "I thought you were supposed to be a goddess."

A nonchalant flick of the wrist. "I will be reborn."

He glanced right and left, but saw very little in the master suite other than the closed bathroom door, the nude woman on the bed, and the heads staring sightlessly toward him.

"Where's Stevie?" Joe asked.

"Does it matter?" she replied, a hand sliding to her bright red snatch.

"Hell yes, it matters."

"Your priorities are poorly ordered."

"Says the woman who's diddling herself while her house burns down around her."

"Come to bed."

Joe went to her, positioned the blade against her throat. "Tell me where the kid is."

Bridget looked up at him like there wasn't a Celtic sword held to her throat. "Touch me and I'll tell you."

Joe didn't know what to say to that, and it didn't matter. Because at that moment a figure burst through the door of the master bath, a figure holding something long and slender aloft. In the moment before the object flashed down at him Joe identified it as a towel rod.

Mitch Martin's aim was off, so much so that the towel rod would have likely missed Joe even if he hadn't brought up the sword to protect himself. But the steel rod glanced off the sword and Mitch smashed straight into him. It knocked Joe back a foot or two, but not enough to steal his balance. Mitch had lost hold of the rod and was slapping at Joe's face now, flailing like a berserk schoolboy. Joe realized what he'd suspected earlier was true – Mitch Martin was jealous. His wife was beyond his control and obviously had a hankering for other men. And despite all the talk about rebirth and sacrifices, at the heart of it, Mitch Martin was nothing more than a cuckolded husband.

One of Mitch's blows broke through Joe's defenses and gave him a painful clout on the cheek. Gritting his teeth, Joe bunched his fist and aimed a fierce uppercut at Mitch's face. It caught him lower than he intended, but when Joe's fist crashed into Mitch's larynx, the well-dressed stockbroker squealed like a kicked puppy. Clutching his throat, Mitch went blundering toward the dresser, and in his periphery Joe saw Bridget rising from the bed, her body still gliding with the languorous ease Joe found so off-putting. He thought of interrogating Mitch to see if the man would reveal Stevie's whereabouts, but he suspected that would be a dead end. And anyway, Mitch was turning to face him again, his jealous rage apparently endowing him with superhuman powers of recovery.

Mitch lunged at him just as Joe swung the sword, bringing it around as though he were hammering a high fastball. The blade snicked off three of Mitch's fingers before slicing through the sides of his open mouth. Mitch brought both his good hand and his mangled one to his lips, garbling out strange oaths Joe couldn't hope to translate. He knew he should put the man out of his misery, but his nerve suddenly failed him. The sight of the mutilated man turned his stomach, made him sick with dull rage.

A hand fell on his shoulder.

Joe whirled, the sword raised, and saw Bridget Martin smiling at him, the wantonness in her expression advertising plainly that it made no difference whether or not her husband was sobbing in agony a few feet away; she was still up for some good, smoky sex.

"Tell me where Stevie is," Joe demanded.

"When you kiss me," Bridget said. She cupped his naked sex. Joe batted her hand away.

A wet arm snaked around his throat from behind.

"*Goddammit,*" Joe grunted, twisting in Mitch's grip. With a hard shove, he sent the bleeding man stumbling away, but Mitch had no sooner regained his balance than he was back on the offensive.

"You stupid shit," Joe muttered and swung the sword. The blade went into Mitch's head at a diagonal and got lodged there, between the nose and the upper jaw. Mitch squeaked once, let out a long, squelching fart, and crumpled.

The sword was wrenched from Joe's grip. Though his gorge threatened to rebel at the sight of Mitch's disfigured face, Joe reached down to retrieve his weapon. His hands were sweaty, and as he tried to tug the sword free, his fingers kept slipping.

"Joe," a voice said.

Joe ignored Bridget, planted his foot on Mitch's twitching head. The blade started to slide out with a vile scraping noise, but the voice spoke his name again, much louder this time. Involuntarily, Joe turned and stared at the woman framed in the doorway.

But it was no longer Bridget.

CHAPTER TWENTY-ONE

The woman gazed at him. He knew it was still Bridget, yet there was something different about her, something fundamentally altered. And it wasn't just the hairstyle, though that had undoubtedly changed – how she'd managed to do that while he had his back turned he hadn't the slightest clue – but her facial structure was slightly more angular. Aquiline. And her green eyes...weren't they just a trifle larger? Joe thought they were.

"I wanted you to see me as I was fifty years ago," the woman who was not quite Bridget said.

Joe shook his head. "I need to find the boy."

"You need to acknowledge there are powers beyond your understanding."

"Look, just tell me—"

"Back in Kildare they called me Anna Blake, but when I settled in Boston, I changed my name."

Joe swallowed, peered deep into the woman's lambent green eyes. "Antonia?"

She smiled softly. "Yes."

He had not the slightest idea what to say, so he asked, "What'd you do to Bridget?"

"I am Bridget."

Joe could hear the crackle of the spreading flames. The odor of smoke was growing fearsome. "Where did that guy take Stevie?"

"For fifteen years I remained in darkness," the woman said. "And then I was reborn as Bridget Martin."

"Are they upstairs?"

"It doesn't matter."

He stepped closer, his grip on the sword tightening. "The *hell* it doesn't. I mean to get that child away from here."

"It won't matter, Joe. Even if you escape tonight, it won't matter."

He made to move past her. "I can't stand here and talk."

"Why do you think Sharon sprinkled ashes on your house?"

"Because she's a fucking lunatic."

The woman shook her head again, and this close Joe could smell her. Fir trees and soil and incense, and beneath all that, the indelible odor of ashes. Joe moved past her, grabbed the knob.

"Your daughter will become like Angela," the woman said.

That stopped him. Without looking up, he said, "My daughter is safe."

"Not from this. All the preparations were made. The ashes, the dolly, the invocation. Have you been having nightmares, Joe?"

Joe whirled and seized the woman by the throat. "*Where the hell is the boy*?"

When she didn't answer, only continued to smile at him with that same placid expression, he pivoted and slammed her against the wall, thrust the sword point to her voice box. Joe brought his face close to hers. The smell of smoke was all around them, stinging his eyes.

"Where did that son of a bitch take Stevie?"

But the woman said, "Lily won't know right away, but she'll suspect something about her is different, she'll—"

"Don't talk about my daughter."

"—become interested in our ways, our past. She'll gaze at the moon, develop an unnatural attraction to fire—"

Joe shook the woman, her head snapping back and forth. "I'll kill you now! Just like I killed the others."

But she pressed on, seemingly in no haste to comply. "She will burn herself alive, just as Angie did."

"*Goddamn you*!"

"That's what the preparations were for, Joe. The same rites were performed on Angie Waltz when she was a child."

"No."

"But her mother didn't think it would happen. And when the urge to immolate herself won out in Angie, her mother blamed you, blamed Copeland—"

"Where is Stevie?"

"—but Sharon made sure she got her revenge. Lily will die so that others may live. You can't save your daughter from her fate, Joe. Enjoy her while you still have her. The suicide urge will one day grow too strong."

He drove the sword point into her throat. The blade pierced her flesh, a rivulet of blood dribbling down her neck.

"Tell me," he said.

"Do you believe me?"

"Where's the boy?"

The woman closed her eyes. "Upstairs," she said.

Joe shoved her away, ripped open the door, and leaped back as something near the floor darted at him. The snake's head grazed his ankle, brought its darting tongue around for another strike. Gasping, Joe danced around it into the hallway. He swung the sword like a golf club. He missed the snake but apparently startled it enough to hold it at bay. It watched him balefully from the doorway, and beyond it he saw the nude woman appear. It was Bridget again – perhaps it had always *been* Bridget – and she watched him expressionlessly now, the smoke enshrouding her, making her look more than ever like some mystical being. Then she turned and moved to the bed. She lay down and folded her hands over her belly. The last glimpse Joe had of her was the beatific look on her face as she closed her eyes.

Joe turned and headed down the hallway.

Around him the second floor became a white-gray haze.

★ ★ ★

On his way toward the stairs, Joe passed several rooms. In each of them he saw a cluster of cult members seated on the floor, holding hands and muttering words he couldn't make out. The sight made him sick to his stomach, but on some level he supposed it was better to have them accepting a fiery death than attacking him like poorly trained kamikazes.

Joe mounted the stairs and within moments reached the third story.

In its dimensions the third floor was a low-ceilinged version of the living room. It was also an unfinished attic that reminded him of some artist's studio, and though Joe hadn't done much work up here – the roofing company had taken care of the new roof and the replacement of the warped joists – he knew the space well enough to guess where Baldy had taken the little boy.

But when Joe glanced into the rear dormer window, he saw that it wasn't Baldy who grasped the child.

It was Sharon who held Little Stevie on her lap.

The pair sat in an old rocking chair, the casement window next to them open and allowing in fresh air.

But moving closer, Joe saw that Sharon looked crazier than she'd ever looked, and that was saying a hell of a lot. Her makeup was smeared, the bizarre flower-child dress torn in several places. The child in her lap was crying, and Joe couldn't blame him. Sharon had the carving knife pressed to Stevie's throat.

From twenty or so feet away, Joe said, "Put him down, Sharon."

She tipped Joe a wink. "We've won, you know. Even if we perish here tonight, we'll be reborn. And you will burn with this house, just as your daughter will burn someday."

Joe glanced right and left, stole a look behind him. He was sure Baldy was up here lurking. The soulless bastard had been the one to deliver the child to Sharon. Which meant he could be hiding anywhere. Him and his machete.

"You're weak," Sharon said. "You've failed to protect your family, and you've failed to protect yourself."

Distantly, Joe heard sirens. He peered into the pooled shadows of the attic, saw the glints of nails the roofers had knocked through and not bothered to pound flat.

"I'm not weak," Joe said, "I'm only—"

But he never finished, because a shape flashed toward him, something big and screaming. The sword skittered across the floor as Joe and his attacker landed on the dusty wood. Joe thought at first it was Baldy, but then he realized Baldy would have used the machete. Whoever it was had Joe pinned down, had gotten a forearm under Joe's neck and squeezed him into one hell of a headlock. Joe's consciousness was already starting to dim. From far away he heard Sharon Waltz laughing, egging on the attacker, and perhaps it was this that galvanized him, that endowed him with enough energy to wrench down on the man's forearm and send him flipping over his shoulder.

The forearm came loose of his throat as the man smacked down in front of him. Joe pushed away, gasping for air, and saw Kevin Gentry scramble to his feet and prepare for another rush. Joe glanced to his left, realized the sword was a good eight or nine feet away. He wanted to behead this peeping bastard, but Gentry was coming at him already, the man's face a mask of vengeance. Gentry was feebleminded, Joe knew, but he had momentum and a good deal of strength. Before Joe could recover, Gentry was on him, so Joe did the only thing he could think to do, which was to let himself be tackled and then use his legs to lever the man up and off. When

Joe rolled back on his burned shoulders, white-hot spires of pain sizzled through his body, but he leg-pressed Gentry anyway, the man's wrath turning to confusion as Joe drove him toward the low, slanting ceiling. Then Gentry flinched and howled in pain, and after a moment Joe realized why. Gentry collapsed onto him, but his aggression was gone, eclipsed by the agony in his back. Joe stared up at the dripping nail points that had punctured Gentry's flesh. He pushed Gentry off and scrambled on top of him. He knew Gentry was hurting, but the wounds wouldn't be fatal. No, unless he took care of the shithead now, Gentry would be right back at him, endangering Joe and Little Stevie.

Joe wrapped his hands around Gentry's throat and began to throttle him.

At first Gentry's eyes bugged out, the severity of his situation perhaps finally dawning in his pea-sized brain. Then his sooty eyes shifted to something over Joe's shoulder, and Gentry's mouth split in an ugly grin.

Joe sucked in air and dove sideways just as the machete whooshed down. He didn't see Gentry's face in that last moment, but he was sure the man had looked as dumb and cowardly as ever as the machete plunged into the middle of his chest. Joe did see Gentry's arms and legs go ramrod straight, did hear Sharon bellowing in indignation. Most of all, he saw how furious Baldy was to have slain the wrong man.

Joe clambered over to the sword, grabbed hold of the hilt just as Baldy stood to extricate the machete from Gentry's gushing chest. Baldy tugged the machete free as Joe swung, but Baldy wasn't deft enough to block Joe's sword. It cleaved through the muscular man's left arm just above the elbow. Forgetting all about the machete, Baldy grasped his spraying stump and squealed like a hog at slaughter time. Joe cocked the sword again, noting as he did that Baldy seemed to have forgotten all about Joe's presence. It was just as well. Sharon shrieked at Baldy to *turn around, turn around*, but Joe was already letting loose with his hardest swing yet.

Baldy turned to run at the last moment, his broad back facing Joe, but the blade caught him in the side of the bicep, crunched through his humerus, and embedded six inches deep in his side. His huge right arm fell to the floor with a squishy thud. There was a gruesome whistling sound as the man's perforated lung struggled to take in air. Baldy slouched forward, Joe's sword slithering out of him with a wet slurp.

Thinking of Copeland, Joe decided to let Baldy bleed his last moments away.

"It doesn't matter," Sharon said. "You and your family will be dead soon."

Joe noticed how close Sharon held Stevie to the open casement window. The attic was swirling with smoke now, the air becoming noxious. Joe coughed into his arm, saw Stevie coughing too.

He stepped closer, the sword clutched before him. "My family's still with me, Sharon. You're the one whose daughter burned herself alive."

She whirled, her face wild with rage. "Don't you say that. Don't you dare talk about my baby that way."

"Your *baby*?" Joe asked, ten feet away now. "How about your *grandchild*? Doesn't he matter? Look at his face, for chrissakes."

"He's as much to blame as you," she spat. "My Angie would be alive if it weren't for the two of you."

Joe clenched the steel hilt. Despite the burns on his back and the fatigue and the smoke he'd inhaled, he felt a tremendous power surging through him. A breathtaking vitality. He said, "You're the one who let them use Angie."

A look of horror spread over Sharon's features. "*How dare you*? How dare you accuse me of…of…"

"Of letting them spread ashes around that tenement of yours? Of providing them with something of Angie's to use on a corn dolly?"

Sharon's smeared lips trembled. "I didn't…I would never—"

"But you did," Joe said, only five feet away now. "You did, you miserable bitch. Why'd you do it? So they'd let you back into the group? So they'd forget Angie's dad wasn't one of them?"

And now something ghastly came into Sharon's face, which contorted in the billowing smoke, the tears streaming down her cheeks.

Sharon's gaze hardened.

Joe reached for Little Stevie, but Sharon was too fast for him. With a crisp jerk the little boy was suspended out the window, Sharon's hands grasping him loosely about the armpits. Joe's stomach gave a sick lurch, and he froze where he was, his feet leaden and rooted to the floor. Behind him, smoke continued to flow up the stairwell, the room now draped in a misty white cowl. Joe coughed into his wrist, fought off the tingling in his throat, the deep burning in his lungs. God, like the worst case of bronchitis ever.

The wailing sirens drew nearer, but Joe had little hope the fire trucks would do them much good. The house was becoming an inferno.

Dangling three stories above the earth, Little Stevie screamed in terror, but his cries weren't nearly as intense now as they'd been that first day at the gas station. It was as though something had been removed from the boy. Something irreplaceable. Joe thought it could be the loss of his mother, but it seemed even deeper than that. A part of the child's psyche that had been damaged by all the trauma, a part that was beyond healing, beyond love.

"Don't come any closer!" Sharon shouted, but her voice was pinched with grief.

Joe had thought to snatch Stevie out of her hands, but now it would only take an infinitesimal error to send the child plummeting to his death. Sharon's body was turned mostly toward the window, though Joe could still see her profile limned against the unbroken tapestry of the night sky. Sharon's hands looked slick with sweat – either hers or Stevie's or both – and her head was bobbing up and down as though she were nodding off. But Joe knew it wasn't fatigue but sorrow that was draining her, and she was so far past caring about the child that his life and death were interchangeable.

Joe kept his voice low so as not to startle her. "Sharon, we need to get out of this house."

She only shook her head, mumbled something he couldn't make out.

He stepped nearer. "Sharon, it's—"

"It won't matter," she said tonelessly. "They never cared about me."

Joe hesitated. "That's right, Sharon, they never cared about you. They just used you and Angie."

She was crying now, mucus and slaver dripping from her chin. "I never thought it would happen," she moaned. "I never thought Angie would get burned."

Joe inched forward. "That's right. They used you. How could you have known it would happen? You just wanted acceptance. It was your grandmother's group after all, not yours."

The moment the words were out of his mouth, Joe regretted them. Because at mention of Antonia Baxter, Sharon's eyes shot wide, her face coming round to glare at him, her features drawn taut like a carapace of loathing. "They'll take her too, you son of a bitch. They'll take your Lily."

And to Joe's horror, Sharon brought a hand around to poke a forefinger in his direction. Which left the child supported by only one clawed hand.

Little Stevie started to slide.

Joe dropped the sword and lunged toward the window, his chest smacking the frame. Time seemed to stop as his hands darted through the aperture into the cool night. Sharon's knobby fingers were clenched around Stevie's armpit one moment, and the next her fingers were relaxing, the boy lowering almost gracefully into empty space.

Joe grabbed for the only thing he could – the boy's blond hair. There was an endless, soul-shattering moment when he was sure he'd missed, was sure the child was plummeting to his death. Then he felt the boy's hand slap weakly at the fingers cinched in his hair, the child obviously in severe pain, but no longer falling. He heard Little Stevie wail, and it was one of the most glorious sounds Joe had ever heard. He began hauling Stevie backward when a firebomb of pain exploded in his side.

Sharon had discovered the sword.

CHAPTER TWENTY-TWO

As the blade slid deeper into his side, pain spread through him like he'd never dreamed possible. He had no idea what organs the sword was shearing through, but he had no doubt the wound would be fatal.

At his ear Sharon was growling, "Feel *that*, you worthless fucker. Feel *that*, you sorry son of a bitch."

His whole body clenched in anguish, Joe dropped back away from the window.

With Little Stevie clutched to his chest.

The boy squirmed against him, and though the lancing pain in his side remained, on the floor here at least the air was a tick more breathable.

Sharon loomed over him. "You two can burn together," she said. And she made toward the stairwell.

Joe had a moment in which he was sure his body would not cooperate, that his limbs would no longer obey the commands his brain sent out. Then he twitched spasmodically, the boy on his chest whimpering, and he knew he still had life left in him. Joe reached down, grabbed hold of the blade, and thrust it away from his side. It slid out with a queasy *snick*, and looking down at the sword he realized Sharon must have jabbed it into him rather than running him through like a marauding Viking. It had penetrated maybe two inches. Not good, but hopefully not fatal.

He glanced askance and saw, through blurred eyes, how her gait canted and lurched as she drifted toward the stairwell. Joe recalled the slurry sound of her words, the demented look in her eyes and realized she was on something – alcohol, meth, Valvoline motor oil, something. She was almost to the steps, but even from here Joe could see the orange tongues of flame licking up the stairwell.

On his chest, Little Stevie was coughing. Joe realized he was coughing too, and soon it would be so bad up here you couldn't stop coughing. They had to get out of this furnace, but there was nowhere to go. They couldn't wait for the firemen. He supposed he could bust out the small window that bordered the street, but then what? It would take time for the fire truck to arrive, for the men to spot them, the ladder to be fitted into place. And they were down to perhaps one minute before they both asphyxiated on the smoke. Or were burned alive.

A violent cough racked Joe's chest, doubling him up and forcing the child to the floor next to him.

They might not even have a minute.

Joe glanced about the dim space as if seeing it for the first time. There was a dormer window on each of the four sides of the house. The front and back windows were the smallest, and the front one was strictly ornamental. The back window was cranked open, but they couldn't very well climb onto the roof. First of all, the roof could be ablaze already, and the fact was, there was very little roof there to begin with – perhaps four or five inches before the eaves trough began.

The windows on the east and west side of the house were larger, but they were also ornamental. Neither of them could be opened without shattering the panes, and on the east side there was nothing but concrete below.

Joe swallowed, wishing he had something to cover the child's mouth with. Little Stevie was coughing continuously now, the boy's face tear-streaked and pitiful.

Joe got up on hands and knees, glanced about desperately. Between him and Sharon, who was still standing at the top of the stairwell as though she were debating whether to chance it or not, lay the unmoving corpse of Baldy, the man who—

Joe tensed. Yes, he thought. It would have to do. If it didn't, it was still better than nothing.

Handling him as tenderly as he could, Joe hefted the child and rushed over to Baldy's prone form. He placed Stevie face down on the floor, reasoning the lower his nose and mouth were, the better chance he'd have of taking in a decent breath. Joe grabbed the tail of Baldy's tight black T-shirt and yanked it up. In moments, he'd wrestled it off the dead man, and though there was plenty of blood on it, there was more than enough fabric to serve his needs.

Lightning sizzled across the back of his neck.

Hissing, he whirled and saw Sharon Waltz's fingernails come flashing down at him again. He tried to avoid them, but the razor-sharp talons tore through the flesh at the base of his throat anyway.

Joe stumbled back, but she came with him. He realized with astonishment that she was laughing. Sharon's claws swept down, raked open his cheek. Blood slopped from the mangled trenches she'd dug in his face. His coughing grew uncontrollable.

But Sharon kept up her attack. It was as though she were immune to the smoke, and what the hell, maybe she was. Joe had long since ceased being flabbergasted by the behavior of these maniacs. Joe braced himself against one of the low-angled walls, made to fend off her assault. But he saw with dread that she'd given off the attack, had turned her back on Joe.

And was making straight for Little Stevie.

With a bellow of rage, Joe darted forward and launched himself at Sharon. He hit her like a battering ram, his shoulder squaring up the middle of her back and snapping her head backwards. They landed in a whir of limbs. Sharon spun around to claw at him again, but this time Joe snagged her wrists, slammed his head down into hers. Pain flared in his forehead, but Sharon's bloodcurdling squall told him he'd done the damage he'd been hoping for. She thrashed in his grip, but he hauled her to her feet, dragged her away from Stevie, whose little body juddered with coughs.

"*Let go of me!*" she snarled, kicking at him.

Joe planted, heaved her over his hip, and cast her into the blazing maw of the stairwell. Her warbling scream only lasted for a few seconds, but the sound of it echoed in his brain even after he reeled away from the jetting flames.

The third floor was so clotted with smoke now he could scarcely make out the tiny pink figure of the naked child. But he found Little Stevie, found him and wrapped him up in Baldy's blood-soaked shirt. It wasn't great, but it was the best he could do. Maybe the moisture of the blood would serve as extra protection.

Joe strode toward the eastern window, did his best to snatch one or two more decent breaths from the befouled air. To his left, in the direction of the stairwell, the floor sagged, then dropped away completely, the flames beginning to devour the attic. Through the turbid smoke, he couldn't even see the other side of the room, but he knew where the other dormer was, where the other window was situated. It was six feet high and began a foot from the floor. The dormer faced his house, but before that there were pine trees, the thick, cushioning needles lining their boughs.

Giving himself no more time to think about it – the very floor had begun to blister the soles of his feet – Joe started forward. It was awkward going with the boy bundled into his chest that way, but he had to get up a head of steam, had to propel himself out of the window, had to launch them both if they hoped to make it to the pines.

Joe halved the distance, picking up speed. The floor behind them fell away with a *whump*. Under the shirt the boy was coughing, but the spasms of his body had mostly abated.

Three quarters of the way there and it was an all-out sprint. A hole appeared in the floor ahead, but it wasn't directly in Joe's path. The window was only six feet away now, but it was still barely glimpsed, a navy blue obelisk that looked as though it would take a wrecking ball to shatter it.

Joe took one more stride, and as he pushed off the floor with all his might, he twisted his body around so he'd strike the window with the back of his shoulder.

For a split second, there was resistance against his shoulder, the flat chill of the glass. Then his body crashed through, sailing through dead space and continuing its revolution. He'd closed his eyes upon impact with the windowpane, but now he opened them, watched the shattered dormer as it seemed to rise into the night sky. Shards of glass glittered in the air around him, a few of them spinning like pinwheels, but the bundle against his chest and stomach had grown still, Little Stevie seeming to understand that, at the very least, they wouldn't be burned to death.

Joe had time to wonder if he'd leaped out far enough. If he'd fallen short of the trees, it was almost a certainty he would die of a broken neck, and there was a good chance the boy would perish from the impact too.

Then the first pine bough slapped his back, the needles puncturing his skin like metal skewers. He smacked the second branch. By the time they'd fallen two stories, their momentum had diminished, but Joe was still too heavy for the third branch they hit, which gave way with a bone-crunching snap. The concussion of the broken bough sent Joe's body tilting sideways. Eight feet from the ground he realized he might land on top of the boy.

With his last ounce of strength, Joe twisted his torso, shielding the child from the earth with his right shoulder and arm. They landed, the impact considerable but not, he prayed, fatal.

At least not for the child.

Little Stevie wriggled against him, the boy spluttering and gasping within the swaddled shirt. Joe's right side was totally numb, but after a good deal of effort, his left arm responded to his demands. He seized the black shirt, unwrapped the child. Joe coughed, tasted something hot and coppery on his lips, and though he knew it was a bad sign, he opted not to think too much about it now. Because the boy was coughing too, coughing violently.

But also, Joe saw with a leap of hope, sucking in breath. Drinking in the oxygen like he'd been buried alive. Which in a way, Joe supposed, was sort of the case.

As the shouts and, eventually, the footfalls drew nearer, Joe realized he'd closed his eyes, had perhaps even lost consciousness for a few moments. But when he opened them again he saw that the boy wasn't coughing much anymore, and further, the kid was staring at him.

Don't know if I'll be around for you, he thought but was unable to say. It was just as well, he figured. After being subjected to Sharon Waltz and the rest of the psychos, the boy probably welcomed the quiet.

Joe and Little Stevie regarded each other in silence. The boy didn't smile, but he didn't look afraid. And that was something, Joe thought.

That was something.

CHAPTER TWENTY-THREE

It took a good while for Joe to understand just what the doctors were telling him. His ears felt crammed with gauze pads, for one thing, so that the sounds he could make out were absorbed through a dense membrane of white noise. It reminded him of when he was a little kid, holding a seashell to his ear.

Secondly, he couldn't keep his eyes open. The medicine they were pumping into him kept him in a perpetual state of drowsiness. Sometimes Michelle was there, and once, he saw Lily peering down at him with huge eyes.

It was more than forty-eight hours after he'd leaped out of the third-story window that he was at last able to carry on a semi-intelligible conversation. But he had to do it without his voice, which didn't want to cooperate.

So he mimed scribbling a note and was given a pen and paper. Joe wrote, WHY CAN'T I TALK?

The solemn-looking doctor, who spoke with the trace of an Indian accent, said, "You were intubated because you were having trouble breathing on your own. Your throat was already badly inflamed from the smoke, but the breathing tube irritated your throat tissue further. You shouldn't try to speak."

Joe wrote, HOW LONG WILL IT LAST?

The doctor was in his fifties, Joe thought. He had thinning black hair and a concerned look that seemed sincere. "You still have some airway edema, and—" Seeing Joe's befuddled expression, he explained, "That means your trachea is still swollen. We need to make sure that doesn't grow worse. If it doesn't – and I have no reason to think it will deteriorate, given your good health and your medical history – you should be able to talk in a couple days."

WHERE IS THE BOY?

The doctor frowned, and Joe felt his heart stutter a little. "He's also in intensive care. In addition to the smoke inhalation, Steven suffered from dehydration and a great deal of bruising." The doctor smiled. "Of course, his wounds were nothing compared to yours, Mr. Crawford."

Joe barely heard that last part. WILL STEVIE BE OKAY?

The doctor shrugged. "He should be. It's difficult to know for sure, but he seems to be recovering nicely. As I've said, Mr. Crawford, I'm more worried about you."

Something in the doctor's tone broke through. Joe wrote, AM I RECOVERING NICELY?

The doctor smiled but hastily recovered his reserve. Joe finally noticed the nametag, which proclaimed the man to be Dr. Ravi Ahsan. The doctor's expression sobered. "I'd counsel you to be patient, Mr. Crawford. It's surprising you lived through the ordeal, and it will take time for you to convalesce. The back of your body was badly burned and lacerated. We may have to entertain the possibility of skin grafts. There were three fractured vertebrae incurred in the fall. Your hip was fractured. Your ankle as well. The wound in your hand…there will no doubt be some nerve damage. And when you were stabbed in the side, the blade missed your colon by only a centimeter. That is good, but there was still internal bleeding, the risk of infection." Dr. Ahsan shook his head. "Yet despite all these things, your vital signs are promising."

FEEL LIKE SHIT, Joe wrote.

The doctor laughed. "I can only imagine, Mr. Crawford. We'll get you something for the pain—" He stopped at Joe's look.

NOT TOO MUCH. WANT TO TALK TO WIFE.

"I understand. And I also want you to know…" Dr. Ahsan glanced over his shoulder, perhaps to make certain the door was still closed. "I want you to know that I think you did a fine thing. A very fine thing. A boy is alive because of you."

Joe wrote, WILL I BE ARRESTED?

Dr. Ahsan sighed. He seemed to consider. "There will be questions to answer, yes. But I can tell you this: Those people, they killed three police officers. They murdered the boy's foster parents. They tried to kill you and the boy, not to mention your wife. They were bad people. I cannot believe anyone will prosecute you for what you did."

Joe knew he should have felt relief, or at the very least, hope at Dr. Ahsan's words, but it wasn't until that moment that he realized he'd been suppressing all thoughts of Darrell Copeland and his gruesome death. And then Joe was staring up at the ceiling, the tiles up there doubling because the tears were coming fast now, and he couldn't very well hide them from the doctor.

He heard Ahsan say, "I am sorry, Mr. Crawford. I'll give you time to rest."

You do that, Joe thought. He closed his eyes. He missed Michelle and Lily badly, but at that moment he didn't mind the solitude.

I'm sorry, Darrell, he thought. *I'm sorry you aren't here right now.* He tried to swallow but found the task too daunting. So he lay there and waited for some of the sorrow to dissipate.

It didn't though. Not that night, not the next morning.

The only thing he could think about was Copeland's basement and how it would never get finished now.

★ ★ ★

It wasn't until the third afternoon that Joe found his voice, but even then it was weak and raspy. His difficulty in speaking combined with the howling agony of his scorched flesh caused him to reluctantly consent to a more powerful pain medicine. And that, in turn, led to a prolonged period of sleep. So it was that seventy hours after he'd been admitted, Joe was finally able to carry on a decent conversation with his wife.

"How's my baby girl?" Joe whispered.

Michelle, sitting at his bedside, cupped his hand in hers and smiled. "She's great. My parents are home with her now."

Joe's pulse quickened. "At our house?"

"With a state trooper monitoring them," she quickly added. "They think the fire killed all the cult members, but they're not taking any chances."

"One got away," Joe said. "I let him."

He thought Michelle would be appalled by this news, but she only nodded. "Shaun Peterson. The police know about him."

"They catch him?"

She shook her head. "The Murphys – our neighbors across the street?"

Joe nodded. "I owe them a beer. Or whatever their kids drink."

"Probably beer. Anyway, the mom, Jenny, she was watching out the basement window when Shaun exited the Baxter house. She said he went down the road a spell, got in his truck, and left."

"The police haven't tracked him down?"

"Not yet, but I'm sure they will."

"The Murphys see anybody else?"

She shook her head. "Not a soul. None of our other neighbors did either. The state police are still in the process of finding and identifying all the remains and matching them to the folks staying out at the compound. When I said the police were monitoring our house, I really meant it. They've got the whole property next door cordoned off as a crime scene, and every hour or so, one of them checks in with us to make sure nothing suspicious is going on."

He relaxed, but only fractionally. "I don't suppose they're having much luck identifying the bodies."

"Some. It seems a number of the cult members had flown in from Ireland for Angela Waltz's funeral, then decided to stick around."

"Wanted to be there for my barbecue."

She gave him a wan smile.

Joe smiled at her, marveling at her pluck, her constancy. "So you were the one who shot the chain? The one who killed Grayman?"

Michelle smiled. "I've been going to the range. You didn't think I was just shopping all those times, did you?"

"I'm impressed."

"You're alive too."

Joe chuckled, then winced at the intense pain it awoke in his back.

"Sorry," she said. "You've got to rest."

He grimaced. "Not my specialty."

"No fooling around, Joe. It's not negotiable. Your lungs were damaged and need to heal. Your throat...your back might require some surgeries."

"That's what the doctor told me."

Her wry smile reappeared. "He's pretty impressed with you."

"He's the one with the title."

"And you're the one who leaped out the third-story window of a burning building in order to save a child's life."

Joe shrugged, then regretted it when a freshet of pain pelted his back. "I was saving my life too."

Michelle sat forward, her voice breaking. "You went back inside for him. The social workers were really moved by that."

Joe glanced at her. "You've spoken to them?"

She nodded. "There've been five different ones handling the case, including the original lady."

"Where's Stevie gonna live?"

Michelle drew in shuddering breath, regarded their interlaced fingers. "Right now it looks like it'll be a state facility."

Joe felt his heart sink. He knew it had been a long shot, but still, he'd hoped…

As if sensing his train of thought, Michelle added, "They're not shutting the door on anything. Like I said, what you did…that counts for a lot. At least to some of them."

He glared out the observation window. "But not enough, apparently."

Michelle didn't say anything to that.

He turned back to her. "Hell, honey. I just realized I haven't even asked how you're doing. That big bastard really rang your bell."

She rubbed the back of her head. "Mild concussion. I've had a headache on and off since I woke up in the Murphys' basement, but that's about it."

"You remember saving my life?"

"Of course I do. I also remember your winky hanging out for everyone to see."

He tilted his head, winced at the pain even that small movement caused. "Do you have to call it a winky? Isn't there something a little more flattering you could come up with?"

"Sure, when we're getting intimate. But when you were handcuffed to that swing it looked more like a shriveled peanut."

"Thanks a lot."

"I love you."

He looked at her, swallowed. "You're more of a hero than I am."

She shook her head, and this time her smile was serene. "We love each other. That's what people do."

Not all people, Joe thought but didn't say. Instead, he squeezed Michelle's hand, let his head loll back on the bed, and closed his eyes.

CHAPTER TWENTY-FOUR

It was a few months later, toward the tail end of September, that Joe worked up the courage to tell Michelle the rest of it. The dreadful things they'd promised him about Lily.

That his daughter would someday take her own life.

Lying next to him in bed, Michelle listened with an air of patience. He'd figured on her being aghast at the information – perhaps even insane with worry – but far from these reactions Michelle only watched him with a frank gaze that revealed absolutely nothing.

"Is that all of it?" she asked when he'd at last fallen silent.

"Pretty much. Well, that and the fact that depression runs in my family. My dad shooting himself doesn't exactly reassure me."

When she didn't speak, he said, "You act like it doesn't add up to much. Like we don't need to worry about our daughter."

"Do we?"

He tamped down the surge of agitation her words brought on. "The day Angie Waltz came on to me at the Hawkins place—"

"You never said she came on to you."

"Sorry. She didn't get anywhere, and I didn't see the need to worry you about it."

Michelle gave him a sardonic look but waited for him to go on.

"That day by the pump…when she moved up against me…I swear I smelled ashes on her."

Michelle nodded meditatively. "The same way Lily smelled those times this summer."

Joe watched his wife and waited for her to come unstrung. He was perilously close to freaking out himself. Though his body was healing just fine, it was the emotional scarring that still gnawed away at him. He was sleeping less than ever, most nights lying awake and listening to their quiet house for the slightest noise. Or brooding over the possibility of his daughter being irretrievably marked by Sharon Waltz's preparations.

He said, "What do you make of it?"

"You smelled the soot in Lily's hair after Angie's death?"

He nodded. "After Sharon scattered our son's—" He cut off, clamped down on the quaver that threatened to hijack his voice. "—Ben's ashes. I smelled it a couple times. Once when we were playing trains, once in her crib."

"And have you smelled ashes on her since that night at the Baxter house?"

Joe thought about it. Then he shook his head slowly.

"So maybe it's over," Michelle said.

"I want it to be. But I'm afraid that's just wishful thinking.

Michelle chewed her lip. "So...how does this change things? I mean, what does it do to our life going forward?"

Joe grunted. "From where I sit, not a whole lot. I mean, I'm already the world's most paranoid dad. This is just one more thing for me to worry about."

"But you don't..."

"Do I believe Lily's in danger?"

Michelle waited. He saw what might have been an inchoate fear in her big brown eyes.

Joe sighed, rubbed his jaw. "Look, Angie Waltz had every reason to be depressed. Raised by that witch.... Sharon was all Angie had growing up. No father, no other relatives to speak of. So right there you've got a girl with very little support, not to mention the fact that she inherited her mom's nasty disposition. Factor in the drug use, the messing around with that sick cult. All that weird shit. Cannibalism, human sacrifice..." Joe shook his head. "And then you take away the one good thing she's got going – her child – it's no wonder she did what she did. There might even have been some mental illness thrown in for good measure."

Michelle did not look reassured. "What's that got to do with Lily?"

"That's just the point. It has nothing to do with her. Angie has nothing to do with her. Sharon bought into that whole legend about preparing a person for sacrifice, but all the evidence points to the more rational explanation – that Angie made the decision to kill herself. Granted, her mind was probably clouded at the time, but she was still the one who did it."

In his wife's eyes he could see the avid yearning to believe, the naked hope that the nightmare really was over.

Michelle chewed her bottom lip. "You're sure you don't want to move to a new city?"

"I thought we decided that."

"I know. It's just—"

"Do you love this house?"

"Of course I do."

"And the neighborhood? The schools? The town?"

She nodded. "You know it isn't any of those things."

Joe took her hand. "What you're talking about, they're memories. Those are gonna follow us wherever we go. This place is where Lily's lived her whole life. Where you and I dreamed of living when we first got married. Leaving here would be the worst thing we could do."

Michelle said, "And you don't think we have anything to worry about?"

"I think it's a scary world. I think there are plenty of things to worry about. I also think some of the stuff that happened can only be explained by the supernatural. Or maybe I'm just nuts." He shook his head. "But Lily one day up and deciding to take her own life? That's not gonna happen. Not with our girl."

She searched his eyes for a long while. Evidently satisfied by what she saw there, she laid her head on his chest and nuzzled into him. "You think love is strong enough to undo the curse."

Joe caressed his wife's arm, inhaled the warm smell of her hair. "I do," he said. "If there is a curse, I believe what we've got is stronger."

★ ★ ★

When he was sure Michelle had fallen asleep, Joe peeled back the covers as gingerly as he could and crept out of the room. September had been hotter than usual, and to combat the heat, Michelle had taken to reducing the temperature to sixty-five degrees every night. His wife loved the chill, but the cold made Joe's balls shrink. As furtively as he could, he bent to the digital thermostat and raised it to sixty-seven, a compromise he considered just.

He crossed to the hearth, where the pewter urn sat atop the mantel. Joe had been sure Sharon had disposed of it, but during the investigation of the cult, they'd found the urn on the floor of her van.

Joe let his fingertips brush the cool surface of the urn and said a prayer for Ben, his unborn son.

Then he went to the basement and contorted his body around the furnace until his groping fingers located the key. Moving briskly now, he crossed to the padlock covering the small crawlspace door. He unlocked the door, pocketed the key, and let the padlock hang. Joe took a moment to move the footstool into place, then he squirmed into the crawlspace entry, which was just wide enough to accommodate his broad shoulders. He crawled forward on elbows and knees until he reached the gun cabinet.

Michelle told him he was crazy for storing it under the house, and he supposed he was. But he'd heard all kinds of crazy stories about kids breaking into their dad's gun safes, messing around with them, and blowing themselves or a friend away.

But it's a combination lock, Michelle had argued.

You saying those things are foolproof? he'd countered.

Michelle suggested he keep the safe in his bedroom closet. Then, she reasoned, he'd be able to access the guns in case of a home invasion. What the hell did he think he was going to do, she added wryly, tell the invaders to hold on a second while he crawled under the house to arm himself?

Joe sighed, dialed in the proper numbers, as he'd done every night since returning home from the hospital. Yes, she was right. Of course she was right. There was no earthly reason to keep the safe under the house. But what she didn't take into account – and what Joe refused to articulate, though she knew it just as well as he did – was that the events of the summer had taken that part of him, that raw, misshapen tumor of irrational paranoia, and caused it to metastasize, its writhing black tendrils extending now to his every thought and deed.

I won't let them hurt my baby, he thought. Gritting his teeth, he wrenched open the cabinet door.

To the replacement .38 the insurance company had provided, Joe had added a Remington 12 gauge and his own personal favorite, the .44 Magnum Colt Anaconda. He knew it wasn't the same one Dirty Harry had used, but that's how the gun made Joe feel whenever he gripped it.

In the gloom of the crawlspace, he only debated a second or two before selecting the Anaconda.

Taking care to lock the safe and return the key to its hiding place, Joe tromped up the stairs with the Anaconda at his side, its weight like a talisman against the skulking shadows he encountered on the way to the second floor.

Once there, he went to the room that had once been their office but was now a second nursery. Joe left the light off. Beyond the translucent baby blue curtains – Michelle had decorated the room almost entirely in baby-blue – Joe could make out the dark void where once had stood the Baxter house. He didn't like for the boy to sleep so near the site of where they'd both almost died, but it was preferable to having Lily on this side of the house. Lily, he reminded himself, was the one who needed the most protection. Lily was the one who'd been prepared, as Sharon and Bridget had claimed. Lily was the one Joe needed to keep a constant eye on.

Joe reached the crib, peered over the railing at his son. Little Stevie was sleeping soundly, he saw. The boy nearly always did. Joe had worried the child might suffer from nightmares, from recurring memories of that terrible night, or even of the many terrible nights the boy had no doubt experienced while living with Angie and Sharon. But Stevie slept like a stone, just like Michelle did. It was almost as if, upon adopting Stevie, Michelle had transferred to him her tendency to zonk out the moment her head hit the pillow and to remain in that position until early morning.

Joe reached down, stroked the boy's forehead.

Stevie did not stir. Only continued his smooth, peaceful breathing.

Joe caressed the boy's forehead one more time before heading down the hallway to Lily's room. Four feet from the closed door, he realized he was holding his breath. You did that, some part of him argued, you wouldn't smell anything you didn't want to smell, and as long as you didn't smell it, you could believe it wasn't there.

His whole body trembling, Joe allowed himself to inhale.

The atmosphere outside Lily's door seemed clean.

Without the faintest tinge of ashes.

Joe reached out, twisted the knob. And let himself into his daughter's room. Again, he realized he was holding his breath, so again he forced himself to breathe normally. Still no whiff of smoke or cinders. Still clean air.

Joe bent down, placed the Anaconda on the floor, making sure to point the barrel toward the bathroom rather than one of his kids' rooms.

He made his way around to Lily's cribside and peered at her through the gathered darkness. Joe reached out to touch Lily, her little shoulder snug within the warm polka-dotted pajamas she loved. He smiled down at her.

Snatches of Sharon Waltz's hateful words battered at his mind:

You've failed to protect your family.

Joe's smile faded. The hand on his daughter's shoulder tightened involuntarily.

You and your family will be dead soon.

His airway began to constrict. In her sleep, Lily stirred at the grip on her shoulder.

They'll take her too, you son of a bitch.

Joe squeezed his eyes shut, thrashed his head from side to side, but Sharon's voice reverberated in his brain, like the toll of malefic church bells.

They'll take your Lily.

Joe realized he was sobbing. He knew the sound would awaken Lily, but it was as if his body had seized up entirely, prohibiting all but the slightest movements. Just like the goddamned Tin Man, only there was no oilcan sitting nearby to cure what was ailing him. There was only Sharon's infernal voice and his own impotent tears. Copeland was dead. Lily was promised to the cult, or at least whatever remained of it. The police claimed they were all dead, save Shaun Peterson, who'd been found and arrested. But if other cult members were alive, wouldn't they want retribution? Wouldn't they do all they could to ensure Joe paid, and paid dearly? They would make sure Lily died. They would go after Michelle and Stevie too. Wouldn't those monsters—

"Daddy?" a voice asked.

Joe stared down at his daughter, became instantly aware of how hard he was gripping her shoulder.

"Sorry," he said, though his voice was so husky the word was indecipherable. But it didn't matter. He relaxed his grip, and Lily had shown no sign of discomfort, was showing nothing at all but concern for him. Her lucent brown eyes picked up some of the starlight slanting through the sides of the curtains, and in them he saw the same look Michelle often wore when he was beating himself up for something.

He cleared his throat and whispered, "Sorry, honey. I didn't mean to wake you."

His voice broke on the last word, the sobs still refusing to completely abate, and all of a sudden Lily was rising from her nest of pillows and toys and reaching for him. He stooped over to meet her, thinking she wanted to be held, but rather than simply resting her forearms on his shoulders as she ordinarily did, this time her slender arms enfolded his neck, hauled him down into her embrace with astonishing strength. Joe scrambled for some comforting word or phrase, but his chest was still quaking, the wet heat in his throat scalding him, robbing him of speech.

But his daughter, he now realized, was speaking, was repeating something over and over, her voice a soft, soothing whisper.

"You're safe," she said. "You're safe, Daddy."

Joe clenched his arms about her, a violent sob racking his body. But though he'd leaned into her, she somehow supported him, somehow helped him remain upright. Worried he'd collapse the whole crib and send her to the ER, he made to pull back, but she only tightened her hold on him, said, "Shhhh. Shhhh, Daddy."

"Lily," he tried to say.

"You're safe," she repeated. "You're safe."

Tears streamed over his cheeks, and though he fought it, the silent, quaking sobs took him then, rendered him powerless. He leaned against his daughter and wept, wept as he hadn't since the miscarriage. The heat in his chest became a boiling inferno. It spread through his shoulders, his arms, down his abdominal muscles all the way to his toes, and now he let it flood through him, gust out of him, his daughter whispering to him all the while. She had turned three earlier in the month, but in her voice, in her unwavering, loving embrace there was something maternal, something ageless. She whispered to him and nuzzled her lamb-soft cheek into his neck, and told him he was safe, and when he'd finally regained control of his emotions, when he was at last able to draw back slightly and gaze into her liquid brown eyes, she was making a face at him, a face she often made when he'd fallen silent and she wanted to make him laugh. They called it her surprise face.

Joe looked at his daughter's wide eyes and open mouth and began to smile, despite how messy he was with tears and mucus.

"Are you better, Daddy?" she asked.

He chuckled, nodded.

"Are you happy?" she persisted.

He wiped his nose and said, "As long as you're safe, I'm happy."

And without pause, as though it was the most obvious thing in the world, she said, "I'm safe, Daddy."

His breath caught in his throat. Their foreheads only two inches apart, they stared into each other's eyes.

"Honey, we—"

"We're safe, Daddy."

It was as though a pair of brutal fists suddenly relaxed within him.

A sweeping sigh of breath expanded his chest. Lily's grip on him relaxed infinitesimally, but still she held on to him.

He was panting a little, his heartbeat still throbbing, but maybe not so painfully now. Her breath was sweet on his face, her gaze unwavering.

A little embarrassed at his display, he ventured a smile, but her answering smile was so patient and understanding that even his embarrassment began to drain away.

"Are you okay, Daddy?" she asked.

He nodded. "Daddy's good. Are you okay?"

"I'm tired, Daddy."

And she yawned. One of those vast, face-contorting yawns only toddlers can manage. Her sweet breath caressed his cheek.

He brought his lips to her forehead for a kiss, but the moment his lips touched her skin, she reached up, placed her hands on his cheeks. Drawing his face lower and rocking up on her toes, she kissed him softly on the lips. Then, she released him and yawned again.

"I'm tired, Daddy," she explained. He lowered into her pile of blankets and pillows and toys. One knee skimmed over her Glo Worm, which lit up and played its gentle lullaby.

"Get some sleep, sweetie," he said.

"I love you, Daddy," she said, on her side now.

"I love you too, sweetie."

He saw her lovely silhouette and allowed himself a long, luxuriant intake of air. The only scents he detected were the laundry detergent Michelle used and what might have been Lily's baby shampoo.

He moved into the hallway and bumped something with the tip of his big toe.

The Anaconda.

Joe bent to retrieve it, and holding it at his side, he returned to the basement, where he went through the process of stowing it away for the night. As he squirmed out of the crawlspace, he decided Michelle was right. It was silly to keep the gun cabinet down here. He'd move it up to his closet tomorrow and make certain he kept the combination a secret.

Another thirty seconds and Joe was crawling into bed. He yawned, feeling drowsier than he had in a good while. He closed his eyes and within moments began drifting into sleep.

He frowned, an unpleasant notion arising in him. He'd locked the front and back doors earlier, but he'd neglected to double-check them. Or triple-check them, which he did nearly every night.

He waited in the darkness for the urge to overtake him, for the anxiety to spread its ulcerous fingers through his chest, through his mind. Waited for the voice of Sharon Waltz to laugh its witch's cackle and declare to him his failure.

Joe waited, waited.

And then, in a soft undertone, he heard his daughter's voice.

You're safe, Daddy. You're safe.

His thundering heartbeat began to relax.

I'm safe, Daddy.

Joe's fists unclenched. His jaw too.

We're safe, Daddy.

We're safe.

Joe breathed. He let his arms go limp, his chest to rise and fall on its own. He thought of his wife, who slept like a wintering animal next to him. He thought of Stevie, of his son, upstairs and dreaming about who knew what. Maybe Thomas the Train. Maybe tractors. They were his favorites.

As sleep gathered him into its velvety embrace, he thought of Lily, of her voice, her brown eyes, her strong little arms.

Joe slept, and even as he dreamed he fancied he could feel his daughter's breath on his cheek.

ACKNOWLEDGMENTS

The first person I want to thank is Mr. Joe R. Lansdale. He influenced this book, and his writing continues to influence me. He tells a story like nobody's business, and he also happens to be an uncannily generous human being. If you enjoy this book, you'll enjoy a Lansdale book. If you hate this book, you'll enjoy a Lansdale book. He's a national treasure who will be read a hundred years from now. So read him. And thank you, Joe, for doing what you do.

Thank you to my pre-readers Tod and Tim for their help on this book. Thank you also to Don D'Auria for an extremely helpful suggestion he made about the structure of this novel. Also, I want to thank Brian Keene, Tim Waggoner, Jeff Strand, Paul Tremblay, and Mary SanGiovanni for their continued support.

Lastly, I want to thank my family. My wife endures this strange writing addiction and does a great job of bringing me back into the real world with love and patience. My three children fill my world with laughter and joy. I don't know where I'd be without you four, but I thank God every day I get to be with you. Thanks for all your love, and please always know how much I love you back.